W9-AFE-306

0 00 30 0351076 9

RECEIVED

MAY 1 9 2004

BY:_____

MAIN

HAYNER PUBLIC LIBRARY DISTRICT
ALTON, ILLINOIS

OVERDUES .10 PER DAY MAXIMUM FINE
COST OF BOOKS. LOST OR DAMAGED
BOOKS ADDITIONAL $5.00 SERVICE CHARGE.

MERIWETHER

BOOKS BY DAVID NEVIN
FROM TOM DOHERTY ASSOCIATES

Dream West
1812
Eagle's Cry
Treason
Meriwether

Visit his Web site at:
www.DAVIDNEVIN.com

MERIWETHER

A Novel of Meriwether Lewis and
the Lewis & Clark Expedition

DAVID NEVIN

 A TOM DOHERTY ASSOCIATES BOOK · NEW YORK

HAYNER PUBLIC LIBRARY DISTRICT
ALTON, ILLINOIS

This is a work of fiction. All the characters and events portrayed in this novel are either fictitious or are used fictitiously.

MERIWETHER: A NOVEL OF MERIWETHER LEWIS AND THE LEWIS & CLARK EXPEDITION

Copyright © 2004 by David Nevin

All rights reserved, including the right to reproduce this book, or portions thereof, in any form.

This book is printed on acid-free paper.

A Forge Book
Published by Tom Doherty Associates, LLC
175 Fifth Avenue
New York, NY 10010

www.tor.com

Forge® is a registered trademark of Tom Doherty Associates, LLC.

Library of Congress Cataloging-in-Publication Data

Nevin, David.
    Meriwether : a novel of Meriwether Lewis and the Lewis & Clark Expedition /
David Nevin—1st ed.
        p.   cm.
    "A Tom Doherty Associates book."
    ISBN 0-312-86307-1 (acid-free paper)
    EAN 978-0312-86307-4
    1. Lewis, Meriwether, 1774–1809—Fiction.   2. Lewis and Clark Expedition
(1804–1806)—Fiction.   3. West (U.S.)—History—To 1848—Fiction.
4. Explorers—Fiction.   I. Title.

PS3564.E853M47   2004
813'.54—dc22

                                                                2003069457

First Edition: May 2004

Printed in the United States of America

0   9   8   7   6   5   4   3   2   1

F
NEU

AEQ-9779

On August 18, 1813, almost four years after the death of Meriwether Lewis, Thomas Jefferson wrote of the explorer, "Of courage undaunted, possessing a firmness & perseverance of purpose which nothing but impossibilities could divert from its direction, careful as a father to those committed to his charge . . ."

This book is dedicated to a modern-day man of undaunted courage and perseverance of purpose —

Battalion Chief Orio Joseph Palmer,
New York City Fire Department,
who died on the 78th floor
when the South Tower fell
on
September 11, 2001.
His remains were never found.

PART ONE
THE MAN

1

For years he had dreamed of this, speculated, imagined, planned; he had lived it in his mind, how he would assemble his party and supply them and the adventures they would have and the wonders they would see. A recurring image haunted his youth, himself at the head of a column of men that crossed a broad valley, climbed a far ridge, and disappeared into the mists beyond. But that was then; now he was a man, strong and ready. Now it was real.

So in this October of 1803 Meriwether Lewis floated down the Ohio River in a keelboat made to his order. Ahead lay the Falls of the Ohio and just below was Louisville, and across the river, Clarksville, Indiana Territory. There he would join William Clark whom he had invited to share the command of the trek into the vast unknown. With a handful of men and all the supplies they could carry—which Lewis already worried would not be enough—they would set out from St. Louis to be gone two years or three or four or perhaps forever. They would cross the uncharted continent, going where no man had gone before. Indians traveled their own terrain but they didn't travel the whole distance.

They paused at the Falls, three huge limestone ledges over which water poured as the river dropped some eighty feet in a mile or so. Then, on Lewis's shouted command, they plunged ahead, down a narrow chute to the right, and fetched up shaken and whirling in the rapids that boiled below each ledge. The boat was strong; it was intact but for maybe a split hull plank. Clarksville appeared ahead and in a minute Lewis made out Clark's stalwart figure on the landing, legs spread and arms akimbo. Before they could get lines over Clark leaped aboard and swept Lewis into a bear hug, pounding him furiously on the back. It had been six years since they had met, Clark then commanding the First Infantry's Chosen Rifles, Lewis his lieutenant.

Lewis's letter inviting Clark to join the expedition had sketched out the vast magnitude of what lay before them. Follow the mighty Missouri up to its source that surely was in the Stony Mountains. Leading thinkers, the president of the United States among them, held that these mountains— sometimes called the Shining Mountains and more and more often these days the Rocky Mountains, and always stars of dreams and myths—would match the Appalachians in the East in height, complexity, and roughness. Lewis had to wonder a little at that . . . as if the continent needed opposing mountain chains of equal size for balance, lest it all tip over.

"You know how folks work things out on paper," Lewis said, "and it always comes out just right? And then you go on the trail and—well, you ever found the trail went the way you figured?"

Clark laughed, that go-ahead laugh, full of confidence and, yes, happiness, too, happiness at something new. "Ain't never what you expect," he said. "That's what makes it fun."

By God, that was the ticket—going somewhere new. Ma told Lewis he was a rambling fool, but that was when she was hot at him, trying to get him back to Virginia to run the plantation. Anyway, he put it right back on her, told her it was her fault, naming him Meriwether. That was her maiden name and the Meriwethers were famous ramblers, packed their wagons in Virginia and poured through the Cumberland Gap and spread over Kentucky. Hell's fire, Ma, that's real rambling! And she would say don't you cuss in the house but she'd be smiling and he'd kiss her cheek and laugh and be gone again. Clark understood him. They knew each other well, knew how their complementary strengths melded to a whole of iron.

Clark was Lewis's height, good six feet, broad in the shoulders, big in the hands, looked like he could heave a two-hundred-pound hog over his shoulder, genial but very dangerous when riled. Like Lewis overall, comparable size, strength, willingness to fight. Maybe not the genial part, Lewis couldn't really call himself genial, he'd admit that, but the rest of it, certainly. Clark's good humor evened out Lewis's moods. They were a natural pair.

When they reached the mountains their orders were to find an easy portage. All the best thinking from Mr. Jefferson on down, learned men who'd never seen the country talking to other learned men who'd never seen the country, said that after a modest climb there ought to be a nice level. It would be like a saddle, probably, perhaps a mountain meadow, with two streams a mile or so apart or maybe nearer. One stream would run east to form the Missouri, the other west to form the Columbia and thence on to the Pacific. This based on a century or more of thinking, wondering, hearing rumors, analyzing, working it all out in logic. If a stream ran one way from a height, why shouldn't another run the other way? It just stood to reason. Go up one and down the other. Didn't that make sense?

Well, it was different, sitting in Mr. Jefferson's study, sparrows chirping on the outer sill, cows wending up L'Enfant's classic oval for milking in the barn behind the President's House, painters chattering as they laid another coat of white on its yellow sandstone walls. It was different, sitting there while the president's easy voice plotted an expedition thirty years in his own dreaming. Then it was like a sorcerer's spell and you could hardly doubt that it would be just so. This even though any man who had walked into wilderness, as Lewis had done all his life and the president had never done, not once, knew full well that the day you found things just as you'd figured you'd better start all over because something had gone wrong.

It really was one hell of an undertaking.

"You know, Merry," Clark said the night Lewis arrived, "we might just make us some history, we get to the Pacific and back."

"Might just do that," Lewis said. "Might just." Yes, and might do more than that, too, lots more. Their success would help anchor the new democracy that the election of Thomas Jefferson in 1800 had brought to the country and that had been under siege ever since. Come back in triumph and democracy would have another feather in its cap; die in some coulee and the expedition never heard from again, and the hounds and hyenas always ready to attack the noblest concept since Moses took down the commandments would be baying and snapping. Failure would shake confidence in government that not only believed but that acted on the basis that free men could live in self-control, stand free and yet hold to stable and reasonable government. But if they returned in triumph it could only strengthen democracy.

And then there was the West, American settlers steadily advancing through the woods beyond the Appalachians. Lewis, on the president's behalf, intended to open the way to the Pacific. A rising West seemed to terrify the East—certainly it would dilute New England's power. But the West was where free men could flourish—more so than the Northeast with its gray factories rising to chain men to machines. Of course, Lewis had to admit that this was Democratic Party dogma but it made sense to him.

And the British were making trouble again. Couldn't seem to accept the fact that we won the Revolution and kicked them out. They harassed our shipping for reasons that made sense to them and none to us. Now they were eyeing the Pacific Northwest, their navy charting the waters, their traders on the move. Wanted to beat us there.

But he didn't burden Clark with such political geography. It was enough to contemplate the real geography lying before them. It was simply awesome—and that suited Lewis just fine. He'd always had a sense of holding himself apart, of being different. He was happiest when he was alone and moving, long strides carrying him for miles—maybe he really was a rambling fool. But he felt an inner capacity to do great things and the certainty that they would come along. Destiny? Too grand a word for a Virginia plantation boy or an infantry captain? Call it what you want, but now the grand and spectacular lay before him—he was going to walk across North America and he was going to anchor his country as a continental nation and anchor its new democracy as strong and solid and successful.

All this if he came back at all . . .

Now, on this October day, a bite in the air signaling that winter was impatient in the wings, the keelboat was floating downstream toward the Ohio's juncture with the Mississippi. Waterbirds swooped and plunged and fought each other with shrieks of rage. The two men sat forward, backs to the cabin structure, sun on their faces, scanning the way ahead.

"So, Merry," said Clark, "how'd this all come about?" Clark had been privy to none of the planning which had been held a careful secret, and had only learned of the idea of the expedition in Lewis's letter of invitation. The letter had come out of the blue maybe a month or so before, drop what you're doing and walk across the continent, Will, how about that? Clark had rolled it around in his mind a bit before answering but he'd known by the time he'd finished reading the letter that he was going. What could have held him back, after all?

"I know you was the president's secretary," Clark said, rapping his corncob pipe on the gunwale and refilling it, "and maybe that's how you was chose. But how come Mr. Jefferson picked you for secretary anyway, a soldier like you? Writing notes, carrying paper, serving tea? Don't sound much like you."

Lewis sighed. "Take me a while to tell it right."

Clark smiled. "We got time." They were alone on the broad river, no other boat in sight, riding the current. Men with poles stood by fore and aft to fend them off when the boat veered toward shore. The day would come when there wouldn't be time for talk.

Meriwether Lewis cleared his throat . . .

2

Albemarle County, Virginia, Winter, 1779

He thought that he had always had that sense of the greatness of nation, of vast spaces awaiting crossing, of endless possibility, of freedom to strike his mark in the world and conviction that he would do so. He'd never been like other men or other boys with all their limits and narrow views. He'd always been different, for better or worse.

Pa came home from the war that winter. He was there two weeks, working hard and still falling far short of bringing the plantation into real order, Ma working beside him, Merry following them around. A thousand acres wasn't a big plantation but running it still took some doing, even with a passel of hands, as they always called the slaves.

Merry was five that winter—yes, that was right, born in 1774. He listened carefully to everything Pa said, and Pa talked of nothing but the war, how it had changed and the country was taking hold and growing up, just like his boy Merry was doing. He made Merry memorize the great names so he could recite them, Washington and Greene and Gates and Putnam. He talked of places that would forever hold mythical cast in Merry's mind: Lexington and Concord where farm boys stood to Redcoats, Bunker Hill and Boston, New York that the damned British still held, Philadelphia where they had marched in and marched right back out, how Charleston held them off with cannon fire and spared the South for a while, Valley Forge where men's feet froze off, and Trenton where General Washington crossed the Delaware and gave them a Christmas present they didn't expect. And Saratoga—Pa said that was the big one, the victory that counted, men in red surrendering right and left. The French saw we meant business and joined us, always happy to smite an old enemy.

Of course, in afterward calculations when he was older and the Revolution was won and the British went home and left us alone for a little while, he better understood the importance of Saratoga as a turning point. That was all before Tarleton's Green Horse came to ravage Virginia, Bloody Tarleton, before Daniel Morgan and his rifles settled Colonel Tarleton's hash at Cowpens. Before the British were herded into a fortified bivouac at Yorktown, Virginia, and the Americans circled for the kill.

But for Merry, all the gallant names focused back on the time that Pa was home. The night before the warrior went back to his regiment the house was full of people, laughing, talking, drinking, eating, come to see Pa off. In Merry's view Pa was the most important man in Albemarle County except perhaps Mr. Jefferson down the road two or three miles and he was off being governor.

Sometime late in the evening, Pa sitting at the scarred old oaken table, Merry awakened and came down from the loft in his nightshirt and crawled up on Pa's lap. Pa wasn't a lap-sitting sort of man but this was a magical night charged with all possibility. Ma wrapped a blanket around him and he snuggled against Pa. There were a dozen men at the table drinking from pewter tankards, the women in the next room. All at once Merry reached for Pa's tankard and Pa steadied it while he drank. It was bitter and it burned his mouth and he almost spat it out, but then he decided he liked it, or at least, he liked drinking from Pa's tankard with all the men cheering and he reached for it again. But this time Pa laughed and pushed it away. Merry snuggled closer, Pa rubbing his back absently as the talk swirled on.

It was about the war, what else, and he remembered Pa explaining how at the start the American forces had been ragtag shirttails facing Redcoats with glittering bayonets but over three years they had steadied into tough-minded fighting men. Tough-minded fighting men — Merry remembered how the phrase had stirred him that night. And it had seemed to him there on Pa's lap that the world was his and great things would happen and he would grow up and stride out into the future in the seven-league boots the storybooks all talked about. He could be and do and go anywhere when-ever he chose, the wide world beckoning.

When they drank to free men with tankards crashing against the table and shouts of "Hurrah!" Merry had piped right up. "Me too, Pa! I'm a free man too. Ain't I, Pa? A free man too?"

"Damn right, son!" Merry could still recall the very timber of Pa's voice full of pride, the feel of his big hand curled behind the small rib cage.

Across the table sat old Colonel Drumfries playing with his long white beard. Drumfries had been with General Washington in the French and Indian War and everyone said he knew a thing or two. And he shouted, "Why, hell, Lewis, you got yourself a regular Yankee Doodle Dandy! Ain't that so, boy?"

"Yes, sir," Merry cried, "I'm a Yankee Doodle," and to prove it he stood on Pa's lap and started to sing and then Pa's deep voice picked up the words and everyone was singing. Pa hoisted him onto his shoulders and the men all stood and paraded around the room thundering the famil-iar verses:

"Father and I went down to camp
Along with Captain Gooding;
And there we saw the men and boys,
As thick as hasty pudding.

Yankee doodle, keep it up,
Yankee doodle dandy,
Mind the music and the step,
And with the girls be handy.

There was Captain Washington
Upon a slapping stallion,
A-giving orders to his men,
I guess there was a million.

Yankee doodle, keep it up,
Yankee doodle dandy . . ."

He was so proud. He could still remember the flush of sheer joy and
that sense of—what? Destiny? Yes, that might not be too far astray, that
sense that great things lay ahead, awaiting him but challenging him, too.
Then sleep must have overtaken him. He had a dim memory of Pa carrying him up to the loft and tucking a blanket under his chin. And in an
instant it was morning and Pa's bedroll was lashed to his saddle and the
big bay gelding was stamping its feet, breath coming in clouds in the cold,
ready to go. Pa lifted Merry high, then pulled Ma into his arms and kissed
her, and before Merry could even restore the image of the night before,
Pa was gone. Off to war, off to whip the enemy.

Two days later he was back, hauled in on a pile of straw in a wagon, shivering like to die. There had been a melt and the creek was near flood stage.
There was no bridge so he had to swim the horse. Maybe the water was just
too cold, but anyway, the horse began to fight—this in moments of feverish
lucidity, his throat closed to a whisper. All of a sudden the horse had folded
up like its heart had stopped somehow. Its head dropped into the water and
it sort of rolled to the right and Pa went in the water. The current was swift
right here and it swept him along for a mile or two before he could lay a
hand on some brush and drag himself ashore and then he lay there, too
froze and too weak to move, and it was a day or more before anyone found
him. When the wagon stopped at Ma's door, he was out of his head, laughing and crying. She laid her hand against his cheek and said the pneumonia
had taken him while he lay freezing on the bank.

Merry remembered those days too vividly, for they were tinted with
shame. The sight of his father crying out in delirium in the big feather bed
terrified him, for Pa looked strange and awful. Ma sat by the bed and
wiped his face with a damp cloth. Four times the doctor came and dosed
him with various nostrums and each time bled him, the shiny lancet with
cup attached glittering in candlelight, cold and sinister, the stream pouring into the cup almost black and ever smaller.

At some point it came to Merry as settled conviction that Pa would die,
and then he was terrified that it would happen while he was in the room.
He imagined his father's spirit lifting from the inert form and seeking a
way out of the closed room to rise to heaven. Once he opened the window
so the spirit could go untrammeled.

Ma slapped him. He tried to explain and she slapped him again. "You
want to kill your pa?" She left him curled and sobbing on the floor as

much for the terrible injustice of her attitude as for Pa. She didn't talk to him again that day.

Pa died two nights later. When Merry awakened that morning he lay still in the dawn's pale light, knowing something had happened, something bad.

So it was that Lieutenant William Lewis died in the war. He died as a soldier fighting for his country, a patriot. That was the thing to remember. He had helped set the nation free.

Two or three months later Jesse Rentfro came to visit with his parents. Jesse was a cousin, second or third, it was hard to keep track. He was seven and stood a head taller than Merry and spoke with great authority on all subjects. Merry admired him. After dinner at the usual hour, three in the afternoon, Merry took Jesse to the barn to see his pony. He pointed out the stall where Pa's big bay had lived and Pa's dress saddle on a peg and above it the dress bridle. He showed the loft where the hay was stored, how you could lie up there and see all that went on below and no one knew.

Jesse didn't say much so Merry told him about Pa, that he was a hero who had died in the war to set his country free, gave his life to make a new nation. At which Jesse smiled. Merry gazed at him, chilled and amazed.

"Your pa wasn't no hero," Jesse said. "He didn't die in the war. Fell off his horse and fell in the creek and froze to death. Got the pneumonia because he couldn't handle his horse. He wasn't no hero, you little poop."

Jesse looming over him, his big nose hung on an ugly grin like he'd been waiting all day to say this, and Merry hit him. He drove his fist right into those flaring nostrils and even as he swung he knew it was no boy's swat. All his force and rage and fury and fear combined in an explosion that years later he could still feel. It must have busted something inside because blood flashed out of Jesse's nose in a spray that got all over Merry as the bigger boy fell on the ground rolling about, hands clamped on his nose, howling and crying. That brought the folks running from the house. Jesse was sitting up and he crawled to his feet with snot and blood still coming from nose and mouth and bawled, "He hit me!"

"Merry!" Ma cried. "What in the world?"

"He said Pa wasn't a hero. Said he didn't die in the war. Said—" But the very memory of that sneer, that ugly grin, so infuriated Merry that he lunged again ready to smash the rest of Jesse's face. Ma caught him and he plunged and twisted in her arms. She shook him. "Now, see here, young man, you be quiet and mind your manners." And to Jesse, her eyes cold and hard, "You watch your tongue, boy. Don't be saying things that don't need to be said. Not around here."

Even then, Merry knew he had grasped in some dim way the reality that Jesse had attacked not just Pa but Merry's own image of himself and that mattered most of all. The Rentfros got in their wagon and left and never came back. But the jolt of his fist against that boy's nose stayed with him a long time until the memory became a talisman that told him he would do things and go places and make his mark. He wasn't like other boys. Sometimes that pleased him and sometimes it saddened, but there it was. Maybe destiny was too grand a word but there were places to go in this world and things to do and he was going to do them.

3

Broad River, North Georgia Frontier, 1784

"All right, Ma," he said, "what is it?"

She had said in the morning that she would speak to him that evening and her expression had told him it was serious. Now she had fed everyone and the sun was near gone; it was summer and the odor of honeysuckle lay heavy on the soft air here on the veranda. A pair of milk cows were lowing impatiently from the barn, wanting milking, their teats stretched taut. He would have to see to them shortly, get after Simon, get his lazy butt moving. Simon was a black boy Merry's age, which was ten. In a few more years the plantation would belong to Merry under laws of primogeniture and his manner was already proprietary.

"Captain Marks—" Her voice quivered and she stopped.

Merry struggled to keep distaste from his expression. Marks was a tall, skinny man with surprising strength in his arms. He'd been with Pa at Trenton when they whipped the Hessians. Took a rifle ball in the knee that night and hadn't walked right since. Soon as Pa died Marks had turned up most every day and it wasn't six months before Ma said she would marry him. It seemed like Pa was scarcely in the ground. Uncle Nicholas Lewis, Pa's older brother who'd been lending a hand to plantation operations, drew Merry aside and explained things. Most widows, especially if they were young and pretty and had some property, took one of the men who tended to present themselves. Woman needed a man, he said. Didn't say for what. It hadn't occurred to Merry that Ma might be young and pretty—she was just his mother. Look at General Washington, Uncle Nick said, grinning, he married him a widder woman. Did right well for himself, too. Ma was a Meriwether and that gave her resources beyond the plantation, which ultimately would be Merry's. She didn't need to marry Captain Marks unless she wanted to.

It had bothered Merry. Anybody raised around farm animals had a pretty good idea of what went on in the bedroom, and the idea of Ma and Captain Marks—but that wasn't it, really. It just didn't seem right, like it wasn't fair to Pa. But when Ma set her mind there wasn't any changing her, and he didn't try.

Before it was all settled Marks had invited Merry down to the barn. None of the hands were near and they stood in the center, the man towering over the boy. "You don't like me much," Marks said. "Ain't that right?"

Merry, tongue-tied, stared at the tall man.

Mark's voice gentled. "Say it, son. Am I right—or maybe wrong?" Merry heard a note of appeal, but it didn't make any difference.

"Well," he said at last, "I reckon you're right. But I don't aim to give you no trouble."

He saw the start of a smile fade. "Fair enough, then. Your ma thinks the world of you and I think the world of her. You stay out of my way, I'll stay out of yours. We'll get on."

"Yes, sir," Merry said.

And they'd stayed out of each other's way, more or less. Now five years had passed, Merry was ten, the war had been over for a year, the British whipped and driven to their ships. The final climactic battle had been over at Yorktown here in the state of Virginia, British troops bottled up, surrendering, marching to their ships under American guns. In New York General Washington graciously waited for the Redcoats to board their ships and go before he mounted a fine white horse and led his troops in to the wild cheers of the people. Merry, who was a strong reader by this time, had exhausted the local papers. Then General Washington stepped down, went home like Cincinnatus when the need had passed.

Folks said the general could have been king but he refused, great man that he was. Merry's first reaction was a hollow pit forming in his gut: Washington had been their protector since before he could remember. What would happen now? But that was a year past with 1784 dawning bright and optimistic. Soon Merry began to hear talk that the Continental Congress didn't know what to do, its members all canceling each other out, and everything would be up to the states and they were always quarreling. But Uncle Nick said they'd get on all right and that eased Merry's mind; Uncle Nick was right smart.

The sun dropped below the horizon, leaving hazy light perfumed with honeysuckle. Merry would always remember that. "Captain Marks," Ma said, "has a claim up in North Georgia, on the Broad River. Indian treaty just opened it up. That's where we're going."

"Ma! Leaving here? No—I don't want to go!"

"We're all going, sweetie." She touched his cheek, a caress that yet signified her command. "This plantation will be yours before so very long,
Merry. You can see Captain Marks wants land of his own, can't you?"

"But we'll keep this place too?"

"Of course. Cheer up, darling boy. You'll enjoy yourself. It's wild country, very fertile, full of game. You'll love it."

Well, maybe he would. Really wild country, eh?

After a rough passage past Cape Hatteras a brig landed them at Savanna.
Ma said the word properly had an "h" on the end and Captain Marks told
her not to come here as a stranger and tell folks how to spell the name of
their own town. For once Merry agreed with Captain Marks.

In a caravan of three heavily laden wagons they followed a plainly
marked road to Augusta, a village with maybe a dozen houses and there
the trail ended. Captain Marks hired a guide named Jack McIntyre, an old
coot probably as far along as the captain himself, even getting a little gray.
Mr. McIntyre wore buckskin breeches and a homespun shirt, both so
greasy they amazed Merry until he saw the scout wipe his hands on shirt
and pants after attacking pork chops. The man chuckled. "Waterproofing,
young feller." Merry often rode with him, especially when it became plain
the scout and Captain Marks had taken instant dislike to one another.

This was fine country, Merry thought, though hot and sultry. There
were huge black oaks. Throw a rope around one at five or six feet, Mr.
McIntyre said, and you'd find they measured a good thirty feet or more.
They flushed bear and a dangerous-looking wildcat with tawny coat and
long curling tail that Mr. McIntyre called a tiger but that looked to Merry
like a plain old panther. It was quiet country, few settlers having yet
invaded while the Indians—Cherokees, Mr. McIntyre said—had abandoned villages that from their remains looked to have been right prosper-
ous. He wondered where they had gone and how they had fared when
they got there. When Mr. McIntyre asked him what he thought so far he
mentioned the things he'd seen except his reflections on Indians—something told him they wouldn't be well received.

"Shit, boy," the old man snapped, "you're looking but you ain't seeing."
His beard was long, his hair uncut, and he stank with an odd smoky out-
doors sort of stink like an old bearskin. Merry liked him more every day;
the last thing he wanted was to appear dull in Mr. McIntyre's eyes. "Now,
look at this here ground we're covering. What do you see?"

Merry hesitated too long, then said, "Well, we're climbing."

"Look, son," the scout said in more kindly fashion. "You want to open your eyes. Look around. This here is the Great Ridge, a pretty much level stretch of high forest except it's rising to meet them mountains up yonder. Look at the soil, dark and rich, it'll grow anything. Most anywhere along here you can dig down two or three feet and you'll hit a rock underlay. Look at all them rocks popping out to the surface."

Indeed, though the ground seemed almost level and Merry had felt rather smug to realize on his own that it was rising, it did have all sorts of rock outcroppings and shelvings.

"All them rocks," the scout said, "don't you figure there's some hid out of sight? Well, that controls how the water flows. All these little hills, creek running off right or left from each, that's what feeds both rivers."

"Both?"

An exasperated glare. "Savanna this way, Alatamaha that. Damn, boy—don't you know where you are? Open your eyes!"

The magnificent oaks rose like stately columns thirty to forty feet before the first branch, he could see that much. Mr. McIntyre rode alongside explaining things. That pretty little tree there, that's what they call the silver bell, its flowers make little white bells that look like they're ringing you to camp meeting; Merry thought that surprisingly poetic, though he had a hard time imagining Mr. McIntyre at worship. Look at all the trees, the hackberry and the beech and black walnuts and locust trees trailing their long white pods. Yonder were tulip trees and over here sycamores, and close by ash trees with their strong bow wood. See yonder, that's a hornbeam, you don't see so many of them, and—look, hold up here, get you a handful of this fruit—that's the mulberry . . .

"You look at those trees one way, son, you see 'em all alike. Some tall, some short, yes, but they all have green leaves unless they have green needles and they all have a woody trunk and throw shade and so forth, but you look close and you see every kind is different from every other. Well, shoot, every leaf is different, every bark is different. Just look—some bark is brown, some gray, some white, some smooth, some rough, some in plates look like they want to fall off, some bark tight as the skin of an apple. No tree is exactly like any other. The woods are like them big books a lawyer'll have in his office, look at things close and it'll tell you all you want to know."

Suddenly he sprang off his horse and crouched by a small bush. "Git down and look at this. See the little fruit—we call it the Indian olive or sometimes the physic-nut, that being how the Cherokees use it, for charming or conjuring. See what I mean?"

Merry shook his head.

"Carry the fruit with 'em on the hunt, figure it'll draw the deer by magic. They got a lot of magic, Indians."

Merry knelt beside him, noticing the way the gnarled old hands with their blackened nails delicately separated the leaves and drew forth the fruit that sure enough had the shape of an olive with an olivelike pit inside. Mr. McIntyre said they went bright yellow when ripe. Merry was memorizing plants as he went. The leaves were deep green in color, smooth in texture, broad but tapered at each end. Each leaf seemed to have a single fruit rising on a stem . . .

He took a small booklet from his pocket and wrote out a quick description.

"Well, I declare," Mr. McIntyre said, "getting the description down so you can remember, eh? That's right smart. I'd give a pretty, I knew how to write something down on a piece of paper. That's something."

Merry looked up in surprise. "Why, I reckon I could teach you," he said, but Mr. McIntyre simply smiled.

A few days later they reached the Broad River and Captain Marks's claim. They would stop here. Mr. McIntyre merely nodded to the captain. He raised his hat to Ma. "Ma'am," he said. Then, still mounted, he reined close to Merry. "You're going to make a good man in the woods, young fellow," he said. "Here's something for you — carry it and it'll save your life someday." It was a short knife, four inches, in a scabbard that Merry had seen on the scout's belt. Merry choked back tears. "Now, you mind," Mr. McIntyre said, "keep your eyes open. And luck to ye." He shook Merry's hand and wheeled his horse and lifted it into a trot and then he was gone.

"Well!" Ma said.

Captain Marks looked like he'd bit into a sour apple.

It took a couple of months to set the place for winter, planting a late vegetable garden and building cabin, barn, and corral, and Merry worked long, solid days. Then he was free to look around. He made sure he was there and working hard during planting or harvesting or butchering, and he saw to his lessons that Ma directed, but soon as he could he was off again, rambling the deep woods. At first he explored nearby but one day he rolled a blanket under his pack and told Ma he might not be back tonight. She frowned and so did Captain Marks but in the end she let him go, judging him a fair woodsman already.

He turned eleven and then twelve and figured he was pretty much a man by now. He went off for several days and then a week and then two weeks and presently they didn't know when they would see him again, just that when he came he'd have a doe over his shoulders, and that was enough to pay for his powder and shot. Pack a little fry pan and a coffeepot that was also good for venison stewed with roots the Indians taught him to dig. Pack a little piece of sowbelly for seasoning and coating the pan, a little cornmeal or even flour when times were flush. That and the game he took, sometimes with his rifle that had been Pa's, sometimes with a snare, made solid meals. He ate well and buried his ordure before he moved on. Each day along about four in the afternoon with the sun tilting down but a long way from dark he'd start looking for a ledge over-hang or a cave, watching always for the rattlesnakes that infested sun-warmed rock. He would cook his meal and have the fire doused before the light faded. When dark came he would roll in his blanket and listen to the night sounds and sleep the sleep of exhaustion and growth. Long before the first tendrils of gray showed in the east he would be up, alert, no fire, chewing a bit of meat—venison, squirrel, coon, possum—from the night before, ready to move at first light.

He was tall and lean and lanky now and he walked with Pa's old piece always in hand, taking game when he needed it for that night or when he was homeward bound, but never wasting. His notebook was often in his hand. He walked on trails when they were available but went cross-country as he pleased. He traveled in Cherokee country and stopped to visit when he came on one of their villages. They seemed like good folks; he suspected he amused them, lone white boy prowling the woods with a long rifle, causing no trouble, paying his way by arriving with game for their tables. They raised corn and beans to go with venison and seasoned it with hickory milk made by boiling hickory nuts and straining off the aromatic oil. When he encountered a feast day he stayed as a guest. He entered the wrestling matches and held his own, and learned enough of the Indian ball game not to make a fool of himself; indeed he became quite adept at catching the rawhide ball in the net at the end of his stick and hurling it accurately enough.

Everywhere he went he looked. He enumerated trees, studied their bark, their leaves, their shape. In the villages he studied the uses made of this plant and that. Ma was a natural herbalist, often doctoring neighbors, and he sucked up her knowledge. More notes. Gradually the role of each plant and each tree became clear, how everything fit into God's whole. He saw bears and wolves and wildcats, wolverines and coons and possum, deer and elk. This had been buffalo country once but they long since had departed before civilization that always thrust westward. He saw "tigers" that still looked like panthers to him. He often thought of Mr. McIntyre. The little knife hadn't saved him yet but now he was experienced enough to know that under the right circumstances it certainly could do so.

Every day there was another wonder for his notebook. He saw glass snakes, snakelike but somehow wrong, too, a critter that he finally figured out really was a limbless lizard, its tail of glass because it broke off easily and the resourceful little fellow soon grew a new one. In shoal waters flowing over a gravel bed he espied crayfish building little pyramids that came close to the surface. Small goldfish roved among them seeking the crayfish young they held. But from time to time veteran crayfish would sally forth in phalanx with claws snapping, and then the goldfish would flee in a furious cloud, flashing gold like lightning streaks. Each little fish was about four inches long, head ultramarine blue, reddish brown on back, flame-colored belly, eyes huge, the iris like burnished gold. When the crayfish had made their point they returned to their citadels and the goldfish came swarming back.

Wonders. A bear cub crying like a human child when its mother was killed. A spider that attacked, killed, and carried away a bumblebee twice its size. Or the skeeter-eater plant that much later he would learn had a Latin name, *Sarracenia.* Now it was enough to know it in detail, the gorgeous yellow flowers, the big leaves that turn over in the rain lest the weight of the water break them and their fragile parallel nerves, the stiff hairs that prevent the escape of insects drawn to its scent. These trapped creatures were swiftly covered with a sort of slime that drowned them and then drawn into the plant's maw. Watching closely, he concluded the plant literally *ate* them. Ma had brought a copy of Mr. Webster's great new dictionary of the American language and Merry, spending hours in perusing it, came by chance on the term for the plant: insectivorous. He felt education had come full circle.

But formal education also had reached Ma's limits. He was thirteen, tall, muscular, quite the strapping fellow. Uncle Nick was tending the plantation, but it was Merry's property and it was time he took hold and he judged himself old enough to do so. And the need for formal education beyond Ma's powers was growing.

The country was changing, too. It was 1787 and it was entirely clear that just like folks had feared, the old Continental Congress couldn't handle the new nation. Each state was on its own—its own money, own customs officers, talk of passports to travel from Virginia to Maryland. States quarreling to beat the band. Were we one country or thirteen?

General Washington to the fore, once again. He called for a meeting that soon led to a constitutional convention at Philadelphia. At the end of a long hot summer a constitution emerged. Captain Marks said it took too much from the state in favor of the federals, but when Merry heard that the brilliant Mr. Madison, who lived maybe twenty miles from their plantation, had just about wrote the whole thing he figured there wouldn't be much wrong with it. Merry had figured Mr. Jefferson certainly would be there. But no—he was in Paris, it turned out, serving as ambassador but soon to return.

So Merry was thirteen, full manhood coming on, the nation in new turmoil, an important property to manage, new scholarship to master, and it was time to go home. Say good-bye to the deep woods and all its wonders and all its teachings. They had a new crop of colts and Merry would ride one to Savannah, sell it and book passage for Norfolk. He lashed his bag with an oilcloth slicker behind the saddle. When he was ready he hugged Ma. She clung to him a long time, full of tearful admonitions.

When at last she loosed him he turned to Captain Marks.

"Well, Merry," the captain said, "I haven't done you so bad. You're nigh on as tall as me now, you'll be heavier than me when you get your growth, you're a skilled woodsman, you're a good naturalist. I judge you can make that plantation prosper."

Merry gazed at him without answering and Marks flushed. "Come on, damn it, admit it—I didn't do you so badly. Not near as badly as you once expected. Now, ain't that right? Say it."

Something in the man's worn eyes told Merry all at once that this mattered as he hadn't understood before.

"Yes, sir," he said, "you done me right fair. And I thank you." He put out his hand and Captain Marks took it and then suddenly drew him into a tight embrace, which had never happened in all the years they had been together.

"I wish you good fortune," the captain said, rather formally, Merry thought. "You'll be a lot of man someday. And I believe you can do anything you set your mind to."

So Meriwether Lewis rode out of the Georgia mountains bound for Virginia and great events in the future. He was on his own, loosed like an arrow from a bow, and again he had that sense that he was somebody, somehow special, that great things awaited him. He rode on, feeling full ready for all that lay ahead.

4

Albemarle County, Virginia, 1792

The dream lived on, but sometimes he had consciously to summon it and sometimes conjure it whole to combat low spirits. He was going to be somebody, do great things, stride in those seven-league boots across a vast and endless plain where the sun set in a golden puddle and stars were diamonds in the night and the man alone made camp on a height and cooked his spare meal and lit his pipe and watched the gorgeous night fall all around him. Yes, he could still summon that vision from nowhere and make it almost real, but it took more doing these days.

For it seemed that his rambling days were over. He had a plantation to tend. Uncle Nick Lewis came by every day and told him what to do and how to do it while good old Aunt Susie who once had been his wet nurse cooked for him. Her best wasn't as good as a hunk of venison roasted on a springy stick and a pot of stew made of Indian roots, though he knew better than to tell her that. After a month of Uncle Nick telling him what to do he was considerably wearied.

"Why don't I tell you what I aim to do and you tell me if it's a mistake?"

Before long Uncle Nick was stopping in now and again but Merry was in charge. It was 1788 by then and he was fourteen going on fifteen and confident he didn't need much advice on anything. He had plenty of opinions, too, and didn't mind voicing them. Like on the new constitution. It was written in 1787 under General Washington's benign eye, their own Mr. Madison being a principal author. Mr. Jefferson complained it didn't spell out American freedoms sufficiently and Mr. Madison pushed through the first ten amendments that made it all crystal clear. Then it went to the states for ratification. It would take effect when nine states ratified.

Virginia was all set to serve as number nine and reap the honor of confirming the Constitution when New Hampshire burst in ahead of the Old Dominion and seized the prize position. By a mere four days Virginia had to take the meaningless tenth place. Merry thought it a damned disgrace and at Saturday market he said so loud and clear.

A stout man in a rich coat, handkerchief in his sleeve, took offense. "You goddam snot-nose, who the hell are you to talk of our great Virginia in such terms? Next you'll be talking agin General Washington. By God, I'd slap your head off if you wasn't still in diapers."

Diapers! Merry was ready to lunge when a tall boy maybe two or three years older stepped in front of him. "Let me handle him, Pa," this oaf said. "Teach him a lesson."

The older boy had weight and strength and reach and knew how to fight, not a good combination. Merry took four hard raps around nose and mouth, two that knocked him down, before he thought, shoot, I can hit harder than that. He bounded up and rushed the boy, punching his body till he howled. The boy fell, scrambled to his feet, and rushed. They went down, rolling together in the dust, and bounded up, punches flying. Still, Merry was beginning to wish he'd kept his mouth shut when a tall man in a black coat and a pastor's collar stepped between them and said to stop it before someone got hurt. Merry figured he already hurt plenty but he'd have died before he'd have admitted it. His opponent, older and heavier, seemed as glad to quit as Merry felt so maybe it was all right.

He walked over to the well to wash his face in the horse trough and returned in time to hear Doc Granby say to Uncle Nick, "That boy of yours, Nick, he can fight. Let him get his growth and he'll be some man." The throbbing pain in Merry's face disappeared.

Mr. Jefferson was still in France these days, member with John Adams and Benjamin Franklin of the commission charged with negotiating treaties of commerce between European nations and the new republic across the water. Merry wasn't an old friend, exactly, but he knew Mr. Jefferson; indeed, the expectation of seeing his neighbor had been an anticipated pleasure in returning.

The Lewis plantation was seven miles west of Charlottesville and hence but a few miles from Monticello. Mr. Jefferson long had bought hams from Ma's smokehouse. Years past — Merry figured he was about eight then — Ma had started entrusting him with delivering the hams. Mounted on a blooded horse, hams tied two and two and slung over the withers, he had ridden off to Monticello proud as a peacock. Much later it struck him that some of the man's kindness to him at that particular time might have grown from his own emotional devastation as his wife, to whom he was famously devoted, approached death. Of course Mr. Jefferson never said a word about her to Merry or to anyone else outside his immediate family and circle, but everyone knew it crushed his spirits.

At any rate, he well remembered the day Mr. Jefferson had said, "You're a bright lad. Do you have your letters yet?"

"Yes, sir," he'd said, "Ma learned me to read."

"Taught," Mr. Jefferson said. "Try to use the correct form."

Mr. Jefferson was tall and skinny, hair an odd rusty blend of red and brown beginning to gray, his eye deeply penetrating. You felt he could peer into your soul and Merry just naturally stood straighter when he talked to the master of Monticello. One day Mr. Jefferson led Merry into a room with an incredible array of books neatly shelved. Now, it was common talk that this was about the finest library in America — years later he realized it was this same library that Mr. Jefferson turned over to the government to form the nucleus for the Library of Congress. Mr. Jefferson stretched to a top shelf and seemingly at random pulled down a book and put it in Merry's hand.

"Next time I see you I'll expect the book returned and a good discussion of what you draw from it."

The book proved to be a pioneer narrative with the emphasis on bear hunting in the wilderness beyond the Blue Ridge. Bear were becoming rare in the plantation country but Merry had been on a couple of hunts. About halfway through the book it struck him that the author had never really seen a bear.

He said as much when he returned the book and the tall man clapped him on the shoulder and cried, "Very good! The writer's a patent fraud and you are a perspicacious young man to sense that." Merry was delighted, the more so when he and Ma sorted through Mr. Webster's fat dictionary and figured out what "perspicacious" meant. For two years, until Captain Marks moved them to Georgia, Merry had had the run of Mr. Jefferson's library, the only stipulation that he must discuss each book when he returned it. It was considerable education.

Merry had been back in Virginia a good year when Mr. Jefferson returned and by then he knew the world had changed substantially. He was fifteen, studying the classics in Pastor Maury's school and running Locust Hill on his own but for his uncle's occasional advice. General Washington was president, elected a couple of months after the ratification of the Constitution in 1788. That was part of the deal, really; folks said the Constitution never would have passed as it did, rapidly and after much debate but little dissension, had it not been clear that General Washington would ride in on a white horse and rescue them.

The general named Alexander Hamilton secretary of the treasury. Congress told Mr. Hamilton to take a couple of months and invent a financial system that would put them on their feet. After seven years of war and four disastrous years under the squabbling and powerless confederation, folks were living by barter, specie was scarce as hen's teeth, and the men around the market, among whom Merry now listened carefully and kept his mouth shut, were saying that a nation that can't pay its bills ain't no nation at all, it's an international laughingstock, and more than that, if we don't get some cash money moving we ain't never going to get on our feet.

So Mr. Hamilton opened a bank that was part U.S. Treasury and part private, which Virginia's own Mr. Madison said gave private hands a lot of power over public money—too much power, too much opportunity for moneymen to feather their own nests. Mr. Madison lived up the road a piece, beyond Orange, on a plantation he called Montpelier, an easy day's ride from Locust Hill, though Merry had never actually met him. Folks paid a lot of attention to what Mr. Madison said. They figured he knew his onions since the way he'd handled the Constitution. When he said that was an overstatement they laughed and waved their hands. They knew. They also knew their own Mr. Jefferson had pushed from France to get the Bill of Rights added, spelling out the rights of citizens in a free society.

Mr. Jefferson said that was his price for supporting the document and Mr. Madison hammered them through.

The men Merry knew were already suspicious of Hamilton's intentions when Mr. Jefferson returned from Europe to be secretary of state in the new government. At least, General Washington offered it but Mr. Jefferson took his own good time in accepting. Seemed strangely unpatriotic for a patriotic man, but then everyone knew Mr. Jefferson never minded being out of step with what folks in general were thinking. Only reason he finally agreed, the men at Saturday market said, spitting knowledgeably, was that Mr. Madison rode down from Orange and put the wood to him.

The wise heads at the market were saying that maybe they should give Hamilton, the New Yorker, more slack given that he had to move fast to keep the country from bankruptcy, but damned if he didn't seem downright hungry to shape an American system just like that in Britain with its lords and ladies and the right people taken care of at the expense of all the common folk. Joe Singleton said that was just a little too much like what comes from the wrong end of the horse and there was a chorus of ayes. It looked like Mr. Jefferson and Mr. Madison saw it the same way and before you knew it they were going hand-to-hand with Mr. Hamilton. Virginia had all the lords and ladies it needed . . .

But when Merry heard that Mr. Jefferson was actually back at Monticello he rode over with a ham and heard no such talk. Mr. Jefferson welcomed him as if he had nothing more on his mind than to chat with a neighborhood youngster. He asked a few questions and Merry heard himself pouring out his adventures in the mountain forests of North Georgia. Soon they were talking of the plant and animal life that Merry had seen and when it was clear that he had encountered plants unknown to Mr. Jefferson, who was certainly the most prominent botanist in Virginia, Merry had to fight to keep pride from his manner.

The next time he went to Monticello he took his notebooks filled in those lonely mountain camps and Mr. Jefferson read with growing wonder. Why, he told Merry, you're on the way to being a first-class naturalist, or somesuch, Merry too rattled by the praise to remember exactly.

Then, head cocked back and long nose pointing at Merry like a spear, he asked if he understood the Linnaean system of plant and animal classification. Whereupon a whole new world opened. Class, order, family, genus, species—the strange terms whirled around in Merry's head but gradually he got the hang of it. A kingdom, animal or plant, divided into phyla. Phyla divided into classes and so forth right on down to species, and even more finally, subspecies. Latin names given arbitrarily but within the rigid rules of this classification system meant that any plant could be listed or identified in such a way that you saw where it fit with every other plant.

Within an hour Merry grasped the magnificent order the system imposed, and he could see that his rapid comprehension pleased Mr. Jefferson. His mentor said it was the work of Carl von Linné of Sweden and handed him a book from his shelves, Linné's *Systema Naturae*. He said it first was published in 1735 but had run through many editions of which this, the tenth, was the best. Merry took a month on that, polishing his Latin in the process so thoroughly that Pastor Maury pronounced him a scholar without ever knowing the cause of this new proficiency. Then he was ready for Linné's *Species Plantarum* that Mr. Jefferson said would complete the picture. He said that one of his most powerful disappointments in Europe was to learn that Linné had died not long before he arrived.

Mr. Jefferson was often in the capital at New York and then when it shifted, Philadelphia, and what was being talked of as a new democracy seemed to be taking shape under his leadership. But when he came home and Merry rode over with a brace of hams and they talked, it was of plants and the forest. Merry could hear something like envy in Mr. Jefferson's questions about the simple act of taking one's rifle and a sack of flour and a piece of sowbelly to grease the pan and flavor the bread and set out across country one had never seen before. Young Lewis turned sixteen and seventeen, as tall as Jefferson, as heavily built, and the older man's longing for a life of nature instead of a life of men stirred a matching longing in the younger man to be up and about and gone . . . where he didn't know, how he couldn't tell, but striding out in those seven-league boots. Inchoate longing burned in him.

Merry heard it at the market, utterly stunning news, different from all that had gone before. Instantly his dreams, sometimes incoherent and often fantastical, came into clear focus like turning a brass telescope till the distance came bright and clear.

It was 1793 and he was nineteen years old. Everything had changed and yet, depressingly, nothing had changed for him. He now ran the plantation with sure authority, but the dark days when life seemed a narrow rut of endless routine, season by season, came more often. Captain Marks had died and Merry had gone to Georgia and brought Ma back to Locust Hill. He told her she would always have a home here.

General Washington had been elected to a second term in 1792 but now the reverence for his name had passed. Criticism came hot and heavy, open season on a great man from a thankless people. Factions were taking hold, government was divided, and parties were forming. Political parties, that is, heretofore unknown in America. Everyone said it was a pity but everyone also cleaved to one or the other.

New York, led by Hamilton, and New England collectively, the manufacturing center of the nation, were becoming known as Federalist. Once the term had meant those who argued for ratification of the Constitution, but now what once had been a unified populace began to split against the rocks of policy differences. Folks in Albemarle County saw it plain enough—the Federalists seemed to feel it only right and proper for government to be in control of and operated for the benefit of the wise and the good, which turned out to be those with position, wealth, and power. After all, why would God reward them with wealth if they weren't wise and good?

The poor old general was trying his best to steer a steady course, Federalists on one side and what came to be called the Democratic Republicans led by Mr. Jefferson and Mr. Madison and Aaron Burr on the other. The Democrats wanted to give the common man a voice in government, wanted a fair shake for everyone, at least everyone male and white. The hotter things got the more the old general tried to hold to middle ground, but that satisfied neither side and he was attacked from all around. Great man that he was, he maintained the dignity of silence but people who knew said you could read the pain in his eyes.

But all this was nothing compared to the wonderful news. It was all over the market when Merry rode in that afternoon, everyone talking. Why, it even had been confirmed in the Richmond *Enquirer*, which was that rarity, a paper you could usually trust. Merry burned with excitement, for clearly this affected him more fully and directly than anyone in America, or at least in Virginia. And instinctively he knew that there was one person, just one, whom he must tell. That he felt so raised a distant question in his mind but he thrust it aside. As soon as Ma got them fed he saddled up and rode over to Mary Beth's place.

Mary Beth Slaney was eighteen, hair honey-colored, freckles that she didn't like and he did scattered across her face and across her nose like they were assaulting a height, eyes that seemed to him to know more than she ever said in that smooth, low voice that made him think of a fiddle crying. They had been keeping company, sort of, for two years and he had the feeling that she was waiting, though she never said much that was direct.

But when they went to dancing parties that the gentry gave in round after round—it being the duty of every young man to be as skilled at dancing as in horsemanship, boxing, and farming—she was the one he sought out and he felt she waited for him. She fitted in his arms, she really was just right, and that scared him. He wasn't scared of much but he was scared of Mary Beth. And drawn, too, like a honeybee to a flower. She smelled like a flower, smelled so good that he took to plunging into the pond for a swim that washed him off just fine before he went to call on her.

But tonight he couldn't wait. Bolted his food and mounted his horse, tied the critter to the fence her daddy had raised around their garden and said, "Let's walk. I got something to tell you."

There was a full moon, good as a chaperon, and they stayed in plain view, walking down the fence line of her pa's pasture. She sat on an upper step of the stile, skirt wrapped about her knees, looking at him with a slight expectant smile. Well, he reckoned this news would thrill her to her very core.

What it was, Mr. Jefferson was planning an exploring expedition that would cross the whole blamed continent! Can you imagine, he cried, knowing his voice reflected the exaltation that shook him like a rag doll, crossing territory no white man had ever covered? It would cross deserts and floodplains and gardens and forests and finally come to what they called the Shining Mountains or sometimes the Stony Mountains that lay in the West like the Appalachians in the East. Across those mountains they would find a river running down to the sea and would end up on the Pacific Ocean!

Mr. Jefferson was secretary of state—he could order such things if he wanted. Never mind that everything beyond the Mississippi was Spanish territory and the Spanish were known as jealous guardians likely to toss intruders in the dungeons folks said they kept handy for trespassers. Mr. Jefferson could figure out how to work around that. And anyway, how many soldiers could they put on thousands of miles of trail? Maybe an intruder could avoid them just by keeping his eyes open.

Pacing back and forth in his excitement, beating out points, fist into palm, he decided a dozen men should do the trick, just about, big enough to defend itself if necessary but not so big that it would look like an invasion or something. It would take two, maybe three, maybe even four years, see, there's no real way to tell—

Mary Beth's smile was gone. He could see that, though her face was turned down, expression scarcely visible in the moonlight's shadow. Later he remembered that blank and empty look she turned on him and how her freckles seemed to have disappeared, how small and distant her voice had gone.

"And you want to go along," she said in scarcely a whisper.

"More than that," he cried, "lots more. I intend to *command* it."

And then—ah, God, he would never forget this—she laughed. Bright as a bell, musical as a lark, and he stared, fighting rage that rose in his throat to choke him.

Looking back, he remembered there was relief in her voice though he couldn't recall her words, something to the effect that he was just nineteen, how did he expect to command things? Said no one would take him seriously.

He roared like a bear, infuriated. "Why not—I know the woods good as any man. I know plants and trails and tracking and the way animals do. He said so himself!"

She tried to protest but he bore her down. "I run the plantation and folks mind what I say. I reckon I could lead men, they'd do what I say or get a fist in the mouth." He was shouting. Take the Indians in the West, he'd dealt with Indians, they were good folk, he knew how to get along with them—

Quick as it came his anger vanished. Think of it, he cried, "Across a whole *continent*—going where ain't nobody but Indians have gone and not many of them, opening hundreds of miles, maybe thousands of miles nobody knows a thing about—"

She was crying. He stared at her, aghast. "What?"—his voice faltering—"what?"

Then in a motion so fluid it seemed like magic she was off the stile and in his arms, her body pressed to his, her open mouth lifted to his. His arms locked around her. And then, loud and wild, she said—Lord, he would never forget what she said, he didn't know women even talked that way—she said, "God, I want you, Merry. Don't talk so. It frightens me bad. Let's get married. I want you— I wake up in the night wanting you. I dream you're inside me—"

She laughed, he remembered how loud that laugh in the still night, and said Ma would kill her if she heard such talk but she didn't care, and she cried, "Let's get married and make love and have wonderful children and teach them all you know—"

He stared at her, appalled. Surrender the great dream? The silence lengthened and she stepped back. Without a word she picked up her scarf where it had fallen on the stile and turned to walk back to the house. He paced beside her, the silence now so loud he felt his ears shattering. He stopped at the gate and she went up the walk alone with her back straight and he watched her, voice frozen and yet somehow hoping she would turn. But she opened the door and went in and never once looked back. The door closed softly, not even slammed, and that made it the more final.

But he had, at least, the dream. He wrote Mr. Jefferson in full confidence that the command was his. He waited a year before he could accept the fact that there would not even be an answer. Then he read that some

Frenchman had been chosen and had turned out to be a secret agent of
the French Revolution and the whole thing had been dropped, and that
was the end of that.

The next year, when he was twenty, he joined the army.

5

Western Pennsylvania Wilderness, 1799

That year before he joined the army, awaiting day by day the answer from
Mr. Jefferson that never came, took on a miasmic gray quality in memory. Gloom settled over him. Since he was twelve or thirteen he'd been
having occasional low, dark periods, but now they seemed worse. He
knew himself that he smiled less often, laughed more rarely. He fought off
bouts of inexplicable sadness—what the hell did he have to be sad about,
he asked himself. Shattered hopes didn't really serve. Ma said he was like
his pa who'd been given to fits of melancholy for no reason anyone could
see. Lewis had some reasons but they didn't measure up to how he felt.
Like his pa, that melancholy streak.

He liked the plantation well enough, but at nineteen he already had
mastered it to his own satisfaction. Was that all there was to be? Maybe
Mary Beth—but then, hadn't she said exactly that? Get married and
make babies and raise them, life no different at twenty-nine or thirty-nine
or fifty-nine, except probably he'd be dead by then out of sheer ennui—a
word he'd picked up from Mr. Webster's tome. Good word, too; he liked
Mr. Webster's book because the variety of words with all their intricate
meanings spoke of a great wide world awaiting him.

In 1794 when he was twenty news came from out beyond the mountains in western Pennsylvania. Men stood around the Saturday market
with the Charlottesville paper rattling in their hands as they gripped it in
outrage, shook it for emphasis. Western Pennsylvania was in revolt! It
was hard to believe but apparently the farmers there really were kicking
up sand, objecting to a special tax on the whiskey they made from their
corn. It seemed they had tarred and feathered a couple of tax collectors
and burned the house and barn of a couple more. When you stopped to
think it didn't sound so deadly but General Washington was all upset and
was calling out the army to march on the rebels.

The army . . . suddenly the future opened like one of the flowers Ma raised. Where to go and what to do was solved. The general calling for volunteers. The nation imperiled. Time to rally around the flag, three cheers for the stars and stripes. A recruiting sergeant came through and set up on the square. He was a big fellow in a gorgeous uniform with a romantic scar slashed down his cheek. He walked with a limp and said he'd been all shot to hell but he'd never give up the joys of the soldier's life. Portentous as a keeper of the gate at Mount Olympus, he dropped silver dollars on a drumhead one at a time, loud thumps in the silent square. Pick up your dollar and join the army to serve your country. Lewis heard his own nails rasp on the drumhead as he took up one of the coins.

He rode home, marshaling arguments to present to Ma. He'd be defending his country, soldier gone to war like Pa, his little brother Reuben was old enough to care for the place, this was duty. Ma's lips drew tight as string but he bade her good-bye and was off to camp with a Virginia company. Soon he was an ensign—he was a Virginia planter, after all, and hence a gentleman and thus officer material even if he was only twenty. Class was rampant in the army. The rebels burned a few more haystacks and chased a tax collector into a lake but weren't militant enough to go in after him and get wet. When word reached them the army was massing they went home, put away weapons, and swore they had never been part of no rebellion, no siree. By then Lewis was reveling in the army and he seized a chance to sign up for the regulars.

A long time passed before he explained this last move to Ma. He also said nothing about meeting an old farmer at the livery stable in the village of Pittsburgh who had looked him up and down with contempt. The old gent said the rebellion was just some ragtag farmers protesting an unfair tax on whiskey that happened to be the only form in which they could get their corn to market, the cost of carting a wagonload of corn over the mountains to the east obviously prohibitive. He said the whole thing was a plot by that fellow Hamilton to further impoverish the honest yeoman who wouldn't vote his way in a hundred years. The treasury secretary was fixing it so the wealthy could eat still higher on the hog and make common folk pay.

So the way the old dog saw it—he said his name was Jack Staring and he didn't give a damn who caught him staring, he would speak his mind as he chose—he figured Jefferson and Mr. Madison, they had the right idea. Government that was able to see plain folks. "You mind, young fellow," he said, hawking and spitting and rubbing the phlegm into the dirt floor with the toe of his boot, horses moving restlessly in their stalls, "we let 'em keep going and one of these days they'll set it up so when you get your snout properly in the trough you can pass your spot on to your son and he to his son, keep all that power in the family, don't you see? Hereditary, that's what we're talking about, holding power to your class, making it part of the law. Aristocracy, lords and ladies like in Britain pissing all over little men."

A horse neighed suddenly, startlingly loud in the stable's confines. The old man rapped the stall door with a snaffle stick.

"Hyah! You settle down in there, God damn you."

The horse snorted. It turned to and fro, tail lashing. By chance its rear was toward them when it farted loudly.

"Damn educated horse," the old man said. "Tells you what he thinks of Mr. Hamilton and his plans. He's setting up for a king one of these days, Hamilton is."

"King?" Lewis said. "But Washington specifically refused a crown."

"Yes, back in the days when he still was a great man—before he got old and didn't care no more and slid right into Hamilton's pocket. Now he does what the big boys tell him—and I can tell you, the people don't like it one bit, send the army to crush 'em underfoot."

The old gent raised a worn finger, nail black-rimed and broken, and said, "I tell you this—we don't get Mr. Jefferson and Mr. Madison in there before long the whole blamed country'll go to hell."

Well, that made sense. Lewis decided that the Whiskey Rebellion wasn't much but he didn't let that dim his new affection for the army. He loved the long marches, horse's hooves thudding, sergeants counting cadence in trilling singsong, men looking to him for orders, guidance, and their care and tending. He was learning to separate leadership from command, to put his men's comfort ahead of his own, to give orders so they would be obeyed. He was learning to tap the vast knowledge locked in old sergeants' skulls, which meant first of all earning their respect. It wasn't quite striding off to the far horizons but it was a start, fluid and open and moving where anything could happen, well beyond the hobbles of plantation life.

But he paid more attention to politics, too. Looking back at his days on the plantation, to say nothing of the forests of Georgia, he could see that his vision hadn't gone much beyond his own immediate self. The way of childhood, perhaps, but now he was moved to look around and decide where he stood in the world. More and more clearly he was finding that the Federalist persuasion didn't persuade. He was a Democrat pure and simple.

Newspapers cut and slashed at one another in wild exercise of the rights of a free press. One side said Democrats were spawn of the devil sure to explode as the common man movement in France had done, every chestnut tree in Philadelphia to be adorned with the corpse of one of the better people swinging on a rope. The other side affirmed the strength of a free people in charge of their own destiny and insisted the sole aim of Federalists was to fasten a hereditary aristocracy on Americans that would assure that the powerful and the wealthy would stay that way, and from that, in time, give the United States a king. Poised between the extremes, the old general caught hell from both sides and Lewis already was enough soldier to understand what General Washington had given his country.

Quarrels raged through the officer's corps, conducted with a gentlemanly veneer that often ran thin. France and the excesses of democracy was in everyone's mind. Within a year of the fall of the Bastille and crowds dancing in the streets and the most noble sentiments on every man's lips the terror had started, the grisly instrument in Guillotine Square dropping like a metronome and the streets slick with blood. Louis XVI whom Americans had seen as a rather decent sort of fellow who tried to support the democratic impulse was dragged to the guillotine. The nobility was executed without reference to any crime, simply because they were of the aristocracy, whereupon the surviving nobility fled to neighboring nations. Soon war was boiling in Europe, the British leading the rest of Europe against the French. And Napoleon stepped in from the wings to establish a military dictatorship.

A good bit of grog was consumed in the officer corps arguments. Most officers were Federalists, the government having packed the ranks as it was packing the courts in its favor. The excesses of France, these officers said, proved the common man to be a brute who must be controlled by the rigid governance of the best people, call them aristocrats or whatever you please. Lewis insisted that the American experience of government by and for the people was the best refutation of that erroneous idea and sometimes he added that those propounding it were horses' asses.

Thus it was that he came to the attention of Stinker Elliott, a pudgy young lieutenant. Stinker—perhaps his mother had named him something else but no one Lewis knew called him anything other than Stinker—announced that Ensign Lewis, occupying the lowest officer rank in the army, was a perfect example of the perils of democracy and letting common men into the company of their betters. Ensign Lewis should be assigned to latrine duty since the content of his speech so closely matched the purpose of the latrine. This witticism drew wide approbation. It was repeated to Lewis on a Sunday afternoon when he and friends were considering philosophy as they bent their elbows.

Lewis marched immediately to Stinker's quarters. They were on a small post a hundred miles west of Pittsburgh and quarters for men of rank were log huts. Lewis was sleeping in a leaky tent, which did nothing for his mood. He kicked open Stinker's door, told him he was a pus-gut son of a bitch, and drove a fist into his face. Then he became aware that Stinker had guests, three other officers who threw Lewis out into the street.

Lewis picked himself up, brushed himself off, and hurriedly penned an enraged challenge. Let them meet under the smoke of dueling pistols and see who proved the better man. In Lewis's view, Lieutenant Elliott settled that question immediately: the pus-gut coward rushed straight to the provost marshal to demand Lewis be arrested and held for court-martial on charges of assault, drunkenness, conduct unbecoming, and issuing a challenge—the last being against a regulation that everyone else ignored.

General Wayne had no choice but to call the court-martial. Mad Anthony, as the general was widely known for the utter ferocity of the charges he led during the Revolution, opened the trial by saying that he hoped this was the last time he must convene such a body over a trivial quarrel that officers with any guts would settle privately with pistols. With that as preamble the members of the court listened gravely to the evidence and gave a full five minutes to reaching a verdict of not guilty. Then, since it was plain that Ensign Lewis and Lieutenant Elliott would have trouble serving together, the general further demonstrated his feelings by giving Lewis a rich plum of an assignment—he went straight to the Chosen Rifles, an elite unit of sharpshooters, Captain William Clark commanding.

When Lewis presented himself at Clark's compound he was on his best military behavior. He dismounted, saluted the flag, saw the captain emerge from a tent, and saluted him with rigid formality. Clark returned the salute with a finger brushed against his forehead and said, "At ease, Ensign." Lewis decided he had found a home.

Over the next six months Lewis grew steadily closer to Clark, who ran the Rifles with easy informality but never left any doubt as to who was in charge. Rouse him, Lewis saw, and his voice crackled with command and men leaped to obey. Lewis earned his lieutenancy and the departure of other officers soon had him working directly under Clark. They became close friends with a deep sense of trust that Lewis saw cut both ways. When Clark left the army, his teeth rattling with malaria and his family in deepening financial trouble out in the Indiana country, formally known still as the Northwest Territory, there seemed a chance that Lewis might succeed to the command. Instead the Rifles were subsumed into other groups and Lewis began a rambling tour of the army that brought him to duty here and there and in the end gave him the assignment he'd been waiting for.

Now a captain, he was named regimental paymaster for the First Infantry. The regiment was scattered over the vast forests north of the Ohio River and on west to the Illinois and the Mississippi. Heading a small detail, five men and a sergeant, he roamed from tiny post to tiny post across the great expanse. For a genuine rambling man it was a glorious assignment. At each post he rested the horses a day, doled out banknotes from the store he carried on a pack mule, took count of the men on hand, and drank with the officers as he gave them the latest gossip. At every post his arrival was cause for celebration among lonely men posted as guards on a restless frontier, Indian troubles and white renegades frequent problems, all under the threat of British intrusions over the still scarcely defined border with Canada.

It was fine, long rides through shadowy woods on the alert for white renegades interested in the banknotes they carried, taking game as they moved. Choose a campsite in the late afternoon, cook a spare meal, post guards, smoke a final pipe over the last cup of sugary coffee, take the second watch himself, visit the two guard posts a last time, and finally roll in a blanket to listen to the creak of trees and the chatter of night creatures and drift away.

Rambling again—it was almost as good as being back in the woods of northern Georgia.

General Washington stepped down as president. Gave his farewell address a couple of months before the election in 1796, making it certain he was going home to rest. Lewis figured he had good cause to be tired but likely his heart was broke as well by all the dissension and attacks. Mr. Jefferson had resigned as secretary of state and gone back to Monticello. Mr. Madison said he would give up his seat in the Congress and go home to Orange. Apparently his days as the main advisor to General Washington had come to an end. By now the general had selected the site on the Potomac for the new capital that everyone figured would bear his name. It seemed the location was part of a deal: Jefferson and the Democrats would accept Hamilton's new bank even though it put a lot of power into establishment hands, while the Federalists would agree to shifting the capital south. Lewis figured that was a canny bargain. There seemed no alternative to the bank so the Virginian had milked advantage from accepting the inevitable. It took a smart fellow to swing that.

Still, so Lewis speculated to himself, maybe the nation had profited from the attacks on the old general, all the charges that he had lapsed into imbecilic senility and was more to be pitied than censured. If the reverence once shown him had never abated, wouldn't they have been rudderless and bereft when he quit? The country was growing up.

John Adams became president, Mr. Jefferson the vice president. They ran without parties, sort of a popularity contest, the Constitution having been written before parties existed. Jefferson posted second but he was coming up fast. Mr. Adams was a great patriot, no doubt about that, but in Lewis's view, he was much too much the Federalist. Adams gulped a little but then brought himself to sign and enforce the Alien and Sedition Acts that made it a crime just to criticize the government. Newspapers were closed, their presses smashed, if they didn't toe the administration line. All this arising from the fear that flowed from the downward spiral of the French Revolution.

"But don't that knock the Constitution into a cocked hat?" Lewis was back at headquarters at Pittsburgh talking to his friend, Tom Sutton, a line captain. Tom's father was a judge about thirty miles east of Pittsburgh; Lewis had fallen briefly in love with his sister, Matilda, until she broke off the relationship without explanation. Tom had just shrugged and Lewis didn't visit the Suttons again.

Anyway, Tom had studied law before he decided the soldier's life suited him better, and he said, "Well, sure, these laws rough up the Constitution but who's going to enforce that document, noble though it is. Supreme Court? Hell no, it's scarcely functioning. You'd think that was its purpose but maybe someone has to get it organized first. Hell, I don't know, but I'll tell you this, if it ain't unconstitutional I'll kiss your ass on the Pittsburgh square and give you an hour to draw a crowd."

Just before Lewis was set to go off on another round, he and Sutton spent a Sunday afternoon strolling about the square winking at the pretty girls and catching their flirtatious smiles. Lewis was thinking about Matilda who had kissed him once in a way that suggested endless possibilities when he saw a burly constable snatch an old man with white whiskers from a wagon. An old woman on the wagon seat screamed and children in the back began to bawl.

"God Almighty," Lewis said. "It's Mr. Staring!"

"What? A friend of yours?"

"I know him," Lewis said. He stepped forward as Staring lost his balance and fell. The old man reared up and bellowed, "I been saying what I believe for fifty goddam years and I ain't likely to stop for the likes of you!"

"Seditious son of a bitch," the constable said and drew back a boot, ready to kick the old man in the chest. A boy, maybe Staring's oldest, jumped off the wagon. Lewis stepped close and bumped the constable. Off balance, a foot raised to kick, he staggered.

"That will do, Constable," Lewis said in his best command voice.

"Merry," Sutton said softly, "you're a U.S. Army officer. Don't be getting involved."

The constable hesitated. "I'm just enforcing the law," he said, a faint whine entering his voice. "He's clearly seditious. Been saying all over town the government has its head up its ass and France ain't no threat at all. Now, judge wants him hauled in—"

"Well, take him if you must," Lewis said, "but you'll answer to me, you abuse him."

Mr. Staring suddenly found his voice. "Seditious, am I? 'Cause I tell my friends what I think? Have a glass of ale and speak my piece? This here is America, you oaf—how dare you tell me I can't offer an opinion."

"Well, you goddam can't and that's the law and I'm taking you in." He turned to Lewis, the whine back, and said, "It *is* the law. I didn't write it, I just enforce it."

Sutton tugging at his sleeve, he turned away. A letter from Reuben told him that Mr. Jefferson was saying that since Alien and Sedition couldn't be corrected judicially it would have to be done politically. Throw the rascals out, in other words. That struck Captain Lewis as exactly right. The way things were going, Jefferson would be the next president.

Well, in the end it was closer than he had expected, not decided until near the end of an election season that stretched across the fall, each state setting its own polling date. So it was that Lewis and his little detail, the pack mule carrying enough banknotes to satisfy most anyone's dreams, he and his men with eyes cocked and pieces ready to meet anyone whose dream might be to convert those notes to his own use, were deep in the Ohio woods when the final word came. A storekeeper said a fellow had been through the day before with a Pittsburgh newspaper that said it was settled—Jefferson had defeated Adams. Now the thought that Lewis had been nurturing for a year or more burst into the open, filling his mind. Now the man who seven years before planned an expedition to the Pacific as a tentative exploration would have the power to *order* an expedition.

Ten days later when he rode into the headquarters cantonment at Pittsburgh he found a letter awaiting him. It was from Mr. Jefferson and it asked Captain Lewis to serve as the president's private secretary. He was tired, dirty, hungry, and short-tempered, and his first reaction was anger. Private secretary? What the hell did Meriwether Lewis know about secretary-ing? Scribbling copies of letters all day, taking dictation, serving tea—he reread the letter. Don't worry about letters, Mr. Jefferson said, explaining that he wrote his own letters; well, that took care of that. But still. Serving tea, for God's sake? Dancing the foreign service minuet?

And then—thirty seconds had passed and he hadn't looked up from the letter—the vast import of it all dawned. Of course. With the power to act the new president was calling for the expedition before he even thought of anything else. He didn't say so, but look at the reality. The expedition would be crossing Spanish territory as soon as it struck the far side of the Mississippi—naturally the president wouldn't confide his plans in a letter that anyone might see before it reached Lewis. But why else would he invite a raw frontier officer to serve among the fancy-drawers of Washington and the diplomatic world? Only one reason made sense: Mr. Jefferson was answering the boy's letter of long ago. At last.

6

Washington, Spring, 1801

Having settled himself in office, the president had gone home to Monticello, as he said he would do at every opportunity. Lewis followed, astride an army mount and leading a packhorse. He crossed the Potomac by ferry and rode into the sweet Virginia countryside marked by warm odors and memories, passing freshly turned fields and flowering orchards and occasional plantation houses with pillars and formal gardens.

The closer he came to the welcome he expected from the president the more excited—well, energized, he decided that was the better word—he felt. His memories of Mr. Jefferson were not quite that of son for father but close: the great man opening his door to the boy with a smile, the free run of his famous library, the schooling in multiple subjects. He remembered how the man had admired the boy's woodcraft, those hard treks up Carolina mountains, taking game as needed, drinking from icy springs, checking for rattlers under a rock overhang before spreading his blanket, dousing his fire before dark.

An image of Mary Beth Slaney popped unbidden into his mind. She would see that the dreaming boy had not been so far off. It was all coming true now. His memories of her were still alive, hair the color of honey, the way her breasts swelled her gown, that wash of freckles on cheeks and nose, Ireland and Scotland at war in her face, her sweet smile reflecting inner purity.

Remember the stately way she walked away that night after she'd downright proposed to him and said things he'd never imagined she'd even considered, the memory stirring him even now. How she had gone inside her house and closed the door and never looked back. How lonely he'd felt, staring at that closed door, wanting it to reopen. She was smart;

that quickly she had grasped that he wasn't the marrying kind and accepted it with grace and dignity. She'd been more the adult then than he had been, really, a boy with wild dreams. Now he could see her strength, different from but not less than his own strength.

Of course, she was older now . . .

He wrenched his mind back to what lay ahead. He must be alert to deal with the startling intellect of the man to whom he reported. Think of Mr. Jefferson's ethnicity studies of Indians, the way he collected vocabularies of their multiple languages and searched out the connecting links even as he could see they must give way before the onrush of settlers, Stone Age men confronting men of the Industrial Revolution. Years in the frontier army had shown Lewis the force of that tide of American settlers. Land west of the Mississippi was still Spanish territory but that would change, too. Still, with the British pushing in their hostile way from the north, Lewis could see that the nation would never be whole until it was anchored to the continent and the continent would never be secure until American soldiers marched across that vast unknown territory and made the connection real. And now he would set that expedition in motion.

God, wouldn't Pa be proud of him? Pa, hero who had mounted his horse and ridden to war and given his life to protect his country. And now the son rode for the far horizon to ensure his country's solidity and wholeness. He found himself whistling the old strain, remembering the last time he'd seen Pa whole and healthy, he perched high on the big man's shoulder, a regular Yankee Doodle Dandy. And so he still was, ready to conquer the continent and make his nation whole. Yankee Doodle making hay!

A few miles from Monticello he stopped at a tavern for the night. He would report in the morning, ready for duty. His dress uniform was in the pack but he decided to report in civilian garb as befit civilian duty. That night he scarcely slept for excitement. For most of his life he'd felt the sense that something grand lay ahead, something spectacular to mark his future. Now the feeling was in full flower. He would start as the president's aide, at par with great men: cabinet ministers and generals and senators who spoke only to each other and now would include Meriwether Lewis in their ranks. Then, after a period of preparation, the westward march. His name would be woven into the fabric of his country's history—or his bleached bones would lie unremarked somewhere beyond the farthest horizon, wind sighing through his rib cage.

On the long ride he had studied the expedition, the men needed, the supplies, instruments to fetch a position from the stars, weapons, foodstuffs, trade goods for purchases from Indians. How much powder and how much lead? Why not seal powder in lead cases that would melt down into exactly the balls that the powder inside would fire? What about a unique boat he had in mind? His notebook was often in his hand as he rode.

Next morning, freshly shaven, coat sponged, boots carefully brushed, he rode up to the familiar white house atop the hill, early sun peeping among trees. The president greeted him with a shout of pleasure and an embrace, bade him welcome to the official family, sent him inside to see Mr. Madison, and bounded off on another experiment in agricultural science.

Not a word was said about the expedition.

Mr. Madison, visiting by chance, apparently, was at the breakfast table reading the Bible. It was the first time Lewis had met the secretary of state though both were nearby plantation owners, and he found him distinctly unimpressive. Small, wispy, pedantic, dried up—they said he had married a beautiful woman, toast of Philadelphia, and Lewis wondered what she had seen in him. Position and wealth, probably; many a woman had married for no other reason.

Mr. Madison placed a bookmark in his Bible, squaring it carefully, and began talking about what they wanted from Lewis. Federalists under John Adams had built up the army, packing the officer corps with far too many men for the troops on hand, appointing only Federalists. Democrats now intended to cut the army by half. As First Infantry paymaster Lewis had visited all the remote little posts and knew most of the officers. His role would be to separate out those worth keeping. Stinker Elliott, he saw immediately, would be among the discards.

But then the little man said with an anxious frown, "We're not just cutting Federalists and keeping Democrats, you understand." Lewis detected an odor of pusillanimity: why not dump Federalist en masse? But no, seemed that was just the point—that's what Federalists would do, they were famous for their excesses, while the whole Democratic idea was for the opposite, a balanced and fair government honoring the individual.

As he listened a horrible suspicion grew. Maybe they did want him for just what they'd said—to separate wheat from chaff in officer ranks. Maybe they would drain his knowledge and then put him to paper shuffling. Minding the teapot. Hustling messages. That's what clerks did, after all.

When he finally reached Locust Hill disappointment had settled into melancholy. He'd been dreaming a fool's dream. They weren't even considering an expedition. And then he had to hold a cheery face for his family and force down a huge dinner Ma had whipped up in celebration.

Then, carefully casual, he said he might ride over and see Mary Beth and immediately there was one of those leaden silences that tell you something bad is coming. Well, what? Looking as she might at a funeral, Ma said that Mary Beth got married last year, one of the Slocum boys, and had just had her first baby. They all looked at him like they figured his heart was broke. It wasn't broke, hell no, far from it—no, what bothered him, it looked like everything that mattered was being tossed down the privy.

But this darkened mood lifted quickly enough and in fact proved one of the lesser of the surges of melancholy that did indeed take over his feelings more often than he thought natural. He had no idea what lay behind them, just that they made him miserable and he had to struggle to conceal them. Ma told him Pa had been afflicted the same way, it was a strain that ran in the Lewis family. Told him not to worry, it was just the way he was.

The president said to take a few days with his family and then repair to Washington; the main party would be along shortly. Lewis roamed about, seeing acquaintances and catching up on gossip. Saw Mary Beth, in a carriage with her husband. The husband was a smallish man who drove staring straight ahead as if he feared the horses would get away from him. Her baby had been nursing and as the child finished she tucked her breast away, but not before Lewis glimpsed a nipple wet and swollen from the infant's lips. The sight disturbed and repelled him about equally; she was heavier now, her face fleshier, the dust of freckles less apparent. She made him think of Ma, somehow, though he couldn't say why.

As ordered, he started north toward Washington, his mood continuing to improve. After all, a new administration had a lot on its mind. It was understandable that an expedition wouldn't head the list. Such a march called for special planning and astute analysis. And there wasn't great hurry.

He was leading a docile packhorse on a long line and was mounted on a big buckskin from his own plantation. Old Buck was mean as a snake, but had great stamina and explosive speed. The horse looked more suited to the plow, and many a fancy fellow on a blooded mount had made the mistake of offering to race. In fact, one did just that out near Manassas; Lewis stood the chap drinks and a tavern dinner on the proceeds.

There was dancing in the tavern and Lewis took a few turns. He loved to dance. This made him think of Mary Beth; he'd seen her a second time, at Colonel Rogers's after the steeplechase. The music was lively and he saw her alone by a table of sweets and asked her to dance. She shook her head. But she loved to dance, she'd been a feather in his arms. She shook her head again and once more something about her made him think of Ma. She said Billy Slocum didn't hold with dancing, which somehow opened the idea he'd been avoiding, of that little man lying with her, the sheer physicality of the act. As for dancing, it seemed the Slocums had joined one of those little Christian branches that had sprung up after state religion was outlawed and their preacher said dancing was a lure of the devil.

From the ferry over the Potomac Lewis stared at what had been the new capital of the United States for six months. Log buildings clustered at the ferry landing with untouched forest all around. He led the horses up the steep bank and rode into the new city. He saw streets distinguished mostly by marking stakes and a swath of trees cut so that a carriage could just pass over the stumps. He began to see houses, mostly of logs but some of brick with two or three stories. It had rained and water stood in mud holes that the horses stepped around. When the streets dried clouds of dust would rise; the undersides of fence rails were thickly coated. He passed cornfields and one of wheat. Sign boards marked open spaces as squares where someday statuary might stand. Avenues named for states and now mere open swaths linked these squares. Gradually an idea of the capital's shape formed in his mind.

It was magnificent in conception but he saw it would be centuries living up to its dreams. He decided its French designer, Pierre L'Enfant, who'd grown famous for his obsessions before General Washington gave him the boot, must be both genius and madman. The avenues and squares and radials linked to the Capitol and the President's House told the story of a dreamer who saw towers and spires, domes and cupolas in visions, saw broad avenues filled with carriages drawn by matched teams from which pretty women nodded to men in fine dress — saw all this where plain folk of unclouded mind saw ruts and stumps and untouched trees and a village that could have been compressed into a dozen square blocks to its own advantage.

You had to hand it to a man who thought so grandly. But then, was his own dream any less? Yankee Doodle Dandy ready to walk across a continent and tie eastern ocean to western? Set the stage for a continental nation? No less grand, surely. But not, he hoped, so fever-struck.

The horses picked their way slowly among stumps. Dogs burst into the road bawling and the horses danced about skittishly. He spied the unfinished Capitol rising on a hill in the distance. Approaching, he saw that the building was as magnificent in conception as the plan of the city itself. But only part had a roof, a dome had been started but apparently abandoned, the grounds were all mud with stacks of building material scattered willy-nilly, brick and stone, lumber in piles under canvas, carts and barrows and horses who seemed no more eager for work than the men he saw here and there moving slowly and inexplicably. The building would be years in completion but it would stand forever.

Here, surprising him, Washington abruptly took on the look of a town. Flanking the Capitol were two rows of well-built houses, their broad verandas lined with comfortable-looking rockers. He quizzed a harried clerk he met in the street; these were boardinghouses where congressmen and senators would live during the brief sessions.

He turned onto a boulevard marked Pennsylvania Avenue. Lewis recalled the president saying he would see this street graveled if he accomplished nothing else in his presidency. Well, a load of gravel would make it a street among streets in this dismal capital. It connected Capitol and President's House where Lewis would be living. Along the way more houses were rising, some quite handsome.

Reining up before the mansion, he saw a boxy place with big pillars and high windows, like the city it graced grand in concept but far from done. It had the barren look of grandeur rising in a mean setting and needed a portico or wings or outbuildings to relieve its angularity. Its walls were of a yellowish sandstone and blocks of sandstone rested on logs next to a stone saw. The grounds were pitted with mud holes and cart tracks where rainwater stood and mule dung gave an ammoniac tang. No workers were about save a leathery fellow with a chaw of tobacco tucked in his cheek who sat a bay that stood with its forelegs splayed. He was slapping a folded carpenter's rule into his palm. Nodding to Lewis, he spat a long brown stream and said he was the foreman on this here job. With a leg cocked over the saddle pommel he explained the place with careless gestures.

"This here, what you're looking at, north side, front side, don't you see, it'll be all grass and then on in front a formal garden like they say the Frenchies have at their palaces, fancy plants from all over the world, oh, it'll be something. Someday, understand." He pointed with his rule. "And all these sheds and shanties and the stone saw and the brick pit with its firing kiln, all that'll be gone. But it ain't finished now, you know. President Adams, he come in last year and lived in it four months, and the new president, he just came to look around."

A curious mix of the finished and the unfinished awaited inside, grandeur and bare bones, some walls plastered but scarcely dry, others with bare laths, some windows with high-quality glass, some merely barred for protection. The foreman slid off his horse and walked Lewis through the house.

"And this," he said in a vast chamber at the east end, "is where Miz Adams hung her washing, so they say." He paused to spit through an open window. Tobacco juice spattered the framing. "The Adamses, now, they didn't think much of the house or the town and from what folks say, they didn't go to no pains to hide that fact, neither."

Yet the room's rough-hewn look, scarcely touched, suited Lewis's uncertain view of his prospects. The eighteen-foot ceiling soaring overhead looked about as close to the open western sky as he was likely to be for some time. He ordered a couple of small rooms framed out with canvas walls, the larger for an office, the smaller as a bedchamber. It would be as ascetic as any officer quarters in a frontier fort.

When the president arrived four days later Lewis was installed and ready. Mr. Jefferson talked of cutting the army properly. He said nothing about what really mattered.

7

Washington, Fall, 1801

Days passed and still there was no sign that the expedition was more than a figment of his own invention. Not a word, not a hint. He was a clerk. He bought a black suit of cheap broadcloth and slippers with pewter buckles and cheap cotton hose that quickly took on a gray tone. Glimpses caught in mirrors told him he looked like every other poor soul wandering Capitol Hill. There was a difference, though, if you looked. He was somewhat bigger and he walked with an outdoorsman's tread, swifter and bolder. And maybe there was something in his face that said better not disturb him, or so he suspected from the side glances tossed his way. Which in fact, way he felt these days, would be good advice for any citizen not interested in trouble. Stand clear of the clerk, by God. Daily he pored over officer rosters, marking who stayed and who went. On the last day of this duty he shifted Stinker Elliott from the drop to the keep list—it wasn't fair to let personal animosity decide.

The president did write his own letters as promised, but Lewis was the messenger boy who hurried them up to the Hill. He played receptionist to men the president chose to avoid, nodding gravely to complaints. It was the worst duty he'd ever had. Two months passed. Still no word. Cutting the army was finished and forgotten. He settled into routine chores. Drank a little whiskey at the end of the day. Struck a cautious friendship with Johnny Graham, a Kentuckian for whom laughter came easily. Johnny was a clerk in Mr. Madison's department. Cheer up, he often told Lewis; said it's as easy to be up as to be down and a hell of a lot more fun. Johnny was a friend and then Mrs. Madison, too. He reckoned he could call that lady a friend.

Lewis long since had come to recognize an inherent power in Mr.

Madison, a steely interior strong in decisions that quite belied his pale voice. Except for the voice, you encountered this quality of command in colonels and some sergeants, which quality Lewis knew he possessed himself. Plainly Mr. Madison was a man of power, loyal to the president but fully as intelligent as Mr. Jefferson and probably somewhat wiser.

The clerk's unkind reflections on why a beautiful woman might marry a colorless man now shamed him. Mr. Madison wasn't really colorless while Miss Dolley possessed a kindness and breadth of spirit that made Lewis glow in her company. Since the widower president had pressed her into duty as official hostess for state dinners she often was in the mansion overseeing preparations and—well, just being near her made Lewis feel good, he didn't quite know why. She was fully as beautiful as people said, her black hair in ringlets offset by eyes the color of sky when a cold front has just passed, her figure certainly as it should be if not more—but he didn't see her as an attractive woman. She was, after all, some years older than he, she had been widowed before she met Madison, she was a mother. She was, well, *used*. Like his own mother, so to speak, like Mary Beth now, so clearly no longer the fresh girl he remembered. What drew him to Miss Dolley was her calm and her air of approval.

One morning when he had a batch of messages for the Hill, duty he loathed, she called to him as he started out. She was here to oversee a dinner for Senate committee chairmen.

"Merry, come sit a moment. We'll send down for a pot of that fierce French coffee Mr. Lemaire makes." She laughed. "Fortify myself before I go down and wrestle with him."

The president had imported Etienne Lemaire from Paris as his chief steward. Mr. Lemaire had learned his trade in the service of French nobility and it was a struggle to make him see the virtue of plain democratic American fare. Miss Dolley was winning the battle but the very idea of this little Frenchman who needed to have his nose pinched sassing her raised Lewis's hackles.

They sat on wicker chairs on the south terrace. He could see the Potomac in the distance.

"He's giving you trouble again," Lewis asked, "the Frenchman?" It came out a growl that he should have softened.

"No, no," she said quickly, "all is in control." He heard alarm in her voice and too late remembered an earlier discussion about Lemaire. Now, as before, he had brought frontier instincts to the President's House. Was his own excess some of the reason for his trouble on the Hill? The thought was like a lantern lighting a dark room but he didn't push into the room.

He settled back into his chair and thought of the messages awaiting delivery. The president would suppose he was on his way by now. This spasm of guilt angered him—God, he was beginning to think like a clerk!

"Do you miss the army?" she asked. She was diverting his attention but the question popped open a wave of yearning. Miss the army? He who had traded a rough-handed life in the open among men like himself for a rotten clerkship? Yes, ma'am, missed the army and missed the West, too. In another moment he was rhapsodizing on western weather and the people with their go-ahead attitude, on the feel of open land and endless forest and vast opportunity, all new and waiting, beckoning to men and women of strength and courage who came with visions and dreams.

It was opening fast, too, unfolding league by league. He hurried along, trying in a rush of enthusiasm to make her see it and believe in its immense potential. Along the Ohio below Pittsburgh the country already has a settled look, farms separated by split-rail fences zigzagging away from the river, fat cattle and good horses and well-tilled fields. But it thins out pretty soon and by the time you've floated to the Falls of the Ohio and on beyond you'll see mostly raw forest, now and then an Indian village. But come back the next year or the year after and likely you'll see a little settlement built around a store that's half tavern and half dry goods emporium.

He was clipping along, telling her how the early settlers pushed the Indians aside and then got uneasy themselves when the new crowds came in and they too figured it was time to move on. Land they had cleared and planted in corn, raising a log house with split-rail fencing, now would sell for five and even ten dollars an acre and that seemed a fortune and anyway, it was getting too crowded for a man who wanted to walk the woods as he pleased. He'd sell and hold the money in gold and move along . . .

"What would his wife say?" Miss Dolley asked.

He looked at her, surprised. He'd never thought of that. "Well," he said slowly, "maybe it's hard on her. She's gotten a home together, made a log cabin comfortable, maybe prettied it up with flowers and all, and her man comes home and says, 'We're going.' Yes, ma'am, plenty of pain I don't doubt."

He wondered if her sense of outrage would rise. More than once when the president asked them in to take tea and included Lewis he had heard her anger at laws that made a woman's property legally her husband's the moment they wed. She had a friend, a pretty widow, whose husband had left her a shipping company; if she married she would turn his company to someone new and that she would not do, condemning herself to a life alone. It's just not right, Miss Dolley would say. But today she let the issue ride and he was relieved.

"Still," he said, "lots of folks do stay. You see, every little town figures to be the next Pittsburgh. They look around full of hope, they've got a courthouse now with a jail or at least stocks and a flogging post; they've got churches and a couple of schoolhouses, couple of taverns, breweries, livery stables, someone cooking out busthead whiskey with a copper coil fetched from back East—" He stopped himself just in time from saying that these folks were full of piss and vinegar.

That was what the Spanish couldn't fathom, he told her. That vast tidal movement sweeping over them. When they said all west of the Mississippi was theirs they didn't reckon with American settlers. Spanish would be gone in another decade or two.

"Vanguard of America," she said with a smile.

Yes, that was it, the ever open West where a man could make his way with a sack of flour and a little sowbelly in his saddlebags, make his way forever toward the sundown out ahead.

"Sundown," she said. "Westward, then."

She was tapping his deepest yearnings, perhaps purposely, and it released a tide of talk. He told her about the idea of an expedition to the Pacific, its importance, how it would tie East and West together in a continental nation, how certain he was that the East could never prosper fully without the West, and couldn't have the Far West until some Yankee Doodle Dandy went there and planted the flag. Yes, an American ship had entered the vast mouth of the Columbia River and hoisted the stars and stripes, but a binding claim on the Pacific Coast depended on men walking across deserts and forcing passage through mountains and running rivers until they came again to salt water—crossing by land. Then we would be a continental country.

"This isn't a pipe dream, you know. The president planned it years ago. I wrote him—wanted to command it. That was in 1793." He paused. "He never answered." He wondered if his voice betrayed hurt, but then, quite unable to stop himself, he added, "I guess it was foolish. Presumptuous, you know. Mary Beth, she laughed. I can still hear it, like a silver bell. Like to tore me to pieces I got so riled up, but I guess it was foolish and she saw it."

Mrs. Madison gave him a keen look; he was talking too much. "Well," he said, sounding lame in his own ears, "she was just a girl then. Girl I used to know. She's married now. Has a baby."

Another quizzical, knowing look and he burst out, "Well, what does he want of me? I'm a soldier, not a clerk. I thought—I mean, when his letter of invitation came, I thought it was a mistake and then I realized the only possible reason for using me was to answer that letter of long ago—to have me make that trek to the Pacific and connect West to East."

"Maybe that's exactly the reason," she said.

He stared at her, a wave of hope rising. Did she know things? And he burst out, "Then why don't he say something?"

She gazed across the expanse south of the mansion, the grassy plain running finally into swamp. A keelboat came into view on the river, men slowly poling upstream toward Georgetown. The silence stretched.

At last she said, "Tell me about the army. You went in, you were right at home, I suppose."

"Yes, ma'am, I loved it."

"And handled everything well, just coming naturally, so to speak?"

He laughed out loud. "No, really, I was green as grass. Didn't know it then, I guess, but looking back I made one mistake after another." He thought of Stinker Elliott, but decided that could well be left unsaid.

Miss Dolley smiled. "The president tells me that you are a botanist of some skill."

He flushed with pleasure. "Maybe I wouldn't put it that way, but I do know something about living in the woods, yes, ma'am."

"On your own, you mean? With a rifle, I suppose, and some food, but no one guiding you?"

"Yes, ma'am, that's about it."

"Overnight, sometimes?"

"Yes'm. Not at first and then overnight and then a week and then two or three weeks at a time."

"How old were you when all this started?"

"Ten."

"Just ten?"

Her smile was warmly approving and soon he was rattling away about the North Georgia woods and Mr. McIntyre, the old scout. "Taught me to see—thing is, that's three-quarters of woods wisdom right there, seeing what you look at, really seeing it and hence what it means." He thought of the knife Mr. McIntyre had given him; he had carried it in a boot until he came to Washington.

By now he saw where she was going. She asked about taking charge of the plantation at thirteen. He agreed—plenty to learn there. And the army? Oh, my God, growing into the capacity to make men want to obey his orders was hard-handed training.

"So," he said softly, "you think maybe it takes a little training to deal with the high muck-a-mucks around here?"

"It does make sense, don't you think? This expedition, you'd be on your own, I take it. Out beyond settled country, out beyond mails and messengers and all, really on your own."

"Yes'm, and you think knowing how government works—"

"I was thinking more of how power works. Power is the issue, isn't it? I mean, you'd be dealing with men of power there too, wouldn't you?" She shrugged. "Are Indians any different? In manners, attitudes, customs, of course, but power is power. I think it's the same everywhere."

Suddenly his ignorance was showing. He knew the army but what did he know about real power?

He smiled. "I guess instead of whining about the expedition I should work on the education of Captain Lewis."

She clapped her hands. " 'The education of Captain Lewis.' I like that, Merry."

"And you think maybe the president—"

"Is waiting to see your progress? Doesn't that make sense?"

Riding to the Capitol, old Buck feisty and full of fun, he marveled at how much better he felt. The education of Captain Lewis—that would stand off melancholy.

8

Washington, Early Summer, 1802

John Randolph—congressman from Virginia, chairman of Ways and Means, and de facto leader of the House since the Speaker preferred to remain in the shadows, a tall man thin to the point of emaciation, his skull-like head perilously mounted on a stalk of a neck—strode through the rotunda like a sultan surveying his realm. Men stepped quickly from his way, bowing to his cool nod, paying obeisance to power. Three fine hounds were beside and slightly behind him, looking neither right nor left, as conscious of their kingly presence as was their master. Mr. Randolph carried a dog whip coiled in one hand and had been known to use it on men who stood too long in his way.

Lewis, a steaming cup of tea in hand, slid quietly toward an opposite corner. Spring had eased into summer, May come and gone, and sultry weather was creeping over Washington. But it was still cool within the massive stone building and hot tea appealed. Not enough, though, to warrant another encounter with the gentleman from Virginia.

There was a fury in Mr. Randolph that loosened fire in his tongue. An old hand at the dueling ground out on the Bladensburg Road, he stood ready to meet anyone who objected to his vitriol. Few such meetings were fatal. He was so thin that bullets fired at him usually perforated his coat-tails but not his hide, and he rarely bothered to aim. But he was a terror in debate, excoriating Federalist members and those in his own party too for the ultimate sin of letting their own mouths prove them fools. And he counted Meriwether Lewis a special target.

Few men cared to challenge that vitriol; this is what gave him much of his power on the House floor. Once, so Lewis had heard, Sam Smith of Maryland, the burly congressman now moving to the Senate, having been goaded beyond endurance, had roared, "Mind your tongue, sir, or I'll take that whip away from you and lash your skinny ass." That silenced Randolph for a full week, not from any concern that Smith might carry out his threat, everyone agreed, but because of the reference to his person about which he was highly sensitive. His voice was strange, a whispering high-pitched whine as if his vocal cords had been damaged. There were stories of a grievous accident in a steeplechase, testicles crushed against a saddle pommel when the horse went down on a water jump. No one knew; like a king, Randolph never explained himself.

So with the House in brief recess and members in the rotunda drinking tea or Madeira or beer brewed down the street, eating sausage or oiled sardines on crackers or gnawing on a roasting ear slathered in butter, here came Mr. Randolph with his regal dogs and his princely manner. Swallowing hastily and wiping his mouth, Lewis cut toward an opposite corner. But Mr. Randolph had seen him and swerved to intercept. There wasn't a man alive from whom Lewis would run; he turned and faced the congressman, arms folded on his chest. Here we go, he thought, and instantly the thought followed: I brought it on myself.

The first time Lewis had carried a presidential message to the chair-man of Ways and Means the clerk's role was chafing onerously. Still under the mistaken impression that a president could do as he pleased and certainly could order an expedition to the West, it hadn't occurred to him that congressional approval would be necessary. When he finally found the chairman's office, having been too proud to reveal ignorance by asking directions, he was in no mood for a pasty-faced little clerk telling him to drop the message on the desk and leave. The clerk's name was Simon Pink and since then he and Lewis had become friends, but now one word led to another and soon the little clerk was squalling furiously as he crouched behind the desk with a glass paperweight for a weapon. Mr. Randolph came boiling from the inner office and started a tongue-lashing that went on and on.

All right, Lewis had been at fault, he'd known that immediately though he would never admit it, and when the chairman finally ran down he had departed with what shreds of dignity remained. But ever since the man had dogged him, making it an ordeal just to take a message to his office. The clear pleasure the chairman took in these tirades made them the harder to accept. And now the gentleman came charging across the rotunda.

"Aha, Captain Ferocity," he shrilled in that strange but penetrating falsetto, "once again comes the ferocious captain, the military arm of the ferocious president here to discipline humble members of the House and bind them to his iron will."

"Actually, sir, to purchase a sausage with sauerkraut," Lewis said. Someone tittered and Randolph's face reddened.

"Toy with me at your peril, sir," the chairman snapped. "You will find that your president's power doesn't extend to Capitol Hill. You'll find something called the separation of powers that clearly has been outside your comprehension. When you return to your kennel, look in on the secretary of state, the esteemed Mr. Madison—he wrote the bloody Constitution, after all, and it establishes the Congress as a separate body, fully as powerful as the executive. 'Pon my word, the executive can't move without the gentlemen on this noble hill, can't spend monies he doesn't have—but come, don't take my word for all this, check with Mr. Madison, see if the contempt that the president shows in sending his ferocious military arm to the Hill to cow members who only do their duty is likely to produce benign results."

He took a deep breath. Was Lewis to respond to this folderol? But immediately the chairman plunged on.

"But perhaps I whistle past the graveyard, for isn't Mr. Madison the same little Federalist manqué who guides the weak president down the paths of peril, romancing Federalists who are past all romance, so bitter their hatred? Isn't the rotten little man who revels in the title secretary of state the same villain who would undermine the Democrats at every turn? And aren't you here to further that very deception? I see you wherever I go, prowling like a hunter, unaware of the trail of slime you leave behind you as you attempt to convert—nay, to force honest men who know better—oh, porter, porter! Where is that damned porter? Summon him from the building's bowels. He must scour clean the trail of slime that follows Captain Ferocity over the floor of the Capitol lest its odor drive members to nausea—"

It was disgusting but typical. Lewis had listened to Randolph rant on the House floor, members tittering uneasily at the extremes, the butts of his attacks considering challenges. But as he heard a member put it, "Just old John in idiot mode."

Randolph led an extreme wing of the new Democrats that took Jefferson's victory in 1800 as a voter demand to hurl out all vestiges of the defeated Federalists and start anew with their own people and plans. But the president wanted a balanced way, keeping both people and plans of the old when they were useful but canting them toward fairness to the common man and away from the Federalist trend toward a hereditary aristocracy. That the Federalist banking system was still in place set Randolph foaming even though its preferences for the elite had been stripped. But criticizing a popular president was dangerous, so Mr. Madison was tagged as the villain who led the great man astray.

Such hypocrisy! Randolph had fought the Constitution as had the old patriot, Patrick Henry, and others who felt more Virginian than American and now they fought Jefferson's moderate course in hopes of shifting most federal power to state hands.

Sensing he was losing his audience, Randolph shouted, "You stand silent, sir. No wit to answer? No courage?"

Lewis hesitated. Among equals such talk would put them on the road to challenge. But a clerk challenging a man of power would be ridiculous. "Ah, sir," Lewis said at last, "what is there to say in the face of such bombast?"

Randolph stared. Abruptly he turned and stalked away. In the watching crowd someone laughed out loud and several smothered grins. Randolph walked faster, his neck reddening.

If Lewis had won it was a small and painful victory.

Obviously the president was in a vile mood. He rode in silence, mouth turned down, moons of sweat staining his cambric shirt at the armpits, his coat lashed to the saddle behind him. A broiling sun bore down on them, the air felt thick and syrupy, the only breeze was that made by their own motion, and the flies were out in pestiferous numbers. It looked to be a tough summer, Lewis observed, and quickly wished he'd kept his mouth shut. Mr. Jefferson turned in his saddle and glared.

"What did you expect?"

Immediately Lewis felt the fool, though his comment still seemed reasonable. It did look like a tough summer, at least so far. Tougher than most, damn it. That wasn't so foolish. They rode on in glowering silence. Behind them came two servants, each leading a packhorse. They were going to Monticello because the foreman there had some concern about grafts in the orchard and that was enough reason for the president to hurry home. Brady's creek was low and at the ford the bottom had gone to mud. Lewis led the horses across, splashing and floundering, boots sinking deep in mud, while the president walked upstream and found a fallen tree that let him cross with dry soles.

Lewis considered a jocular note and thought better of it. That night they stopped at Sam Bailey's plantation house. The reception was cordial but after an hour of halting conversation, their host suggested a round of whist. When Lewis wasted a trump the president stiffened as if insulted.

On the ferry over the Rappahannock the next day Mr. Jefferson handed Lewis a folded dispatch. Rufus King, ambassador to Britain, reported that Napoleon Bonaparte planned to reclaim the Louisiana Territory from Spain. France had lost the vast territory that stretched from the Mississippi to the Stony Mountains to Britain in the French and Indian War and Britain had passed it to Spain. Now Bonaparte had the power to take it back. That was explanation enough for the president's temper.

For it put Kentucky and Tennessee—indeed, all the ground between the Appalachians and the Mississippi—at risk. Spain controlling the river was no problem. It was weak and knew to mind its manners. But Napoleon's eagles were different. France on the Mississippi would strangle the American West, which must export through New Orleans. Lewis didn't have to be told that we would never tolerate this; we would fight first, and where would that leave an expedition? Forgotten in the groundswell of history, that's where.

The president told Lewis to go visit his own plantation. Lewis walked Buck up the hill to the roomy log house and saw a neat little shay drawn up under a shade tree, a water bucket set out for the horse. He walked into the house calling and heard Ma's voice from the kitchen.

There he found her spooning a black liquid from one glass to another half full of some other black liquid, mixing the herbal remedies that treated folks for miles around. Then, greatly surprised, he saw Mary Beth Slaney—no, Slocum—standing against the wall. Her hands were clasped together as if she were trying to crush one with the other. He saw Ma's glance cut sharply from him to the young woman.

A basket he hadn't seen before lay on a table and he realized that in it was Mary Beth's baby, apparently asleep. A boy named William for his father.

He kissed Ma's cheek and turned to Mary Beth. Just as he took her hand, Ma said, breaking the silence, "Mary Beth, I'm afraid she's a widow now. Billy Slocum got killed."

"My Lord," he said softly. "I'm so sorry." He heard Ma leave the kitchen. Mary Beth looked pale but composed. There was a dash of gray at the temples in her hair that looked less honey-colored now, and her skin had coarsened, as if it lay heavy on her bones somehow. Hadn't her nose been a slender ridge when they were young? She looked different, thickening a little in the body, breasts more than filling her gown.

"What happened, Mary Beth?"

"Galloping his horse on a fox hunt and was looking back when his head hit a low-hanging branch. He lived two or three hours but he died before they could get him home."

"That's sad," he said, "and you with a new baby."

She nodded. He didn't know what to say. The silence in the room seemed to weigh on him, made it hard to breathe. She stepped from the wall, stood in the middle of the room. She glanced toward the sleeping baby. He could hear her breathing.

"I guess your heart is broke," he blurted.

"No," she said, "it's not. Billy was a good man, decent, honest. He was kind to me and he loved the baby. And I was true to him and wouldn't never have changed. But I didn't love him. I think he knew that."

"What?" He was confused. She had married him but didn't love him? Made no sense.

She was gazing into his eyes and suddenly she looked as old and strong as Ma. And she said, "I never loved no one but you, Merry. Didn't you know that?"

He was speechless. At last he said, "Then why . . ."

"Because you wasn't going to marry me. You made that plain. And a woman don't want to grow old alone, without a man."

He stared at her. It seemed kind of terrible, woman marrying a man and taking him to bed and having him inside her and having his baby, all when she don't love him?

As if she could read his mind her face closed down and she nodded and scooped up the baby's basket, one hand clamping it to her hip, the other lifting her bag. At the door she turned. "Good-bye, Merry," she said. And then she was outside and in a moment he heard the carriage move away and still he stood, motionless and somehow dismayed.

Ma came back in the room quietly. "Beth left?" she said. "She has the makings of a good herb doctor. I'm teaching her all I know. She'll need it before she's done." She gazed at him curiously. "She was supposed to stay for dinner. What'd she say when she left?"

"I don't know, Ma," he said. "I don't know."

9

The French threat swept Washington and Mr. Randolph grew even more impossible. His office door hung open, dogs poised to alert him to appearances of the hapless clerk, or so it seemed to Lewis. With the clerk in his sights he loosed fury at the president and Mr. Madison, that lickspittle lackey who wagged his tail in hopes Mr. Hamilton would pat his head. Yes, indeed, it was Madison who led the weak-minded president astray, while the French threat proved the need to plunge ahead on the true path of democracy, by which Lewis knew he meant his own extreme concepts. And here was Captain Ferocity himself, useless as teats on a boar hog in a society that honored civilian over military—

"For God's sake," Lewis roared one day, surprising himself almost as much as he surprised Randolph, "why don't you tell the president, tell Mr. Madison? What in hell can I do about it? I'm a mere clerk—do you really think I'm going to give the secretary of state a tongue-lashing in your name?"

Then, knowing he was burning bridges, he spoke frankly. Mr. Randolph stared—even his dogs sat down as if wounded by such impertinence. Outside Simon Pink was gasping. As Lewis whirled from the inner sanctum he heard Simon's anguished whisper, "Oh, Merry, you can't talk to him that way. Nobody does."

Lewis hurried off. He turned onto a small balcony and gazed across the swamp that lay between Capitol Hill and the mansion. Gradually his breathing slowed. He sighed and shook his head. What a start on the education of Meriwether Lewis.

A shotgun banged in the swamp and he heard the distant cries of dogs barking in sudden fury. A polished black trap with the top thrown back appeared on the road that wound around the base of the hill. Sunlight flashed off a gleaming black gelding in harness and to his surprise he saw the driver was a woman alone with gloves to her elbows, bright-colored hair glinting, bonnet cast back on her shoulders. She was too far to see clearly but immediately he imagined her young, beautiful, daring. Yes, alone in her carriage, holding herself far above society and its opinions but chaste and virginal too, what would she think of the mad Captain Ferocity and his fruitless yearnings?

His stomach rumbled. He was hungry and angry at himself. He wandered into the Rotunda for its food stalls. The floor was fine marble but the roof was still sloped canvas. He saw a brewer with a keg ready to tap, boiled eggs on the counter, a grog shop across the way, here rows of teacups on a plank atop sawhorses with a teapot simmering on a brazier, there a fellow in a leather apron peddling hot sausage wrapped in a bun. Newsboys shouted and a boy did tumbling tricks, his cap out for coppers.

"Captain Lewis, I believe."

He turned to find a tall, slender man bearing down on him, his voice soft but commanding.

"At your service, sir."

"Timothy Pickering of Massachusetts. Come, let me buy you a sausage." Lewis came immediately alert. Pickering, aspirant for a Senate seat, former secretary of state under Washington and Adams until Adams dismissed him in a rage, was a thunderous Federalist. He raised two fingers to the sausage cart and with dripping buns in hand they stepped into an alcove. Munching, the other studied Lewis, who returned the stare.

At last Pickering said, "We know why you're here, Captain."

"Sir?"

"Obvious. For secretary the president chooses an army officer from the Far West who knows nothing of Washington. Why? This town is full of men who know more—and certainly know better than to get on John Randolph's dark side. Eh?"

"You heard about that?"

"Hell's fire, young fellow, whole damned town's heard about it." He laughed. "Ain't Brother Randolph a gem? I do my best to keep him stirred up all the time. If he keeps on trying to put Federalists to fire and sword he'll pop us right back into office. He's my secret weapon." His voice dropped. "But enough of that. The question is, why Captain Lewis?"

"Suppose you tell me, Mr. Pickering."

"That's just exactly my intention, young fellow. It's why I lavished my coppers on the sausage you now consume. He wants you here because he has great plans for the West."

Lewis stared. Did this long-nosed Federalist know things still held secret? "What do you mean, sir?"

"He's always hungered after the West, dreamed and plotted. Why, some years past, way before your time, he had some idiotic scheme to send an expedition clear to the far ocean. Overland, for God's sake. Point is, he's always seen the West as important, which it ain't, especially now the French want Louisiana."

He waved aside Lewis's protests. "Point is that Federalists won't let western adventures happen. We don't need more terrain, we've got too much already. All those bloody acres of wilderness, infinitely more than we can handle now, he wants to add to them? It's madness. Kentucky and Tennessee already states, Ohio next—why, 'twould be a blessing, the French come and take it all."

He wadded the paper wrapper from his sausage, hurled it at a can, and missed. He shrugged.

"You underestimate the West and its value," Lewis said. He thought with longing of those trackless forests, the savannas that ran for miles with grass higher than a rider's stirrups.

"Pshaw! You're like all the westerners. Big talk. Hell's fire, it's just land. But manufacturing is our future and that's all in the East. And believe me, when it comes to feckless dreams about the West you'll see we have the votes. We'll kill it dead."

Lewis bowed. "Thank you for the sausage."

Better report all this, Randolph and Pickering. But the president was visiting a friend and Lewis turned toward the State Department on the mansion lawn. Try it out on Mr. Madison—he saw more clearly on some things than did the president. He found the secretary in a plain chair by a window, late-afternoon sun on a dispatch in his hands. Through the window Lewis could see the guard pacing before the mansion. Mr. Madison peeled off wire spectacles and squeezed the bridge of his nose.

Lewis mentioned Pickering first, delaying Randolph.

"Old Timothy," Mr. Madison said, and chuckled. "He's a mad dog on nearly everything. Certainly on the West."

Cautiously Lewis asked, "Do you think, if we were to plan something there, would the Federalists—"

"Oh, yes, they'd fight western expansion. They fear the West because it draws off the most enterprising, entrepreneurial men, the ones they most want to keep for their factories. Men who prefer independence to pulling their forelocks for meager wages."

He smiled. "But then, Mr. Pickering is a poor patriot. You know he heads a secession plot? Wants to split New England off with New York and set up a new country?"

"Good God! And western moves would make it worse?"

"Probably . . ." Then, with a subtle cooling of tone, "But there's more to this, I suppose?"

Lewis colored. His voice sounded strained even to himself. "Well, yes, Mr. Randolph. Attacks me constantly as a way of getting at you and the president, calls me Captain Ferocity—"

"Captain Ferocity?" A faint smile crossed the other's face. He was watching sparrows pecking on the windowsill and Lewis saw that he had laid out crumbs to draw them. Lewis explained his own irritation that first day that had triggered Randolph's venom.

"So what happened today?"

"Well, I'm afraid I told him he should calm down lest he fall in a fit and the president blame me for his demise."

"Was that all?" Mr. Madison said. "That's not so bad."

"Well, I did say a little more."

"I thought so. What else?"

"He was in a tantrum, two-year-old throwing food on the floor. And I told him we'd had young fellows in the army who frothed as he did but we just sent them home to their mamas."

Madison didn't answer and feeling more and more uncomfortable, Lewis blurted, "Sir, this man is impossible."

"Oh, granted, he can be infuriating. Most every time I see him I seem to lose my temper."

A burst of relief. "So you've told him off too?"

"No. Growled to myself, but there are bigger issues afoot here." He gazed at Lewis, who could feel his own face reddening. Then, to the clerk's surprise, Mr. Madison said the sun was near over the yardarm, close enough to break out the Madeira. He took bottle and glasses from a cabinet. Lewis thought the wine, from the south of Spain, was the best he'd ever tasted and in combination of nerves and awkwardness he rapidly emptied his glass. With a glance in which Lewis read amusement, Mr. Madison refilled the glass. This time Lewis merely wet his lips.

"Bigger issues . . ." Mr. Madison said. And then, "Do you understand why this really is a second revolution?"

Of course he understood. But sure enough, here came the litany of events, new government, country going broke, Alexander Hamilton inventing a system that rescued finances . . .

"Have you met Alex? No? Able man, clever, very quick-minded, handsome, dashing, his least attractive trait his contempt for those who don't keep up with him. Plus his general contempt for the common man. But he did get control of the debt in jig time."

Lewis's lips tightened; he was being patronized. The revolution in

France, noble aims souring, mobs in the streets, guillotine whacking aris-
tocratic necks—and how eerily slogans there about the common man
matched Democratic slogans here. But then the secretary did surprise him.

"So, the question is, does the common man have the self-control to
govern himself or will he explode without a controlling hand holding him
in place? The Democrats say he can control himself, the Federalists that
he can't. Democracy terrifies them—do you know, I once heard Mr.
Hamilton call democracy 'the greatest evil.' Heard it with my own ears
and there was no doubt he was serious. He still sees Napoleon's military
dictatorship as the natural consequence of common man government.
That's why the Federalists are so bitter. That talk about saving the country? They mean saving it from us."

He was watching the sparrows again, obviously using them as a diversion, for he turned suddenly and gave Lewis a look that as clearly as a
crier in the streets told him to listen, now we talk business. "You see the
rhythm? Why faith is so essential? In casting aside old patterns of control
and hereditary authority, we've put ourselves on an uncharted course.
Think of it, real power, a radical reversal of theory and belief, and it
shifted without bloodshed—that's the American genius and I'll warrant it
hasn't been accomplished without blood since classical times."

He shrugged. Then, smiling, "Of course, it does mean we stand alone,
the only popular democracy in the entire world."

Lewis felt oddly stirred, Yankee Doodle Dandy at attention.

"But this is bigger than any single nation," Mr. Madison said, twirling
the Madeira glass by its stem. "I think we stand at the hinge point of a vast
transition in human society. The world has started moving from centralized
and tightly controlled monarchies to a broadly diffuse form of democracy,
shifting power from a wealthy elite to a broad base of the common man.
We're just leading the way. In time we'll be seen as a model for the world.
But for the moment don't forget that we do stand alone—and are under
huge pressure from Britain to join it in its war with Napoleon."

There was a long silence. Lewis felt the hot stir in the mind produced
by new ideas. Mr. Madison made it all ring with truth and Lewis saw rapture in his face.

"We set the movement up, you see, with a constitution that institution-
alizes the rights of the common man. The French shook the world because
at just the right moment they articulated all the glorious possibilities of
human freedom in this new form. And in their disastrous outcome they
illustrated the dangers of freedom—loss of control and consequent chaos
are inherent in self-governing as opposed, say, to a king whose function
has always been to control people who couldn't control themselves."

Mr. Madison's gaze locked on to Lewis's eyes. The man had startling impact. "This is noble work," he said. "Bigger than any of us. You see where this takes us?"

Lewis swallowed. "Well, I suppose it makes reacting to Mr. Randolph a bit penny-ante."

"Exactly. We walk a narrow path between extremes, Mr. Pickering and his rebellious secessionists, Randolph's radical Democrats seeking opposites that American voters would surely reject—either in charge could finish the great experiment."

Lewis walked back to the mansion figuring that the vision of a continental nation paralleled that of a democratic nation, and continentalism depended on hard men taking the trail. Could no one see this? Randolph who controlled the Congress that controlled the money was no friend. Federalists feared continentalism. The president said nothing. But what the hell, war would sweep Lewis back into uniform anyway—

Simms, the day guard, hailed him. "Miss Dolley's on the south terrace," he said. "Wants to see you if you come in."

He found her in her shady alcove. A brewer's dray was poking along the road at the end of the president's yard where a couple of sheep kept the grass in check. The driver shook his fist at a passing horseman who swept off his hat in mock salute and scampered away. Miss Dolley had tea makings on a tray, a novel in hand. French novel, he saw, squinting upside down.

He bowed. "You wanted me, ma'am?"

"Just to offer you a cup of tea."

"Gladly, Miss Dolley," he said, and let her pour. The sun had soaked the building in heat that the stone walls now returned against the cooling day. He rolled his shoulders, feeling tension ease. There was gingerbread that didn't exactly go with tea but he put away three pieces, feeling better with each. He listened to her describe ways to decorate the mansion to make what she called a great national house. Decorating didn't come naturally to him, but the place certainly was shabby. And Miss Dolley's plans sounded bang-up—furniture and drapes and molding and different shades of interior paint and inlaid parquet floors—and he told her the place would be grand when she finished. A great national house—he liked that too. She smiled, as pleased as anyone by approval, and this was a bit of a revelation to him as well.

The sun settled but by now the stiffness in his shoulders was gone. Yes, things would have to be settled and objections met, but the expedition made such sense to the growth of the nation that it must come to pass. Could the new democracy even survive without it? Didn't it need to keep growing?

He smiled, spirits restored. Would he have the last piece of ginger-bread? Oh, no—certainly she should have it. She didn't want it? Well, if she wouldn't think him greedy . . .

10

Washington, Mid-1802

The scandal struck with an impact that Lewis could scarcely believe. And to make it all infinitely worse, he had to ask himself, was it his own hot temper that had precipitated it?

That wretch of an editor, James Callender, published it in his Rich-mond rag and it spread paper to paper as a forest fire jumps from tree to tree. Now newspapers from Maine to the Carolinas were serving it up weekly full of salacious glee. Federalist papers trumpeted the story with ardent clucks of tongues, seeing the moral collapse of the nation under way. Democratic papers treated it as just one of those things, repugnant, perhaps, but really no more than distressing appetites. But everyone rev-eled in the details, the dark little damsel coming to the great man's bed in the still hours of the night for him to have his way on her lush young body. Sally Hemings in the same paragraph was dusky temptress supreme and innocent maiden broken to use by the vile slave master.

And underneath it all was the hoot of laughter, the great man with his noble ideals caught in a story as prurient as the least of us might entertain, drawers at half-mast.

The president said nothing. A dark silence settled on the mansion. Cur-rent business was conducted in clipped voices. Lewis didn't see Miss Dol-ley for days; had she stopped visiting the mansion? In disgust, perhaps? He prowled about, hoping she would appear to arrange another dinner, though he knew entertaining had almost stopped in the gloomy silence.

But perhaps he was overimagining, for when she did appear her eyes lit at sight of him. She called for the tea fixings, as she put it, and sat down on the terrace overlooking the south lawn. A dogwood was in full bloom, its creamy petals like an antidote to the poison staining this great house.

"This business in the papers," he started as she handed him a teacup. But her face hardened and she raised a hand to stop him.

"My word," she said with new sternness, "surely you don't propose to discuss that, here—or anywhere, for that matter."

"No, ma'am," he said hastily, "not at all. The details, I mean."

"You know nothing about the details or the lack thereof, or so I should think." Her voice was harsh.

"Yes . . ." he said, "but you see, I fear I'm partly to blame—"

She gazed at him, waiting.

Sally Hemings, now being celebrated in newspaper doggerel that passed for wit as Monticellian Sally, Black Sally, Dusky Sally, was Mr. Jefferson's housekeeper. She was a beautiful woman, servant and slave on the one hand, honored and authoritative figure on the other. The allegation was that Mr. Jefferson had fathered a number of children on her. Everyone who visited Monticello knew Miz Hemings. Among other things, in the tangled ways of big Virginia families, she was half sister by a slave mother to Jefferson's beloved wife, Martha, now long in the grave.

Miz Hemings had several handsome and light-skinned children who looked like Jefferson, but that was an old story. Visitors to Monticello noticed how the young people serving table resembled the master, a point to which Jefferson seemed serenely oblivious. The whispered explana-tion—never from Jefferson himself—was that various blood nephews had liaisons with various women on the plantation; Sally herself was said to be the mistress of a particularly favored nephew.

Miss Dolley's frown deepened. "Your fault? How could that be?"

"You know about Callender, the editor in Richmond?"

"Vaguely."

"James Thomson Callender. Had this little sheet that pilloried Presi-dent Adams to a fare-thee-well. Federalist thought police jailed him and fined him, stripped his purse, evidently. Finished his prison sentence about the time Mr. Jefferson was elected and of course he looked to us for recompense. This was all right, the president was prepared to make good all his financial losses. But he had developed grandiose ideas. Seems he'd fallen in love with a young woman from a prominent Richmond fam-ily. Very unlikely match, he being usually drunk, middle-aged, linen filthy, shaves only when he happens to think of it—well, he demanded that Mr. Jefferson name him Richmond postmaster. Said that would win the lady's hand, the title and position, don't you see."

"Really? Postmaster? Oh, my goodness." Miss Dolley shook her head. That was the ranking federal office, much sought after. The president had sent Lewis to tell Callender that such an appointment just wasn't possible.

"I found him half drunk in a tavern where he'd taken lodging. Soon as he realized I hadn't brought his appointment he began to threaten. Threaten the president. Said he would tell the world the whole dirty story if we denied him. Imagine, drunk in a tavern shouting that he'll destroy the president."

"And you?"

Lewis could feel his face reddening. "Well, I—"

"You roughed him up."

"I suppose you could say. Gathered up his shirtfront and snatched him out of his chair and was about to knock his head off when I remembered I was there in a tavern as presidential aide, so I dropped him back on the chair."

"And you think that set him off?"

"Well, another time he came to the mansion repeating the threats and I kicked him out."

"Um . . . metaphorically, I hope."

His face felt bright red. "With my boot, actually. Dragged him out to the street and knocked him sprawling."

She gazed at him a long moment. "Do I understand you to be saying that in retrospect you see better ways of handling it?"

"Oh, yes, ma'am." He knew the fervency in his voice was real. He was a different man today from the subaltern who was ready to knock the oaf's head off in a crowded barroom in the name of the president of the United States.

The night was dark and they rode slowly and in silence, Lewis more than a little irritated. Simon Pink hadn't spoken for twenty minutes; when he did all traces of alcohol had passed from his voice. Lewis and Mr. Randolph's little clerk had dined together. Simon, who could never hold liquor, had managed to get into a scramble with a crewman from a flatboat, a stocky fellow heavily muscled from working the sweeps. He had a bad scar under one eye and towered over Simon. When they stood to go outside he wore a look of pleased anticipation—big man against small. But when Lewis stood too it turned out there was a way to settle the matter quietly. The boatman offered it and Lewis forced it down Simon's throat and that was that.

Now, liquor traces gone, Simon said, "That fellow was a mean son of a bitch, Merry, you know that?"

"I noticed."

"He was looking to do me some damage. Real damage."

Lewis shrugged, still irritated. "He calmed down, though."

"Because you took a hand. You know, Merry, there's something about you that gives a man pause."

Lewis didn't answer and in a moment Simon said, "It's sort of a quality, an inner sense. Man looks at you, he sees danger. Maybe he'll take you on, it means enough to him, but not just for the hell of it."

"Danger?"

"Something about you, that's all. I noticed it that first day."

They rode on in silence. Well, it wasn't the first time he'd heard that observation. He was a big man, well over six feet, shoulders set wide, lean muscles, big hands. And yes, he knew there was something there in his eyes. Don't get in my way. He thought of it as determination. Don't get in my way. A hank of black hair fell over his pale forehead and he tended to go bright red when angry. That was often enough, too, as if a tide of anger lay behind him, wanting to spill over. But dangerous? He swung down at the stable a block from the mansion and watched Simon disappear along Pennsylvania Avenue toward his boardinghouse. He didn't consider himself a contentious man but this wasn't his first dustup in the Washington night. And that seemed not to his credit.

"Captain Lewis, you do put on airs for a clerk." The remark was delivered so gently, the speaker elderly and avuncular and so likable that Lewis could hardly take offense. Baker Broadbent, his long white hair caught up in an old-fashioned queue, was himself a clerk on the Senate floor.

But the remark disturbed Lewis—he wasn't a clerk. Or was he? He served as one, didn't he? Close to power but a functionary like Mr. Broadbent, allowed to comment but never to decide. This came as revelation and that it did revealed further.

Across the rotunda with boot heels clicking, out the door, walking fast on noisy gravel, he faced the reality: he'd been fooling himself. He was a block beyond old Buck before he remembered he was riding today, not walking . . .

More than ever he was convinced that the expedition was inevitable. Nothing new was said but he was learning and growing. The president had transferred much of his library at Monticello to the mansion and Lewis read avidly. He read European accounts of travel in North America— everyone who came here rushed home to write a book about it. But what most drew him was insight into how the world worked, how nations functioned, how politics and human decisions were inextricably intertwined.

What was old Broadbent really telling him? That the ways of politics are utterly human and utterly mysterious. That clerks have a righteous place in the world; it's just not the place of masters. He remembered the revelation he'd felt when he saw that to challenge Mr. Randolph for his vulgar abuse was out of the question. Clerks don't challenge chairmen, nor chairmen clerks. The town would rock with laughter and Mr. Randolph would incorporate a challenge into his witty diatribes. Witty? Well, looking at it properly, yes, witty was the right word. But chairmen can't challenge clerks and, indeed, can't even wound clerks. The chairman's abuse was meaningless, amusing himself but doing no damage. Not unless you believed you were at par with the abuser. Unless you doubted you were a clerk.

So he pondered Mr. Broadbent's meaning and incorporated it into the ranging study in which he found much new pleasure. Now he grasped the meaning of the metaphor that nature abhorred a vacuum. And he saw that the unexplored center of the North American continent was just such a vacuum, static while the world changed swiftly. In the last quarter century the world had turned over. Our own revolution, the cataclysmic French Revolution that told Europe a new day had come, Napoleon now resting, momentarily, after demonstrating a new art of warfare, Britain's Royal Navy dominating the seas with ever greater authority, the Spanish empire terminal as the new American Republic gained strength and position and authority every day.

So it was that Lewis came to see ever more clearly that the United States was destined to dominate the continent. Yes, Napoleon was amusing himself with notions of establishing a new French empire in North America and such was his fighting nature that perhaps only war would dissuade him. But in the end Lewis was confident that if it came to war, he would lose. He couldn't dominate the massive American continent; England with the Royal Navy as its tool understood it couldn't dominate America. If France carried out its mad hopes, we would defeat it. In the process we probably would destroy our own new democracy and who knew what would arise to replace it and that could be a tragedy of major proportions, a chance at human perfection shattered by French caprice — or maybe by human fate. But whatever the future brought, Americans would not surrender the North American continent. And the next essential step was the march that would tie West to East. Yes, the expedition was crucial. Why couldn't everyone see that?

Elsie Carpenter was eighteen, he hoped, but more likely sixteen. He feared to ask. She was tall, slender, willowy, and there was fetching modesty in the way she braided her chestnut hair and folded the braids atop her head. Dark brown eyes peering from beneath heavy brows gave her an impenetrable air of mystery and when she smiled his heart seemed to turn over. She danced with all the fervor he felt. Sometimes the tip of her pink tongue slid over her lips as she executed this difficult step and that, and a sheen of moisture stood on her brow. Both struck him as charming in the extreme.

She had sought him out, her gaze locked on his until he took note and approached her in the dance. Instantly he was swept with the sense of her decency, her purity, her guileless manner. He had stepped on the slippery slope and soon was plunging, his heart all tangled and racing, reading her reciprocation in every glance, every soft murmur. He called, she led him into a darkened parlor where a chaperoning auntie dozed, and her kisses were fiery. He knew it was going too fast but it was a toboggan there was no stopping.

Then her father met him at the door. Jack Carpenter seemed to have built half the buildings in Washington and had the wealth to prove it. He was a burly man in boots and breeches, an outdoor flush in his face, a man used to command. This was all entirely too serious, he told Lewis; they were not to see each other again.

Lewis walked into the night, consoled at least by the heartbroken letter that Elsie doubtless was penning even now. But he heard nothing and gradually came to realize that there would be no letter. And he saw that Mr. Carpenter had been acting for his daughter. The romance had become inconvenient and she lacked the courage to say so. Had she been playing with him too? Like Miss Dolley's little sister that strange and wonderful night? She had seemed so real, so ardent. Playing? He just didn't know.

Lewis was in Mr. Randolph's anteroom. Simon Pink was at his desk, an anxious eye on clock and door. "Don't hang about, Merry, really," Simon said. "He'll be back any minute now. You know how he gets with you."

"Maybe he'll turn over a new leaf."

"Hah! That would be a day to remember."

The door opened. Both men stood abruptly. Mr. Randolph entered in full stride but stopped when he saw Lewis.

"Ah, Captain Ferocity."

"Mr. Chairman."

The chairman took a deep breath as if to launch a tirade but then shrugged, smiled faintly, and went quietly into his office.

"Well, I'll be damned," said Simon Pink.

"Simon, do something for me. Ask the chairman if he would be so kind as to give me a few minutes this week at his convenience. For myself, not for the president."

Simon stared. "You want to talk to him?"

"I have something to say, yes."

"And that is?"

"I'd as soon tell him first. Will you ask him?"

A slow smile spread on Simon's face. "Like I said once, you've got the balls of a cougar. Certainly, I'll ask him. Be interesting to see what he says."

Late that day a note in Simon's distinctive hand. "Friday at ten—good luck."

Lewis was there ten minutes before the hour. He waited. When the big brass clock on a bookshelf touched ten Simon nodded.

"You may go in," he said. A quick sardonic smile flashed, the look one might give a man going blindly to the lions.

Lewis entered, bowed to Randolph's nod, and closed the door. The dogs came to their feet; Randolph murmured something and they seemed to relax. The chairman sat with hands folded on the desk. A portrait of a beautiful woman hung behind his head at a level that would let him see it each time he rose. A landscape of a handsome plantation, presumably his own, was on an opposite wall with a portrait of three good hounds, probably predecessors of the current guardians. Through an open window to the left of the chairman's desk Lewis could look down the grassy slope of Capitol Hill to the swamp that dreamers said would be a great ceremonial mall some bright day in the future.

Gesturing to a seat, the chairman said, "Captain Ferocity. Braving my very own den—"

"Yes," Lewis said, "it took a certain amount of nerve—"

"Courage, I'd say."

Lewis smiled. "I like that. Thank you."

"Ah, me," Randolph said, fingers forming a steeple under his chin, "your manner today is so much milder than your usual ferocity that I suspect something's afoot."

"Well, it is, in a sense. But I must protest—I really was only ferocious, if you insist on the term, on my first encounter. And one other time, I suppose, when I felt unduly strained. Since, it is you who has been abusing me."

"Ho!" The congressman laughed abruptly. "Say you so—walk right into my office and say you so?"

" 'Tis but the simple truth."

A teasing chuckle. "Possibly. Possibly. I will admit, at any rate, I've had a good deal of sport with you. Is that your complaint?"

"Oh, no," Lewis said. "In fact, I have no complaint."

"A petitioner for a meeting who has no complaint? That is very close to an oxymoron, sir."

Lewis laughed. "Perhaps. But if no complaint, I do have purpose."

"Ah, we come to the nub. Say on, sir, always with the understanding that I may use whatever you say as a lever to heap more abuse on your head."

"Then you do admit your abuse," Lewis said quickly.

Randolph laughed. "Don't play the lawyer with me, young man. You will learn in time that one of the perquisites of power is that one may admit one's sins without losing advantage."

"I have learned a great deal about power over the last year, sir. Which is why I sit in your office today."

"Well, well, enough of this fiddle-faddle. State your case, sir, or move on."

"I'll tell you my story, sir. A year ago I was deep in the Ohio woods with a load of cash on a packhorse and squad of riflemen guarding the money. Payroll, you understand, for isolated little army posts all over. Rode into the cantonment at Pittsburgh and found a letter from the president-elect inviting me to serve as his secretary."

"At which you clicked your heels and felt your fortune was made," Randolph said.

Lewis resisted the sharp retort. He was here for a purpose, after all, and he was in the man's office.

"No, sir, neither. But I noticed in particular that he said I would retain my rank and title in the army. Now, you may not be aware of this, Mr. Chairman, but captain in the United States Army is a significant title. It is the highest direct command position in the army—rise beyond it and you are in more executive levels, no longer directly leading troops."

Randolph sighed. "This is fascinating, Captain, but not especially new. Your point, please."

"The point, sir, is that I was in a position of command. I thought I was being invited to a similar position."

"And found you weren't."

"And found I wasn't. And it took a bit of getting used to."

"Why do you think you were chosen, Captain Lewis? Knowing nothing of what your duties would require."

"I'm not sure, now."

"I am. You came expecting a great move on the West, none has emerged and you're confused."

"Something like that, I suppose."

"And you want me—"

"Oh, no, sir, not at all. No, what I want you to do is accept my apologies."

"I think you'd better explain yourself."

"Well, I felt more captain than clerk a year ago. That's how I expected

to be treated. There was a roughness in my manner that first day, I have
to admit that. And yes, I did have a dispute with Mr. Pink over, in effect,
my status. That opened the way—I might as well be frank here, Mr.
Chairman—opened the way to more abuse from you than I really
enjoyed. And it took me a long time to understand the problem and even
longer to admit it. Now that I do understand and do admit the error,
apology becomes essential."

Randolph gazed at him in silence. Lewis heard one of the dogs sigh and
then yawn. "And you suppose that will save you from, as you term it, further abuse."

"Oh, no, Mr. Chairman. Amuse yourself as you choose. Abuse away.
In many ways, this apology was more for me than for you anyway—I
needed to acknowledge reality and pay whatever price that entailed. So,
yes, sir, abuse me as you wish."

Randolph laughed, the sound startlingly loud in the small chamber.
"You damned young imp, you—what the devil is the pleasure in abusing
you after you tell me to fire away, you deserve it. Eh? Tell me that, Captain Lewis."

Lewis smiled. "If you choose not to abuse me, that will be perfectly sat-
isfactory, sir."

Still laughing, Randolph cried, "Begone, Captain, out with you, sir.
One thing, though. I think your hopes vis-à-vis the West, whatever they
are, won't be disappointed." Another hoot of laughter. "Out with you,
young man, out with you!"

Lewis bowed, opened the door on the congressman's laughter, and
stepped into the anteroom. He saw Simon Pink staring and winked as he
left.

"That must have been an interesting meeting," Miss Dolley said. She was
sorting through silver in the dining room, rejecting the pieces inade-
quately polished.

"Pardon, Miss Dolley?"

"I assume you connected somehow with John Randolph. Caught him
feeling less manic than usual, I suppose. At any rate, the president tells
me that Mr. Randolph announced you were a fine young man. 'Damned
fine,' I believe he said."

Lewis smiled. "That's pleasant to hear," he said.

"So we further our dreams."

He shook his head. "That wasn't my intent, madam."

"Probably I'd like you less if it had been," she said. "But I think your
dreams have advanced more than you know in this year."

11

The president was happy, as he always was at Monticello. You could hear it in his voice, in his easy laughter and light quips. He was home . . . and he seemed to regard the cavernous mansion in Washington as a gilded cage, his time there a sort of penance.

He had summoned Lewis to announce some pretext for going home that the subaltern already had forgotten. They had spent three hard days on the road, picking up remounts at the plantations they passed, everyone pleased to accommodate the president whose mood was steadily improving.

Miz Hemings met them at the door and within an hour the cook produced a dinner that Lewis felt made up for all the hard travel. It was that kind of day. The president inspected his wine cellar and chose two bottles of his best and afterward there were excellent cigars—a meal to remember.

If any embarrassment passed between the president and Miz Hemings, Lewis missed it. She was an extraordinarily handsome woman and Lewis found that the very sight of her stimulated unworthy thoughts. As for the talk, the president had made no public response and the fire was slowly dying for lack of fuel. Lewis had followed Miss Dolley's advice and kept his mouth shut.

Now, working on second cigars and fresh glasses of Madeira, they sat where a breeze sweeping up the little mountain at Monticello drove away mosquitoes and watched fireflies dance in the grass. And they fell into a conversation about the West that delighted Lewis all the more because he was the traveled expert, Mr. Jefferson the wondering novice. The president knew a lot but it came from reading and talking, not forking a horse and riding out to see. In most of their conversations Lewis was the supplicant, Jefferson the source; it was good to reverse that balance now and again.

They talked of the region's rivers, the sweet ease of flowing downstream, the brutal effort of going up, cordelles dragging boats from the shore, poles sinking in silt, paddles making some headway for a rhythmic hour, then nose her in and tie to a tree to save that precious distance gained. Flatboats

forty by twenty and some bigger, riding the current downstream clear to
New Orleans and there broken up, the planks used to build houses.

Those aching little towns along the way each dreaming of being the next
Cincinnati, the next Pittsburgh, each with its rope walk and distilleries and
sawmill and general stores, the mail routes passing through, the taverns
that serviced stage passengers roughly indeed. They talked of crops, which
always fascinated Mr. Jefferson, why wheat was good here and not there
but corn was good most everywhere. The cattle and milk cows that pros-
pered and those that didn't. Clearing land by burning and selling potash.
Indian tribes and how they fitted and how they didn't, their natural resentment, the settlers recognizing them as fundamental enemies, their languages and customs and habits and feelings for each other, and the
inevitable clash of a Stone Age people with men from the Industrial Revolution. Taking two and even three squirrels with a single ball. Log court-
houses, trials by jury in a land with few jails and no prisons, punishment by
stocks or by flogging or branding or cutting off the tip of the nose or hanging or tar-and-feathered exile for the guilty. Land speculation as the real
engine of commerce. Fights where eye gouging was the critical mode, dig
your thumbs into the eyeballs till they popped out on their stems and sometimes they popped back in and sometimes they didn't.

Lewis was in full swing when the president interrupted and for a
moment he felt a sharp spasm of irritation. "I suppose," Mr. Jefferson said,
"that all these men and women and children heading west by flatboat or
wagon or even handcarts crossing the Cumberland Gap, going out to find
new land and new adventures—I suppose they really are acting out the
same westering dream that has driven men since the start of time."

Lewis frowned. They had been talking real things, hard things, tools
and weapons and crops and the way towns grew, and he was finding that
he was a regular storehouse of information, and it had dawned on him
with real pleasure that he knew a lot more than he had realized. And here
was the president lurching back into his dreamy speculation. It pained
Lewis to surrender the floor but he managed a soft voice. "I rather think
they go out to better themselves."

"Oh, yes," Mr. Jefferson said easily, "people always go west to improve
themselves. That's the significance of all the ancient tales." He fixed
Lewis with a gentle smile and added, "Now, Merry, when I spoke on
these matters at dinner a few months ago I believe you were preoccupied
with a pretty woman and heard very little of what I had to say. This time
I want your attention because you can't understand the westward movement without grasping the heritage that underlies it."

Lewis felt himself going crimson in the dark. Had he been so obvious?
It had been at the big dinner for the diplomatic corps over which Miss

Dolley had labored so hard. Came just after he had met Anna Payne, Miss Dolley's little sister. He remembered that meeting so well—it had been on the walk leading to the mansion and Miss Dolley had introduced him and Anna had smiled. Young and sweet and pure and untouched by man or life, he could see that in a glance, and her smile told him that she was reacting to him in thunderous fashion. He had felt wobbly in the knees and short of breath.

Then when she arrived for the dinner she had given him another ravishing smile and he had hurried to her side. The president had instituted what he called the pell-mell approach to dining as a mark of American democracy. Gone was the custom of seating guests by rank; now when dinner was called each man was expected to take the nearest woman to table at whatever seat he could find. Made for some hard feelings with significant figures like the French and British ambassadors who might find themselves well below the salt, but it played well with plain Americans and it permitted Lewis to claim Anna as his dinner partner. She responded with a smile that almost stopped his heart, or so he felt. Only later did it occur to him that he had been the only other young person in the room.

Then at table she had done the most amazing thing and left him dazzled and shaken. If he had been in love before, now he was besotted. And just as he was rising to new heights of rapture it had penetrated his mind that the president was talking about the West in a way that went directly to the subaltern's interests. He had struggled to pay attention in the midst of joy and love, but without much success. And then, when the dinner was over, Anna had departed without a word to him and thereafter she avoided him as if he were covered with some excrescence and slowly he had been forced to the sad conclusion that for her it had all been a game. She had played with him, amusing herself at his expense. Well, he was a country boy, God damn it, not used to the wiles—but enough of that, it was just that he had taken her play seriously, that's all. He was over it now, no question about that, though still—but forget it. Doesn't matter. Done.

He had a sudden sense the president was eyeing him in the dark and he felt his face heat again. At last Mr. Jefferson sighed and said as if turning a page to a new chapter, "Well, I was intoxicated over a pretty woman a few times in my youth. But these concepts are important—ideas with which a man of the West such as yourself should be familiar."

No answer seemed expected and Lewis drew on his cigar and waited. A night bird cried softly in the darkness and then there was an excited chirping, babies clamoring for a worm.

"Look beyond the immediate, Merry," Mr. Jefferson said. "Beyond terrain and homesteads and flatboats on the river. And you see what has always been in a cosmic sense—that since man's vision reached beyond the distance he could throw his spear the place that swallows the sun has stood as monument to his desires, symbol of his dreams, and root of his yearning."

Lewis did remember now hearing this at the dinner and the near over-whelming moment of self-consciousness the idea had produced, even as his feelings still whirled from the woman's attentions. He had felt some-how exposed, as if his head had been opened and dreams he had never stated clearly even to himself had been snatched out and laid on the table for all to see. It had seemed a violation and he had had to stop the protest that had formed in his throat before he realized that this went straight to his deepest interest. Perhaps the westward march would begin clothed in rhetoric; perhaps only in rhetoric could it begin.

But there was honest passion in the president's vision of the West. "Look across the flow of history," he said, "and you see enchantment lying westward. In every age seers have looked there, convinced that beyond that border place where the sun escapes the sky lies a place of romance and mystery where hopes and dreams and ambitions come true and men live a life of laughter and peace and death is given no place."

Now, sitting in the dark where the Blue Ridge loomed unseen in the distance it struck Lewis again as it had that night how remarkable that Mr. Jefferson who had never ventured westward could grasp the rover's passions and show them as universal dreams of mankind. Lewis remem-bered how he had felt the night of the dinner, his mouth open, breath short, fork forgotten on his plate.

A small candle lantern glowed on the ground at their feet and when Mr. Jefferson reached down to place it on the table beside him Lewis saw several small books in a stack. A paper slip in the top book marked where he'd been reading and he slipped his finger between the pages.

His voice had a pleased, anticipatory note. "And think of our own West and the passions it raises, the absolute westering hunger that makes a man yearn to go and see—to know what was only guessed at before. Always been so. Listen to old Horace, fat, easygoing old Horace and his genial poetry, writing at about the time that Mary was wrapping Jesus in swaddling clothes—

> "See, see before us the distant glow
> Through the thin dawn-mists of the West
> Rich sunlit plains and hilltops gemmed with snow,
> The islands of the blest!"

Islands of the blest—Lewis loved the idea—by God, it fitted his view of the whole matter to perfection.

"Think about that, Merry," Mr. Jefferson said. "It has real bearing on how we view the practicalities of our own West and what we want to realize from it. Go back to the great minds of ancient times, to Virgil, Aristotle, Seneca, Strabo, and listen to the poetry of the Elysian Fields and the Fortunate Isles. This isn't science, of course, but general truth lay in their dreams. Their view of the world was small and they placed these wonders but a few days' sail to the west. Of course they didn't know—and maybe it wasn't very good business to suggest such marvelous visions were too far away to be useful. But the assertion was, sail westward a few days beyond Gibraltar, then known as the Pillars of Hercules, and you'd be there."

The night bird sounded again and the president paused, listening to its lament. "What's bright in the morning can be sad at night—interesting, isn't it, tells you how we are conditioned by surroundings."

"Or by dreams," Lewis said.

"Dreams! Exactly—and very well said. For dreams and commerce mixed perfectly when medieval merchants developed a real market in Europe for oriental teas and spices and silks that had to come via a dreadful passage by caravan across the steppes of Asia. Naturally they turn to the classics and the dream interlocks with commerce.

"So listen to Homer, the blind poet writing eight hundred years before Christ, as he places the Elysian Fields, the place to which heroes of Greek legend came to their final resting rewards, places them in the misty West."

He opened the leather-bound book in his hand and held it near the lantern. "A place of joy, the West—you remember this, I'm sure, from Homer. Where 'life is easy to man, no snow falls nor rain but always ocean sendeth forth the breezes of the shrill west to blow cool on man.'"

He closed the book with a little snap, smiling with pleasure, and abruptly was off on the subject of medieval maps, long since superseded for geographic knowledge but filled with imagery, strange names and strange places that shouted of ancient tales of sea dragons and castles of gold and races of men of immense size—and the Amazons, consider those amazing women, did Lewis know it was said that they cut off their right breasts the better to draw their bows, and didn't he think that really was an analogous expression of the power of women? Such a thought Lewis had never had in the stretch of his life but he knew that power in his own mother and he knew enough to keep his mouth shut.

"All of it, you see, looking westward, all the dreams and myths and hopes of fortune, all looking westward. Valhalla beyond the setting sun where Norse heroes go to meet Odin and their reward. Mallory placing Arthur at last on the mystical Isle of Avalon where—I always read this with such pleasure—'falls not rain, or hail, or any snow, nor ever wind blows loudly . . .'"

He chuckled and took a sip of the fine Madeira, holding it momentarily in his mouth, inhaling its fragrance. This westward thrust was universal he said in a moment, warming again to his theme. Here in our country Native Americans see the great spirits beyond the setting sun, in that land of mystery where departed souls return to their maker.

"You've read Cabeza de Vaca's account of his wanderings over the North American plains — remember how he says that going west — "

"Yes," Lewis cried, memory suddenly stirred, "says that going toward the sunset we must reach our goal or find what we want, somesuch — "

"Yes — 'find what we desire.' "

The night bird was quiet now, the chattering babies fallen silent. The president sighed and bent forward to relight his cigar from the candle lantern. "So," he said, "when these medieval merchants developed a market for the wonders of the East, the advice of the ancients was to look westward for all good things — including water passage to the shores of China.

"Now, a key point here is that the medieval mind conceived of a world about half the size we now know it to be. And they knew where they were and roughly where China was, so when Columbus made landfall on what so clearly was not the Orient, of course they believed that this land mass could be no more than a narrow ridge."

Miz Hemings appeared in a doorway, a single lantern bright behind her. She carried a tray with a teapot and cups. For a moment Lewis thought the president would call for more Madeira but then he laughed and said tea was just what they needed, it fitted their conversation, you could ascribe to tea the very discovery of America, assuming you didn't mind stretching your point just a bit.

Miz Hemings smiled and Lewis had the idea she had heard a lot of such rambling musings and knew better than to answer.

"Tea, now," he said, cradling the warm cup in his hands, "as motivator for America, that's not so far off. Not so close, either, but a thought to toy with. For really, this westward dream that has infused the world, what is it but the Garden of the World, that place of human joy, that Eden where all cares are lost and innocence can be reclaimed, where man can live in peace and plenty, forever content in gentle sunlight, at one with God or, as I pointed out the other night, the gods, as the case may be. From Homer on it is the idea of the garden of human perfection that has driven the western image. Now, in that last talk, perhaps I went too far in suggesting that the Edenic garden of glory where lieth all good might await us in the distant reaches of our own continent. Still, it's an interesting idea."

Lewis thought it so interesting he was near blurting his own hopes, but the president went smoothly on.

"At any rate, we can see why this untimely land mass between Columbus and the Orient was perceived as a narrow ridge. And instantly, riding the power of the western dream, it became clear to everyone that there would soon be found straits through this ridge. They even had a name, these straits—the Straits of Anian, the passage that ultimately was called the Northwest Passage, as we know it today."

The president nattered on, voice low and ruminative now. The teacup in Lewis's hand had gone cold as he listened. Verrazano thought he had seen the western sea across a narrow spit of land; perhaps he was off the barrier islands of the Carolinas, there's no telling now. Cartier sailed into the St. Lawrence and was sure he had the strait. Henry Hudson sailed up his river confident that he had beaten everyone in settling the mystery.

So the shifting ideas born of the dream. When finally it was clear that there were no straits, no connection per se, everyone turned to the rivers. Perhaps the major rivers of the world, thought to rise on a single huge height of land, bore the answers. Perhaps there was a vast inland sea that fed the rivers. You could run up one at the east end of the continent, sail across the inland sea, and shoot down a river on the far side to the western ocean. But the inland sea was never found and the idea faded to a great lake with eastern and western outlets and then to a mountain lake and finally to the rivers themselves.

"As each theory was examined and discarded the aim never changed—to find a way through this untimely land mass blocking the way to the riches of the East. And so came the answer we believe today. We know the Mississippi runs to the Gulf of Mexico and provides no western avenue. But the Missouri comes from the west and carries such a volume of water that it must flow from the mountains which more and more evidence suggests are there. Stony Mountains or Mountains of Shiny Stones or Shining Mountains, all rough translations from Indian tongues, oh, call it as you like, but this must be the source for the Missouri. Now, if a river pours eastward from the slopes of those mountains, doesn't logic insist that a similar river must flow from the opposite side, flow toward the western ocean?

"For years we have postulated that such a river exists—we call it the Great River of the West—and now we know it does and that it has been claimed for the United States. Our own Captain Robert Gray out of Boston in a merchant brig bound for China rounds the Horn and runs up the west coast of both Americas in search of sea otter pelts that produce a fabulous price in China. And well up the North American coast he finds a river pouring into the Pacific with such force and velocity that it seizes his ship and drives it far out to sea. He beats his way back to find the river's mouth is blocked by a barrier reef so complete that it looks solid—yet there's that tide of water flowing out. So he searches, finds a place where he can breech the reef, throws his ship across, and finds himself in a gigantic estuary. The Great River of the West. And he takes possession for the United States and he names it for his doughty ship, the *Columbia*. The Columbia River, running westward from the Shining Mountains, at about the latitude of the Missouri entry to the Mississippi. D'you see, Merry? The solution to the mystery is at hand.

"And so, isn't it logical to suppose that they originate not far from each other and that to go up one is to find oneself in a gentle saddle from which streams pour westward as well as eastward? An easy portage might well link these streams—why, we might find that portage would be a mere half mile.

"And there lies our Northwest Passage at last."

The president was smiling, craggy face illuminated by planes and hollows in the light of the candle lantern, the book closed in his lap, finger still holding the place. It was a beautiful dream and Lewis could see that the older man loved it. But the subaltern had ridden hundreds of miles on faint trails through silent forests east of the Mississippi, and he saw it through a haze of skepticism. What hard experience long since had taught him was that when you walked the ground it never was quite what the charts showed. The dreams he had heard tonight, beautiful as they were, had come in the main from book-lined studies across the ages. Now it was time to go and see, once and for all.

Then we would have our Northwest Passage. Or wouldn't.

The time was getting close. Before long he would have to do something to move things along. He had come east to run an expedition, no matter what Mr. Jefferson's aim might have been. Sooner or later, and better sooner, he would have to force the issue, win or lose.

12

Albemarle County, Virginia, Early Fall, 1802

The president was in a vile mood, which was very unusual given that they were still at his beloved Monticello. But he spent this day alone in his office, summoning a fresh pot of tea from time to time, silent when he did emerge. He took a light supper with Lewis but scarcely spoke. When they were leaving the table he pushed over a leather-bound book.

"Here," he said, "read this. Finish it by morning—we'll talk then."

By morning? It was a substantial book, pages freshly cut, cover stiff and bright. Lewis glanced at the title on the spine in gold leaf. *Voyages from Montreal, on the River St. Lawrence. Through the Continent of North America, to the Frozen and Pacific Ocean.* By Alexander Mackenzie of the North West Company. Fur company, trapper country. Part of Britain's international trade that gave the little island nation the power to dominate the world with one hand while holding the brilliant Napoleon at bay with the other.

That title on the spine struck Lewis like a sudden chill breeze on a summer evening. Mackenzie . . . he hefted the book and sighed. He would need a lamp with a good supply of oil and a big pot of tea he could warm on a candle. The president went off to his study and Lewis took lamp, book, and teapot to his guest cabin and settled into a chair bottomed in rawhide.

The book had been published late the year before in London where apparently it had created a stir. Rufus King, our ambassador there, dispatched a copy and here it was in Lewis's hands after obviously having upset Mr. Jefferson. To his surprise he saw that the events Mackenzie described had taken place in 1793, years past. And all that time, Lewis and the president had been sitting on their hindquarters supposing that they might hold time itself to use as they chose.

Mackenzie proved to be a young Scotsman of vast hardihood who dreamed great dreams of penetrating the wilderness to find the Northwest Passage—but in Canada, with all that that would mean in giving Britain standing to claim the Far West. British fur interests already gripped much of the Canadian wilderness and no boundary existed between Canada and the United States west of the Great Lakes. Lewis stared at the words flowing across the page, the book beginning to feel like a bomb.

Mackenzie had set out from the fur company's westernmost post, a tiny community on Great Slave Lake, striking westward into the deepest wilderness. He went looking for fur, oblivious to the geographical insight that Mr. Jefferson saw as the natural aim of exploration. No sense of botany, no feeling for the meaning of terrain, blind to the implications of his travel. Eventually he came to a major river to which he affixed his own name. But it soon turned north and in time delivered him to the Arctic Ocean, which Indians told him froze over but for a month or two in summer.

Mackenzie rallied himself for a second try, this time from Fort Chipewyan on Lake Athabaska well to the south. Lewis rested his eyes. You had to admire the man's courage, pushing on with a couple of soldiers, two voyageurs, and two Indians. But then it struck Lewis that the

Scotsman marched directly against American intentions. His eyes popped open and he read on. Night birds were still, insects slept, the quiet seemed thick and lonely. A glance at the stars told him midnight was long past. He screwed up the lamp wick and read on, eyes sagging.

But soon he came to a passage that stunned him. Mackenzie wrote rather casually that he had crossed the Continental Divide at a mere three thousand feet. Why, their own local Blue Ridge outside the back door stood well over that. But that was just the start of marvels. For Mackenzie claimed that on this saddle he had found two streams as if a provident God had placed them there for his convenience, one running west, the other east, a mere seven hundred yards between them. But at so pat and perfect a finding, Lewis's skepticism soared. This Scotsman was finding it all too easy.

The little party from Fort Athabaska pushed westward and reached a major river that Mackenzie took for a north fork of the Columbia. They built canoes and floated downstream. But in a few miles waterfalls and wild rapids made the way impassible. Mackenzie scouted ahead for miles and found no improvement. Supplies grew dangerously low and he decided to abandon the river and march westward until he reached salt water.

The search for a water route to the West had failed but that hardly mattered to Lewis, for on a rock ledge overlooking what certainly was the Pacific, Mackenzie had mixed a paint of vermilion and bear fat and inscribed a yell of triumph. In bold block letters he had printed a legend that struck Lewis squarely in the breastbone. It said: ALEXANDER MACKENZIE, FROM CANADA, BY LAND, THE TWENTY-SECOND OF JULY, ONE THOUSAND SEVEN HUNDRED AND NINETY-THREE.

By land . . .

"Well, look who's here," the president snapped. "Up at last. Congratulations." Lewis stiffened. He had slept barely an hour, and while he could function efficiently on an hour's sleep, it left him in no mood for sauce from anyone, even the president.

Dawn had fairly broken and he found the great man at the breakfast table, a teacup in one hand, rasher of bacon in the other, a scowl on his face. "Did you see it? That 'by land' business?"

Lewis stared, the question not worth an answer. He took a seat at the table, poured tea, held the cup in both hands. The president folded the bacon into his mouth and glared as he wiped his fingers. He was clearly furious, apparently the more angry for having slept on Mackenzie's assertions. "Well, what do you think?"

The right answer was to voice similar outrage but that wasn't exactly what Lewis felt. It struck him that since he'd been a tad every encounter with the squire of Monticello had been designed to please the powerful man. But the ground had shifted and the subaltern found himself at a precipice that he knew Mr. Jefferson couldn't even see.

"What I think," he said, "I think this Mackenzie is a pretty clever fellow."

It wasn't at all what the president had wanted. His cheeks flashed scarlet and he started half from his chair. "What the devil do you mean? Don't you understand—"

Power in full flush of rage is awesome and Lewis was momentarily shaken. But yes, he understood all too well, and then, abruptly, he was tired of the whole long game. He was tired of watching his step, tired of service to Mr. Jefferson, tired of the big white mansion and fancy men who danced in silk hose and buckled slippers and lied to your face and ridiculed common men. The Randolphs and Pickerings and all the others.

He paused to gather himself, then said, "Well, Mackenzie had the wit to see what was needed and the gumption to do it, anchoring a claim that we can't make on the single instance of our Captain Gray sailing into a river and naming it for his ship. Granted this Canadian trapper failed to find a commercial route, but he managed a foothold for Britain in our Far West. Who's to say his masters aren't following up right now?" He almost stopped himself but there was a wild wind in his sails and he blurted on, "In short, sir, he up and did what we should have done. Stole a march on us."

Mr. Jefferson glared. "And the corollary of his cleverness is our dullness?"

"Or slowness. Yes, sir, I guess that sums it up."

Long silence. A ray of first sun slanted across the table and sparrows whispered under the eaves. "And what do you draw from that, Captain Lewis?"

Lewis noted the formal address and wondered if he had burned all his bridges. But he had cast off shackles that were of his own making and, newly liberated, he saw that once embarked, he had no choice but to drive ahead. "What I get from this man's exploits—well, I guess that we are far behind when we need to be far ahead. And what that means, it means we should put together our own expedition and damn the French, damn the British, forge ahead, and put our own mark on our own West. By land, sir, by land. We should go ahead with what you planned a decade ago."

He hesitated through a long, pregnant moment that the president didn't interrupt. Then he went the rest of the way. "I wrote you about it, if you remember."

"I remember." The president's mouth was a thin line. "Nine years ago, actually, 1793, same year that Mackenzie was at work, it now turns out.

Rather than you, we engaged a French scientist to lead the party and before he went far he unmasked himself as an enemy agent, more or less, and that was that."

"Well, sir," Lewis said, riding the crest even if startled by his own bluntness, "that you chose the wrong leader doesn't invalidate the idea." Again he saw that quick, angry tightening of the mouth, but now the president had himself in control.

So, Lewis thought, in for a shilling, in for a pound. "I wrote you then to ask for the command. Now I can see that at the time I hadn't the faintest idea what was involved. But today I know exactly how to handle it. We should mount the expedition anew and I should lead it."

The president stared at him. Had he ruined everything, destroyed all his dreams and hopes in a fit of impatience? But he knew he was right— Mackenzie's book left them no choice. As for the command, they would find no one better than he. And if it was not to be his, there were other things in life.

A long silence. A servant loitered in an adjoining room. The president folded his napkin and stood. "Finish your breakfast," he said, "and let's walk."

A couple of bites, a last bacon strip downed, a gulp of tea, a biscuit in his pocket for later, and Lewis was ready. Down the hill they went, the president setting a brisk pace, long flowing sleeves flapping in the wind he created, Lewis following, neither speaking. By the road they turned, followed the shoulder, found a narrow lane uphill, passed through a field of experimental corn, a little weather box in the corner where a diary was kept to record each day's activity in that field.

As they came to the orchard the president said over his shoulder as if there hadn't been a moment's interruption, "Well, it was an old idea even in 1793." He said his own father had planned such a trip. Peter Jefferson, famed as a surveyor and explorer, a powerful figure in colonial Virginia. He and a handful of planters had planned a two-man expedition up the Missouri to search for a Pacific connection. Lewis quickened his pace to come alongside Mr. Jefferson.

"Too ambitious by far and of course it failed, but you see the trend of thought even in the 1750s." They passed over a stile into an orchard, peaches at the near end, robust apple trees at the far end, the fruit beginning to redden. The day was warming and Lewis felt a trickle of sweat in the small of his back. Still focused on the early days, the president reminisced about the wanderer who opened the Cumberland Gap far down the Shenandoah Valley as a gateway to the West. "And to think, Daniel Boone followed on, passed through to the bluegrass country, and hordes of settlers followed and today Kentucky is a state.

My God, how things have moved! Anyway, the trip to the Pacific sput-
tered out, much too grand for the day, I suppose." At the end of the
orchard another stile led to a wheat field. The president paused to
examine low-hanging apples, then sat on the top step of the stile, gesturing to Lewis to sit on the lower steps. Gazing up at the great man, in
short. Lewis remained standing, a boot cocked on a lower step. He saw
that the president noted the move.

In 1781 a British trader had tried such a trek and failed. A couple of
years later, full decade before what Lewis had assumed was the first
thought of the Missouri as roadway to the Pacific Northwest, Mr. Jefferson had invited General George Rogers Clark to lead such an expedition.
General Clark had saved the West in the war but bankrupted himself and
his family in doing so, and had to refuse. General Clark was Will Clark's
brother, Will the youngest, the general the oldest of six.

The president slipped down the second step, resting elbows on the top of
the stile. Then he started up with a curse, rolled up his sleeve, and extracted
a splinter from an elbow, all without a break in the conversation. He talked
about the Royal Navy on the Pacific Coast, Captain Cook making the
soundings on which the world's perception of the rugged Pacific Coast was
based, a decade later Captain Vancouver dispatching Lieutenant Peter
Puget to examine the waters now known as Puget's Sound . . .

The meaning of all this seemed pretty clear: Lewis's dreams were nothing new. Don't get above yourself, young fellow. The old melancholy was
seeping in, darkness at the edges. Now his forceful talk to the president
took a different color. More naive than heroic. He suspected that was a
false feeling, but he felt it anyway.

Then there was John Ledyard, a young American who had been with
Cook and proposed to find the Northwest Passage from the opposite
direction. From London he would cross Europe, then Russia, then the
Pacific Ocean to North America where he would set out west to east. The
president seemed entranced by the idea, Lewis struggling to keep from
laughing. Mr. Jefferson, neither adventurous nor daring, had nonetheless
a romantic streak that made dashing young men so equipped seem vitally
attractive. He recounted how Ledyard got nearly across Russia before
the czarina's police seized him and bounced him back to Paris. Where, the
president said with a chuckle, he got a new idea and new sponsors and
was off to Cairo where he contracted some mysterious ailment and died,
poor fellow.

"A gallant young man, if not the most practical," he said.

Lewis kept his more realistic surmise to himself. Likely someone in
Cairo had slipped a blade between the gallant young man's ribs.

In the distance hounds were baying, probably on their own business, given the time of morning. "Sam Barker's dogs, I expect, slipped the kennel and on the run." He laughed, his mood restored after having put Lewis in his place. "Sam will want to work them this evening and they'll be wore out from the morning." He sat up straight on the stile. "Now, why don't you pull that biscuit out of your pocket and we'll share it." Then, munching, he added, "So, you see, the idea is not all that new."

But this wasn't just a casual idea; this went to the country's future. Lewis folded his arms across his chest. "All you've said just proves my point, Mr. President. Makes it a disgrace that we know almost nothing of our own West."

Mr. Jefferson leaned back on his elbows. He crossed a leg, half reclining, toe of his boot aimed at the sky. "So from this you conclude—what?"

"That we should mount a new expedition to track that river to its source and make a connection with the western ocean. Of course there's a connection of some kind, has to be. Let's get on with it, find the Northwest Passage, make that connection once and for all. We should start planning right now. Start with this—it should be military and should be small, maybe fifteen men."

"This very morning, eh?" The president didn't smile but he seemed amused and this refreshed Lewis's anger.

"Finally," he said firmly, "I want to command it."

" 'Want'?"

What the hell did that mean? Lewis hesitated, then said bluntly, "I'm your most qualified man."

"Are you? Well, go ahead. Make your case. Most qualified—or like Ledyard, do you simply want it?"

That angered Lewis and he knew his face showed it. Ledyard had been a fool and Captain Lewis wasn't at all the fool. He said as much but Mr. Jefferson brushed this aside with a motion. "Make your case, sir."

"Gladly, sir." Lewis began folding down fingers. Suddenly he felt good, confidence flowing in like elixir. Already on his feet, he began to pace. "This should be a military matter and I'm a soldier. I know small unit command. I know how to lead men, when to discipline and when to overlook, how to read maps, how to follow the stars, how to choose campgrounds and set proper watches for the night and have men ready to repel attack as daylight breaks. All the various ways you stay alive in the woods. I'm a professional, Mr. President—and that's what you need.

"Departing St. Louis, this party will go a couple thousand miles through sheer wilderness. Now, sir, I've spent a lot of time in the wilderness and I'm comfortable in it. Not everyone is, you know; indeed, I'd think you yourself are not of a wilderness turn of mind."

That got the man's attention. Lewis saw it in the flash of his eyes. No one likes the idea of something he can't do. "Well," Lewis said, "doesn't your mind flourish in the context of ideas and people? Quite unlike wilderness life with its loneliness, that sheer silent absence of other voices, other faces. It weighs on a man but anyone figuring to travel two thousand miles from St. Louis to salt water had better be ready for that silence." He raised a finger and added, "Be different for the men—they'll have each other. The commander is alone."

Need he explain so obvious a point? No, the president nodded, but it was clear he was hearing things he hadn't considered. Lewis's spirits rose another notch.

"And, sir, who's to seek out the new in plant life, separate the known from the unknown? Determine suitability for agriculture? Relate wild grasses to domestic grain? Not many army officers are botanists and I am—at least an amateur."

Congressional support? He'd had some experience with Congress. "I was slow to grasp the humor of dealing with Mr. Randolph, but I learned."

"Yes, you learned."

"And it came to a fair conclusion."

"It did. And yes, Congress will be crucial to any such expedition. Paying the bills, authorizing the penetration of foreign territory—we can't do without congressional approval."

Thank goodness for giving him the wit to offer that apology. Then abruptly he realized the proof of maturity in having done so, and just in time stopped himself from asserting the obvious.

The climate seemed to be improving. The president sat forward on the stile, elbows on his knees, close attention in his expression. "And then," Lewis said, "I'm young and strong—march through the night when needed. Next night too and keep right on going. Now, stamina will be important in a venture where the odds on even returning are no more than fifty-fifty." He saw the president's eyes flick open at that. Another thought the armchair explorer hadn't really addressed. "So," he said, "an older man for all his experience, when trouble starts he may not be the one you want after all."

There were more arguments he could make but instinct told him he had said enough. "So there you are, Mr. President. I'm not the best botanist, not the most conversant with Washington's ways, not quite a Daniel Boone in the wilderness. I've dealt comfortably with Indians; I'm a good small unit soldier but without pretensions to greater command; I'm sturdy and stalwart, persevering and very hard to stop; I'm perdurable as my old ma liked to say of herself—she was and so am I."

He made the comparison with calculation—he knew the president admired Ma Lewis. Mr. Jefferson smiled and nodded but didn't speak.

"Well, sir," Lewis said, "I guess that sums up my case. I'm schooled in a multiplicity of things that taken together add up to fitness for this command. And then, intangible but I think important, I've dreamed of this for much of my life. Who else can say that?"

"Well, one other, at any rate."

"Sir?"

The president punched his chest with a thumb. "Me. I can say that. Thirty years of planning . . ."

Lewis smiled. "But you have other duties."

The other didn't answer and Lewis had no idea if he'd been persuasive. He waited expectantly but Mr. Jefferson merely said quietly, "Let's talk about how an expedition might go."

Well, what did that mean? But he'd made his case; now he must wait.

The president stood, stretched, and moved off, explaining over his shoulder that he wanted to see a field of experimental corn lying beyond the wheat field.

"Start with Congress," Mr. Jefferson said. "You're right about that. I won't move without its approval. So what we're proposing has to be clear. How big?—a dozen men should do it, eh? Then the cost, first thing the House committee will want to know. So, can it be done for twenty-five hundred?"

Lewis quickened his pace to come alongside the president. "Twenty-five hundred dollars?"

"What else?"

Lewis looked away to hide his smile. That much would buy a lot, but to carry a dozen men or more for two, three, four years in the wilderness? A party beyond any source of supply that must carry everything with it, weapons, ammunition, foodstuffs, medicines, fresh clothes—they would be in buckskin before long, but buckskin alone is poor dressing—and maybe above all, the presents. Presents, what everyone called trade goods, ribbons and beads, blankets and shirts, scissors, looking glasses, things of everyday practicality in developed societies, wonders in less developed. They would go up the Missouri by boat but at the mountains they would have to acquire—buy—horses, and trade goods were the medium of exchange. Each new item a new expense. Twenty-five hundred dollars was ridiculous.

But this was no time to cavil. "Probably," he said.

"Lay out a budget to that amount."

"Yes, sir." Time enough later to increase it by ten.

"Such an expedition must be military but can't appear warlike. Among other reasons for counting our men soldiers, they're paid anyway—won't distort our budget." Lewis nodded; so the president did understand the money problem. Very reassuring. With a smile, Mr. Jefferson added, "And for command and discipline issues, and even combat should it come to that."

For congressional ears emphasis would be on trade. The villages of the Mandan Indians up in Dakota country were the farthest known point on the river, identified by French traders. Now the villages functioned as a fur entrepôt for the British. That should be our trade, an idea that would appeal to Congress.

"But the paramount aim—the Northwest Passage. I suppose Mackenzie's most vital point was his assertion that he found a three-thousand-foot crossing of the western mountains. Could that be, three thousand? Could he measure with any accuracy, alone in the field with a handful of men all more ignorant than he? Seems much too easy to me. But I must say, if he's at all accurate, that's good news indeed."

But I doubt it, Lewis thought and debated saying it just as the president said, "But frankly, I doubt it."

He turned abruptly and stopped, facing Lewis. "And his other claim, that he was on a north fork of the Columbia, I just don't believe that. He's almost certainly letting hope and dreams take over, the desire to put the best face on his ventures. But he's at least six hundred miles north of our Columbia and I don't doubt that that claim will disprove readily. A river running parallel to the ocean for six hundred miles? Damned unlikely, wouldn't you say?"

"I would indeed, sir."

He paused to examine the wheat, then went on to the corn, talking all the way. Now, he was saying, an American expedition would be different from Mackenzie's in all ways—Mackenzie sought one thing, commercial advantage. But the American expedition would be recording everything new. Certainly new plants, perhaps new animals. Were there new species? Species believed extinct still alive? Mastodons as rumored? White Indians, lost tribes of Celts so often reported but never seen? The lost tribes of Israel? Volcanoes, to account for the pumice stone reported? Many, many things to tax the human imagination.

Lewis was beginning to see what the president meant when he said he had been thinking of such an expedition for thirty years. And it was becoming clear that anyone chosen to lead would have months of study ahead. He must be proficient in astronomy, navigation, ethnology, surveying, mapping techniques, all in addition to botany.

"I could train him in botany," Mr. Jefferson was saying, "but there are men in Philadelphia who have devoted their lives to such studies, and they'll be anxious to help."

He rattled off names that Lewis knew only from afar. That the president

would call in favors from so distinguished a group told Lewis how much
weight he attached to an expedition. It seemed they would pour knowledge
into the leader as with a funnel. This leader must know the stars but must
understand celestial navigation as well, must position his party daily, placing them on the accurate, detailed map of the Missouri River the expedition
must produce, all two or three thousand miles of it. Lewis saw that his own
calculations had been naive. He had supposed that leading his men successfully over hundreds upon hundreds of miles that white men had never penetrated would be enough. That and explore unknown mountains that
appeared on conjectural maps as a modest little ridge but that in reality
probably were huge considering the amount of water they poured into the
Missouri, and never mind the Canadian's views. Oh, and discover the
Northwest Passage, too, or disprove it, which possibility the president
refused to consider. But no, all that was just the start.

Consider medicine, a crucial need when the leader must be doctor as
well. Lewis thought of Ma instructing Mary Beth in natural medicine and
wished he'd put more account on her knowledge. The president said he
would call on his old friend Benjamin Rush to give the leader a tutorial
that would see him through. Rush was about the most famous doctor in
America, signer of the Declaration, hero of the yellow fever epidemic that
felled one out of ten in Philadelphia that terrible summer of 1793. The devil of a fellow, really.

A great expedition was unfolding. Lewis's spirits soared. It was thrilling
in its vastness, its significance, the possibilities and potential inherent in the
very idea. This sudden awareness seemed to deepen his own senses. A powerful intuition came to him, richer and more sophisticated than he had ever
felt, that life would never be the same if he made this trek and returned triumphant. Confidence soaring, he felt it was his to take and make his own.
But ten minutes later, spirits plummeting as he noted the president's tortur-
ous circumlocutions to keep the identity of the leader open, he saw that
quite the opposite was true. And the president talked on.

But presently as the tumult in Lewis increased Mr. Jefferson stopped
at a stile leading to a pasture where a good-looking mare was showing a
colt the ropes. He threw his arms overhead, stretching, then said, "I
expect that's enough for now. Good start, though, don't you think?"

Suddenly outrage swept Lewis. All this talk circling around the crucial
point, the man dangling it, playing with him—

"No, sir," he said, "I'd say it was downright piss-poor."

"Oh?" The president's voice went cool again. "Because?"

"Because for two hours we've been talking of something that
becomes increasingly real. I made my case for this command—I think I

deserve at least a hint, am I in or out? And I'll tell you this, too—put someone else in command and nine chances of ten the expedition goes out crippled."

"My," the president said. "You're demanding it."

Lewis hesitated. "Well," he said slowly, "I suppose I am. But it has gone too far—I owe it to you, I owe it to myself, to say it in so many words—I want that command."

Walk into the lion's den and stick your head in its mouth. His own temerity surprised him but he knew instinctively that he was right. If the president couldn't see it, it was a mark against the president. An odd sort of comfort flowed through him. The time had come and he had made his move for better or worse, but he was sure that if he had not done so everything from here on would have been downhill. It might be downhill anyway but so be it.

There was a long silence, the president's expression stern, perhaps offended, perhaps uncertain. But at last he nodded. "Yes," he said, "you are to command it."

Despite his defiance of a moment past, Lewis now felt such a wash of emotion that he had to brace himself. His eyes blurred and he blinked. Perhaps tears weren't what you'd look for in a commander, but he didn't care.

"It's what I'd always intended," the president said. "That's why I offered you your present post—to get ready."

There was a long silence. The president seated himself on the stile, this time on a lower step so Lewis, still standing, was looking down at him. "You know," he said, "you made a strong impression on me as a youth. But you've been a frontier soldier for a good many years now. Done well with a captaincy, but nothing truly outstanding. I went over your record pretty carefully, too. Some men grow on their own. Others grow against circumstances. I judge you to be in the latter class. So I had to see. Throw you into strange, difficult situations. If I had determined that in the end you were no more than a good frontier soldier, we wouldn't be having this conversation."

The mare and the colt approached and stood motionless. They seemed to be auditing the conversation. Lewis waited.

"Now," the president said, "you handled yourself well with Mr. Randolph, and others too. Kept your balance. You'll be on your own, far from any counsel—you'll be dealing with Indians, dealing with traders from other nations, perhaps with troops from Spain or Britain or both, and in every possibility you must remember who you are, whom you represent, the larger realities all aside from the immediate. I don't want to start a war, but neither do I want American troops knuckling under to Redcoats.

You may find yourself in situations that demand a highly sophisticated response. Now, Merry, I don't want you to take this amiss, but when you came you were well short of sophistication."

Lewis smiled, feeling sunny. "Agreed, sir."

"So, you've grown. Handled yourself well or well enough but more importantly, developed real skills in a new and taxing milieu. It's what I had to know before we went further. And you did well in a tough new situation with little preparation."

The mare had a sore behind her rib cage, gouged herself on something, likely. Mr. Jefferson murmured that they'd have to get some blue ointment on that. He glanced up at Lewis.

"Another thing. Temper can be an asset, but you have more than you need. It will always be up to you to restrain it, use it when you need it, but always in control, never to be indulged."

Fair enough: Lewis had reached the same conclusion.

The president gazed at Lewis. "But there's another issue, too," he finally said, "and I believe it trumps all others. I had to see how you dealt with your melancholy. I know you had to struggle with it as a boy. It plagued your father too. Runs in the Lewis family, actually—I know two of your uncles were affected. So I needed to know—can you control it, or will it control you? I thought your point about the loneliness of command in the wilderness was apt but I can tell you that loneliness is never melancholy's friend. So I've been watching for that, too. I see it attacking you, see you withstanding it—indeed, a couple of times this morning I believe you've had to fight it. Control of this is critical; I judge you can do it, and it is on that basis that I give you the command. Now, Merry, if you have the slightest doubt you must say so. Withdraw now."

Lewis stared. My Lord, the man knew him well, perceiving the dark days that Lewis had believed he was keeping hidden. Sometimes it was perilous—every now and then he felt himself in a hole, daylight a mere patch of blue far overhead, walls of the hole seeping water and utterly slick, he with no tool but fingernails staring at that patch of blue and knowing that this time there was no escaping. And he would shut his eyes, clench his fists, and will himself out of that hole and into the sunshine, gasping with relief when he made it. And make it he always did. Always did. He controlled it. But those were days that came with the bark on, no doubt about that.

He saw the president was awaiting an answer and he said quietly, "Yes, sir, I am subject to melancholy. But I don't surrender to it. And won't."

"Very well," Mr. Jefferson said with a smile. He bounded to his feet. "So it's settled. I'm glad. There'll be lots to talk about, much to be planned, and we'll have time for that. But we know where we stand." The president offered his hand and again Lewis caught that quick flash of hidden humor in his eyes.

"Sir," he said slowly, "you were waiting, weren't you? Waiting for me to ask for the command. Weren't you?"

Mr. Jefferson laughed out loud. "So, young man, you caught me out." Then, more seriously, "Yes, I was waiting. A man who can't bring himself to ask for something of this magnitude, demand it, really, hardly deserves it. And probably would botch it. So of course I was waiting. I didn't want to give it to you — I wanted you to take it — to force it. And you did."

PART TWO

THE TRIUMPH

13

On a sunny Sunday afternoon in September of the year 1803, George Shannon sat on the boardinghouse veranda watching the women of Pittsburgh go strolling by, many with little parasols and others with bonnets, many indeed seeming to swell right out of their gowns, walking with a swaying motion that seemed immensely attractive to Shannon. He started to mention this to John Colter but John was enough older he'd probably make light of Shannon's interest, which was innocent as could be, after all.

Just then John Colter looked up from the newspaper he was reading. He gave the paper a shake for emphasis and said, "Listen here, George— this feller's talking about walking across the whole blamed continent. Clear to the Pacific Ocean."

Shannon sighed. You could never tell when John was joshing. "How come he's going to do that?" he asked.

"Grab us some new territory, I wouldn't doubt. Why else would you mount such a trip as that? Whole damned continent, I mean, that's something! Look for the Northwest Passage, too—find him a water route to the China trade."

"Go on. Is that possible?"

"Hell, I don't know. But it sounds like more fun than a barrel of wildcats and I aim to go with him. You got any sense, you'll come too. I hear he's looking for men."

"Really? Reckon he'd take us?"

"Don't hurt none to ask. Meriwether Lewis, his name, captain in the army, I think, and he's over at Mrs. Johnson's boarding. Let's walk over and let him speak his piece."

Walk to the Pacific! God Almighty, wouldn't that be something! A sight better, anyway, than going back to his uncle's farm in central Pennsylvania, Uncle Homer kicking his ass around, Ma puling and mewing about how Pa done went off and left her and died in Ohio of the valley ague. Poor Pa, struck down in his prime. When he'd known he was going he'd pulled George close.

"Go back to your ma." It was a whisper but an order, too.

"Oh, hell, Pa—"

"Don't argue. Sixteen, that's too young out here alone—"

Too young? "I do a man's work, I'm big as most men, most I meet I can whip if it comes to that . . ."

Long silence. Then Pa had said, "You'd pass for eighteen anywhere. I don't hold with lying, but if you was to say you was eighteen 'twouldn't be too far from the real truth . . ."

But in the end, once he put Pa in the ground and sold out for a few twenty-dollar gold pieces that he sewed into his waistband, he started back to Pennsylvania because he didn't know what else to do. Taking slower and slower steps, dreading more and more, stopping finally here in Pittsburgh, not deciding anything, just stalled. Pittsburgh, tucked onto the point where the Allegheny and the Monongahela formed the Ohio and sent it cascading down toward the Mississippi, brick buildings on narrow streets hugging the river, grog shops and rope walks, a nail factory and a foundry. He hired on at a warehouse on a wharf and met John Colter who led him to Mrs. Sandovar's boardinghouse where they now sat with their feet on the porch railing belching off the pressures occasioned by her Sunday dinner.

Captain Lewis proved to be a tall, handsome fellow, maybe thirty or so, hank of black hair and kind of what you might call a hatchet face, narrow with a long nose. He was broad in the shoulder and his hands looked hard and he moved with an ease and flexibility that meant strength. That and a look in his eye that said you'd be wise not to provoke him. Yes, he intended to march to the Pacific, down the Ohio and up the Missouri River, and cross the mountains he said were supposed to be there and go down some river or other, and yes, he was looking for good men. Said right off selection wouldn't be final till his co-captain down the river, name of William Clark, had looked them over and then it would mean joining the army. This was a military affair.

The captain asked Colter so many questions that George's heart sank—he'd never be able to satisfy this man with the air of whipcord command about him. At the same time, his respect for his friend shot up—seemed Colter had been everywhere and done everything and him not yet thirty, knew the river and knew the woods, could read sign and track like an Indian and was a dead shot agin man or beast. But Cap'n Lewis frowned at that and said the whole idea was to go in peace so Colter confessed he'd never killed no one unless once when Indians attacked at first light, and that what he really meant, he was some hunter.

Whereas George was just off the farm. But no matter, he talked right up when the cap'n turned to him, putting the best face on everything—and then the cap'n asked his age.

His eyes opened wide. "Eighteen, sir."

Cap'n Lewis went right on but after a bit asked suddenly for the year he was born. George had worked it all out and smooth as glass he said, "'Eighty-five, sir," instead of "'Eighty-seven."

The cap'n rubbed his chin. "Pretty young," he said.

"Sir," George cried, "I don't take a backseat to no man. Down the Ohio and up the Missouri—I can paddle long as any man you'll find, I can shoot, got me three squirrels with one ball once, I can cook a venison stew to set your mouth to running, I don't drink and I don't hardly smoke and I don't fight long as I don't get pushed and I can start a fire in a driving rain and—"

Lewis laughed. "Think well of yourself, eh?"

"Well, my pa said you don't think well of yourself, nobody else will either. I generally finish what I start. I won't give you no cause for dissatisfaction and if I do I'll turn back without a word anytime you tell me. You won't find me lacking, you won't hear no complaining, I get along good . . ."

So both of them became members of what was to become the Corps of Discovery and George sent those gold pieces to Ma and told her his fortune was assured. The cap'n put them right to work, rounding up supplies while he stayed after the drunken scoundrel who was building his keelboat. It took George a few days to realize how much store the cap'n set on that boat and by this time he was following his new leader around with what John Colter said matched the devotion of a hound to his master. But John could go to hell—Meriwether Lewis was a kind of man George had hardly known existed, such was his inner power and authority, that sense that he knew everything worth knowing and could do anything he decided to do and do it better than most anyone else—why, he made you feel good just being around him, made you sure of yourself and wanting above all to please him. Disappointing the cap'n, that would be the worst thing you could imagine . . .

Sam'l Hawkins had the only real boatyard in Pittsburgh, but George heard he was a drinker and you could never tell when he would finish a boat, just that it would be good when he did. It had been a hot summer and ol' Hawkins had boils on his backside and couldn't hardly sit down so he was drinking away his misery instead of turning to the cap'n's keelboat.

So here was the boat with ribs still unplanked. It was big, fifty-five feet in length, eight in the beam, able to carry tons of supplies for men cut off from all civilization. But every day came a new excuse and George watched that flush creep up the cap'n's face a little faster. The delay was dangerous. Autumn was coming on and naturally the river was falling.

There was a gauge at Pinkham's Wharf where old Pinkham sold little river fish fried to a turn and Shannon, who was always hungry, watched that gauge go down and down. Soon the river would be too shallow — even now you'd be fetching up shoals . . .

On a morning when hammers should have been ringing and saws whining George followed the cap'n into the yard and heard nothing but angry voices. Wrangling instead of working. Then here came all seven workmen storming out of the yard —

The cap'n stopped the leader with a hand on his chest, a big fellow with carrot-colored hair who cried, "We ain't going to work for that drunken devil no more, always on your ass, whining and complaining and changing his mind and taking it all out on us — why, he accused me of slacking, me! Lighting my pipe, I was, paused between hammer strokes and he —"

"Shut up," the cap'n said, and any fool could tell he meant business. But the fellow reared back. "Now, see here —"

The cap'n slapped him. Knocked him down openhanded. And he said, voice not loud but crackling with command, "This yard is under contract to the United States Army. Push me, I'll have you working at bayonet point."

"Well," said a heavy fellow with a black beard and a hammer in his hand, "you better tell ol' Hawkins —"

George didn't like the looks of that hammer. He scooped up a stick about as thick as his wrist that would make a right handy cudgel. It had a nice balance. Cap'n Lewis led them back into the yard, George off to one side watching his back, and found old Hawkins reeling, his face near purple with rage.

"Whoreson scoundrels," he was bawling, "walk out on Sam'l Hawkins, I'll sack you all —"

The cap'n gave Hawkins a shove. The boatman reeled back against the door of his shed. He was taller and heavier than the cap'n and when his workers crowded forward George stepped up with his bat. But quick as a wink the cap'n grabbed Hawkins and dragged him to the horse trough, threw him in and rammed his head under. Hawkins bobbed up and a stream of vomit shot from his mouth. Minute he was done the cap'n shoved his head under again. This time the boatman rose slowly to his knees in the water, staring at the cap'n.

"Mr. Hawkins," the cap'n said in what George took as a right civil tone, considering everything, "you're under contract to the United States Army and I intend to enforce that contract. Don't let me find you drunk again." He looked around. "You men, no more sloughing off. Give me honest work and I'll have a ten-dollar gold piece for every man the day the boat is done." He glanced at Hawkins who was crawling from the water. "And you—stay at it and I won't put you out of business."

The cap'n watched with his arms crossed as the men went back to work and the ring of hammers and the whine of saws started up and Mr. Hawkins stood wiping his face with a rag.

Later, his bat still in hand, George said, "Could you really put him out of business?" But Cap'n Lewis only smiled.

14

Pittsburgh, Early October, 1803

Pounding along a rocky trail that followed the Ohio, long stride eating ground, Lewis was walking hard as he always did when troubled in mind. A dark shape moved on the edge of vision. His grip tightened on his stick and then a black dog appeared from the brush and fell in beside him. A Newfoundland he was and big, already well over a hundred pounds and probably still shy of his full growth, pushing thirty inches at the shoulder but lanky, not yet filled out. Looked eager and companionable as he trotted along, lolling tongue a splash of color against dense black coat.

Lewis laughed. "All right—we'll tramp together."

The dog looked up with a curl in his lip that would do for a smile and gave a brief wag of the tail that was courteous but not effusive. He held pace with the man, wide head swinging from side to side, ranging. Lewis felt he'd been adopted. He considered Newfoundlands unusually able dogs, and this one clearly had a mind of his own. All right, big boy, let's see how long you last. Then it struck him the dog might be thinking the same thing and he laughed again.

Thirty-odd miles was a good day's ramble. It shook out the kinks and let off pressure when you burned inside. It wasn't so much the boat that bothered him now. It was still slow but taking strong shape, though time was running dangerously short. The river fell a little more each day. Already this morning he was seeing schoolboys only ankle deep on shoals as they took fish with hand nets. His boatmen would have to drag the heavy vessel across those shoals with sheer muscle.

He had Colter at the boatyard to keep things moving. Colter didn't say much but a wildness flashed in his eyes when he felt he was being crossed, and that livid scar on his cheek stood white as bone. He had been with Simon Kenton in the latter days on the Kentucky frontier when the British were arming the Indians and there was hell to pay around most any corner; this was a man who could handle himself.

Shannon, at the moment out collecting supplies the cap'n had ordered, he might work out. Big solid youngster, ruddy look of old Ireland on his broad face, blue eyes that glittered when trouble threatened. Looked more like sixteen but Lewis admired the way he had taken note of that bastard with the hammer and picked up a bat. Of course, another step or two and the fellow would have been looking down a pistol barrel, but Shannon had gone a long way toward proving himself in that moment. As it happened the worker had glanced at the hammer as if surprised to find it in his hands and had laid it gently on the ground. But Shannon had shown good stuff.

No, what pressed him so hard now was a critical new problem. His invitation to Will Clark to join the expedition had gone out weeks ago and there had been no answer. Maybe enlisting Will was a harebrained idea from the start. Will had made himself a power in frontier trade in Indiana—how could he drop everything to go marching across the continent no matter how much the adventure of it might appeal? There had been no answer because Clark was embarrassed, wouldn't want to turn down his old friend and yet probably was finding it all impossible. But Lewis must have an answer soon for if Clark refused a substitute must be found quickly. He didn't like the idea at all, but soon he would have no choice— he must make a new selection. He remembered telling the president he wanted another officer. A lieutenant, the president had said brightly, an able assistant capable of bringing home the journals should an evil mischance befall the leader. Very good. But Lewis had shaken his head. It must be a man of proven ability. And applying the sense of the politic he had absorbed in Washington, he had said he wanted General George Rogers Clark's little brother. William Clark, youngest of a great family, very much in the mold of his older brother, older now than the brother had been when he saved the West.

Excellent choice, the president had said, puzzled that there was any question. But there was. Lewis had served under Clark as a raw lieutenant. Since Captain Clark left the army he had become an important man in civil life. He would never serve as subaltern to a former subaltern, roles reversed. Only a co-captaincy in a joint command would do.

The president had nodded. There were problems but Lewis saw no need to raise them. So he sent the invitation and now awaited an answer with growing anxiety.

They walked on, the man and the dog, the latter's long tongue lolling, keeping a steady trot beside his companion.

A year of intense preparations flavored with anxiety had passed since Lewis won the command. The president told him to get ready to go, but the unwavering French intention to take over the Louisiana Territory inhibited every move. Foreign troops landing on North America would mean war and forget the expedition. Lewis wrestled with melancholy.

In every way he could, Mr. Jefferson told Bonaparte that the day French troops landed in New Orleans would strike the low water mark of the Napoleonic career. The huge American merchant fleet coupled with the Royal Navy's dominance of the seas must sink his hopes on the continent. There was no response. The president offered to buy New Orleans, since the French needed money to prosecute war and the mouth of the river in American hands would at least keep it open for western commerce. The silence from Paris continued, so unreasonable it seemed eerie.

Lewis had no doubt the French faced humiliating defeat in the Americas. The Royal Navy would blockade the Gulf Coast and starve out French troops. Denied resupply, they must eventually collapse. The British long had pushed America to join their war against France. But doing so would slide the new nation back under John Bull's thumb, sad end to the Revolution. A conundrum.

Indeed, much of the quarrel between Federalists and Democrats that had put Mr. Jefferson in office turned on just that question—how like the British with their hereditary aristocracy were we to be? Alexander Hamilton swung toward the British connection, Mr. Jefferson away. Federalists admired Britain for its stability, its financial expertise, its centralized power, and its codification of rule by the right people. Of course Hamilton didn't talk such rank heresy directly, but Democrats, Lewis among them, didn't doubt that a system like Britain's, aristocracy entrenched, was the logical outcome of the Federalist view. Joining Britain would be fatal. Only thing worse would be knuckling under to France in Louisiana. But the irony was that Bonaparte would drive us into Britain's arms.

"Cutting his own throat even as he cuts ours," Lewis had cried to Miss Dolley. They had been having tea and scones on the south terrace of the mansion where the sun warmed the stone walls and he was denouncing stupidity in high places. A slight smile curved her lips and for a moment he saw that he was stating the obvious, stupidity in high places being not unusual.

But momentum swept him on—saw it all the time in the army, he cried.

Soon she was chuckling over command missteps left to subalterns in the field to correct. And here was the great Napoleon who was changing the face of modern warfare doing the same thing. Amazing. Life is full of such ironies, Miss Dolley observed quietly.

"Which makes them no easier to bear."

She laughed and said, "I suppose not," and something in the very timber of her voice seemed to warm him.

Never mind the French, the president had said, and Lewis plowed ahead as a grim air settled over Washington. The president was distant and silent, the easy manner that some people mistook for weakness rarely seen. Detail proved an antidote for worry: he sat in his office with its canvas walls flexing to errant drafts and calculated. Those bickering gentlemen on the Hill would never give him monies without limits. Set a total of twenty-five hundred dollars and work backward. That sum wouldn't get them far on the ground but would move them right along with Congress. On separate sheets rougher and rounder figures built new totals. He added, subtracted, recalculated. He balanced his list of weapons, ready to fight if they must but never seeking a fight. How many weapons? Well, how many men? How to strike between too few and too many? The president had mentioned a dozen. Say fifteen for a start?

One day it struck him that while he worked daily with the president he rarely saw Henry Dearborn, the rotund secretary of war. Odd . . . it was an army expedition and Lewis would be reporting to the War Department. Suited him, though; he didn't like Dearborn who treated him with a stiff formality in which Lewis read disdain. And the president was in charge.

His penciled budget grew. Foodstuffs, how much, what kind? Beans and flour for starches. Hunters would keep them in meat but he would need sowbelly preserved in salt to grease the pan and flavor the meat. You could eat elk meat till you dropped and still feel hungry, so lacking was it in fat. Someone was making a condensed soup in Philadelphia; how was it packed, how long did it last, how much did it cost? Find out . . .

How many hundredweights of beans, of flour? Well, how long would they be gone? Two years? Three? Four? But how could you say? More question marks. How much firepower all told? How to keep powder dry? The old idea, sealing it into lead canisters, each shaped to melt into exactly the number of balls the powder inside could fire, worked just fine. Then new calculations. A supply of tomahawks, once the word for the stone fighting ax of the Algonquins, now adopted into the white world with an iron head. Equally handy for campground chores and close combat.

And the iron boat, don't forget that. He would put skilled smiths to work at the national armory at Harper's Ferry. He considered it his most brilliant idea, a framework of iron rods that disassembled and bundled could be carried by one man, but bolted together and covered with skins would float a couple of tons. Portable boat: a work of genius.

They were to map the Missouri mile by mile. That meant parchment and paper, pencils and rules, dry ink, goose quills. It meant instruments for star sights that would position them and a chronometer of highest accuracy since star sights depended on precise time. How to fit all that into a budget? Borrow instruments? Buy them as a War Department, not an expedition, expenditure? It took finesse, this business.

The president produced a dilapidated sextant and introduced Lewis to its mysteries, catching the afternoon sun through the little 'scope, the boiling globe slipping rapidly from the mirror, twirling the thumbscrew. Basic navigation, a sight easier standing on solid ground than on a ship's rolling deck.

Lewis considered himself an adequate botanist but Mr. Jefferson showed him his inadequacies. Prowling the fields around Monticello they looked at plants in all their varieties and multiple seasonal dress, each with its distinguishing characteristic, an oddly shaped leaf, a varying color, imperviousness to or susceptibility to cold, the order in which leaves lay on stems, stems on branches. At Monticello they prowled woods and meadows, from Washington they walked the banks of the Potomac, the president lecturing as Lewis desperately drank in knowledge that must equip him to deal alone with plants unknown to classical botanists, though Indians absorbed their form of the science with their mother's milk.

The president's library on North American geography was widely held to be the finest in the world. Lewis immersed himself in books there, his clay pipe alight, a pot of tea at hand. He pored over Captain Cook's account of his third voyage, his pulse thundering with the special joy of new ideas, new discoveries. Bartram's great account of his botanical travels in the Carolina mountains was just out, as was Vancouver's report on his voyages to the Pacific Northwest following Cook's work. Though it was forty years old, Antoine Simor Le Page du Pratz's *History of Louisiana* proved so valuable that Lewis rounded up a copt for the expedition library to be packed in a sealed chest.

And that was just the start. He studied maps and the art of mapping. Every map of North America was essentially speculative since no one with mapping skills had gone to see. Lewis memorized wildly conflicting ideas. The Stony Mountains, that great challenge that fed the Missouri to the east, the Columbia to the west, appeared on most maps as a single narrow ridge. Sort of a Blue Ridge of the West. The president liked that idea but Lewis clung to skepticism. Take just those two rivers—that was a hell of a lot of water for a western Blue Ridge to produce. But skepticism was difficult with every new map asserting new facts with not a hint of doubt.

Late in the year the president drafted a bill through which the Congress would authorize the expedition. For a mere twenty-five hundred dollars a small and peaceful delegation would map the Missouri, cross the mountains on an easy portage, and run down the Columbia to the sea, this with its hint of the China trade. It would present itself to Indians as a trade partner to challenge French and British traders. A handful of men out one year, back the next. It couldn't be less offensive. Or further from reality.

Lewis called on Mr. Randolph, who would manage the bill. Tall, awkward, the three hounds sniffing and sighing at his feet, the chairman examined Lewis who stood in respectful silence. "You are to command?"

"Yes, sir."

"Then, sir, you shall have it."

The bill came to the floor. Mr. Pickering, now a Senate member, rose with angry Federalist rhetoric on the waste of money, the undue attention to the West, the concern that France would be the only beneficiary, working himself up to full foam. House Federalists ranted. When they ground down to irritable muttering, Mr. Randolph called the vote. As the "ayes" went swiftly into the majority, the chairman gave Lewis a languorous wink. Thus the explorer's dream was authorized as a matter of law, the Senate sure to follow. They drank champagne that night and no one mentioned the French designs on the Mississippi.

Christmas of 1802 came and went. The revelry was austere, shadowed by the French crisis. As soon as the bill passed the president heaped more study on the subaltern. He enlisted the nation's leading scientists, most of them in Philadelphia, to offer tutorials. Lewis felt himself a sausage, learning tamped into an ever tighter skin.

He set out via Harper's Ferry to arrange for weapons and the iron boat. Then to Lancaster on the road to Philadelphia to visit Andrew Ellicott, the nation's leading astronomer and mathematician, who tutored him in celestial observation and its relationship with precise time. At the University of Philadelphia Robert Patterson lectured on the modern chronometer. He guided Lewis to the purchase of a gorgeous instrument made in London. The explorer paid $250 to a clock maker on South Third Street and sent the piece back to Ellicott to be regulated. In the end this marvel of precision varied by only fourteen seconds per twenty-four hours. When properly wound the works could be stopped and held in place with a hog bristle until accuracy's precise moment could be captured by star sight.

Benjamin Smith Barton lectured on fine points of botany with special emphasis on collecting and preserving specimens in the field. Barton was just publishing the first text on American botany; Lewis had read it in draft form at Monticello. Dr. Caspar Wistar, professor of anatomy and author of the first American treatise on anatomy, gave him a grasp of the human body that would be critical for a leader who must be a doctor to his men.

Benjamin Rush, far and away the leading physician in America, hero of the ghastly yellow fever epidemic that had decimated Philadelphia nine years before, lectured on medicine as a practice. He explained sound maintenance of health, Lewis listening carefully: at the onset of illness keep the patient prone, bathe his feet in cold water, and purge him with a special pill of Dr. Rush's own concoction designed to blast free the most compressed and resistant bowel. Lewis ordered fifty dozen of these "thunderclappers." The next day he paid $289.50 for 193 pounds of condensed soup—"portable soup" as the maker, Francois Baillet, a clever cook over on North Ninth, called it. Would it soon spoil? No one knew, but it might save their lives in starving time.

Meanwhile, Lewis and his friend Mahlon Dickerson were cutting a wide swath in Philadelphia society. They dined often with the governor, frequented the best homes, danced the night away at frequent balls. He fell in love, or at least thought that might be happening, to a willowy young woman named Charlotte Sinclair who seemed to dance with feet not touching the floor. Her eyes were a clear and wonderful blue, her hair light brown touched with auburn, and she listened to his pronouncements, laughed at his jests, responded to his stolen kiss even though she professed herself shocked—and then it was all over. She broke it suddenly, no real explanation, she was going to New York with her mother and no, he was not to follow. She shrank away as she told him this and he had the sudden impression that she feared him, at which all his ardor fled.

Then, abruptly, the French crisis ended. The wall of indifference around the French leader collapsed. He was losing interest in his American empire—rebelling slaves in Haiti had destroyed one army and awaited the next. But more importantly, war was recharging on the Continent and he needed money.

So it was that the foreign minister called in the American ambassador, who had been trying to buy New Orleans for months.

"What would you give for the whole?" Manner offhand, eyes sharp.

"The whole? Louisiana Territory entire?"

"Of course. What good is it to us without New Orleans?"

Church bells rang all over America. Baring Brothers in London issued

the bonds by which Americans paid a total of fifteen million dollars for the
rights to more than a third of North America. And Meriwether Lewis was
free to set out for the Northwest Passage, water route to the China trade.

A rabbit flashed across the trail and the dog went booming after it. Good-
bye, dog. Lewis felt an odd disappointment, feelings a little hurt as if he'd
been rejected somehow, the way women seemed . . . but how women
acted, that was another matter, for God's sake. Good-bye, you black bastard. But on impulse he put two fingers in his mouth and whistled a shrill
blast. A crashing in the brush and the dog bounded back to the trail, looking pleased with himself.

"You walking or playing the fool?" Lewis said, voice stern. The dog's
tail wagged, but slowly, doubtfully. He eyed Lewis, not sure if he liked
the tone. Lewis touched his head. "Come on, mate, let's go." He walked
on, strong and steady, the dog keeping pace. He didn't need any more
tomfoolery; the silence from the West was enough. He had written Will
Clark at Clarksville on the Ohio in Indiana Territory—the name gave you
an idea how potent the Clarks were.

The expedition had been held secret long after Congress authorized it
lest it upset the French maneuvering. Only recently had Lewis been free
to write. He had tried a half-dozen drafts to bring things to focus; then
he'd cut a fresh pen and started.

Dear Clark,

*From the long and uninterupted friendship and confidence which has sub-
sisted between us I feel no hesitation in making to you the following communication under the fulest impression that it will be held by you inviolably
secret until I see you or you shall hear from me again.*

*During the last session of Congress a law was passed in conformity to a pri-
vate message of the President of the United States intitled "An Act making an
appropriation for extending the external commerce of the United States." The
object of this Act was to give the sanction of the government to exploreing the
interior of the continent of North America, or that part of it bordering on the
Missourie and Columbia Rivers. This enterprise has been confided to me by the
President and I have been engaged in making the necessary preparations . . .*

He then continued to explain supplies, preparations, and authoriza-
tions before laying out his plan:

*. . . it is to descend the Ohio in a keeled boat of about ten tons burthen,
from Pittsburgh to its mouth, thence up the Mississippi to the mouth of the*

*Missourie, and up that river as far as its navigation is practicable . . . and
proceed to its source, and if practicable pass over to the waters of the Columbia or Origan River and by descending it reach the Western Ocean . . .*

He listed various objectives—to anchor the geography via celestial
observation, to present the United States to the Indians now in the new
territory, to report flora and fauna, rainfall and water flow—and above all
to find the fabled Northwest Passage that would open direct trade with
the Orient. Then to the real point . . .

*And so, my friend, you have a summary view of the plan. If therefore
there is anything in this enterprise which would induce you to participate
with me in it's fatigues, it's dangers and it's honors, believe me there is no
man on earth with whom I should feel equal pleasure in sharing them as
yourself . . .*

And finally, the president has authorized him to say that a captain's
commission would be forthcoming, and that,

*. . . your situation if joined with me in this mission will in all respects be
precisely such as my own.*

Co-captains for an epic journey. Up the Missouri a thousand miles,
cross mountains of God only knew what complexity or even how many
chains. Persuade mountain tribes to sell horses to haul gear and supplies
after water travel ran out. Debouch on the western slope, find the head of
the Columbia of which nothing was known now but the mouth and follow
it to the sea, begging information from Indians through sign language and
maps drawn in dirt with sticks as they passed on a trek that Indians had
never even had practical reason to consider. He had dreamed for years,
but now the dream had become reality and yes, now he knew with certainty that he needed Will Clark.

Gradually, striding along with the black dog beside him, a good thirty
miles behind them as they retraced their route with no real sign of tiring,
a new calm overtook Lewis. Action always soothed him, moving and
stretching. Now he saw that things would work out. The boat would be
completed and they'd muscle their way over the shallows in the falling
river and get on to St. Louis. Will would answer, yea or nay. He wasn't a
fool nor at all indecisive. He would know immediately if he could venture
so and would send an answer.

Shadows were longer and the town was not far ahead. At a bend in the river he saw a cabin backed to the water, the road swerving to pass near the front gate. Late flowers spilled red and white from hanging pots under the overhang. A woman was watering them with a cup. A man sat on a rawhide chair tilted against a post, his arms crossed. Lewis raised a finger to his forehead in courteous salute just as the man leaped up with a cry and ran into the yard.

"You!" he shouted, pointing at the black dog. "Where you been, you black son of a bitch?"

He was wiry and looked tough, maybe forty or so, going bald, wearing a deerskin vest that was near black with grease. A fighting knife in a worked scabbard was thrust under his belt.

"Been rambling with this here fellow, eh? I'll take a stick to you, teach you a goddam lesson."

The dog glanced at Lewis once, then at his owner. He was crouched, rear legs spread and braced, ready to fight or flee. But his tail wasn't tucked. Lewis sure as hell wasn't going to see his walking companion beaten before his eyes, or maybe it was that business about rambling. The black dog was a rambling fool and the only other rambling fool Lewis knew was himself. "Why don't I buy the dog?" he said, surprising himself. "He don't seem to cotton to you."

Instantly the fellow's scowl gave way to a winsome smile and then a look of cupidity so open that Lewis had trouble keeping a straight face.

"Well, I don't know. I been raising him careful, training him, don't you see, bringing him along. Maybe I'd sell him but you got to understand this here is a special dog. He can herd sheep or goats, he'll nail a squirrel before the little bastard can make a tree, he'll fetch a downed duck or a goose, don't make a tittle to him. He's—"

"How much?"

The fellow hesitated, then swallowed. "I'd have to have . . . twenty dollars. In gold."

That was robbery. "This here is a dog we're talking about. We ain't talking ten acres planted in corn, for God's sake."

"But he's very special." The whiny, scratchy voice continued, making up ludicrous claims for the dog's merit. Lewis stopped listening. He went to a knee and ran his hands over the dog's shoulder muscles and flank and along his tail, raised a lip to look at his teeth. The dog gave him that curious turn of lip that Lewis saw as a smile. And after all, he'd made a fine companion for a day—why not for a dog's life? "I'll be moving by boat," he said. "How you think he'll do on the river?"

"Do?" the fellow cried. "Why, he'll be perfect! You couldn't have chose better, for he's a river dog. A traveling dog. Why, hell, I took him to New Orleans on a flatboat and he was a regular seaman!"

That was so obviously a lie that Lewis laughed out loud. He scratched out a bill of sale for the owner to sign, handed him a twenty-dollar piece that might be his own or might be the government's, he was losing track as supply purchases mounted, and whistled up the dog. They went down the trail, Lewis still laughing.

"Regular seaman, are you? All right, suppose I call you that. Seaman. Think you can remember that? Seaman? Seaman?"

And Seaman looked up with that grin of his and wagged his tail and Lewis saw that the dog's doubts were gone.

The next morning he stood in line at the post office window. Seaman flopped at his feet and dozed. When he reached the window the postmaster's chief clerk brightened at the sight of him. "Yes, sir, Cap'n, got one for you this time. Hope it's what you've been waiting for all these days."

Surprised, a little displeased that he'd been so obvious, he took the letter. Yes, from Clark! The clerk grinned and said, "Yep, I reckon that's the one."

The letter hot in his hand summoned an image of Clark, hearty, intelligent, face ruddy, permanent outdoorsman's squint to blue eyes, four years Lewis's senior and probably heavier now, a natural commander of men. What would his old friend say? Ask a man to drop everything and set out on a march of two years or three or four or maybe ending dead in a box canyon somewhere, and what would he say? Ask out of the blue and say we must leave immediately—could a man of affairs just drop everything in a finger snap? Suddenly he saw that it would never work. Yet damn it all, he must have a man he could trust. His mood, brightened by the dog, sagged again. He ripped the letter open, thinking that he was too damned moody. The president had warned him, Ma had warned him, why, hell, years ago when he'd been subaltern to Clark's captaincy, Clark himself had warned him. Roughly he unfolded the sheet, ready now for rejection.

Dear Lewis

    I received by yesterday's mail yours of the 19th ulto. The Contents of which I recived with much pleasure. The enterprise &c. is Such as I have long anticipated and am much pleased with—and as my situation in life will admit of my absence the length of time necessary to accomplish such an undertaking I will chearfully join you in an 'official Charrector' as men-

tioned in your letter, and partake of the dangers, difficulties and fatigues, and
I anticipate the honors & rewards of such an enterprise, should we be success-
ful . . . My friend, I do assure you that no man lives whith whome I would
purfur to undertake Such a Trip . . .

Lewis sank into a chair. His heart was racing. Good old Will! At a second glance he focused on that phrase "official Charrector." Yes, as he had
known Clark would do, his co-captain was tying down the promised
equality.

A few days later a second letter, sent to Washington to be forwarded in
case Lewis had moved on. In this one, after making the same stipulation
of equality "as offered in your letter," Clark had written and then crossed
out — Lewis could see his old friend shaking his head, deciding the phrase
was a little too sentimental — "My friend, I join you with hand and heart."

With hand and heart . . .

15

Clarksville, Indiana Territory, Late October, 1803

Lewis gazed ahead at violent water. The big keelboat had come down
from Pittsburgh, his temporary crew often over the side to hoist her over
shoals. Now it poised just above the Falls of the Ohio, chief impediment
to navigation on this artery river. He nodded to the bowman and they
pushed into the maelstrom. It went well and his heart rate was already
slowing when near the bottom she took a ferocious lick from a hidden
boulder. Was her bottom gone? Colter and Shannon hurled bundles and
boxes aside; then Shannon looked up with a triumphant grin.

"She's dry, Cap'n! There ain't no leak!"

They slid into gentle current. Just ahead lay Clarksville . . . and Will
Clark. Yet this didn't bring the joy he had expected. Niggling little doubts
had arisen. Had his old friend changed — had he grown? Remember Mr.
Jefferson saying that if Lewis had proved to be no more than a sound
frontier officer there would have been no conversation. Lewis knew he
had matured and steadied in the cockpit of Washington. How would
Clark have handled the infuriating Mr. Randolph? Clark was well
respected on the frontier but that had been true when he left the army.

Now they were embarked on something so filled with the unknown that they must rely on their own instinct and experience. Lewis had grown to the challenge, but what about Clark? All the way down this concern nagged him.

Another anxiety, too . . . they were running late and departing St. Louis before winter now looked doubtful. Leaves were turning to gold, mornings brisk, afternoons flooded with bright light, birds all southbound. One day flocks of passenger pigeons heading away from winter just about blanked out the sun and on another day squirrels by the thousands were swimming madly across the river, hell-bent for the south bank, though the north bank seemed equally carpeted in acorns. Seaman jumped among them and snatched up dozens of the little critters for a rich squirrel stew when they camped that night, Seaman getting his share.

He had sent word ahead. Sure enough, when Clarksville came into sight just below the falls he saw Will on the wharf, recognizing him instantly, a solid, strong, wide figure, shoulders broad, height to match Lewis's own, feet planted with such firm strength that those drawings of a colossus with the world on his shoulders sprang to mind. Here was a man for great deeds. Half of Lewis's doubts fell away. But half remained.

Before the boat stopped Clark vaulted aboard and enveloped Lewis in a bear hug. Stepped back, shouted, "My God, Merry, but you're a sight for sore eyes!" and embraced him again.

Then, at once, Clark was to business. "How's the boat? Banged around coming down?"

"Took a hell of a lick at one place."

Clark laughed. "That boulder's sunk more than one boat. Is she taking water?"

Shannon was crouched nearby, gazing at them raptly. "No, sir," he said with a wide smile, jumping up, "she's dry." He hesitated. "Or was . . ."

Clark gave him a long, withering look, at which Shannon shrank back, face gone deep red.

"We're all set," Clark said to Lewis. "Boys at the yard are ready to haul her and check her bottom." He glanced about. "Nice—I figured you'd have a good one." He was just as Lewis had remembered, direct and immediately practical. See to the boat.

That was Will Clark, bluff, hearty, a courteous man with a little edge in his manner that warned you not to test courtesy, a bit heavier now as was Lewis, his face mobile and expressive of a generally but changeable good humor. He was clear-eyed, steady, confident, but assuming little—a man to go to the well with. You heard that crackle of command in his voice that made men ready to follow without question. Lewis heard it in his own voice when he listened.

Will said he had seven men standing by as candidates for the march to the Pacific; Lewis would meet them the next day. Lewis introduced Colter and Shannon. Clark nodded to Colter and turned to Shannon. A flash of amusement in his eyes, he said mildly, "Don't raise a hell of a lot of beard, do he?"

Lewis saw Shannon color and start to speak up, then think better of it. Good—the lad was learning.

Clark seemed in a joyous mood. He bounced about getting the boat unloaded and onto the ways. He was the first to spot the crack in a starboard hull plank and told Lewis that the plank could be cut out and replaced easily enough. Dusk was edging in when boat issues were settled and Clark took Lewis off to the inn for a private dinner he'd ordered.

"Salt-cured ham, sugared yams, grits, biscuits and honey, washed down with hot grog—been a while since you've had salt-cured ham, I'll wager!"

As they walked up the hill from the riverfront Lewis noted a subtle shift in Clark's manner. Celebration was done; time to be serious. The inn was a handsome place of peeled logs, two stories, a big barn out back, a smokehouse giving off rich odors. Inside Clark made for a corner alcove curtained off.

"Be private here," he said as they took chairs. "Now, Merry, did you bring my commission?"

Lewis knew he was coloring as he said, "Secretary Dearborn hadn't drawn it up when I left. It was supposed to follow me but hasn't so far—I've written three times about it."

Clark gave him a thoughtful look. "Something wrong, you think?"

"Don't see how it could be. I told the president I wanted you and he was delighted—knows your brother well and I told him you were cut from the same cloth. He personally approved it."

"You'd tell me if there was a problem?"

"Well, of course. Probably it got sent on to St. Louis."

Clark spread his hands. "We'll wait and see, then. But you have our orders, at least. You did bring them along, I hope."

Lewis didn't like the edge of sarcasm, but maybe he deserved it. He should have worked harder to have that commission in hand. He saw clearly now what he had surmised before—that equality of command was crucial to Clark.

He took a packet wrapped in oilskin from a shoulder bag that also held a pistol. Clark unfolded the sheets written in the president's tight hand and began to read. Lewis's doubts continued to dissolve, though they didn't vanish totally. The smiling young captain of the Rifles had given way to a man of substance and weight. As had Captain Lewis.

The orders noted the legislative act that gave the force of law to the expedition and then it continued, "you are appointed to carry . . . into execution."

The object of your mission is to explore the Missouri river, & such principal stream of it, as, by it's course and communication with the waters of the Pacific Ocean, may offer the most direct and practicable water communication across this continent, for the purposes of commerce.

Beginning at the mouth of the Missouri, you will take observations of latitude and longitude, at all remarkable points on the river, & especially at the mouths of rivers, at rapids, at islands & other places & objects distinguished by such natural marks & characters of a durable kind, as that they may with certainty be recognized hereafter. The courses of the river between these points of observation may be supplied by the compass, the log-line and by time, corrected by the observations themselves . . .

The interesting points of portage between the heads of the Missouri & the water offering the best communication with the Pacific Ocean should also be fixed by observation, & the course of that water to the ocean, in the same manner as that of the Missouri.

Your observations are to be taken with great pains & accuracy, to be entered distinctly, & intelligibly for others as well as yourself, to comprehend elements necessary, with the aid of the usual tables, to fix the latitude and longitude . . .

They were to make several copies of the resulting journals, including one on birch bark as less susceptible to injury from damp, these copies to be held by various members of the party that their chances of getting through be improved. The paper crackled in Clark's big hands. The text moved into Indian matters, where Clark's experience would be crucial.

. . . you will . . . endeavor to make yourself acquainted, as far as a diligent pursuit of your journey shall admit,
    names of the nations & their numbers;
    the extent and limits of their possessions;
    their relations with other tribes or nations;
    their language, traditions, monuments;

their ordinary occupations in agriculture, fishing, hunting, war, arts, & the implements for these;

their food, clothing, & domestic accommodations;

the diseases prevalent among them and the remedies they use;

moral and physical circumstances which distinguish them from the tribes we know;

peculiarities in their laws, customs & dispositions;

and articles of commerce they may need or furnish & to what extent . . .

Other objects worthy of notice will be

the soil & face of the country, its growth & vegetable production, especially those not of the U.S.

the animals of the country generally, & especially those not known in the U.S.

the remains and accounts of any which may be deemed rare or extinct;

the mineral productions of every kind; but more particularly metals, limestone, pit coal & saltpetre; salines & mineral waters, noting the temperature of the last, & such circumstances as may indicate their character;

volcanic appearances;

climate as characterized by the thermometer, by the proportion of rainy, cloudy & clear days, by lightning, hail, snow, ice, by the access and recess of frost, by the winds prevailing at different seasons, the dates at which particular plants put forth or lose their flowers, or leaf, times of appearance of particular birds, reptiles or insects.

Altho' your route will be along the channel of the Missouri, yet you will endeavor to inform yourself, by inquiry, of the character and extent of the country watered by its branches, & especially on its southern side . . .

He was to study especially the North River or the Rio Bravo running to the Gulf of Mexico, and the Colorado running to the Gulf of California, all in frightening detail considering how far these rivers ran from "the channel of the Missouri."

They were to treat native peoples

in the most friendly and conciliatory manner which their own conduct will permit . . . but since it is impossible to foresee how you will be received by these peoples, it is impossible to instruct on how diligently to pursue an object, but . . . we wish you to err on the side

of your safety, & bring back your party safe, even if it be with less
information . . .

Given under my hand at the city of Washington, this 20th day of
June 1803

TH: J. Pr. U. S. of A.

"My word," Clark said as he folded the document into its oilskin wrapping, "doesn't want a hell of a lot, does he?"

"Wants the moon but he'll settle for a water route to the Pacific."

"Still," Clark said, nodding to himself, "this is serious stuff. Starts us
off with high ambitions." So, he asked, how many men, how many boats,
where do we stand on supplies?

Lewis explained the president's reasoning on numbers plus the difficulty in getting congressional approval.

"Fifteen men?" Clark was incredulous. "Hell, Merry, the current alone—
I was in St. Louis last year, and when the Missouri enters the Mississippi it about takes over. Puts its water three-quarters of the way across
before the big river can absorb it. That kind of current eats up men.
We got two thousand miles of it to fight—hard as hell with too few
hands."

Smiling, he added, "Anyway, that ain't the worst problem. You heard
about the Dakotas—the Sioux?"

Lewis knew his own expression was hardening. Plenty of talk about
them in Pittsburgh and down the Ohio. Apparently these Indians were
the chief impediment facing the handful of upriver traders who went each
year to the villages of the Mandan Indians which had developed into a
wilderness trade entrepôt, connecting Plains tribes with French and
British traders down from Canada. Going upstream, the Mandans represented the last place on the Missouri that white men had actually seen.
Lewis assumed it would be his most important stop. Beyond was the
speculative unknown.

Reports said the Sioux, holding ground along the river some five hundred miles beyond St. Louis, were masters of their territory and let
traders pass only as it pleased them, which in practice meant paying them
off with goods if not whiskey. From the traders' view, it was merely
another cost of doing business. But the very thought of paying ransom for
free passage of an American river set up a redness at the edge of Lewis's
vision.

"We'll pay no damned ransom, Will, I can tell you that right now." He
sounded harsher than he'd intended, and Clark's face darkened, a new
sternness wiping away the genial expression.

"Well, of course we ain't going to pay ransom. What the hell did you think? But you don't want to face a few hundred warriors notching their arrows with but a handful on your side."

Lewis explained the financial restraints. Doubling their numbers would double or triple the cost and they already were well over budget. This was serious. Their numbers were built into the legislation authorizing the expedition. It could be changed, he supposed, but it worried him.

Clark hesitated. "Well, we'll see. But how about supplies? That what we unloaded to haul the boat, that's the crop?"

"I've got a pirogue following but basically that's it. Get more in St. Louis—we'll work that out together."

Clark nodded approvingly. His irritation had passed. "I saw ample powder and lead and good weapons except maybe a light cannon would be handy—"

"Think so?" Lewis said. "Good. Maybe a couple of blunderbusses on swivels, too."

"Fine. So what about trade goods? Have we enough? Remember, we'll be dealing with Indians all the way, not just the Sioux."

"Presents, you mean? To pave the way?"

"Well, you can call them presents, many people do, but they're really trade goods. You know, Merry, these are primitive folk in lots of ways—hadn't figured out the wheel, for example—but they have a very highly developed social sense. They understand equality and they trade hard for what they want, even though we look on what they want as trinkets and foofaraw and simple utensils, scissors and the like. They want what they want and they ain't backward about expecting it. One thing, though—what they want most is whiskey, but they ain't going to get it, leastways not from us." He gave Lewis a penetrating look.

"Exactly," Lewis said.

"Good. So I expected, but I wanted to hear it."

Clark long had traded with Indians for furs, basic commerce of the frontier. He understood enough of the intertribal sign language to signal that he came in peace as a friend. Lewis would follow Clark's lead in this area. The trick was to treat them honestly, Clark said. They were naturally honest no matter what many whites believed; treat them well and they would respond. Lewis thought that made sense—like folks anywhere.

"I spent about six hundred dollars on presents, beads and all," he said.

"Beads are good. What color?"

"White, mainly."

Clark shrugged. "Maybe we can swap some for blue—they're strong for blue beads. We get to the mountains, no matter how bad or how easy, we're going to want horses, right? Indians know horseflesh the way they know their own hands—they'll drive a hard bargain and blue beads and good knives will prove valuable. I know what I'm talking about here. Let's stock up good—better too much than too little."

"Agreed," Lewis said. Doubling size and cost would rattle Congress but might be necessary. He felt himself coming around.

All told, the evening had gone well. Lewis now saw that his worries had been miscast. In power and force of personality, Clark was perfect. Lewis understood national affairs and its politics in a way that Clark couldn't, but Clark far surpassed Lewis in experience with rivers, swift water, boat handling, dealing with Indians, and on far western matters in general.

In the end it was Clark who summed it up. "You know, Merry, I wondered what those Washington years had made of you. If you'd be the same man I used to know or what. Well, you ain't, not really. You've grown a sight from what you was. And I suppose I have too, grown and deepened. We're older, been around a few more bends in the road. But this should work well—looks like we complement each other, and that makes a good partnership."

He gazed owlishly at Lewis. "I been worrying about how this was going to work and I figure you been worrying too—be a fool if you hadn't wondered. So I'm content and I hope you are too."

Lewis put out his hand and Will took it. "I'm content. Yes, I worried too. Funny—you pretty much took the words from my mouth. And now—now all's well."

The subject wouldn't arise again. They understood each other.

At the boatyard the next morning a group of young men that included Colter and Shannon stood about watching the boat repair. They were laughing over some private joke but sobered quickly at sight of the two captains. "Morning, Cap'n Clark." A chorus.

"Boys," Clark said, "this here is Captain Lewis. He and I are leading this venture, like I explained, and what he says goes, same as with me. Now, he'll talk to you one by one."

Lewis had an instant impression of collective ability. They were hardy-looking fellows, mid- to upper-twenties but for Shannon, most of them heavily muscled, wearing eager smiles. Will said he'd been swamped by applicants when the papers described the expedition; of some 150 he had chosen seven to present to Lewis. He said each was at least a passable marksman and experienced meat hunter. Each had experience and some skill as a river boatman. Each could pack a hundred pounds without breathing hard and had marched twenty-seven miles without complaint. None was married and all agreed to take the soldier's oath subject to army discipline. Will said that generally they seemed to see this as a grand adventure from which they might reach a measure of fame. All were interested in the rewards, including parcels of western land; land could set a man on the way to wealth.

Clark had singled out two men he saw as potential sergeants, Charles Floyd and Nathaniel Pryor, and he called them first. Floyd proved to be a tall, slender young man with long muscles and a bushy mustache threatening to get out of hand. Lewis found him calm, confident, sharply intelligent. It seemed that Clarks and Floyds had marched together, worked together, fought together about since the frontier began. Charles Floyd, young Charles's father, had marched as right-hand man to General Clark in those brutal days of the Revolution when the British seemed ready to roll up the western country and the settlers formed an army under General Clark and whipped them to a standstill. Floyd looked a stalwart fellow ready to follow in his father's steps, but then it struck Lewis that he looked pale and as they talked his mouth tightened now and again.

"Are you ill?"

"No, sir. Tip-top, sir."

"Really? You look like you're hurting."

"Gut spasms. Had 'em for years—they don't mean nothing. Be gone tomorrow. Ain't bad pain—just takes me by surprise."

"I'll want your assurance tomorrow that the pain is gone."

"Yes, sir. It'll be gone—always is."

Clark cleared his throat. "I know for a fact he's had gut pain for years—it never amounts to anything."

Clark had explained privately that both his sergeant candidates had experience leading punitive raids on warring tribes along the Wabash and had acquitted themselves well, itself a powerful recommendation. They called Nathaniel Pryor next. He and Floyd were friends and almost exact opposites physically—Pryor was thick-bodied, short, very powerful in appearance and doubtless in fact, the sort of man who would readily hoist three hundred pounds of flour on his back in a strength contest. He wore a tawny beard trimmed in military fashion and though he was courteous and soft-spoken he offered little of the charm that marked Floyd even with pain in his gut. But both possessed a distinct command quality; Lewis saw them as natural sergeants.

Then came a solid fellow with yellow hair tied back with a length of scarlet yarn. He looked bright and eager with vivid blue eyes. His shoulders and biceps bulged from a shirt of blue homespun, but otherwise he was of moderate size.

"John Shields," Clark said. "Blacksmith and gunsmith. Carries a small forge and bellows, makes his own charcoal."

A gunsmith would be valuable; few were young and fewer free to travel. "My pa was a leading smith back in Ohio—started me when I was eight. So I've been at it a good while."

"I gave him a musket with a busted firelock," Clark said, "told him to put it in working order. Fired it the next day."

"Good enough for me," Lewis said. A competent smith would be useful around Indians who hungered for knives and fighting axes.

Two men who looked startlingly alike stood next to Shields. Each was tall and broad, each with a hank of black hair that fell over the forehead at the same angle, eyes that looked nearly black. They were brothers, Joseph Field and Reuben Field.

"Twins?" Lewis asked.

"No, sir," Reuben said hastily. He jerked a thumb at Joseph. "He's the old one. Three years ahead of me. Tells me what to do and how to do it pretty often, but shoot, Cap'n, I'm the one gets the girls."

"No boasting, now, Reub—world don't like a boaster," Joseph said. Lewis saw that his brother embarrassed him.

"Oh, Joe—don't get the cap'n thinking bad on me," Reuben cried. He turned to Lewis. "Joe, he's always wondering what folks'll think of him, while me, I just jump in and do whatever lies ahead."

"Reub," Joe said, warning clear in his voice.

"Cap'n," Reuben said, suddenly serious. "I don't mean to do Joe a hard turn. Older brother, see, I got to keep him a little bit in line or he'll order me all over the place. But Joe is the smartest man I know—you can't go wrong in taking him along, nor me neither, 'cause I'm a working fool. Like to laugh but I work hard. You won't go wrong on neither of us, I promise you."

Lewis liked them both. Joe had captained small vessels on the river, which made him valuable and he said Reuben could take down a squirrel at a hundred yards four times out of five. Looking like twins, doubtless they needed means of differentiating themselves. Joe positioned himself as the wise senior, Reuben as the blithe spirit; they would do.

"Say, Cap'n," Reuben said after Lewis had accepted them with a nod to Clark, "let me ask you a question."

"Reub," Joe said, warning again. To Lewis he said quietly, "Reub opens his mouth when he might just as well keep it shut."

"Oh, Joe, I ain't giving sauce. What I wonder, am I right in figuring gov'ment's mainly sending us out to check on this new land—Louisiana—they say we bought from the French?"

It was a common question, the idea behind it obvious. U.S. makes the purchase, sends Lewis and Clark out to look at it. Lewis skipped the diplomatic nuances and simply explained the expedition had been years in planning, while the purchase wasn't even complete. St. Louis was still controlled by Spain as proxy for France.

"See, Reub," Joe said, "just what I told you."

"Well, I didn't doubt you. Just I'd rather hear it from the cap'n." He glanced at Lewis. "You don't mind my asking, sir?"

"No, no," Lewis said, still liking them. "But I don't want to listen to you two wrangling all the way to the Pacific. So I want you to remember, youth has its virtues but so does maturity. And I don't want to hear much chatter from either end, and I'll send you home from St. Louis if you forget that."

"Yes, sir!" they both said, for once in unison.

Two more men made up Clark's selections, William Bratton and George Gibson. They were from over in Kentucky and didn't seem to know the others. But Clark said they had proved out against his rugged criteria and Lewis saw no reason to question that. He presented Shannon and Colter. After a half hour of questions Clark pronounced himself satisfied. Colter with intensive experience in the wilderness was an obvious choice; Shannon seemed to amuse Clark, as if he couldn't believe a man who appeared pretty much innocent of a razor was all that old. But smooth cheeks or no, Shannon stood straight, looked Clark in the eye, and made his case. In the end, still chuckling, Clark accepted him. Lewis saw relief flash across Shannon's face.

Thus the nucleus of a crew, nine men: Nathaniel Pryor and Charles Floyd, potential sergeants, Joseph and Reuben Field, John Shields, John Colter, George Shannon, William Bratton, and George Gibson. A good start, the captains agreed.

The sun was lowering when Lewis found time to show his partner the iron boat. He loved the boat for its elegant simplicity and its practicality. Bolt those iron rods together end to end, cover the resulting frame with elk or buffalo hide, seal the seams with pitch, and you had a forty-foot boat that would float a couple tons of cargo. But a single man could carry the rods when disassembled and bundled, and skins were readily available where they were going.

Lewis adopted a mysterious air that seemed to disturb Clark, but Clark would understand and certainly be delighted when he saw the prize. Its value would be obvious. When the river shallowed as they approached the mountains the keelboat would be too heavy to go farther.

Then they must turn to canoes hollowed from logs; these would be heavy too but not impossible to carry over portages from one creek or one lake to another before they must turn ultimately to horses and leave water passage behind. How much faster, how much farther could they go with a boat that when collapsed one man could carry. Lewis as inventor would surely impress Clark. He ran up the ways where the boat stood elevated for repair, then up to the deck. With Clark following he opened the forward cargo hatch. Clark stood by with arms akimbo, saying nothing, watching Lewis unwrap the bundle of rods. Lewis explained his darling invention. Clark just nodded. Did he even understand the idea, let alone its virtue?

"Come down for a closer look," Lewis said.

Clark shook his head. "I can see from here."

Where was the excitement, the enthusiasm? Yet he couldn't just leave it there. He felt forced to say, "So what do you think? Doesn't this give us a whole new leg?"

"Well, I don't know about that," Clark said slowly. "But it's mighty fine, all right. No doubt . . ." His voice trailed off. Sounded bored, somehow. Without a word Lewis wrapped the canvas about the rods and laced it up. Clark passed from sight and Lewis heard him step onto the ladder.

Clark was whittling on a stick when Lewis came down. They walked off in silence. Lewis was immensely disappointed. They paused at the inn for grog and after a while conversation resumed. But neither mentioned the iron boat again.

General Clark had built his house after the war, long before his excesses had undermined him and Will had been called from the army to restore the family's fortunes. It was a big, rambling place with a broad veranda across the front, part of peeled logs, part of upright siding sealed with narrow vertical lathes. Out back was a barn with twenty stalls and a carriage house that was set to one side. The orchard looked neat and well tended, trees going to gold, bright in late fall sunshine. Will had set off the west wing as quarters for himself, and here Lewis was his guest in the week it took to repair and restock the boat.

This bachelor lair was comfortable, two small bedrooms and a parlor furnished with wooden chairs with leather cushions that faced a fireplace of stone. Hanging over the mantel was a portrait of a young woman that drew Lewis's attention immediately and held it. There was something about the figure; despite her youth, for she appeared more child than woman, there was an elegant air, a depth in the eyes, a warmth in the smile. The artist might have improved her a bit, and she wasn't really

beautiful, just pretty in the way that a fresh young girl may have a lumi-
nance that can pass for beauty until she grows older and the plain woman
behind her emerges.

"Oh," Clark said, "that's Judy Hancock, my cousin. Lives back in Virginia." He smiled. "How old you think she was when that was taken?"

"Fifteen, maybe?"

"Only twelve. But she'll be marrying age about the time we get back
from the West."

"Really? You're betrothed, are you?"

"Nah. She's too young. Says she'll wait for me till she's proper aged but
I want her free so she can pick and choose when she wants to fall in love."

"But you're pretty sweet on her?"

"She'll be the one, all right, if she'll have me when the time comes."

"I expect she will. She looks nice and generous but she has an intelligent look, too."

"She'll do. I been watching her since she was a tyke. But what about
you, Merry? I hear you cut a swath with the ladies."

Lewis laughed and threw up his hands. "Not me," he said, gratified a
little nonetheless.

The talk turned to other things and then there was supper and soon
they were reviewing the list of supplies yet again. But the conversation
remained in Lewis's mind. That swath hadn't amounted to much and
there was an empty gap in him that no woman had filled. He had to
admire his friend—Clark radiated a steadiness and solidity that was nothing like the turmoil forever aboil in Lewis. Naturally Clark had a pretty
little girl all picked out for a wife. Lewis didn't doubt for a moment that
she would be waiting. She seemed so fresh and virginal looking down
from her picture that Lewis felt an anguished cry within his heart—why
did sweetness and joy so elude him? All those effervescent young women
who seemed to glow in his company and just as quickly to tire or grow
alarmed or see brighter pastures. Or Miss Dolley's beautiful little sister
who so stunned him as they sat at the president's table as Mr. Jefferson
droned on about the West. And then the dismal aftermath, he full of
assumptions, she cutting him to leave him feeling a witless fool.

And all of them as pretty and sweet as the Mary Beth of long ago
whom he remembered with an ache. At that point in their lives she'd been
as virginal and innocent as was Will's Judy Hancock now—and then in a
flash she had emerged as a powerful woman. Overnight, one moment a
girl, the next a woman.

He thought of the last time he'd seen her, just a week before he left
Washington for Pittsburgh. The guard had summoned him from his canvas cubicle: two women to see him, Miz Parsons and Miz Slocum.

Slocum? Mary Beth? Sure enough, he found her sitting on a marble bench just inside the door clutching her bag. With her was an older woman with a long beak of a nose, her gray hair drawn into a severe knot, her mouth set in a fierce line. Mary Beth introduced her as Mrs. Faith Parsons, and Lewis bowed. He led them up the staircase to the oval drawing room with the shabby blue furniture that Miss Dolley was so anxious to renew. The president was out riding and they were alone. Lewis sent down to the galley for tea and cakes.

They needed advice, Mary Beth said. Both were widows, each left with a farm she couldn't work alone, neither interested in a new husband. They had decided to sell the land, pool their funds, and invest in a boardinghouse, sharing the cooking and cleaning. Washington had seemed a good prospect with its transient population until they found property values were painfully high for what really was a dusty little town deserted half the year. So they were thinking of going west: how would Captain Lewis advise them? Wheeling? Cincinnati?

"Pittsburgh, perhaps?" Miz Parsons said. Lewis thought her voice harsh as a chicken squawk. He shook his head; they'd find dangerous competition there. "Look westward," he said. "Money stretches further, barter's common and foodstuffs for your table—it's all plentiful. Rougher clientele, perhaps—"

"I have a cudgel and I know how to use it," Miz Parsons said. He saw she meant it.

"What about Louisville?" Mary Beth asked.

"Much better," he said. Both women nodded at that and Lewis saw that they already had decided and weren't here for advice at all. Mary Beth would look like Miz Parsons one of these days; she already resembled her own mother. She was thickening in the body; she would be stout in due time; her breasts were a shapeless bulge inside a plain frock. Her skin seemed coarse and the gray at her temples had progressed.

"We saw in the papers that the western expedition is real now," she said. "So you got your dream after all."

He stared at her, uncertain. Then, voice soft, a vulnerability in her eyes that wrenched him, she said, "That was the greatest mistake of my life, laughing at your dream that night. I should have knowed you had the gumption to make it all come real."

But that was long ago and she was different now. He remembered her bulging breast, scarlet nipple swollen by the infant's suction, remembered the somehow casual way she tucked herself back into her gown, her husband staring ahead as if he feared his team would escape him. Where had she gone, the girl whom once he'd thought he loved?

"But, Merry," she said, "ain't it dangerous?"

"Not really."

The older woman snorted. "Devil it ain't," she said in that harsh squawk. "Like going to war."

"Faith," Beth said, half warning, half entreaty.

"No," Miz Parsons said, "I know something about this so you hush up and listen to me, the both of you." She turned in her chair to face him directly and smiled. At once her whole expression changed, her stern manner gone, the ice vanished. She had big brown eyes and she dwelt on him with love as she might look on a child.

"Me and Jake Parsons, we married up when we both was sixteen and soon after that he went off to war. British shot him all to pieces and if he told me once he told me a thousand times he never would have made it through hadn't he known I was to home awaiting him coming down that road with his sack under his arm.

"Well, one day he did come home, riding a worn-out old mule he'd traded his musket for, him not wanting no more part of war. And right away I seen he was hurt bad. The doctor said he had a British ball laying up against his heart and there wasn't nothing to be done and by rights he oughta be dead. But he weren't dead, and he come home and I put him to bed and cosseted him good, made him soup and kept him clean and petted him. He lived five years when he wasn't supposed to live five minutes and if he told me once he told me a thousand times he wouldn't have had those years without me caring for him. Oh, it was hard, but I gave him five years and he gave me five years and there was enough love there to last a lifetime."

There were tears in her eyes. "You understand what I'm telling you? Man needs a woman and a man in danger needs a woman more. Needs someone to come home to."

She was struggling out of the armchair. "You think on that, young man," she said. "And I bid you Godspeed and good fortune." She extended her hand and he took it.

Mary Beth came close. She took his hand and touched it to her cheek and then abruptly drew him close and kissed him. She smelled good, some flowery scent, and she seemed warm and comforting. He had a sudden feeling she was kissing him good-bye forever and he wanted to cry out but didn't know what he wanted to say and the moment passed in silence. He helped them into their hack, the two horses sighing and switching their tails, and as that other night so long ago Mary Beth didn't look back or speak and he felt cold and abandoned.

Now, embarked on his great adventure, he sat studying the painting of the young woman his friend intended to marry. Trust his steady, sensible, organized partner to know what mattered and to have made his arrangements so life would work to his favor and he would come through it whole. He thought of the older woman's wise remark about love and wondered if the warmth he sensed in the painting flowed from the artist catching that emotion in this young woman's eyes.

He lit a cigar and went out in the chill night and walked under a bright moon. He walked a long time and when he came back to the big silent house and wrapped himself in a blanket he still didn't sleep.

George Shannon was on the wharf where they'd unloaded the boxes and bundles preparatory to hauling the boat. The voyageurs saw themselves as paddlers only and were deeply engaged in a complex game in which small stones served as chips and violent emotions were stirred. John Colter was sleeping off the effects of a wild night; George had no taste for whiskey and he had left John early and turned in and now he was up in bright morning sunshine looking for work. From under a heap of bundles he dragged forth the wooden box holding the short-barreled rifles from Harper's Ferry that Cap'n Lewis prized. He spun the wing nuts on the bolts holding the lid in place. Sure enough, damp had invaded and a sheen of rust showed on the barrels. Shannon found an oil can and a canvas strip and went to work.

He was on the second piece, enjoying the sun, when a shadow fell and he looked up to see a huge black man gazing down at him. The fellow was heavily muscled, broad in the shoulder, with the kind of belly that was more muscle than fat, and my God, Shannon told himself, he'd never seen a man so black. Most black men, they really were sort of chocolate, but this one was like coal.

"Give you a hand?" this fellow said, voice a deep rumble but warm, friendly, not at all threatening. George knew he'd felt a frisson of fear at this massive black figure towering over him and he supposed the other had sensed it.

Now the black man wanted to work and he'd expect to be paid and George didn't know—"I'm York," the fellow said abruptly, "that's my name. I'm Cap'n Clark's man and he told me to get on down here and make myself useful."

"Uh . . . you going along, is that it?"

"Yessuh, that's it. I go where Cap'n Clark goes."

"What do you mean, you're his man?"

"He owns me, that's what."

"Owns? You're a slave, then?" There were slaves in Pennsylvania, but not many and Shannon had never known one.

"What's it feel like, a man owns you?"

Anger flashed on the big man's face. "What the hell do you think it feels —" and abruptly shut his mouth, lips compressed. But then his look softened and George had the feeling allowances were being made for his tactlessness.

"Well," York said, "it's all right. Cap'n Clark he's good to me. Don't beat me, or not often." He laughed. "Not unless I deserve it. I been with him since we was tykes — my daddy belonged to his daddy. He was about a year old and I was five or six, I reckon, when I got him."

"Or he got you."

York nodded. "I suppose. So what's your name?"

Shannon told him. He didn't know if he should shake hands with a black man and since York didn't offer, neither did he. They worked for a while in silence.

Then York said, "You a pretty heavily built fellow. Strong, are you?"

"Strong enough to hold my own." In fact, George was proud of his strength. Back in Pennsylvania he'd been a local champion of arm wrestling, put down some of the biggest, toughest fellows around. John Colter had tried him once and decided he didn't want any more of that, George putting his arm down so firmly it barked John's knuckles. So without really reflecting, he said, "You want to try me?"

York looked surprised. "Try you?"

"Arm wrestle." He gestured, bending his arm sharply to the left.

"Aw . . ."

"Come on. Let's try it, just for fun."

"How old are you, George, you don't mind my asking?"

Shannon hesitated. "How old do you think?"

York gazed at him, expression almost fatherly. "Oh, eighteen, nineteen, maybe more but not a lot over twenty."

George nodded. "Close enough," he said easily. "Now, you want to contest?"

York pulled the lid over the rifle box and planted his elbow. George got ready. He'd never touched a black person and he hesitated a moment before he clasped York's hand. He saw that the black man had noted his hesitation and he was suddenly shamed. He tightened his grip as if in apology and then began the slow, inexorable downward pressure that had defeated so many Pennsylvania farm boys. But nothing happened. The two arms locked together, each straight up, held motionless. A tremor shook Shannon's arm. A vein on the black man's forehead bulged and pulsed but his arm was still.

"Well," York said after a bit, "looks like we evenly matched."

Abruptly George understood. "You ain't giving it your full strength," he said through gritted teeth.

A ghost of a smile flashed over York's face. "What you mean?"

"You're favoring me."

"Well, white man don't like a black man winning."

"God damn it, favoring me, that's like an insult. Like I need babying. If you can put me down, do it. Go on . . ."

George felt like the muscles in his back were being ripped out as he fought to hold his arm upright, but York bent it steadily back until knuckles rapped the box.

"My word," George said, "you are some strong."

York glanced about the empty wharf. Shannon saw something haunted in his eyes. "We won't tell no one nothing about this, all right? Please, George."

They held a formal ceremony to swear the men into the United States Army. General Clark presided as the senior officer, flags snapped, the brothers McAllen broke out the fife and the drum they'd played when they marched with General Clark to hold the British in the West and Yankee Doodle rode once again. Swept Lewis back to that wonderful night when he'd been a Yankee Doodle Dandy himself, riding on Pa's shoulders, and then Pa dead of the pneumonia in scarcely a day—but he cast the gloomy thought aside by an act of will. When they were done the general led them off to the inn and stood them a couple of rounds, privates and sergeants and captains alike. Lewis knew this day had been worth its weight in gold. More than any amount of exhortation could manage, it told these raw country men they were in the army now and subject to its discipline. Rough terrain and rougher tests lay ahead; the day might come when as soldiers they would stand together and prevail where individuals would disintegrate.

By late the next day the boat was repaired and loaded. In the morning they would push off from Clarksville, bound downriver to the Mississippi and points west. The general set up a farewell feed; come up to the house around four. He met them on the broad veranda. Inside, the canvas walls had long since been replaced with planks, as had Will's apartment. Lewis saw a clavichord that looked as though no one played it. The general was a big bear of a man bulging out of denim pants and a red flannel shirt, eyes bloodshot and sad, face raddled from living and liquor. Why, Lewis thought, not for the first time, if I didn't know he was in his middle fifties I'd mark him at least a decade more. But he wrapped Lewis's hand in two big paws with high cordiality and led him to the table set for three and laden with all the bounty of the frontier harvest. They drew up hide-bottomed chairs.

The general had a stone mug he kept full of whiskey and he liked to talk. Soon he was remembering Virginia before the war when the Clarks lived near the Jeffersons and he'd known Tom well. "Older'n me, tall skinny young feller, and I thought he was the smartest I'd seen anywhere and I guess I was about right, too." He sighed and took a long pull of whiskey. "And 'bout the time Will here was getting hisself born, why, Pa went to hankering for the West. Old Boone had been prowling the west end of Virginia, called it Kentucky like the Indians did 'cause they'd fought so many bloody wars over it. Boone sent back some grand stories, and Pa had to go see it for hisself. Packed us up and out we went. But you know, I remember that even then Tom Jefferson was talking about the West. Maybe he wanted to go and couldn't get up the gumption, I don't know . . ."

Well, maybe . . . or maybe Mr. Jefferson's intellect was so powerful and he could live so fully within his own mind that he didn't need to go. Lewis thought that explanation more likely. He often reflected on how much he had learned from this extraordinary man, for nowhere else had he encountered the intellectual awakening that flowed so naturally from Thomas Jefferson. How many times had the president dropped a casual thought that reverberated later as meaning suddenly came clear.

His own thoughts drifted away as he remembered the night the president had delved into the dream that underlay the world's passion for the mystery and romance of the West. Now he could see his own expedition as the latest expression of that combination of spiritual and commercial. Would he try to make his partner understand this causal connection of dream and hard physical travel? He looked across the table at Will and saw him as a man of immense practicality and utter confidence in strength of arm and hand, listening now to his oldest brother's entirely practical ruminations. No, probably he would spare Will explanations of what he only half understood himself and yet knew to be true and real. After all, one dreamer was enough—that wasn't what he wanted from Will—

Abruptly he was startled from reverie. General Clark crashed his stone mug down on the marred table, whiskey splashing.

"Now," he said, voice raw and heavy, "I take it you boys ain't going out just to see where the Missouri River rises and look for this Northwest Passage everyone's been looking for ever since Columbus found this wasn't the place he wanted it to be."

"The president has high hopes for that passage," Lewis said cautiously.

"And well he should. It's a geographical puzzle nagging sensible men for three hundred years and it would be grand if you could find it and if it really exists and if it will give us the trade advantage we need so bad. 'Cause trade is what makes a nation strong and there's what I want you boys to see should be the real aim of your trek. Find you the passage by all means, but don't forget the British want the fur trade much as we do."

Ah, the fur trade, that western pot of gold, now dominated by the

British North West Company that collected furs that Lewis knew should have been ours all along and shipped them to London via Hudson's Bay. Maybe it was tolerable before we bought the Louisiana Territory from Napoleon, but by God, it wasn't tolerable now. And by all accounts British traders like Mackenzie had dug themselves so deeply into the Mandan villages that the Indians didn't know there was any other market. Indeed, French fur men out of St. Louis said that every year Indians of other tribes were bringing their furs to the Mandans to sell to British traders in what was fast turning into a regular bazaar . . . a bazaar that should be aimed straight into the American market in Lewis's view, and let the British traders go to hell.

Lewis had serious ideas about accomplishing this. There were fortunes to be made in western fur that brought incredible prices in the Orient. But don't denigrate the Northwest Passage—without that dream the expedition probably would never have been funded by the narrow, suspicious, parsimonious Congress.

Meanwhile relations with Britain worsened steadily. France and Britain were back at war. Britain wanted us in on her side and gave us plenty of abuse on that count. Sooner or later we must fight them again but he knew Mr. Jefferson was intent on making it later. But, my Lord, they were hard to take. Arrogant, saw only their own aims, and ignored American power. Given that we were the largest neutral shipping nation in the world, both sides depended on us for foodstuffs. But the British plowed right on, and dominating the fur trade out of Canada was just another instance—the bastards.

They were in the Northwest. Cook and Vancouver had explored the vast anchorage at Puget Sound. Yes, Captain Gray discovered the Columbia for the United States but he commanded a mere merchant vessel, hardly official. He told Vancouver about it and the Briton charted it for a hundred miles, a British claim sure to follow. At a reception at Annapolis Lewis had encountered a hard-drinking British admiral who said he intended to take a small flotilla around Cape Horn and make the British claim stick from Canada to San Diego. Put Canadian settlers on the west coast and the conquest would be near complete.

So angry old General Clark was making perfect sense as Lewis saw things. He listened to the rumble of the older man's voice, broken by frequent pulls on his stone mug. "Trade, that's what matters. And I tell you, the British are hungry, they always want more, and us taking over Louisiana, that puts us directly agin them and don't think they ain't looking at just that point on just this minute."

He sighed. No one spoke. "This Northwest Passage, maybe it's real, but it don't sound easy to me. Those mountains sound real. Hell, that's what led to the Purchase, because we had to keep the Mississippi open, only way to get our western produce to market. Maybe there's a passage through those western mountains, I don't know 'cause I ain't been there but my guess is they better be a sight smaller than eastern mountains if we're going to haul produce up one slope and down the other . . ."

He rumbled on for a while, nothing that Lewis hadn't heard before, and gradually the younger man's attention drifted. But then the talk jerked Lewis out of reverie. General Clark was remembering his own glory days when he'd made his name saving the West—and he was remembering the British. The Redcoats had kept Indian raiders well supplied with weapons and food and well stirred to the attack on settler cabins.

"It got worse and worse and God, we hated 'em, but it was the British behind them, really. War parties with British arms and British powder and ball and British hand axes came through every week and they killed anyone they could catch alone, man, woman, child, it didn't make no difference. And then we found that behind it all was a British colonel name of Hamilton, Henry Hamilton, and he was paying the Indians *bounty* for each settler's scalp. Hard to believe, a civilized man paying bounty on human beings, women and children too, like so many wolf pelts. They called him the 'Hair Buyer' and I tell you, I still regret that I didn't kill the filthy bastard when I had him in my hands."

Now Lewis was paying close attention. The dishes had been cleared and they had pushed back their hide-bottomed chairs and the general had set a whiskey bottle on the table. Clay pipes were fired and the smoke and the whiskey on his tongue and the blood in the talk combined to hold Lewis mesmerized.

"War didn't really get out this way till '78," Clark said, gesturing with his pipe, "and by that winter it was getting beyond bearing. And then we heard about the Hair Buyer. Well, folks about went crazy and I up and called for volunteers and two hundred of us formed us a regiment and the boys put me in charge and we set out to fix these bastards was killing us right and left.

"Hamilton, he was holed up in a fort at Vincennes up on the Wabash maybe a couple hundred miles, and there was snow and ice everywhere, ice jams made the rivers flood, and they said the Wabash was out of its banks and the country was marsh for miles around. The Hair Buyer figured no one could come after him in this weather and he didn't even put out spies to keep their eyes peeled just in case, he was that confident.

"Well, the boys was some worked up. Like at a tent meeting, you know the way it is, folks get to hollering and singing and dancing for Jesus, like to tear up the woods, and in that state of mind they can run up mountains and leap rivers and you must kill them to stop them. And we set out marching overland and waded rivers where we had to bust the ice with sticks and found Vincennes surrounded by water. So, by God, we jumped in and came up with our clothes freezing on our bodies and put the Hair Buyer's fort under siege, picked off his marksmen one by one through the fort's loop-holes, firing from outside, you see, the boys that good with their rifles."

He stopped then, gazing at them owlishly, belched and poured more whiskey. His voice was beginning to slur. Neither Will nor Lewis spoke. "A party of Indians come in and we took 'em, captured 'em, you know, and we sat 'em in a circle in plain view and killed 'em one at a time with tomahawks, chopped open their heads, you see, them awailin' their death songs, and their brethren inside seen the British couldn't protect 'em no more and they slipped out in the night and was gone. That left but eighty British soldiers and they saw they was near meeting their maker and they couldn't wait to surrender. We kept their arms and supplies and sent 'em packing back to Canada and if half of 'em froze to death en route, who cared? But you know, I should've killed the Hair Buyer . . ." His head sagged and his eyes closed.

Well, Lewis thought, the general was a hero in his day and that counts for a lot. But then the shaggy old head rose and he lifted his arms over-head as if awakening and the slur was gone and he didn't seem drunk at all as he said, "Well, hell, I'm spinning these old tales when you boys are fixing to set out on just about the greatest adventure ever. But mayhap the old tale and today ain't so far apart, so you listen sharp, Will, and you too, Captain Lewis, you boys remember the Hair Buyer. 'Cause you got to watch out for the British. They want that country out on the Pacific, want it bad. They're pushing into western Canada, we hear about 'em every year, pushing outward.

"Now, I expect Mr. Jefferson thinks Captain Gray naming the Colum-bia after his ship pretty well establishes American title to that country. But my opinion? Gray didn't do much. Not near enough. You know what counts? Going overland. *Walking* the ground, that's what makes your claim stick and that's what that fellow Mackenzie did. God Almighty, he must be much man, other side though he is. Walks out, finds him a river, follows it down, thinks at first it's the Columbia, finds it ain't and goes back and damned if another year or two later he's not back going it again and this time he comes down on salt water. Crossed the continent by land. Was he on our river? Nobody knows but he thinks it. Now I hear he done wrote a book — trader through here last year told me — claiming the whole West for Britain."

His head was down but he was studying them from under heavy eye-brows and he looked like he was challenging them to conquer the world. "Do y'see? Those bastards know no limits, that's what I'm telling you.

Ones out on the far edge, they're all hair buyers. I think they want the west coast all the way down to San Diego. Spanish are weak, you know—their so-called empire don't amount to a fart in a windstorm these days. They'll lose it in another few years and Britain'll be there to pick it up.

"I expect Mr. Jefferson's told you all this—he's sure as hell thunk it 'cause he's nobody's fool. With this purchase and all, we got a chance to stand tall on the continent and you boys are going out to make sure it happens. You plant the flag, put your stamp on the country, you'll make it *American*."

He stood, swaying slightly. "I'm going to take a nap and let you boys get busy. But mind what I'm telling you. Get our claim on this Pacific Northwest fixed solid and you'll do your country service beyond calculating. So I wish you good fortune."

He took Lewis's hand and drew him into an embrace, then did the same with Will, murmuring, "Your turn now, Will. Go with God, li'l bubba."

As they walked down to see to the boat Lewis marveled that colorful language aside, the old warrior had told him just what Mr. Jefferson had said.

The next afternoon, now well down the Ohio, the two captains sat on the boat's bow warmed by the lowering sun, watching the shore rush by, downstream the easy part. So how was it, Clark had asked, that a plain soldier like Meriwether Lewis had been chosen to complete the work that Christopher Columbus had started?

High in the sun-struck sky a hawk rode thermals on rigid wings, a black speck playing a lonely game, canting suddenly to wheel off when the current he rode failed, the game being to find another before momentum was lost and he'd have to break wing stride. So while the bird played overhead as carefree as men and horses on a steeplechase, Lewis told his story.

Clark sighed and said he reckoned they would pull in at the next likely looking open spot in the woods and set up camp for the night. Then in the same easy tone he said, "Well, Merry, I guess the answer is that you wasn't just the plain soldier. Maybe you never were. Maybe your whole life set you on a path for this. Anyway, I take it as a privilege to share in it."

Far overhead the hawk folded its wings and plummeted, black speck against red sky, falling maybe a thousand feet before it braked and floated gracefully to a roost. And Clark said, "You know, we get up the Missouri and over the mountains and reach the Pacific and come back alive and the bulk of our men alive, we might just make us some history."

Lewis often had thought just that but saying it would have sounded pretentious. But Clark had sounded as natural and easy as that hawk falling from the sky. Released somehow, now Lewis could laugh and say, "By God, we might just at that."

16

Washington, Fall, 1803

The cabinet meeting was already going badly in James Madison's opinion. He had given the State Department report to the effect that the Louisiana Purchase was moving slowly. New Orleans would change hands around the New Year, St. Louis the following spring. The president already was glowering — said cabinet meetings were a waste of time. They were gathered around the long, shiny table like crows on a fence rail overlooked by a miserable painting of the capitol with a clumsy dome that might or might not ever be built. Low clouds leaked rain and occasional gusts sent it slashing against the windows.

At last Tom asked the question that Madison knew was close to his heart. "What do we hear from Captain Lewis?"

Henry Dearborn, secretary of war, shifted his massive bulk uncomfortably in the chair, his expression sour. The idea of Captain Lewis seemed to irritate him. "Too little," he said. "The young man has a poor grasp of military propriety or manners."

"Oh?" the president said. Sounded like a warning to Madison; Henry knew full well that Tom was very fond of Merry. But Henry plowed ahead. "Reports pretty much as he pleases—"

"Or perhaps when he has something to say."

But Henry had the bit in his teeth. "Has nothing to say, he should report that. But this business of a captaincy for his partner—most irregular."

"William Clark? There's a problem?"

"We don't just hand out commissions to anybody, Mr. President. Especially not when we're slashing the army." Madison knew the cuts in army and navy imposed by Tom's insistence on reducing Federalist spending galled soldiers and sailors alike. He heard a little retaliation in the words.

"Well," Tom said, "Clark is Captain Lewis's first choice when he needs all the help he can get. Clark's brother—"

"Yes, sir, I know he's old General Clark's little brother and all that." Madison winced; Henry sounded downright rude. Soon he saw that the real problem was the rank, captain.

"Co-commanders?" Henry snorted. "Suppose they disagree—who controls? It's a recipe for disaster."

Robert Smith, the navy secretary who was politically important but inept, chose this unfortunate moment to speak. "Same in the navy, Mr. President. A ship can't have two captains." Smith shared Dearborn's resistance to the funding cuts. Tom ignored Smith who colored and looked at his hands.

In a tone he clearly meant to be decisive, Tom said, "I think we'll follow Merry on this. He feels Clark is far and away the best man to take over if he—"

"You see!" Henry snapped. "To take over if he is killed or wounded or is ill or goes out of his head. That's what a lieutenant is for—for that ultimate role. And lieutenant, sir, is the proper rank for Mr. Clark."

"Let's reflect on this," the president said. A quiver in his voice said he was struggling to control his temper. Hastily he ran over the arguments. The Far West was important, Captain Gray's claim on the Columbia was based on a single visit, the British were moving ahead as witness this fellow Mackenzie's travels and now his book, every reason to think they're looking down the coast at least as far as the little settlement on San Diego Bay—this was not the time for a contretemps over rank.

Henry's face was red as fire. His stare was dangerously close to a glare. "Contretemps, sir?" His voice was shrill. "I know of no contretemps. Clark will march as lieutenant, second in command. That's military procedure because it clarifies command. My God, Mr. President, the idea of split command when the pressures of decision can be instantaneous— why, the whole expedition could be lost if command were frozen in a tight spot. And there surely will be tight spots."

But was that all there was to it? The president had planned the trek with young Merry. It was a military expedition but how much say had he allowed the War Department? Rather little, Madison thought; he suspected Henry was taking his revenge now.

Nettled and yet, Madison thought, somehow uncertain, Tom said, "Well, perhaps, but I want latitude given Captain Lewis. I approved Clark, you know, before Lewis invited him."

"Certainly, sir. There's no complaint about Clark—doubtless he'll be an ornament to the expedition." Dearborn's voice took on a patronizing note. "You'll see, sir, it will work out perfectly and ultimately Lewis will see the wisdom of it."

The president stared at him. "*Will* work out?"

Dearborn's head came up. "I sent Clark's commission yesterday. As a lieutenant. Mailed it to Lewis in St. Louis where he's supposed to go, though he hasn't given me the courtesy of a progress report."

Jefferson had that dangerous look. "I'd have supposed that that was something worth discussing with me."

"I thought it entirely within my discretion as secretary of war, Mr. President." There was warning in Dearborn's tone, too.

Deadly silence fell over the room. Madison could see that Tom was offended but found it hard to quarrel with assertions of military expertise that he lacked himself. Same old story, neither he nor Madison had served and Henry was an old soldier and a war hero, no getting away from it.

Then in a low voice Henry said, "If you give me a direct order, of course I'll obey it." But Madison heard the unspoken threat: resignation might be his next step.

Another silence, and then the president said, "Very well, Henry." He stood. "Gentlemen," he said, and walked out.

"But that's outrageous," Dolley said. They were having a late tea when Jimmy told her about it. She put her teacup down with a loud click. "My word, they're asking him to march across two thousand absolutely uncharted miles! Indian tribes, wild animals, deserts and mountains and storms and who knows what-all, finding his way step by step where no white man has gone before. Has Henry lost his mind? Of course Merry should have Clark as co-commander if that's what he wants. Think of it, Jimmy—going off into wild and dangerous country for years beyond any help or rescue, wouldn't you want at least the comfort of someone backing you up whom you knew well, whom you could trust, who had proved his mettle in one tight situation after another?"

"My, Dolley," her husband said, his expression half amused, half irritated, "you are advocate par excellence."

She smiled but she thought his remark ill-placed. She and Merry were friends. She knew him much better than Jimmy did and perhaps better than Tom did, or at least in a way different from the way Tom knew him. Merry was a man of power and yet she sensed a vulnerability, too. Not just his clumsy relations with women. Many men were clumsy with women. He did seem to connect with a young woman and then she fled or she had Papa speak to him. There was a power in him but with it that dark, depressed quality always ready to break into the open. It wasn't just her imagination, either—Jimmy said that Tom had known for years that his young friend suffered from serious melancholy. He said Tom had held up naming him to the expedition until he convinced himself that Merry could control this dark side.

"I know how much having Clark meant to him," she said. "He told me once that Clark had been his commander and would never accept a junior position now." She poured the last of the tea and took a fat scone onto her plate. "I never met anyone quite like Merry. He radiates power. Walk across an unknown continent? Yes, he can do it without a question. And yet, there was a boyish quality, too, that vulnerability or maybe an uncertainty. He needs his friend. Anyone would, but Merry especially. Jimmy—why didn't Tom just tell Henry to do it?"

"Reverse orders already issued? Well, he could have, I suppose, but that could have precipitated a cabinet crisis." He hesitated a long moment. "But you know," he said, "when I thought it all over I had the feeling that Tom had surrendered rather easily. That somehow in the back of his mind he was satisfied enough with the outcome."

"Really?"

"Well, he could have taken Henry aside and jollied him along, salved his feelings, you know. So it struck me that maybe he didn't because he really wanted Merry to have the total command. The Lewis and Clark Expedition? How does that sound? Diluted, don't you think?"

"Not really. And apparently it's what Merry wanted."

"Well, in his heart, I think the president wanted it to be the Lewis Expedition."

There was no point in pursuing it, but her private thought was that Merry and his friend Clark would have to be very big men if they were to make this work.

Dolley was staring at her sister, whose face had gone scarlet. It was the next morning. Anna had come in with a clutch of materials, for which the dressmaker waited. Even as Dolley readied a tongue-lashing, she had to note Anna's charms. Her sister had cast off the last shards of girlhood while still short of full womanhood. An ardent young man pursued her and probably she soon would succumb, but for the moment couldn't give up the joys of being an elusive goal. Dolley remembered the phase in her own life with nostalgic pleasure.

Still, she managed to maintain her outraged stare. She had mentioned Tom's unwise decision on Clark and Anna was expiating on Merry's nature when Dolley stopped her.

"Are you sitting there telling me you played footsie with that young man at the president's table?"

Half amused, half defensive, her blush deepening, Anna said, "Well, I never would have done it if I'd known how he'd take it. Any other man in Washington would have understood . . ." Her voice trailed off.

"Good God. What did you do, exactly?"

"Well, you needn't make such a big crime of it. Nothing you haven't done in your day, I'll warrant."

"But not when dining with the president."

"That was the trouble, everyone solemn as a goose, Mr. Jefferson droning on about the West—I mean, you just wanted to jump up and ask them if they'd heard the one about Pat and Mike, crack a joke or something. And there was Merry so serious—"

"What did you do, Anna?"

"We were sitting side by side, so I put my foot against his. Gave it a little rub to set him thinking. Rubbed it again."

"And he?"

"He might have been stung by a bee. Jerked his foot away—afraid he was in my space, you see. Well, that was no fun. So I searched around under the table and found his foot and gave it a really good rub. He turned red, then white, then red again, and pretty soon he was pressing harder than I was. You know, like he'd found a route to nirvana. Well, when everyone was near asleep the president finally quit talking and I took my foot away and talked to the people across the table."

"And that was all there was to it?"

The red crept up her cheeks again. "Dolley, you know any other man would have understood—I was just livening a dull evening. But Merry—well, next time I saw him he came rushing over, good Lord, you'd have thought we were engaged. It took me a month of being cooler than I liked to convey the idea there was nothing doing."

In fact, Dolley had introduced Merry to her sister when they met by chance on the street. Anna had given him a ravishing smile that seemed to promise endless delights and Dolley had seen the young man was instantly smitten. She now saw that dinner a week later was the coup de grâce.

Anna shrugged. "Well, had I known him better, I suppose I wouldn't have done it. If I'd known what he was like . . ."

"What is he like?" Dolley said, suddenly curious. She knew him as a mature woman, married, a friend within sharp limits. "He does seem to have trouble connecting with young woman. They like him at first and then it ends. Why?"

"Maybe he goes after them too young," Anna said slowly. "I've wondered myself. He's a very powerful man, you know. I don't doubt he can march west and do all the things he'll probably have to do to keep his men together and reach the Pacific and then find his way back. I expect he can do anything he sets his mind to. But that's somehow threatening, too. It's like he meets a woman and immediately he's in pursuit. She likes that at first but it's scary, like paddling a canoe and finding you're approaching a waterfall—and she balks and pretty soon she runs away, off to New York to see Auntie Prudence."

She sighed, shaking her head. "He's a nice man, decent to the core—but, Dolley, he must be thirty or so, isn't he? Why doesn't he go after an older woman?"

17

On the Mississippi, November, 1803

Lewis had been on the Mississippi before but he hadn't been taking a heavy boat upstream then and he'd forgotten what a vast implacable tide it was, an inland sea with relentless current. They had departed Clarksville, running downstream with little effort. Paused at Fort Massac, the old fur trade fort a bit above the Mississippi now pressed into army service. Departed Massac at dawn, camped a mile short of the Mississippi at dusk, pushed onto the great river the next morning—November 14, 1803.

Clark had said little more about their numbers that he felt were many too few; he said he counted on the power of the river to make his argument for him. A long, tapering point of land marked the intersection of the Ohio and the Mississippi, and beyond this point the whole world changed as they turned the big boat upstream and the current seized them. The sleigh ride was over; now they must labor for every mile. And the Missouri, moving almost as much water much more rapidly would only be worse.

Debris came hurtling down. Huge trees torn from crumbling banks as the river ever widened its turns and re-formed its course traveled with the force of medieval battering rams. They jammed themselves against the bank and rocked there, breaking away from time to time without warning. The trunks gradually became water-logged, rode low in the water ready to punch holes in any boat they met. Finally many became what river men called sawyers. The heavy trunk sank, the lighter wood, often with leaves still intact, remained on the surface; in time the trunks hung near straight down. Sooner or later they dug their roots into the bottom. Held in place, they formed a hinge that flexed and flexed and dug them ever deeper. Then the massive trunk could saw back and forth, pressed down by the current, then rearing like an apparition to impale a boat, then sinking again from view, ghostly bête noire of those who failed to post a watch. Clark placed York, he of the massive muscles, on the bow with a boat hook to fend off the obstacles—sawyers, logs submerged and on the surface, fence rails, broken limbs, debris of wrecked boats, animal and occasionally human corpses . . .

They broke out the sweeps. Nine men on oars. Progress was minute. They could all mark themselves against the bank, creeping foot by foot. Lewis and Clark put their oars in the water. Eleven men. Still foot by foot, two thousand miles or so to go westward. Pain began to build in Lewis's back. It became a berserk throbbing before Clark turned the boat into what Lewis thought of as an alcove of relatively still water where a modest stream reached the river. York jumped ashore with a line and lashed it to a tree. They lay on the oars, sweat pouring though the day was cool, breathing still hard. Lewis noted in a fuzzy way, too tired himself to draw quick conclusions, that even Shannon's youthful face looked newly drawn. They stepped ashore, flexing their backs and wincing. They hardly spoke. Lewis thought they had come five or six miles; more like two, Clark said.

They boarded and resumed. Now blisters on their hands began to break, leaving hands raw. They were at the end of a long lateral passage; now the river began to curve. Lewis saw they were on the outside of a vast bend and the current grew steadily more rapid. Progress as measured by the slowly passing bank slowed and slowed again until they hardly moved.

"We'll cross," Clark murmured and steered into the mainstream. Lewis looked across the sea of a river; he thought it a mile wide, at least. The oars bit deep. Clark cocked the bow into the current lest they lose all they'd gained. As they left the outside of the curve where the river was busily cutting down the bank to widen its sweep the going became steadily easier. They inched across and tied to another tree for respite. Lewis realized that for every mile he covered as the crow flew he would have to cover another mile or two on the water, fighting for every yard he gained. He sighed.

On the inside of the bend the current was indeed slack but soon they were approaching the opposite bend, soon the current grew and they slowed, and again they must cross, another mile that scarcely advanced them.

They pulled ashore and camped at the mouth of another stream, the boat solidly moored. Clark estimated they had made ten river miles, five as the bird would go. They ate ravenously and fell immediately into sleep.

"It will get worse," Clark said in a low voice.

"I understand," Lewis said. "You're right."

"Double our numbers?"

"Or triple."

Clark smiled. "Now you're talking." He rolled over to sleep, then rolled back. "Reckon we can get away with it? War Department, president, Congress, all that?"

"Tell you what, Will," Lewis said. "We'll do it. When it's all over we'll find out if we got away with it."

Clark grinned. "Suits me fine."

Lewis sat by the fire, taking the first watch, Clark to take the second. He fought sleep; he stood, started walking slow rounds about the perimeter of their little camp, down to the boat to check its mooring, back up the bank to circle the sleeping men, come back to the fire, sit for a few minutes until exhaustion crept upon him again. Then up, stand to watch the river in moonlight, listen to its rumbling and sucking noises, see a tree so large that it must have been a century or more in age before succumbing to the current striking at its roots like a hungry animal, now floating south, spinning slowly in the grip of a new force.

As he stood there his brave words of an hour past began to haunt him. Triple his size without a word to the War Department, not a word to the president who must answer to Congress for the errant explorer and must pay the bills? Of course he could do it—he carried a carte blanche from the president promising to pay whatever expense he incurred, whatever funds he drew. But winter was near; already he knew he must delay his start until the following spring. That certainly meant they had time to petition Washington for permission to expand.

Then the matter of the iron boat flashed to mind; it had been a great turning point. Stung by Mackenzie's claims, the president had arranged post-graduate training for the subaltern with leading savants in Philadelphia and told him to get on his way. But first, Lewis had said, he must stop at the armory at Harper's Ferry and see to the portable boat. He remembered the president's expression, harsh and somehow balked as he nodded reluctantly. "Mind that you're on your way within a week," he had said, and waved a hand in dismissal.

But work was slow and resistant at the armory, no one in a hurry to oblige on a project workmen found hard to take seriously. A week passed and another week. And it was problematic, he had to admit that. No one knew how to shape the rods so that when assembled they would make the frame of a forty-foot, double-ended boat. The solution, arrived at slowly, was to build the end of such a boat in wood, then use it as a template to bend individual rods to shape. Another week passed and they were well into the second before the wood shape was ready. Then they had to hunt for rods of the right weight, and then start bending them against the wooden template.

More time gone. Lewis was in an agony. He pictured the president in his mansion eagerly awaiting word that his expedition leader was at work in Philadelphia. He saw the important men who had cleared their schedules for his benefit dashing off angry letters to the president: was his man even coming? He expected a presidential blast with each new mail. Yet he believed in his gut that the boat and the freedom it would give him over mountain portages would be vastly more valuable than a few extra hours of botanical instruction.

The longer the letter didn't come the more his nervous tension grew. When he felt he might explode he seized a walking stick and on sudden impulse headed for a trail he'd spied that ran up the Shenandoah from its juncture with the Potomac. He long had known that nothing soothed his nerves like a long tramp. So many things frustrated him. The stresses and demands of modern society, his infernal awkwardness, women—ah, God, women, don't get going on that. He walked with long thunderous strides, and gradually issues began to clear.

Mr. Jefferson was a genius, so people said. Lewis didn't doubt it. Smartest man he knew, certainly. But genius or no, he was not a woodsman. He had never crossed the Blue Ridge, never walked virgin country, never taken game for his supper or gone hungry if he missed, never made a bed of downed leaves under a rock overhang, never come awake in the dark predawn to meet attack if necessary. He knew plants but he didn't know wilds. He was a walker, but within the confines of civilization.

Nor was he a soldier. He had never commanded a unit, enforced discipline, worried over rations, chosen bivouac spots, never studied small unit tactics or the science of moving men under fire. Indeed, the one time he'd brushed against war, when he was governor of Virginia and Tarleton's Raiders were bearing down on him, he'd been none too heroic, so went the talk.

Mr. Jefferson couldn't lead the Corps of Discovery across the wild unknown to the shores of the Pacific. But Meriwether Lewis could. And nothing was more clear to him than the value of a truly portable boat. He felt this an invention to rank with Dr. Franklin's capture of lightning with those rods, Mr. Watts's steam engine in Britain, the shuttle loom secrets that had leaked from Britain to Boston and were putting fine cloth in everyone's reach.

So he needed it a lot more than he needed a few more botany lessons. Botany and biology were luxuries; what mattered here was a man taking command and bringing it through. And note that if it failed by any of the dangers that awaited, the fault would lie with Lewis and Clark. Mr. Jefferson still would be a great man; soon he would form an expedition anew to wipe out old failures.

So if he and Clark were to fail, let it be their own failure, not because they had been denied what they needed. Didn't matter much what the president wanted, really. The weight wasn't on him; it was on the two captains. Now, sitting in the dark by a guttering fire, the massive throbbing power of the river at his feet, he recalled what a stunning revelation that understanding was. It changed everything for it was the great transition: heretofore the president had led and the subaltern had followed; now the roles were reversed, the subaltern had taken command, the president must wait and hope for results for there was little more he could do.

He remembered how calm and peaceful his spirits had been that afternoon as he strode back to watch the boat's slow progress. Sure enough, the next post brought the president's quiet, thoughtful letter saying he was sure something of merit had created the delay at Harper's Ferry. Within the week the frame was finished. They had covered it with canvas and it had floated perfectly. It was as beautiful as a man-of-war under full canvas.

Now, as Will came awake by instinct to take his watch, Lewis saw that the decision on the Mississippi had been made as he tramped along the Shenandoah. So it was settled.

18

St. Louis, December, 1803

Pretty impressive, George Shannon thought. Cap'n Clark had issued a few orders and now the camp at Wood River was taking firm shape. They had borrowed a dozen soldiers from the garrison at Kaskaskia sixty miles below St. Louis—thank God!—to share the rowing burdens and had made better time.

Cap'n Lewis had stopped off in St. Louis while Cap'n Clark had brought them to the campground he'd found, five hundred acres where Wood River entered the Mississippi a little above St. Louis. No one had quite said they were delaying but December was fair gone and John Colter said they would be idiots to start in the face of real winter. Said they'd freeze their balls off.

Under Cap'n Clark's direction they built a cluster of neat huts each with a small fireplace and housing several men. Then he had put them to work on the keelboat. First he laid benches athwart the boat for oarsmen, making the big sweeps vastly easier to handle. Made the boat look a little like the galley George had seen in a picture in Ma's copy of *Arabian Nights*, only he didn't suppose Cap'n Clark would be cracking a whip over them as the big fellow in the picture was doing.

The cap'n also saw to the construction of lockers right up to the gunwales on each side. They opened from the top and if the lids were up they provided a barricade against arrows; if they were down they made a walkway on which men with poles planted against the bottom could walk them upstream if they stuck to the shallows near the bank. They offloaded the supplies and then reloaded as the cap'n tried this and that distribution for the best balance. He kept them at it for what seemed to George pretty small variations in the way the boat rode in the water.

December slid into January and the cap'n gave them a little extra tot of whiskey for Christmas and again at New Year's. It took George a long time to get his ration down, burning his throat the way it did. John Colter gave him a suspicious look and George said he was savoring it. He'd have given it to John Colter who really did savor it but the others might have figured he was just a kid.

Sure enough, one of the new volunteers from Tennessee did ask him if he didn't fear hard liquor would stunt his growth. That was the kind of talk George couldn't afford to take, so without a word he set down his mess cup with the whiskey and stood up and punched the newcomer so hard he was unconscious near twenty minutes, so long George began to fear he'd maybe killed the fellow. Hell of a note to kill someone you don't even know his name.

That night York sat down beside George. "You did just right. You busted that fellow good and he deserved it." George clapped him on the back in appreciation, and York added, "I may have to bust a couple of 'em myself, they call me 'Hey, Nigger,' again."

Now, you can only load and unload a boat so many times before you figure it's make-work and some of the men were getting hot. John Colter was a leader in drumming up resentment and looking for ways to stir up devilment. John wasn't a bad fellow but he'd been shouting that he'd seen plenty of places and covered lots of ground to find himself sitting around with his thumb up his ass, the way he put it, waiting for something to happen.

So next thing George knew John Colter had heard of a blind pig over beyond the settlement where a man could get all the whiskey he wanted. The settlement was small, a handful of families that seemed fearful of the camp full of soldiers and that let them know in a hurry there wasn't no marriageable girls to be had. Of course, as George pointed out to John Colter, they were sworn into the army and couldn't have married anyway, at which John rolled his eyes and walked off. After a while George figured it all out. He might still be a virgin but it was clear that John Colter sure wasn't—well, anyway, when Cap'n Clark had gone down to St. Louis to meet Cap'n Lewis and Sergeant Ordway was in charge, John led a group of them off to find that blind pig.

Did George want to join them? But Sergeant Ordway had strictly forbidden it and George wasn't one to disobey authority and he shook his head. He was glad when John didn't press him. About an hour after they'd left Sergeant Ordway figured it all out and he was boiling. He was a red-faced fellow who didn't say much. He'd come up from South West Post down in Tennessee leading a party of volunteers. Gotten them lost, too, till a scout Cap'n Lewis had hired found them and brought them in. This scout, Drewyer was his name, seemed to know a lot about Indians, and George liked him, though he had a way of looking at you as if he knew exactly what you were thinking that made George uncomfortable even when he wasn't thinking much of anything.

Most of the Tennessee volunteers had been found wanting and were rejected, but Ordway had survived the cut and for the moment, anyway, retained his sergeancy. So when Cap'n Clark went off to St. Louis he put Ordway in charge. When John Colter and the others came back that night George saw at a glance that John was some drunk. He got quiet and his eyes sort of squinted when he was drunk, and he walked around like a fighting rooster and you had to be a damned idiot not to see he was a dangerous man.

So Ordway took offense and said he would confine John to quarters and John said there wasn't a man alive could confine him to quarters and if he heard more such talk he'd smash Ordway in the nose and throw him in the river, and Ordway ran to his cabin in search of his pistol, and John pulled his rifle and was patching in powder and ball, said he intended to kill Ordway in the next two minutes, and here came Ordway bellowing threats but without his pistol and John stormed out to meet him, splashing powder in the rifle's pan, and George hit him from behind, knocked him down and jumped on him and held him to the ground, John roaring and cursing, George heavy enough that John couldn't move. George yelled to Reuben Field who was a very lively young man to get ahold of Ordway and shut him up before John broke loose and did kill him. Reuben grabbed Ordway and talked some sense into him. Reuben was an absolute pistol when it came to talking, and gradually it all settled down.

"You ain't sore at me, are you?" George asked John Colter the next day, John looking like death itself and moaning as he drank the coffee George gave him.

John managed a grin. "Nah—you did me a favor. I hanker to see that far west country and this is the only way I know to do it. Sounds like fabulous land and I'll just bet a couple of ambitious fellows getting in there early, God knows what they could accomplish. But if I'd taken a shot at Ordway, the cap'n, he'd've kicked my ass out in the cold."

It had been a long time since Lewis had been in St. Louis but it seemed little changed. A thousand-odd people lived here in modest little houses atop a limestone bluff on the west side of the river that overlooked the throbbing riverfront below where boats jockeyed for landing space. Of course he went first to call on Auguste Chouteau, patriarch of the founding family that had settled the town near forty years before. The Chouteaus had made themselves powers of the western fur trade and St. Louis the entrepôt for all the pelts that weren't snatched up by the perfidious British or shipped off to French bastions on Hudson's Bay. The Chouteau warehouses reeked with what folks here described as the odor of money. Periodically flatboats ran from those warehouses to the docks at New Orleans for a ship bound for Europe or, less often, New York.

The old gentleman gave Lewis a roaring welcome: he must be their guest in their baronial mansion that dwarfed the lesser houses crowded against it. The town's leaders would assemble at the Chouteau table that very night to meet the visitor to hear his views on their rapidly unfolding future. For the Louisiana Purchase was taking hold, now that Baring Brothers of London had issued bonds guaranteeing the price of fifteen million dollars. The Americans were coming. Probably New Orleans had already passed to them; St. Louis was scheduled to become American in early spring of 1804.

Chouteau was delighted since his already thriving business could only improve under the new men. He said the Frenchmen here had been thrilled when Napoleon ordered the Spanish to return Louisiana. When they learned their leader had in turn sold them to the Americans there was a near riot. Hence Lewis might encounter a little hostility that soon would pass and was to be ignored. He was an honored guest and if the Spanish, who hadn't actually turned the town back to the French and were nominally still in charge, had their noses out of joint, who really cared? Not the Chouteaus, it was evident, and as his glass was filled and refilled, it struck Meriwether Lewis that he hardly gave a damn himself.

Still, he was an army officer in command of a unit preparing to march through territory that the Spanish still claimed. Common courtesy said he should call on the Spanish commandant and so with an interpreter he presented himself at ten the next morning at the cantonment and was ushered into the office of Colonel Carlos Dehault Delassus. The colonel proved to be a handsome man in a uniform that in sheer gaudiness put the plain garb of an infantry captain that Lewis wore quite to shame.

The man seemed to be glaring at him. Lewis's graceful bow was returned by a scarcely civil nod. A slow simmer arose in Lewis. Before he could state his purpose the colonel launched a stream of angry and very rapid Spanish that Lewis suspected included serious invective that the hard-pressed interpreter left out. But there was no mistaking the Spaniard's tone and expression. The simmer stirring in Lewis grew.

The Spaniard set about making it clear that he regarded the American as an unlawful intruder who violated the norms of civilized behavior between nations. He said the American clearly felt that the miserable treaty that denied the historic rights of Spain in Louisiana gave him carte blanche to appear as an advance conqueror. The captain need have no illusions that the Spanish army was unaware of his aims—it was well known that he came to anchor the American presence onto the West. To use an American expression that vulgarly demonstrated the American propensity for grasping everything about it, he was jumping the gun. It was bad enough that soon the colonel must turn the province over to the hated intruders and take his men and matériel to Cuba, but it was intolerable that the Americans should seek to advance that future event by a single day.

Lewis rose in protest. He was here only in passing, westward bound for the Pacific, with orders to keep an eye peeled as he went for the Northwest Passage. The colonel mistook him; he was a simple explorer. The interpreter pleaded with both men to slow down. Then came the explosion.

"The colonel says he takes the liberty to doubt you."

"Doubt?"

"Says he doesn't believe you. Thinks you're lying. Says Americans lie as a matter of course."

The simmer went to full boil.

The interpreter blundered on. "He says that any attempt to go farther west will be met with force. Until the day the province passes in full to the Americans."

Before Lewis could really react the interpreter added helpfully, "He has two companies of soldiers and a substantial dungeon. Says he'll put all your men behind bars, including you."

Lewis felt such rage that his vision was momentarily blurred. That this puppy should dare—

And then he remembered the president telling him that he possessed an abundance of temper so that his main exercise should be in controlling it, not using it. The Spaniard was arrogantly offensive, but in fact Lewis's men were in winter camp on the American side of the river and the transfer of Louisiana to the United States would come before he possibly could leave.

He stood. "Colonel," he said, "you are offensive. You quite belie the reputation for courtesy the Spanish people enjoy." Then he remembered that Captain Bissell at the cantonment at Kaskaskia who would receive the province for the United States had invited him to take part in the transfer ceremony. "And, sir," he added, smiling, "I shall be there the day you give up command and post and dungeon and all and hie yourself off to Cuba, and it will be a pleasure to see your face on that day."

He bowed. "Until then, Colonel."

"Canoe coming, Cap'n," Sergeant Floyd said. "Two men. One looks like Drewyer."

Clark liked Drewyer and he knew Lewis was quite taken with the woodsman. They had come on him at Fort Massac when those volunteers from down in Tennessee were overdue.

"They're lost, I don't doubt," a crusty old sergeant said in disgust. "Some men never learn the woods. Better send Drewyer here to fetch them, you don't mind the suggestion."

Drewyer proved to be a swarthy, muscular fellow in his middle thirties who had acquired considerable local fame as a scout. He said his mother was Shawnee and his father had been a French trapper who froze to death in the woods when he fell in a blizzard and broke a leg. Drewyer didn't seem to regard this as a serious loss but spoke of his old ma with rich affection. Lewis and Clark liked him immediately. He was solid and strong, didn't talk much, had a way of looking at you that was quiet and inoffensive but told you at once not to trifle with him. He spoke a couple of Indian languages and was highly skilled in Indian ways. An important, perhaps decisive point, he was a master of the intertribal sign language that Plains Indians used to connect to other tribes. He said he had been up the Missouri three times, going as far as the Mandan villages, which he said was as far as anyone sensible went. The captains talked to him for an hour, finding there was simply a quality about him that gave one confidence. They were going to the Mandan villages and beyond; did he want to join them as scout, hunter, interpreter, guide to Indian customs, and all-around useful figure?

"Clear across the continent? To salt water, you say? My, that oughta be something. Hell yes, Cap'n, I'll sign up."

They dickered a bit over salary and terms—he was a hired interpreter, not a soldier—and then sent him off to find the lost troops, final employment conditional on success. When he brought the men in he said, "They was hunkered down in the woods like a covey of quail waitin' on a dog to flush 'em out." In the end the captains accepted only two of the volunteers.

When it was time to enter Drewyer in the records, Clark asked how he spelled his name.

"Drouillard, sir," he said, spelling it out. "George."

So Lewis told him it still sounded like Drewyer and that's what they would call him. Drewyer just smiled.

Now Clark and Sergeant Pryor watched him drive the canoe ashore. The man in the bow vaulted out and dragged the dugout beyond the river's reach.

"Mornin', Cap'n," Drewyer said. "This here is Baptiste, that's all anyone ever calls him. He's been upriver trapping and got in this morning, tells me the Sioux are raising hell. I figured you'd want to know right away."

Baptiste was a wizened fellow who could be anywhere from thirty to fifty and wore shrunken buckskins and moccasins, his graying hair clubbed back with a leather thong. He'd lost all four fingers on his left hand and was smoking a cigar that he held clamped to his palm by his thumb.

"Baptiste, what he says, says they roughed him and his two partners pretty fierce," Drewyer continued. "Told him them furs was their property and he'd have to pay heavy to take them through country they claim as their own."

Baptiste began to talk in rapid French. Clark had a little French but this was a strange patois he'd never heard. He looked at Drewyer who seemed to get most of it and the scout translated.

"Says they knew he was coming. Like they had spies along the river when all he'd seen were a few young boys fishing, so he figures they was there as scouts and had horses in the nearest gully. Anyway, Baptiste and his party turned a bend and there was warriors on both banks with their arrows tipped into their bows, strings pulled tight—they meant business, all right."

"How many?" Clark asked.

"Five thousand, he says. I figure five hundred is closer to it but that's plenty. Would have been their deaths, him and his partners, to have tried to run it, he's sure of that, and anyway, they came out in their own boats and jumped aboard his and took it in and that was that."

"But bows and arrows only? No firearms?"

"A few old muskets the British had let them have back when, but mostly arrows. Course, an arrow'll kill you just as dead."

It seemed the Indians had pretty well stripped the trappers of tools, what little liquor they had left, and the last of their trade goods. Scared them, too; Baptiste apparently was a man who often dealt with Indians and been in plenty of tight spots before, but this was different, both in numbers of Indians gathered and their aggressive attitude. He wondered if they had won some victory, cleaning out a neighboring tribe's horses or perhaps driving a smaller tribe to flee to new territory. Now their news of this unsettling turn was spreading like wildfire in St. Louis.

"You take this pretty serious, then?" Clark asked.

Drewyer gave him a sharp look. "I ain't a'scared of 'em, if that's what you're asking." Clark heard ice in his tone. "But if we're going to bump into five hundred Sioux figuring they're cocks of the walk and everyone'll give in to 'em, I'd like to be sure we have some weapons, and I ain't seen many around the camp."

"So what do you suggest?"

"Well, Cap'n, ain't nothing like a little cannon to get folk's attention."

Clark smiled. "Agreed," he said. "We'll shoot our way through if we have to, but if we're ready I doubt we'll have to."

A rare smile spread over Drewyer's face. "Yes, sir," he said. "Look at it that way and I expect you're right."

19

St. Louis, January, 1804

The fellow was well dressed for a fur trader, his manner crisp and authoritative, his questions on the expedition's aims well couched. Lewis took him for a British Army officer working undercover and felt this was confirmed when the other said, "You may find British troops in garrison if you get that far." There was a nasty twist to his lips that made Lewis think of General Clark's story of the Hair Buyer.

"That's possible," Lewis said, "but we'll make ourselves felt."

"Find yourself in irons, perhaps."

"I don't think so. I wouldn't want to start a war but the United States has valid claims to the Origan Country and I would think it my duty to support those claims. And I bid you good day, sir."

"Good day to you, sir—and may your travels go well."

Well, that was a gracious enough closure on the Briton's part, but the whole exchange was a new goad to get the men moving westward. He was on his way to Chouteau's warehouse and his step quickened. Clark was up at the camp he'd established on Wood River bringing their party to focus as a military unit. Clark was good at that, understood military discipline and knew how to enforce it with balance. More and more he felt that the president's decision to make this a military expedition with the authority and discipline that implied had been wise.

Still, the encounter with the inquisitive Briton had left him restless and irritable when the warehouse clerk handed him a packet of War Department letters. He opened the first, the second, the third. All complaints. He wasn't moving fast enough, he wasn't reporting with the frequency expected—God Almighty, they were getting ready to cross the entire continent and the department wanted daily reports from St. Louis? Having to answer to the department was an unfortunate complication. Of course, the president was commander-in-chief and could do as he liked, but it appeared that in practice Mr. Dearborn intended to have considerably more say than Lewis had any intention of granting him. Hell's fire, he'd report when he had something to say and then he would say it to Mr. Jefferson. Mr. Dearborn seemed to resent him for some reason, and by God, if anyone knew how to reciprocate resentment it was Meriwether Lewis!

So irritation was well on the way to anger when he opened the fourth envelope and found Will Clark's commission. At last! He scanned it, no presidential signature but that would be a later formality, secretary of war would do for now. He started to refold it when a word caught his eye: "lieutenant." Now, bottom dropping out of his belly, he examined it. Yes, good Lord, it named William Clark a first lieutenant in the United States Army!

But God damn it, Will was to be a captain! They were to be co-commanders, all equal. That's what he had told Jefferson, what Jefferson had approved. Of course he'd had presidential agreement before he wrote Will. The president had been delighted, said the Clarks were the salt of the earth and the general a national hero. He'd spun off a few stories from the old days—how could he have let this go through? Lewis sat there trying to remember: had Mr. Jefferson accepted the joint command or merely accepted Clark the individual?

But Lewis had promised. His invitation letter to Will had specified they would be of equal rank and the reply had carefully specified that term. What would he do now? Will simply wouldn't serve as lieutenant and yet he was essential. As they approached departure and the magnitude of what lay ahead became ever more clear, he knew he needed Will Clark.

"Why'd you offer it if it warn't yours to offer?"

"But it *was*," Lewis cried. He had hurried to Wood River and walked Will a mile downstream, well away from the camp, and they were seated on the trunk of a tree delivered by the river. The Mississippi bubbled and swirled at their feet. A doe peered curiously at them through brush until Seaman charged her.

"Warn't figuring to get me in, not tell me till it was too late?"

"Jesus, Will—you know me better than that."

Clark's gaze softened. "Yeah, I reckon I do, Merry. But we done stepped in shit this time." He sighed, then said, "You know, I thought it was kinda funny at the start. Don't make much military sense to have equal commanders—suppose they disagree? Old Dearborn, he saw that right away. I 'spect he went thumbs down the minute it hit his desk."

"But the president has the power. And I worked it out with him."

"Well, you know Mr. Jefferson better'n I do, but he didn't never serve in the military, did he?" Lewis shook his head. "So Dearborn might've found it pretty easy to turn him around. But tell me, Merry, suppose I'd said no right at the start?"

"I did have a fallback candidate, but I wanted you."

"This fallback, he'd have been co-captain too?"

"Lieutenant."

"See, there you go. That's what Dearborn was thinking. And the truth is, Merry, that's what's militarily appropriate."

Will was talking so calmly, so reasonably, that Lewis had a sudden wild hope that he would stay, it wouldn't all come unhinged before they even left the Mississippi.

But then Will said, "Well, the camp's in good shape and the boys are about set. Keep training 'em and they'll do fine. This fellow Ordway, he'll make you a lieutenant."

But Ordway wasn't Will Clark, lacked the intelligence, the judgment, the experience, the force of personality. He was a natural sergeant. Lewis shook his head. "I need you."

"Well, you should have figured that out earlier."

"I did. I had it set. The president—well, maybe he don't know—"

"Don't know what?"

"What Dearborn did. This lieutenant business. Maybe—"

"God, Merry! You're sounding more the country boy every minute. Dearborn ain't going to go against him without telling him."

Lewis knew this was true. Jefferson knew, all right. Then why hadn't he corrected it?

"Will," he said, "please . . ."

Clark's lips were a tight line. "No! I ain't going as lieutenant and that's that. I ain't been a lieutenant in a long time. Been in command of all I done since they gave me the rifle company. Left the army, been in the fur trade and Indian trade, win some and lose some but on my own. I run family affairs to suit myself. What I say goes in all that I do, no two ways about it, no asking permission, none of that. That's long behind me."

His face softened. "You'll be all right, Merry. You got some good men and there ain't nobody I'd pick ahead of you to go conquer the world. Me . . . well, I think this is important and I'd like to have been a part of it, but I ain't taking seconds—"

Seconds? But that was just it—he didn't want Will taking seconds. Suddenly it was like mist clearing. He slapped his knee hard. "God damn it, I never asked you to take seconds!"

"Army did. Made me your lieutenant, ain't that right?"

"No!" Things clearer and clearer. Why hadn't he seen it before? "What the hell do we care what a piece of paper says? You're not going to stay in the army when this is over, and I doubt I will either. Everything is different now, Will."

"Yes, but—"

"But, hell. You agree to go and you're the captain same as me. We're both in command and to hell with military thinking. The men will never get a hint of anything different. Nobody'll ever say you were less important than me because I won't stand for it, I'll jam it down their throats, that's what! I won't stand for it, you won't stand for it. C'mon, Will, don't give it up now. We'll be together all the way. It'll be Clark and Lewis, Lewis and Clark—"

"But that piece of paper—"

"But who cares what's on a piece of paper? If I say you're captain along with me and you say it and the world sees it, what does it matter what's writ on a piece of paper in some goddamned file drawer?"

Clark stared at him and didn't answer. "Look, Will," Lewis said, "it's reality we're talking about, not titles. We share the command, I know it, you know it, the men know it. World won't question it whether we do something big or die trying. Either way, who'll give a shit what's on some piece of paper?"

At last Clark began to laugh. "Merry, you missed your calling. You'd've made some lawyer."

"But I'm right, Will."

Another long pause. Clark's face looked cut from stone. "This is gut serious, Merry," he said. "Ain't no fooling around now."

"Exactly."

"All right. Here's what you're saying. You're talking equal. Really equal. Both of us cap'ns, no fooling. The men don't know, now or later. We both write the report. Report says we decided this and we decided that, not you decided. If rank ever comes up after it's over you step front and center and you say in so many words that that was just a piece of paper, we were always co-captains, equal, fair and square and nobody ever doubted it on the trail."

"That's just what I'm saying."

Clark had a sudden dangerous look. "That's what you're *agreeing* to."

"Exactly. That's what I'm agreeing to."

Clark studied his face. Lewis held his gaze. At last Clark said, "Merry, I've always knowed you to be a man of honor. I'm going to trust you and I'm going to hold you to everything you've said. I want your hand on it."

He held out his hand and Lewis took it in both of his. "My hand and my heart," Lewis said softly. He whistled up Seaman and they started back toward camp.

Suddenly Clark laughed. "Clark and Lewis expedition, eh?"

"Don't matter to me," Lewis said, though it did.

"No, no. Lewis and Clark it'll be. This has been your play for years. I'm just coming in at the last moment. Lewis and Clark—but it will be that, equal in all respects."

"In all respects."

But again Lewis wondered: why had Mr. Jefferson let that stand? He could think of various possibilities, none favorable to the president. It was a betrayal and it had nearly wrecked the expedition at the start and Lewis wouldn't forget it.

20

On the Missouri River, May, 1804

It was time to go. The air was softening and spring was in the wings. The day came when Lewis took his place in the ceremony of transfer, Spain to France, France to the United States. Colonel Delassus officiated for Spain, but Lewis took no pleasure in his discomfort. Spain was fading from the world's stage while the United States was just stepping in front of the footlights. But at least Meriwether Lewis could lead his men westward knowing that now they crossed U.S. territory clear to the Rocky Mountains, as people now were calling them. There was a ball afterward, attendance mandatory, but he and Clark escaped when they could. Too much to do.

The Corps of Discovery now stood at near thirty members, decisions still open on two or three men. A steady stream of applicants had appeared; Lewis supposed they had chosen one out of ten. Lewis had added two pirogues—canoes hollowed out of massive cottonwood logs, in fact—to carry the excess of supplies now needed. He also put on five soldiers under Corporal Richard Warfington who would not be part of the Corps but would accompany it as far as the Mandan villages and then return to St. Louis with reports and specimens of hitherto unknown birds and animals. When all was finally settled, the permanent party had twenty-two private soldiers and three sergeants plus the two captains, and York and Drewyer.

"And Seaman makes thirty," Lewis said when Clark was tallying up totals. "Don't forget old Seaman—he may be our most valuable member."

Clark grinned. "Seaman may make dinner," he said. "We're going into country where people consider dog a delicacy and white men traveling there often acquire a taste for it. Especially in starving time."

Lewis glared. "I'll kill the man thinks he's going to eat my dog." Instantly he knew it was too strong. Clark had been joking, or perhaps not quite joking, but the Indian taste for dog meat stew was well known and more than a few white men had acquired it as well. Clark gave him an odd look and didn't answer. Lewis considered softening the remark, then shrugged. It was how he felt.

The Corps was proving a bonanza for St. Louis merchants. Chouteau's capacious warehouses could supply most of his needs but Lewis tried in fairness to spread his business around. This proved too little for the second-ranked merchant, Manuel Lisa, and when Lisa pushed him Lewis exploded and swore not another government penny would go to that blackguard. Clark asked if he really felt that was wise and though he recognized good counsel he shrugged it off. Lisa bombarded Washington with complaints and hot messages flowed from the War Department. Lewis decided he was too damned busy to tend to such pettifoggery.

His purchases grew. In payment he dashed off chits authorizing merchants to draw on the president.

"You keeping track of all that paper, Merry?" Clark asked one day.

Lewis shrugged. "It'll all get tallied up in Washington."

"God Almighty, Merry, you know the army. End of the day, they'll want a written explanation for everything. You'd better have your records in shape."

But how could he keep track of it all? The decision on their own to expand their numbers imposed all sorts of new demands for supplies—for clothing, foodstuffs, whiskey rations, weapons, ammunition, medications. He bought more and worried that it was not enough. He had ordered 193 pounds of the soup concentrate that was a radical innovation in wilderness supply; chronometer, compasses, sextant and circle; corn, flour, salt, pickled pork, lard, candles, tools, whiskey, tobacco, flint and steel sets. Tutored by the famous Dr. Benjamin Rush of Philadelphia, he bought clyster and penis syringes, Peruvian bark, thirteen hundred doses of physic, a thousand of emetic, thirty-five hundred of the purge pills that Rush called "thunderclappers" and prescribed for every ailment, saying it cleaned out the poisons so the body could heal on its own. He carried strong spirit wine to be diluted for medicine, Epsom salts, sulfur, balsam, asafetida. He loaded all his boats would bear in Indian presents; fish hooks, pocket mirrors, scarlet cloth, tobacco, beads of blue, white, yellow, orange, red; red and checked handkerchiefs of muslin and silk; eyeglasses, burning glasses, bells, scissors, needles, thimbles; knives, tomahawks, copper sheets, rings, earrings, peace medals. He had a supply of American army uniform jackets to present to Indian chiefs. A couple of extra casks of good whiskey that he would issue to his men (and never to Indians) as a commendatory or celebratory ration or when exertion had been especially brutal. Pots and pans, knives, tin plates and cups, salt and spices, blankets, wool coats and shirts, cotton drawers . . .

There . . . that should see him through. But then one night at Chouteau's table he was struck by a sudden certainty that his purchases fell far short of need. How long would they be gone, really? Make the Mandans this year, cross the mountains and come down on the Pacific in the next, home on a down-current run before the ice formed in the third year. There would be no stores, no resupply; there might be a ship when they came down the Columbia to the sea and there might not, and if there was, it might supply them from its stores but it might be in starving condition itself. No, count on it, they would be on their own, relying on what they could carry or could make.

He delayed again. Clark reported that up on Wood River the men were beside themselves with boredom, impatience, anxiety to be on their way. There were fights every day. He said Shannon and York were serving as peacemakers, talking men away from rage, though he added that both gave good account of themselves when pushed too hard. Said his reservations about Shannon had vanished. Didn't matter how old or young he might be—he was a good man and valuable addition to the expedition.

Lewis was as frustrated as his men. He was sick to death of St. Louis that he now decided he'd never really liked. He caught glimpses of himself when he happened past a looking glass, his mouth a grim and humorless slash. Clark told him to ease off, they'd make it all right, but he couldn't. Waves of the melancholy that the president had warned him against swept him like the ocean battering a headland. He rejected this dark emotion but it wasn't helped by the fact that, as he told Will, he felt like a goddam quartermaster sergeant. Will gave him another odd look at that outburst and he resolved to keep his thoughts to himself. But that made them harder still to bear.

Still, the time came when the supplies had to be seen as complete. The boats were repaired and ready to go. The men were as close to soldiers as he could expect, with four months of close-order drill, getting used to unquestioned obedience, learning basic combat techniques, hand signals, moving under fire, digging shelter.

It was time to go. Both men knew they were seriously short of trade goods, the presents that paved the way, but they had collected all they could find here. Clark took the main body to St. Charles, a hamlet four miles up the Missouri and next to the last of civilization going west. Lewis came on by horseback and joined them there. Clark presented two new men whom he wanted to engage. Both were half-breeds, sons of French fathers and Indian mothers. Pierre Cruzatte, born to an Omaha mother, was fluent in Omaha and the Plains sign language. He was small, wizened, of indeterminate age, given to loud bursts of cackling laughter that were quite infectious of good humor. It was hard not to laugh with him. Francis Labiche spoke several Indian languages; he was quiet, reserved, spoke halting English but exuded a quiet competence. Both men were skilled boatmen, veterans of the endless lakes and waterways of the Canadian woods. Soon Lewis agreed—they would be welcome additions. They were sworn in as privates and so the expedition grew, twenty-four privates, three sergeants, two captains, York, Drewyer, and Seaman in three deep-laden vessels. Only the permanent party would man the keelboat. The whole party would winter at the Mandans but then the extra men would return to St. Louis in the keelboat, which would be too heavy when they reached the mountains. It would return with notes and specimens for the president while the main party plunged into the unknown.

Clark said the men had asked him to arrange a final mass before they pushed into the unknown. The parish priest at St. Charles donned his robes, lit candles and incense, the men knelt and the blessings of God and Jesus Christ were called down upon them. Lewis joined them, following the sonorous Latin phrases that invoked their special majesty. At the same time all the prejudices of a Virginia gentleman boiled in him and he felt quite disapproving of this papist clatter. He made no attempt to rectify this disapproval with the deep comfort he felt in calling down God's blessings on himself and all his men and even, he supposed, his dog.

The people of St. Charles, a hundred at least, turned out on the riverfront to cheer as the expedition got under way. It was the twenty-first of May, 1804.

A dozen riflemen fired a three-volley salute and Lewis ordered the flag dipped in response. Then they were out in the swift river, westward bound. It was four in the afternoon. After about four miles they camped on an island. Sometime after midnight it began to rain.

21

On the Missouri, Summer, 1804

So the great adventure began. For a little while, at least, the sense of pressure under which Meriwether Lewis had lived much of his life lifted, to be replaced by near exaltation. He felt so extremely good at leaving behind all the quarrels and confusions of St. Louis and of the pettifogging War Department. Devil take them! He was free, acting out his destiny just as Clark had said, doing what he had been born to do.

The relationship with Clark had deepened somehow, as if bringing it to focus in so many words had solidified and made specific what before had been unspoken and intuitive. Now each man knew where he stood with the other. Lewis sensed in Clark the same confidence he himself felt in having navigated a perilous passage from which each had emerged the stronger.

Two weeks after their departure he and Seaman were tramping along the bluff above the river, the boats slender shapes in the glittering water below. There were three boats—the keelboat and two thirty-foot pirogues or dugouts. The party of soldiers under a corporal handled the larger one, which was painted white, while hired voyageurs paddled the smaller, which was painted red, neither group part of the primary Corps of Discovery and neither going beyond the Mandans.

Lewis walked loose-limbed and easy, rifle slung across his back, spontoon in his hand. He liked the spontoon, a medieval weapon dating to the days when soldiers wore armor. In effect it was a short pike combining iron point and battle-ax on a five-foot shaft of oak that had emerged as a badge of rank for infantry officers before passing from use in the previous century. It served Lewis as walking stick, aid on steep slopes, a handy and immediate weapon, and finally it had a crosspiece on which he could rest the heavy rifle when firing at a distant target. This mattered when taking specimens with the least damage possible to feed science as well as the natural history museums rising in Philadelphia.

Now, leaning on his spontoon and gazing down, he could see Clark in the stern of the keelboat. They already had settled into an unspoken division of labor. Clark, by far the more skilled waterman and boat handler, would stay with the boats. Lewis, by far the superior botanist and biologist, would tramp the banks alone with Seaman or, as they neared the Sioux, with a few well-armed men behind him. They would swap these positions now and then for variety, but the lonely tramps suited Lewis's nature as well as letting him search out discoveries. A major part of the president's intentions turned on finding new plants and new animals or perhaps animals extinct in Europe or the East. He was to keep an eye peeled for mammoths.

Thus he left Clark the more immediate command. It was Clark who chose their campgrounds, usually on an island for greater security from dawn attack, who gave the word to turn in and beach the vessels, who cast them off in the morning. The captains shared equal authority, never any question about that, but in effect Clark was functioning as executive officer, leaving Lewis the broader view. The men were divided into three messes, as Lewis called them since each was expected to cook and eat together, each of these under one of the sergeants. Ordway doled out rations on days the hunters came back empty-handed. Since rations were cornmeal and salt pork on one day, flour and pork the next, hominy and lard the third, Lewis pressed the hunters hard not to return empty-handed. Nothing like a side of venison to brighten expressions around the campfires. They had two horses for packing purposes that followed along the riverbank. Drewyer went out near daily, Colter almost as often, each leading a horse to pack back their kills.

Travel against this fierce river was brutal. They rowed. On days of blessed good luck when a following wind sprung up they hoisted the square sail. They rowed, paddled, or poled, depending on circumstances. Poles had a metal cap on one end, padding covered with canvas on the other, the latter to snug into a man's armpit as he walked along the lids of the lockers and shoved the boat foot by foot up the roaring stream. If that didn't work they ran the cordelle through a ring at the bow and up to the top of the mast and most of the men went ashore and dragged the boat along, with a few still aboard to use rudder and poles to hold off the shore. The cordelle was hemp at the start but wore quickly and soon was mostly elk hide. It had loops into which each man fitted his shoulder. Lewis shared these various tortures from time to time, and so did Clark; the men appreciated the captains grunting and blowing alongside them.

But whatever the means of the day, forcing a heavy vessel up relentless swift current was exhausting work. Everyone ate prodigious amounts, but many still found themselves hungry as they rolled into blankets and passed instantly into sleep. Only the guards moving quietly about the camp, alert to possible attack, watched over by the sergeant of the guard, were awake. After two hours each man awakened his replacement. The captains spent most evenings on the telescope, taking positions to enter in the map growing under Clark's pen. Usually Lewis took the glass, calling positions that Clark would note, combining the chronometer reading. From time to time he would go through the ritual of establishing time from the stars as a correction to their chronometer. Still, the brass clock from London wasn't often far off and Lewis was more than pleased; already it had justified its $250 cost. Often he congratulated himself on summoning the courage to spend that money.

Then the endless fight with the current resumed. The three sergeants manned bow, stern, and 'midships. The half-breeds, Cruzatte and Labiche, had spent their lives on this river and knew it better than anyone. Clark posted them at the bow, one at the all-important bow oar to pull the big boat this way or that to avoid obstacles, the other to thrust aside the massive trees that floated whole down the river and the sawyers that sprang up from the bottom unbidden but able to hole a boat. Cruzatte had a special talent for crossing the river to catch the slack water on the inside of a bend. He seemed able to sense exactly when the current roiling and boiling into the curve would near reverse itself. Caught at the right moment, it might lift the boat clear across and occasionally carry it an extra thirty or forty yards upstream.

The relentless current was worse than that of the Mississippi by a couple of miles an hour. And the river had a disconcerting habit of throwing up sandbars, forming whirlpools, catching whole trees on the shore around which the boat must maneuver cautiously.

Since Clark was constantly on the river he took responsibility for the map the expedition was expected to produce and soon was skilled. At even the slightest direction shift, let alone the great swings by which the water endlessly carved a new route, he took careful compass headings that he entered in a notebook he kept wrapped in oilcloth. Then he entered a dead reckoning estimate of the distance before the next turn. After a few days he could estimate both river miles covered and linear miles with real accuracy. The latter then could be checked by celestial observation.

Lewis usually made the star sights. "Damn, Will," he said, seeing how closely Clark's dead reckoning matched the fact, "you're getting pretty good. Don't let it go to your head, now."

Clark laughed. "Go to hell, Merry," he said.

"You boys know what you're up against with the Sioux?" It was a rhetorical question and the captains just waited for more. Pierre Dorion was a tall, limber old Frenchman, snowy hair and beard, fair command of English, whom they had spotted standing propped on a stick on the stern of a fifty-foot pirogue heavy laden with pelts stacked and bundled. Three half-breed voyageurs served as his crew. They were bound for the Chouteau warehouse in St. Louis; this was the fur trade in action, commercial heart of the West.

It was late afternoon. Clark had chosen a campground where a fresh creek entered the river. The boys had found a catfish pool up this creek a bit and had a fine mess of the delicacy. Clark immediately waved the pirogue in and suggested they camp together. Now the captains were talking over the campfire to Mr. Dorion, everyone having made short work of a catfish dinner.

Without waiting for an answer Mr. Dorion said you had to understand the Sioux were tough and dangerous, firmly set in the idea that the river, at least a few hundred miles of it, was their property and they intended to tax anyone who thought to use it. Had Dorion paid a tax to pass? No, he said, but they knew him pretty well. Turned out he had lived in a Yankton Sioux village for fourteen years, had a Yankton wife who'd been cute as a bug when he married her but had run on to some fat by now, which he found made her even more attractive. She had given him a passel of children who were back in the village eagerly awaiting his return with the sweets and play-pretties he always brought them. Of course he spoke the language.

It seemed the Yanktons were only one branch of a dozen or so branches of the Sioux nation, each autonomous but linked to the others. If anything united them, Mr. Dorion said, it was the conviction that this was their land to be harvested for their benefit.

The captains explained the monumental changes of the last year, the Louisiana Purchase with its transfer of vast terrain, French and Spanish out, no longer a factor, forget them, the Missouri country now American. Now the president of the United States, a tall, genial, and generous patron was the kindly new father of all the tribes from here to the Shining Mountains. Among the captains' duties to spread this happy word. Of course there could be no question of the Great Father's agents paying a fee to travel through country now in the possession of the same Great Father.

Mr. Dorion looked very doubtful at this but Lewis told him firmly that it was not a question to be argued and that his Sioux brothers would put themselves in terrible danger if they chose to contest that. They showed Mr. Dorion the cannon and the heavy blunderbusses on swivels.

At last he said gravely that they needed his services; he would inter-
pret to avoid misunderstandings and try to make his people see the reality before them. He said he would join them now and his men would
take his furs on to St. Louis. Lewis was delighted. He swore Mr. Dorion
in as a paid guide and interpreter. So the Corps of Discovery continued
to grow.

Some four weeks and four hundred miles up the Missouri the expedition
came to a halt at the gorgeous spot where the Kansas River entered from
the left. Here the Missouri made an abrupt turn. Now the expedition would
be heading north instead of west. They had seen no Indians, which surprised Lewis, but Drewyer reminded him that Plains Indians were nomadic
people who folded their conical tents and took them along when they went
west on the annual buffalo hunt that was crucial to their survival.

The Kansas River wound in broad and leisurely loops through a
marshy flat pierced by innumerable little waterways and populated by
vast numbers of waterbirds, many of them white but some with vivid colors. Lewis could see a great city rising on this garden spot, but Clark
hooted and told him to tend to his knitting and save fantasies for his old
age. Lewis decided his poetic instincts surpassed those of his partner.
Partly for the place's beauty but mostly to reward four hundred hard
miles, he and Clark called for a few days of rest. Raspberries were plump
and black, fields of them for as far as he could see, and the men swarmed
through them stuffing fruit in their mouths, juice running down their
cheeks to stain homespun shirts.

It was a time to rest, bathe, wash clothes, roam, explore, try one's hand
at hunting. For the captains, before indulging in the berries and the
beauty and the wealth of birdlife, it was a time to assess their men, for
strengths and for weaknesses. They fired their pipes and savored the last
dregs of coffee that already was running short and went down the roster.

With a couple of exceptions, they were well satisfied. The sergeants had
worked well. They were popular and yet none had trouble commanding
respect and obedience. Floyd was the most graceful of the three and
among the best liked men in the Corps. He laughed readily, and had a powerful sense of irony and of humor that when the going on the river was at
its hardest he had something to say that reduced men under strain to
laughter and eased their pain. But he was dangerous under his easy charm.
If he felt challenged a startling coldness came into his eyes. They would
bulge slightly and the men in his squad would be quiet and cautious.

Lewis often thought of the gut ache Floyd had had on that first day
they met. From his paleness, his winces, the slight stagger when he

walked, the captain had seen that this was serious pain. But Clark had agreed with Floyd's contention that he had always had bouts of such pain, but it would be gone in the morning and signified nothing. And in the morning apparently it was gone and he was bouncing around full of energy and cheer. Lewis thought he'd been afflicted a few times since they left but it hadn't interfered with his duty or curbed his appetite. He was a good soldier, easygoing, balanced, fair, tough when he needed to be, understanding when that was needed.

"Like his daddy, from what General Clark told me," Clark said. "His daddy died young, though."

That put it in the open. "Died of a tender gut, maybe," Lewis said. "I did see Floyd all doubled over the other night, white as a sheet—said it was just a momentary flash of pain."

Clark nodded. "I've seen him looking troubled a time or two but he's always ready in the morning. Just the way he is, maybe."

Lewis said no more. He felt a basic sympathy for a man with a sore gut; he'd had gut aches of his own.

Pryor, Floyd's muscular friend, led his squad with equal success though his manner was different. Lewis couldn't remember having seen him laugh and when he spoke the words seemed measured if not rationed. But he was always direct with his men and always fair. They never had any doubts on what they were to do and seemed to like him, though there was little camaraderie.

Ordway was far more valuable to the captains than he was beloved of his men. There was a little of the bookkeeper in him, pedantic insistence on things being just so that some of his men found hard to take. But he was solid and steady despite a stuffy manner and his men could trust him. Keeping track of things came naturally to him and the captains relied on him. Before they left Wood River Clark had put Ordway in charge of issuing rations and the occasional dram of whiskey when there was cause to celebrate, this beyond the usual daily ration. Handling whiskey was tricky. They all knew spirits would be exhausted long before they returned and each man wanted his share, no more but certainly no less. It was the sort of thing that could make for murderous quarrels, but everyone trusted Ordway. Such was his nature.

When Clark had decided where to land them of a night it usually was Ordway who placed each squad, said where to dig the latrine pit, saw to the stacking of rifles in neat tripods for quick access. Both captains had an infantryman's insistence on high military order in each camp even when you would depart forever in the morning. That was how you kept your men alive and ready to meet attack. Their orders were to offer friendship to Indians, of whom so far they had seen none. But many tribes had a reputation for hostility, so how they would respond to white men climbing the river in relative force remained to be seen. This applied most immediately to the Sioux, whose country they now were approaching. Mr. Dorion admitted that despite his affection for these people, attack was always possible.

Ordway's orderly mind led Lewis to wish he had named the sergeant quartermaster at the start and made him responsible for keeping records on all that was spent. He knew Will was right; when this was over the War Department would want an accounting. But he shuddered to think of trying years after the fact to remember what each one of those bits of paper was for and the rationale supporting it. He sighed and took up the roster.

Shannon . . . he was highly popular with almost everyone. Whatever his age, the brightness of youth shone in his face and he usually was smiling. Clark had told Lewis of an incident back on Wood River when they were improving the keelboat. Moses Reed, who fancied himself a better carpenter than he was, had objected to working alongside a snot-nosed kid, as he put it. Shannon stood up without a word and hit him what Clark had judged to be medium hard. Reed went down but bounced up and rushed the youngster. This time Shannon gave him a ferocious shot that broke his nose and left him unconscious, and that pretty well settled the question for everyone. He gave an equally good account of himself on the oars. He seemed to see the brutal labor as an exercise to build muscles.

His hero worship for Colter bore watching, Lewis said, until it was evident Colter kept it in bounds. Colter was an interesting man, fierce and deadly in a fight, ready for knife play if any were offered, self-contained, independent, and, Lewis imagined, entrepreneurial, though few fortunes would be made on this voyage. He and Ordway appeared to detest each other, rarely speaking and then cold as river ice.

The sergeant hadn't forgotten or forgiven Colter for drawing on him back on Wood River. Clark had called a court-martial on the matter but felt it was all overblown and recommended a light sentence, proforma penance, so to speak. Lewis felt that if Ordway would unbend Colter would respond but Ordway didn't and Colter treated him with a contained, almost polite venom. Lewis said he would regard each as equally guilty if there was more trouble and reminded them of army discipline. So, no fight but no love lost between them either.

On the other hand, Colter immediately grew close to Drewyer. Both were sophisticated hunters. Meat hunting was always crucial and while field duty was somewhat rotated, there being a number of skilled hunters in the crew, Drewyer and Colter were the most often called upon.

As Lewis had expected, the Field brothers, one ebullient and the other

not, were just as able on the hunt as they had promised and were strong
workers. Reuben's busy mouth stretched some of the men's patience thin
and from time to time Lewis told him enough was enough. Still, nothing
serious developed because the older brother stood by to make sure no
weapons flashed and Reuben could take care of himself with his fists.
During their occasional stops Joe Field asked to accompany Lewis on his
field forays and demonstrated surprising ornithological knowledge, all
self-taught, a quality Lewis understood and admired.

John Collins and Hugh Hall had disappointed sorely. They were quiet
fellows in Pryor's squad and all was uneventful until the night Collins was
on guard duty and decided a drink would help him stay awake. He tapped
the keg. The drink did go well and another would go even better. He was
drunk when he awakened Hall to relieve him. Did good old Hugh want a
drink? Why, don't mind if I do. In the morning both were drunk.

Clark called a court-martial. Collins pled not guilty. The court took tes-
timony from Ordway and sentenced Collins to one hundred lashes. Hall
pled guilty. Fifty lashes, the court said. Heavy switches were cut from
willow trees and laid across each man's back with vigor. There was muttering that they should be shot — imagine hogging whiskey that was for all
of us.

And then there was Moses Reed, a natural malcontent who had sold
himself originally on sunny good humor and willingness. He'd been among
the last to sign on and perhaps they were moving pretty fast then. Soon he
turned into a whiner with endless worries, dire predictions of trouble
ahead, all carried over an inherent anger. The work was too hard, they
should have more hands, the food was garbage, the whole project seemed
simpleminded. He hated Shannon but was afraid of him and avoided him.
The other men began to avoid Reed, which added to his distress. The men
all hate me, he told Lewis. The captain told him things were hard enough
without complaint, so his complaints now included Lewis as an inadequate
commander whose frequent forays left Clark to handle it all which put
Clark in a foul mood that he in turn took out on Moses Reed.

Now, the Corps of Discovery under way again, a new bungle. Floyd
presented Reed with a whine that he had lost his knife. Clark had supposed Reed was preparing a theft accusation against someone but no, he
said he remembered sticking it in a tree and didn't remember having it
after that. Clark told him they were beyond supply and knives were precious. He could go back and get the knife or do without. Reed slung his
rifle, requisitioned powder and ball, and started back.

They hadn't seen him since. Of course, it was always possible that he
had deserted, sorry bastard that he was.

They were moving along, north and a bit westward now, the sea of grass that marked the high plains up ahead. Miles and miles of grass that brushed a horseman's stirrups. Lewis couldn't wait to see that. Forest country was passing behind them now. The ash and oak, sycamore and walnut that had studded the river's floodplain now was replaced by ubiquitous cottonwoods. Again Lewis tramped the bluff, spontoon in hand, dog at his side. They were nearing Sioux territory and he had the Field brothers posted a hundred yards behind with rifles poised. All his senses were throbbing as he looked across what indeed was a sea of grass, no other term quite described it. The wind caressed it and swept shadows across it, rising and falling.

It stretched unbroken to infinity, great blue bowl of sky overhead, shade his eyes and a man could see forever and the wind blew with nothing to stop it in all that distance. It sucked moisture from the eyes and roared in the ears, so strong it would flutter a hat brim. The wind was maddening to some, isolating to others, exciting to a few. Lewis fell in the latter group—he liked the idea of air sweeping unbroken across a thousand miles of hard and dusty land to blow in his face.

And then, ruminations forgotten, he came to the damnedest sight—a dusty mound of earth with a swollen, disturbed look that proved to be pocked with holes and that went on and on as far as he could see. And scurrying about collecting grass and seed were hundreds or thousands or maybe millions for all he knew of odd little animals. Probably they would classify as rodents but were not like mice or rats or squirrels. The big dog stared with what seemed equal amazement and then lunged ahead barking—and the little creatures barked back! Raced for their holes, each seeming to know just where it was going, poised themselves looking erect and proud and even belligerent over the holes and barked. You could say it whistled or squeaked but to Lewis it sounded just like a toy dog sitting on a woman's lap and barking his head off. It sat up on its haunches, forepaws clasped together, and with each yelp it jerked its little tail as if voice and tail were one. When the dog lunged toward them they stared for a moment in apparent outrage and then with vast angry squeaking dropped into their holes and disappeared, leaving an eerie silence. The big dog hesitated, then began to dig at the nearest hole.

He was down a foot or more before he gave up and sat back disconsolately with his tongue hanging out while all around the little creatures reappeared and barked at him, sounding collectively furious. Lewis knew he must catch one to examine and dissect so his report could describe it properly. This was just the sort of new and surprising creature that would thrill his scientific mentor in Washington. He halted the boats and they camped on a midstream island. He gathered a party of men to dig out the little beasts with shovels. Dozens of interlocking tunnels were opened. They could hear the animals barking and squeaking in distant dens. When they were down six feet with the tunnels going still deeper, he decided to try water.

They brought up barrels from the boats and filled them with river water carried up in buckets. When they emptied the barrels into the hole they'd dug the water disappeared into still more distant chambers. But only one of the creatures emerged, drenched and sputtering; the others had escaped through the interlocking tunnels. Seaman caught this single specimen; Lewis would dissect it immediately. Back in camp Cruzatte gave hoots of laughter when he saw their prize. The little critters were what the voyageurs called *petit chien*, little dog of the prairie or prairie dog, famous for their elusiveness in their vast villages. But it was new to science, another of their discoveries.

They set off again at dawn, boats pushing against hard current on the northward turn of the river, the land changing as they climbed, Lewis marching ashore again. What wonderful little creatures. How did they drink, so far from the river? Well . . . they must metabolize the minute quantities of water in the vegetation on which they fed. The idea had a pleasing symmetry with the sere country. Prairie dogs . . . the president would be delighted with the very notion of little *chiens* barking at the vast arid sky. They would stir that open, eclectic, far-ranging mind that was so constantly in motion. Perhaps that explained Mr. J's awful headaches where the very light of day seemed to torture him—maybe so active a mind just wore down sometimes. How different from Lewis's own urgencies and doubts and limitations and wondering if he would ever amount to much. You wouldn't catch Mr. J wondering if he had any value in the world. Of course, he was a proven success, but still, Lewis saw no sign he'd ever had a moment's doubt, whereas Lewis—

The old dark was crowding the edges of his mind, the gloomy doubts, the conviction that nothing would ever go really well. That wouldn't do, not now, not here on the great adventure. Then he saw dust swirling ahead on the unbroken wind and presently a figure, a man leading a horse oddly refracted in the golden light. He unslung his rifle, shifting the spontoon to his left hand. Coming close, he recognized Drewyer with a deer carcass on the horse's back. The scout offered an easy way down to the river but Lewis needed longer alone to deal with the very sort of mood Mr. J had warned him against.

As he marched over country that few white men had even seen, distant dust glowing in the lowering sun, spontoon light in his hand, big dog frisking tirelessly, the dark crowding the edges of his mind faded as he worked through dreams come true. A bit of the mood was always there but he could back it off.

The fires would be going below and perhaps they had landed a mess of catfish. Suddenly he was very hungry and at the same time it struck him that he was quite exposed alone on the bluff with night coming on. He whistled to the dog and went back to Drewyer's route down to the river. He saw Clark standing spread-legged below looking up. He waved and Clark's arm came up in an answering wave that said all was well, and Lewis thought there was no place on earth he would rather be at this moment than on this stretch of the Missouri coming up on the Great Plains, westward bound.

22

On the Missouri, Summer, 1804

John Colter's voice was hoarse, Shannon noted, the way he sometimes sounded when he was looking at a woman. It was the day after Mr. Dorion joined the party.

"Did you see them furs? What that white-haired old bastard is sending on to St. Louis. See 'em? Worth a damn fortune."

For a terrible moment Shannon thought John Colter was inviting him to help steal this fortune in furs. But then he remembered seeing Colter talking with the half-breed voyageurs. His friend had a smattering of French, which Shannon envied, having no head for language himself. Out of Colter's hearing, Joe Field said with a touch of contempt that Colter didn't speak French at all, only sort of a lingua franca. Shannon didn't know quite what that was, but Colter understood what the Frenchmen told him, more or less, so what did it matter? Anyway, Joe Field was a prig, so Colter said and Shannon pretty much agreed, talking about books he'd read, or said he'd read. In some ways he was worse than Reuben. Shannon shared Colter's view that both of the Field brothers were a pain in the ass.

"Hundreds of pelts, each one of 'em worth a pretty penny in St. Louis and worth that tenfold in New York if you can get them there," he said in that same avid whisper. "Now, them three Frenchmen, they took every one of them over the season, within the last year — Dorion, he don't trap, he takes care of the Yanktons for them and makes sure they get a fair price in St. Louis. This is wonderful country, George — a man couldn't help but get rich out here in trapper heaven where the beaver got nothing to do but sit in them dams they make and breed little beavers."

"Maybe trapping's not so easy," George said.

John Colter grunted. "Well, of course it ain't. Wading in an icy stream to set traps, knees aching, chilblains on your hands, but thinking of the price each one fetches, that warms you up. Anyway, prices they bring, after a couple or three years you got a stake so big you can take 'em to New York yourself. I been thinking about this and by God, I intend to get in on it. Cut you in, too, never you fear." He smacked a fist into his palm. "I been pore all my life but by God, I ain't gonna die pore."

This made Shannon uncomfortable. Colter was always deciding his future for him before he even thought about it. He shifted to something he'd been brooding over. "John, how come you think the cap'n don't never send me out on the hunt?"

Colter gave him a measuring look, something hidden in his face. "I don't know," he said. "You asked him?"

"No . . . but he knows I'm good. Why, once I —"

"Don't tell me about them damned squirrels again. I heard all I need on that."

Shannon tried to hide his chagrin and hurt. Colter watched him a moment, then said more gently, "You want me to ask him?"

Nothing more was said. They got started, two or three weeks passed, they made some miles, the terrain began to change. Not a word and Shannon assumed it all had been forgotten. Certainly he wouldn't risk another sneer — anyway, everything was different now, for they were coming into buffalo country. The other day Joe Field had shot one of the great shaggy beasts and had come running back to the river to stop the boat and call for the horses to pack in the kill. Turned out buffalo meat was rich with fat and delicious beyond expression, as good as beaver tail and a hell of a lot more of it. Since then Drewyer had killed four buffalo and they had jerked some of the meat.

A week more passed and they were well up the northern leg. Shannon was helping load the boat one morning when Cap'n Clark drew him aside.

"Drewyer saw buffalo about two miles to the east last night. I want you to take both horses to pack the meat and go get one or even two if you can. It's time we started jerking a real supply." He gave Shannon an appraising look. "Let's see how good a hunter you are. When you start back cut an angle that'll bring you up the river a ways and be back tonight."

Yes, *sir!*

That night, while Lewis was shooting star sights and calling coordinates to Clark, he said, "Shannon didn't get back?"

"Nah. Probably the buffler strayed. A night in the woods won't hurt him—says he's some hunter, so he's spent a few nights out, I expect. But Reed ain't back either and he's long overdue. I'll send Drewyer out for him tomorrow."

"Deserted, you think?"

"I expect," Clark said. "He's a sorry son of a bitch."

"Drewyer may need some help."

"I thought I'd send Shields. Fair to give them authority to kill him if he resists, don't you think?"

"Certainly. Desertion in the face of the enemy."

The day had quickly disintegrated for Shannon. There weren't any damned buffalo, that was the first thing. Shannon already had gone two miles. Or more. Probably more. Been a couple of hours, he thought. Even with stops to scan the horizon, he could walk ten miles in a couple of hours. Well, not ten, maybe, but a lot more than two. You could see in this country, too; after you left the cottonwoods along the river's floodplain it was pretty much open prairie, grass a foot or more, damned horses wanting to stop and graze every minute or so, jerking on their lead lines. Looking back it was hard to tell where the river was now, being as it was down in a cut, you might call it.

Of course, the buffalo could be down in one of the little draws set up by small creeks running through the grass. The ground sort of waved like a flag rippling even though it looked level. And then, so he supposed, anyway, buffalo could cover two, three miles an hour while grazing. Did they stop and bed down at night? He wasn't sure. But overall, they could make good time overnight if they chose. Anyway, seemed like they were gone. Which, damn it, wasn't his fault. But this had been his one chance to establish himself as a hunter and he sure didn't want to come back empty-handed. But time had been passing, the sun long since had cracked the meridian and was falling rapidly toward the west. He'd better turn around. Yes, and face the ridicule of the men.

But then he saw disturbance in the grass ahead of him and hurried forward, and he had them. Or had their tracks, at least, grass beat down, cropped short in places, hoofprints where the ground was soft, cow pats here and there. Things were back in control, quarry in his sights—eagerly he hurried on, following the tracks. But he didn't come on the animals and the sun sank lower and then, quite suddenly, it was dark. He came to a small creek and watered the horses, then drank himself. He tied the horses to small but sturdy bushes, ate a crust of roast buffalo he had salvaged from the night before, and eventually, with his stomach rumbling, he slept.

Drewyer and Shields returned with Moses Reed.

"He was sitting in a clearing when we come on him," Drewyer said. "Gave me the feeling he was waiting, expecting us, don't you see. Like he'd gotten scared, all by himself. He's lucky a war party didn't get there ahead of us."

Clark assembled a court-martial, Sergeant Pryor presiding. Pryor looked somewhat drawn to Clark, but maybe that was just distaste for the whole proceeding, for its necessity and for its near-certain result. Pryor asked how he pled, and standing very straight Reed answered briskly, "Guilty." Clark's eyebrows rose at that. The prisoner asked if he might make a statement. Pryor nodded. Reed said he pleaded guilty because he was guilty, had intended to desert, did steal a government rifle with powder and shot, and now asked the court and the captains to be as lenient with him as their perception of duty might allow.

Clark met with the court. Reed's unexpectedly manly candor appealed to them all. Execution, while within their power, clearly would be excessive. The sentence: run the gauntlet of the whole party four times, each man armed with nine switches cut from a willow tree and designed to do considerable but not permanent damage. He was to be discharged from the Corps of Discovery and join Warfington's crew in the white pirogue, winter with that group at the Mandan Villages, and return with it to St. Louis in the spring, separated and disgraced.

Shannon awakened from fitful sleep punctuated with starts awake and savage dreams. The first hints of dawn appeared in the east but the light was strong enough to see that one of the horses was gone. The horse still present, a placid bay, was lying down with legs folded. The missing critter, a young sorrel gelding of rambunctious nature, had left a small hole where he'd jerked out the bush that Shannon had supposed would hold him and had set off dragging it behind him, leaving a clear trail. Unfortunately the horse didn't follow the buffalo trail. Shannon had to choose.

He followed the horse since he would be the more a laughingstock if he lost one of their two horses. He realized he now was seriously hungry. He had seen little or no game though the country was supposed to be full of wildlife. He caught movement from the corner of his eye and whirled to see a fat rabbit. He drew a quick bead and fired. The rabbit jumped but didn't fall. Reloaded and fired again, twice. The last time he clearly hit the rabbit but the damned critter still could hop away. It struck him he might not be either the skilled hunter or marksman on which he had placed such pride.

Better go after the missing horse, ride the bay to run down the sorrel. But there was no saddle or bridle or stirrups, just a packhorse halter. Back on the farm he had ridden bareback, but now he realized that he was no great shakes as a horseman, either. He drew the bay close by the halter rope and tried to jump on its back. The bay moved adroitly and Shannon fell beside it, hanging on to the rope. The horse snorted. He took a dozen tumbles, clinging to the halter rope. He was furious and lashed the horse with the rope. This made the critter more skittish. Still, with the morning wearing on, he managed at last to pull the beast close with the rope, then seize its mane and vault onto its back. It gave a tentative leap as if to buck but gave it up after a few more licks from the rope end.

The trail he followed bore steadily away from the river. The sun was still high when he saw the stray but catching it was another matter. It simply galloped ahead whenever he drew near. He thought of galloping along behind and leaping off to seize the rope, still tied to the bush. But that risked losing the horse he had without catching the stray.

At last, with the sun sinking rapidly, he gave it up at a small stream. He watered the horse, tied its lead line around his waist, and tried to shoot a rabbit. His hands were shaking. His belly felt wrapped around his backbone, so hungry was he. Perspiration stood on his upper lip as he aimed. He fired four times before the rabbit's head disappeared. Shannon skinned the slender little body and roasted it over a fire he struck with his flint and steel. He sucked the bones when he was done and still was hungry. How many times had he fired? He wasn't sure now. He hefted the powder horn and found it still half full. Then, uneasily, he felt in his shot pouch. It was empty. He sat gazing at the waning light to the east. He was alone with an empty weapon, one horse gone and the other fractious, and the truth was he didn't know where the hell he was. Eventually he slept with the horse's lead rope still tied around his waist.

Clark awoke with a start. It was near daylight and there had been no wake-up call. It was the duty of the last guard shift to catch that moment when dawn was ready to break and walk about the camp clicking two sticks together—loud enough to bring tired men to wakefulness but not to signal the whole countryside. Who was on the watch list? Let's see—yes, Willard had the last watch. Just then he saw Sergeant Ordway hurrying toward him, a look of fury mottling his usually even expression.

"Cap'n," he said, voice cast low. "Come—I want you to see something."

Clark followed and in a moment saw Willard stretched flat, hands cradling his head for a pillow, sound asleep! Holy God—the whole Sioux nation could have crept in and murdered them in their sleep!

Alex Willard was a big man. He came from New Hampshire, and was rarely ruffled. He wore a somewhat sleepy expression that was not reassuring and was far from the brightest member of the party, but until now he had been a good soldier, quick to obey orders, slow to make trouble. Now he breathed gently in sleep, making a faint whistle.

Clark stepped close and gave him a smashing kick in the ribs, putting all his weight behind his boot. Willard grunted, came awake, rolled onto his knees in one motion, and looked up in bewilderment. "What happened?" he said.

"You slept on guard, you lazy son of a bitch."

Calculation flashed across Willard's face. "I warn't asleep, Cap'n. I lay down a moment, I admit that, resting, you know, but I was awake, I heard you—"

"On your feet, you lying bastard."

The offense was deadly serious. They were in Sioux territory and had been warned repeatedly that their presence might trigger armed combat with a foe that vastly outnumbered them. Sleeping on guard duty— army regulations made the death penalty an option for this offense. In this case the captains themselves sat as the court, the men listening closely. Willard insisted he had been awake and pled guilty only to lying down on duty, not guilty to sleeping. In the face of the evidence, he swiftly was found guilty. The penalty was flogging, almost the only punishment short of execution that was available on the trail. The captains purposely made it harsh—fifty strokes on his bare back every morning for four mornings with no relief from his duty on the oars. They stopped short of flogging with a heavy leather strap let alone one with studs. Instead Clark cut a switch from a willow that was nearly a half-inch thick and quite certain to stripe his back.

The men were drawn into military formation, squads in three ranks, standing at parade rest to witness this fierce punishment. Willard screamed on the tenth stroke and on nearly every stroke after. He was sobbing when they cut him down. And this was just the first day.

The men were silent, not disapproving but grim. Willard had put all their lives at risk and deserved his punishment but there was no pleasure in witnessing it.

Now a new concern gripped Shannon. He was being left behind. The expedition was moving rapidly upriver, the captains driving the men, doubtless concerned with implacable deadlines. All the time he was dawdling in the woods they gained and gained on him. He remembered that Cap'n Clark had warned him to cut a few degrees to the north on his return. He'd been due back the same night and he had paid little attention. But the river was to the west, he'd been pretty much going east in his pursuit first of buffalo, then of the horse. Cut to the north on return, hold toward the right. What the cap'n had meant, he'd meant they weren't going to wait for anyone and certainly not for someone who didn't know any better than to get lost.

He came to a grove of plum trees and his heart lifted, but the fruit was small and hard, still green, sour beyond bearing. He found berries still green and wild grapes green on their vines, tried to chew them and then spat them out. He might not be as good as he'd thought he was but he was enough of a countryman to know that green fruit would sicken you without nourishing.

He walked in a westerly fashion, bearing a little to the right, leading the horse, watching for game. He had found a small stick that was nicely straight and would just fit in the barrel of his rifle. Rabbits had been sporting about as if word had been passed in the kingdom of rabbits that George Shannon had used up all his ammunition and was an impotent fool and could safely be ignored. Now he stopped the horse and let it graze. He tied the lead rope to his wrist, lay on the ground, and waited for a fat rabbit to appear in his sights. One did. He waited. Just as he was ready to fire the horse stepped way, the line jerked his arm, the rifle fired, the stick flew harmlessly.

He had a sudden startling impulse to cry. Hadn't felt that in years, eyes tearing up. He was dismayed. Thank God he was alone. John Colter wasn't here to see him disgrace himself. He recharged the rifle, pouring powder down the barrel, tamping it with wadding, splashing powder in the pan. He had to look a bit but presently he found the stick and put it back in the barrel. He tied the lead rope to his ankle this time and waited on another rabbit. When he located one he waited for it to come near, then fired. The stick flew true, knocked over the animal, and then shattered against a rock.

Quickly he got a fire going and while it took hold skinned and dissected the little body. This rabbit proved smaller than the one he'd taken the other night but it was just as succulent and rich and he demolished it in short order. When he was done he felt immeasurably better and saw that he had better get a move on. The expedition was hurrying up the river, leaving him farther behind. He trotted a little in his agitation but that proved too much for him and he stopped, dizzy, and then walked on, westerly bearing perhaps northwest by west.

"Shannon ain't back, Cap'n," Colter said. He had just witnessed the third day of Willard's agony and felt distressed. "He's gotten himself lost, I expect. Permission to go look for him? He ain't another Reed, you know."

"No," Clark said, "I thought about that and decided he would never desert. Not Shannon. Maybe he's hurt. Maybe he's not as competent in open country as he thinks he is."

"Yes, sir," Colter said. "That could be."

Rifle in hand, a careful supply of powder and balls in his pack along with a goodly supply of jerked venison, Colter set out, walking eastward, his course bending a little to the south to accommodate the distance the flotilla had covered. Presently he found what he took for Shannon's footprints. Then what might be the mark of a herd, dried cow pats here and there. The sign of a man leading two horses continued eastward. Then where Shannon apparently had stopped, then the mark of a horse moving away alone. Lost one of the horses . . .

Foreboding growing, Colter walked on.

Shannon found no more sticks to fit in his rifle. He paced along, leading the horse, feeling a little weak to try to mount it. He had to be near the river, he was sure he was almost there. When he stopped at dark he felt dizzy, started to lie down, and fell the rest of the way. His gut howled for food. He thought he should be planning his next move, for the expedition was moving away from him, but he couldn't get beyond how his gut could talk to him, speaking English, or so it seemed. When he next focused daylight was bright and he'd slept through the night. He got up and staggered, feeling better but not that much better. He drank from a creek and went on.

Colter was worried. He'd lost Shannon's track in a sandy patch that went on and on and had come back to the boats hoping to find the young man already returned. It wasn't like Shannon not to come back. Maybe he was hurt. More than one man had shot himself trying to get his piece loaded and primed.

"Cap'n," Colter said, "I fear for young Shannon. Me and Drewyer, I think we should go find him. Two of us, we can cover this way and that. Boy's already lost one horse. Sioux probably had a hand in that and they might have Shannon too."

Clark nodded. "So I've been thinking. Go and find him or find sign that something's happened to him."

Shannon had been following a small creek on the theory that it just about had to be heading for the river. It wound back and forth like an imitation river in its own right but he stayed a little above it and was able to cut across its turns. Then, when the gouge it was making in the prairie deepened he looked ahead and saw what looked like a falloff. And sure enough, when he lurched ahead a panorama spread before him and across the floodplain he saw the bright flash of the Missouri, sweeping in long and gorgeous turns. He saw no sign of the boats but maybe they were hidden in one of those turns.

Strengthened by the sight, he hurried back to the little creek and followed it down to the floodplain and across that expanse to the river proper. Still no boats. So, just as he had feared, they had gone ahead. Cap'n Clark had warned him, after all, told him to bear north, and that meant they wouldn't be waiting around for the likes of him. They were going to the Pacific and God knew how many hundreds or thousands of miles that would be, so how could they wait around every time someone wandered off and got lost?

So it was up to him to catch up. He brought the horse near one of the plum trees, its branches full of unripe fruit. Bracing against the tree, he managed to get astride the beast. The boats must follow the river bend for bend but he could cut across those big looping turns and he was bound to catch up. He went on in rising spirits.

"Cap'n," Colter said to Clark, "me and Drewyer, we searched all over and didn't find no sign. He ain't lying hurt somewhere or there'd be buzzard sign. Or dead or dying with his hair lifted, no such sign. Been gone ten days or so now and it just don't make sense. I think the Sioux have him and sooner we find some of them bastards the better. They may be holding him, some kind of bargaining business planned or somesuch, but we find them, I'll go in myself, kill as many of 'em as need be and bring him out. That just about has to be the answer."

"That'll do, Mr. Colter. We'll have no talk of killing no matter what. As to whether they have Shannon, Mr. Dorion can sort that out, I'm sure."

Colter wasn't so sure and if they had Shannon there might be some killing whether the cap'n liked it or not. But he let it go for now, seeing as how it upset the cap'n so badly.

Shannon knew he was coming to the end of his string. He saw a big bird overhead. A buzzard? Those dirty bastard birds knew a dead man even before he was dead. Knew the signs. And that was how he felt, too, like the signs were all around him.

He went all that day, all the next day, and started again. But now he could see the chances of catching up were just about zero. Every time he sat down, even when he fell down, he went to sleep. No clear idea how long he slept. The sun told you the time but now he couldn't remember where it had been before. There were fish in the river but no way to catch them. He tried to creep up on turtles basking in the sun but they waited until he reached for them and then tipped into the muddy water and disappeared.

It was just too much. He had done what he could. They had hurried on and now were far ahead and he was abandoned. The big bird overhead told the story. He awakened and looked longingly up the river as he always did. Nothing. Sheet of empty water. But the sun hurt his eyes and he turned away and looked down the river and now he saw boats. Keelboat and two pirogues. Was he dreaming? He shook his head. No, they were still there. Then he was on his feet, weakness forgotten, shouting in a voice that sounded like a whisper and maybe was and waving his arms, and yes, the keelboat turned toward him, yes, there was Cap'n Clark standing in the stern, John Colter at the bow.

And then he understood. He had been *ahead* of them all along. He had cut too far to the north, in his worry he had assumed more speed than they could manage, and now he had been desperately hurrying along, each agonized mile putting him farther ahead.

His knees were wobbly. The boat ground into the sandy shore and he saw John Colter jump lightly ashore. His knees were really going now and he staggered toward Colter with his arms out and Colter caught him and held him a moment and then lowered him.

"George," Colter said, "where the hell you been?"

23

June slipped into July, July into August. Lewis issued a double ration of whiskey on the Fourth and much good cheer echoed in the camp. But then the weather shifted. Gone were the crystalline skies, the pleasant temperatures with an edge of coolness. Now it was plain old hot, painfully so. They traveled on constant alert for Sioux warriors, more concerned with safety than with the splendors of the country.

They came to the vast Platte River. Dorion repeated the trapper quip that it ran a mile wide and an inch deep. It constantly formed new channels as it broke from old channels, creating a jumble like a woman's braids. Huge hunks of the bank broke off, sand crumbling into the water, throwing full-grown trees into the water to ride the current as so many battering rams that could sink a boat in a single blow.

The constantly moving rivulets dammed themselves into still water frequently and here mosquitoes bred by the millions. At dawn and dusk they buzzed so close, in such mass, that they became a constant snarling threat. The men built smudge fires and sat in the smoke that drifted lazily through the camp. On sheer impulse Lewis had bought a supply of mosquito nets that allowed the men to sleep in relative comfort, sentries coughing in smudge fire smoke.

The sun blazed out of a hazy sky. Half a dozen men were felled by sunstroke. Robert Frazer was out of his head. Sergeant Floyd, gone paler than the white sky, vomited over the side and fainted in a single motion. He was half out of the keelboat before someone pulled him back. He lay on the walkway the locker lids made around the coaming and moaned. After a while he rolled into a ball, arms clutched over his belly, gasping and choking. He moaned and cursed and shook his head when men tried to talk to him. Clark diagnosed it as bilious colic and summoned Lewis.

Lewis was the doctor for the expedition. He knew almost nothing but he also knew that most physicians of the day knew little more. Like most frontiersmen, both Lewis and Clark could deal with a surface wound, set broken bones, extract bullets and arrowheads, and cope with common ailments like croup and dysentery.

Lewis remembered Ma teaching Mary Beth the intricacies of folk medicine; she was famous for her herbal treatments, people came from miles around to consult her on difficult cases and births. He had always figured that Ma's comfortable, confident manner had a lot to do with her cures, and the last time he saw Mary Beth that same quality was evident in her. She would know the right herbal dose for you, the right food to set you straight, when you should lie down and be cosseted and when you should get moving and forget your ailment. Life would be good with Mary Beth and now that he was far from home facing grim realities and responsibilities he was the more sensible to what such a woman could mean in a man's life. But never mind such maudlin thoughts—now he had a man on his hands who surely looked and acted as if he were at death's door, who was looking at him piteously for rescue and for surcease of the pain.

What would Benjamin Rush say? His mind summoned up the spare, limber old man in Philadelphia, said to be the best doctor in America and certainly the most famous. Got back from a medical education in Edinburgh, the acknowledged focus of world medical learning, in time to sign the Declaration that separated us from Britain and had been serving mankind ever since. Lewis had found him bright as a button, full of wit and good cheer. They had sat together hours taking occasional nips from a bottle of rum as the doctor described difficult cases and how he had cured them or whether the uncooperative patient had died.

"I'll tell you, Merry," Dr. Rush said in a flatteringly intimate tone, two men of knowledge, professionals, talking on equal terms, each respecting the other, "the blood is the key to it all. We have too much blood anyway, you know, so naturally some of it goes bad from time to time. Yes, sir, bad blood. I bleed all my patients. Always have my pocket lancet with me." At which he displayed a small folding knife with a razor-edged blade. He said he honed the blade on a stone after each use. "Slit a vein neat and steady, catch the blood in a basin, and then study it. Look for how loose or how tight it is, look at how dark it is or whether some is dark, some bright."

Then there were his patented pills composed of calomel, jalap, and a mixture of six parts mercury to one part chlorine. "Each a purgative of strength," the doctor said happily, "put them together and they blow through a man's bowels like a hurricane. A tornado of the gut, sir. Clean out everything he's eaten for a month, cleans the system as a ramrod cleans a rifle barrel, wipes it clean, sir. All the poisons go."

Lewis swore by thunderclappers. Now he peered into the case he had had made for his medicines. Rush's Pills of course, the milder physic, for milder problems, emetic to induce vomiting, pills to induce the body to sweat, which was another excellent way to rid the body of the poisons afflicting it. In a separate compartment he had lancets, clyster syringe, scapeis, a pewter penis syringe for gonorrhea's discomforts.

But now he had a desperately ill man and no more to go on than his medicine chest and memories of the great doctor making it all sound easy and natural. But it wasn't easy. Lewis was sweating as he thought about it, and not just from the heat. Floyd was watching him with a strange mixture of hope and despair in his eyes. Suddenly Lewis thought of a doe he'd shot once and found still alive but dying. The animal had gazed up with that same resignation, her life ebbing, her eyes crying for help and, he thought, for compassion, life to life. He had put his hand on her head and smoothed it as he might pet a dog, and she had sighed and then the light in her eyes faded. It had unsettled him somehow and he had hesitated a moment before beginning to butcher the now inert body.

He shook his head, not liking the memory as he wiped Floyd's face of the sweat that stood in heavy droplets. He ordered the boat landed and Floyd carried ashore where he could be made more comfortable, but the pain seemed even worse. He remembered the handsome young man's attack that first day but it was nothing like this. He'd been well the next day, and certainly Floyd had pulled his own so far, never shirking, never falling short. But the pain seemed to have come more and more often. He rarely complained but that paleness, the sudden quiet, the tension in his expression told the story. Lewis had asked him a few times if he was ill but each time Floyd had insisted it was naught but occasional colic and Lewis couldn't really challenge him. Maybe the man was simply terrified that the officers would send him back if they thought he was seriously ill. Or maybe he couldn't admit that possibility to himself.

But this had been going on a long time, and it wasn't bilious colic. It had to be something much more serious and now it was worse. Lewis asked him to describe the pain and he could only grunt and cry and writhe. Lewis felt he was seeing whatever it was come to a head and demand resolution right before his eyes.

He hesitated, then gave the patient a thunderclapper. It sure enough cleaned him out. They had to carry him to the freshly dug latrine pit where he voided his bowels in a black gush. But it seemed to make him no better. Put the mosquito netting over him and gave him a sweat pill and the water poured off him. When Lewis held up his head so he could drink warm water he rolled to one side and vomited. And the pain got worse. Whimpers became yelps and gasps. Where, where? All over him, he was a knot of pain from his eyes to his ankles.

He was like a soldier gut-shot in battle. Soldiers made it a point to eat nothing when a battle was expected so if they took a ball in the belly their intestines would be as empty as possible. It was the torn intestine dumping its feces into the abdominal cavity that set up the blood poisoning that gave a gut-shot soldier only hours to live, and those were horribly painful hours.

Clark sat up with him that night. They were family friends, his pa had marched with General Clark, and Clark couldn't bear the thought of losing him and going home to report to the father. Floyd whimpered and writhed through the night. Lewis poured laudanum into him and at last, his eyes getting hazy, he slept.

In the morning he was no better. Yet there was nothing to be gained here so they rigged a stretcher and put him aboard the boat and cast off. He cried and writhed. Laudanum seemed to have no effect now. At about ten in the morning Clark saw his lips moving and bent his ear close to hear.

"I'm going. I want you to write a letter—"

Thus Sergeant Charles Floyd died. Later it struck them that he was the first American soldier to die west of the Mississippi. The thought proved cold comfort.

They landed the boat where a small river entered the Missouri, wrapped Floyd's body in a blanket, carried it to the top of a knoll, and buried it with full military honors, Lewis reading the sonorous words. They cut his name, title, and the date into a red cedar post that they fixed over the grave.

That night Clark wrote Floyd's epitaph in his journal: "This Man at all times gave us proofs of his firmness and Deturmined resolution to doe Service to his Countrey and honor to himself." A soldier's epitaph.

Much later it occurred to Lewis that Floyd might have had an infected appendix. Doctors were just coming to understand that this miserable little worm growing somewhere in the abdominal cavity could get infected with unknown evils and perforate or tear and dump its poisons right into the bloodstream. Maybe that was the functional equivalent of a gut-shot soldier's torn bowels pouring fecal matter into his abdominal cavity and flowing thence as pure poison into his bloodstream. Maybe a ruptured appendix was what had killed Charles Floyd. Apparently this thing in the body had no use, did nothing good or bad, except when it got infected. Made you wonder what God had in his mind, putting something so useless but so deadly in the human body.

24

Dorion's trading fort on Cedar Island stood empty and silent a year after he'd been forced to abandon it. Gates hung askew, grass grew undisturbed, and though its well water was sweet and clear, animals now lived in its buildings. With sad pride Dorion showed the captains the construction, sixty feet to a side, walls of thirteen-foot pickets, bastions at opposite corners for enfilading fire.

With a platoon of regulars and adequate supply, Lewis knew he could hold this fort forever, but Dorion and his trader-voyageurs had been driven out in a year by a chief of the Bois Brulé division of the Sioux whose name translated as the "Partisan." There was an uneasy note in old Dorion's voice when he talked of the Partisan and his eyes flicked about as if that fearsome man might pop from the bushes and abuse him again. As Dorion described him the Indian fitted his name. He was a massive man, very dark, a messianic gleam in his eyes, and he dominated the river up ahead.

Lewis listened carefully; they were entering Bois Brulé country now and Dorion, their language link to the Sioux, was leaving in the morning. Said he was worried about his family back in the Yankton Sioux village; Lewis had an idea he was even more worried about the Partisan. The Bois Brulés were the most threatening division of a tribe already notorious for abusing traders. And indeed, Dorion looked ready to weep as he described the chaos the Partisan had worked.

Lewis understood only fragments, so fractured and accented was Dorion's English, but apparently the Indians landed on the north end of the island at night and slipped through the woods to burst onto the fort with yells and sudden loud drumbeats. The Partisan would stride into the fort as the traders offered food and drink. Laughing, the Partisan might pinch out the candles and turn his men loose to loot in the darkness. In another mood he snatched blankets and other goods from the shelves and tossed them to his men, eyeing the white men with menace.

The Partisan announced that an Indian need only lay hand on a vessel's mooring line to claim it for his own with all its contents. Seizing every vessel would have killed trade, but Dorion had lost two pirogues with most of their contents. These were the folks the Corps of Discovery was advancing to meet.

They were coming into the short-grass prairie that marked the start of the High Plains. Suddenly game was everywhere, elks in stately herds, deer in every copse, buffalo abruptly common. They began seeing a small deer with long and sharp pronghorns that looked a bit like paintings he'd seen of African antelopes. This critter surely was new to America; it ran like the wind, too fast for Lewis to clock but he estimated the swiftest race-horse couldn't catch it. He called it an antelope for lack of a better term.

The sun was bright sky but the debilitating heat had passed. The air was cool at dawn and Lewis watched geese forming vast V's overhead, soldiers honking angrily to straighten the lines. Fall was in the air as they came into the Partisan's country.

The Sioux were the most important tribe on the known part of the Missouri, which was to say this side of the Mandan villages. Mr. Jefferson had made that point repeatedly—bring these Indians into the friendliest possible relationship with the new proprietors. Naturally, he went on—a favorite idea he seemed to cherish—the Sioux were equally anxious for a warm relationship with us. Clark's eyebrows had shot up over this. Really?

Further, Dorion had said the Partisan was working for British traders. If he could put the Sioux fur trade in their hands they would make him a power, meaning replace the cheap shotguns they once had offered with fine rifles and supply the Partisan's men with good quality powder to replace the weak stuff that was all Indians could lay hands on, powder that often misfired or gave a disgracefully weak *poof* and struck so light a blow that the buffalo galloped right on over the horizon. So the British were offering him wealth and wealth is power in any society. Other tribes must bow before Sioux with superior arms.

While Mr. Jefferson's hopes for the Sioux might be wishful thinking, the facts underlying them were realistic. The fact that Napoleon had agreed to sell and this was now American territory made the young nation on the Atlantic a full-fledged rival to the old European nations—the dying Spanish empire, Britain holding the frozen north and wanting more, Russian seal hunters carrying their flag within striking distance of Puget Sound. If the body of North America was to be none of the above and American instead, a connection to those who called it home was important. And here was Meriwether Lewis and his men in a keelboat and two pirogues on the forefront of American policy, so to speak. It was sobering.

And then there was commerce. Indians, just moving from a pure hunter-gatherer society to a mixed society hungry for industrial artifacts, were new to the game and had nothing but fur to offer. Most of that now was draining northward via British and French traders. With the United States suddenly interested in the whole North American continent, that no longer would do. Trade from American territory belonged in American hands. Let Indian fur come down the Missouri via traders to St. Louis and thence to New York, London, and ultimately the vastly higher prices American wilderness fur brought in the Orient.

Clark smiled as Lewis brought recitation to a close. The night was cool, and they sat near the fire. "Sounds like you're telling me this Partisan is a mighty important fellow."

"Better we make him a friend. Shoot him only if we must."

Something awakened him. A noise, certainly, but what? He couldn't identify it. Ashore he would think of an animal in the brush and almost immediately he would think of a man crawling closer for the attack. But he was aboard the keelboat as were most of his men and it was anchored midstream. He had reserved a spot for himself on the roof of the boat's cabin, very conscious that he was in at least potentially enemy country.

He rolled on his belly, his head up, listening. The moon had buried itself on the far horizon but bright stars cast a pale light. He saw no movement on either side, no shadows gathering on the shore, no bulky rafts or slender canoes poised to enter the river. Clark had been asleep in the cockpit astern of the cabin and Lewis saw the noise had awakened him, too. He glanced up at Lewis and shrugged. A shuffling noise now and Lewis turned to see Colter picking his way among sleeping bodies. Colter had the watch and he'd seen Lewis studying the shore.

"Fish, I think, Cap'n. They been jumping the last half hour. One just hit the boat. Might be there's a gar down there."

Lewis nodded. Not gar but maybe a pike on the prowl, little fish darting out of the way. Then the noise again and yes, it was a wet slapping sound. Clark glanced up with a smile and settled back into blankets. Lewis, wide awake now, rolled on his back and rested his head on laced fingers and watched the stars reel overhead, assessing once again the distance they'd come, the vastly greater distance that remained.

They were two days beyond Cedar Island. Dorion had departed, and they must rely on Cruzatte for translation at the meeting set for today.

The little one-eyed half-breed said he was fluent in the Sioux tongue but Lewis feared the worst. Both Drewyer and Cruzatte had resented Dorion for his language skills.

They had toiled upriver and had seen no Indians, though atavistic intuition told him they had been under observation. Then three youths fishing from the north bank swam out to greet them and reported there were two temporary camps of Brulés on the next entering river. Clark gave them two carrots of tobacco and sent them off to say the white men came as friends and wanted a meeting. Now with dawn breaking in the east, the captains expected the Brulés just before noon. A sailcloth awning held aloft by tent poles gave them shade and the flag waved overhead from a slender pole.

The Brulés arrived about eleven bearing slabs of well roasted buffalo and pemmican made of lean venison strips pounded into paste with bear fat and dried fruit and formed into patties. The Americans had salt pork fried crisp and tasty with hominy and heavily sugared tea. With the food Lewis arranged a half-dozen carrots of twisted tobacco on a bed of fresh leaves. He and Clark wore dress uniforms complete with cocked hats. The Corps of Discovery wore enlisted men's blues. The guests were dressed too, in clean buckskins, the tunics painted in wild abstract forms. The older men wore feathers in their hair and a few had the full headdress, feathers sweeping down their backs, won through exploits in battle. Dorion had said the Brulés had just won a war with the Omaha tribe, killing many warriors, taking many prisoners, seizing many horses, and consequently were likely to be unusually cocky.

Before the introductions, Cruzatte already struggling with translation, Lewis had singled out the Partisan. He was a big man, standing well over his fellows, thirty years old or so, taller than Lewis and substantially heavier, certainly well over two hundred pounds, dark face with jutting hook nose that gave him the predatory look of an eagle. He wore a feather headdress and was bare above the waist, pectoral muscles rippling.

His very manner was irritating, an arrogant bastard who swaggered about, made you want to take him down a peg or two. A stone ax was thrust in his belt beside a glittering English fighting knife, the two together making a clear statement. He wore a necklace and anklets made of bear claws, each claw representing a single bear killed at close range with arrow or knife, so Clark said in a whisper. That these hadn't been easy was clear from livid scars on arms and shoulders but not, Lewis checking to see, on his back.

Black Buffalo and Black Medicine carried themselves as chiefs but more modestly. They dined, each side complimenting the other on its food, the Indians exclaiming over the sweetened tea. The Partisan barked something in a sharp tone and a slender woman with a soft smile that struck Lewis as delightful appeared with a stand holding a half-dozen pipes cut from red pipestone and fitted with long reed stems. The Partisan raised a hand and the woman shrank as if she expected him to slap her and Lewis felt an instant visceral sense that here was a man richly deserving of chastising. The pipes were filled with American tobacco and passed around the circle of men until each pipe had completed the circuit twice. Then it was time to talk, and then the trouble began.

Lewis opened. By now he had spoken to several such councils with good results and he was taken aback by his audience's sour expressions. They were bored! The Partisan muttered something and the men around him grinned. Encouraged, he spoke more loudly, pointing at Lewis, and his group laughed out loud and one of them shot back a quip that the Partisan answered to still louder laughter and enthusiasm. They were enjoying themselves now. Lewis was beginning to burn; by God, he'd like to put a pistol ball between that bastard's feet, little lesson in manners. Then he remembered he was to make friends of them.

Cruzatte was having trouble translating abstract ideas, the Purchase, the transfer of sovereignty, the connection to nations still more foreign across water vaster than they could imagine. But you could see it working in their eyes, this leader known as the president and the Great Father who sent emissaries to lay down the law to warriors whom they addressed as "Children"—who could keep from laughing?

"They ain't getting it, Merry," Clark said in a low voice. Just then the Partisan broke into loud gabbling like a duck and his men roared with laughter. The two older chiefs frowned and impatiently gestured the younger men down, but Lewis saw they were having trouble suppressing their own smiles. He shifted to the plans for an army of traders who would follow this first party with rifles and powder, knives and scissors, beads and looking glasses—all the artifacts of an industrialized nation that would far surpass what they were getting now from French or British traders. They listened, sleepy-eyed.

Lewis broke off the talk. He assembled his men in their blue uniforms with rifles on their shoulders and led them in close-order drill, a skill that Clark had pounded into them over the winter at Wood River. By the left flank, by the right flank, to the rear, left oblique, right oblique, halt, present arms! There is something impressive, even frightening, for an individual watching uniformed men under arms marching in unison, power of the individual massed tenfold. But after a momentary stir of alarm at possible betrayal, the warriors watched with scarcely a flicker of interest. One, a sleepy-looking fellow with a jagged scar down his left cheek, yawned loudly.

Lewis called off the military maneuvers and broke out his air gun,
which fired a pellet on the force of air compressed by a little pump, a
recent oddity of industrial America that was immensely popular in the
East. Audiences before had been enthralled but the Brulés watched
impassively. You'd think each one of them had a duplicate back in his
lodge. Slow anger began to bubble in Lewis.

Clark's face was red and strained. "I might bust some heads afore this
is over," he murmured.

"Ain't it tempting?" But they both knew that was just talk. They had
clear orders to conciliate and so Lewis moved on to the next step, naming
the chief-in-charge, so to speak, with whom the Americans henceforth
would deal. Clark had shaken his head over this, saying it wasn't the way
of Indian society.

"But how is government to deal with a tribal entity if it doesn't have
someone it can address?" Lewis remembered saying.

Clark had laughed. "Well," he said, "let's see you get that idea over in
their language."

Now Lewis saw he was getting nowhere. He stopped explaining and
told Black Buffalo he was the main chief of the Brulés with Black Medicine and the Partisan second and third. The Partisan clearly was the man
of power around with loyal followers but one shuddered to think of him
with his bear claws visiting the new Great Father in his white castle.

Now they were at the part the Indians awaited—presents, trade goods,
largesse from those canvas-wrapped bundles that filled the white visitors'
boats. A sense of eager anticipation swept the newly bright audience and
Lewis saw that they had merely put up with the long and apparently
tedious preamble in expectation of golden rewards. Lewis produced an
infantry officer's jacket festooned with gold braid and helped Black Buffalo don it. It was too big, sleeves draping over his hand, but too small to
button comfortably over his gut. Lewis shook out a cocked hat, sort of an
ultimate honor, and fitted it to the Indian's head. He tried to explain the
significance, but Cruzatte foundered over this abstraction. For the other
two chiefs he had medals on silk ribbon that he fitted over their heads
with as much ceremony as he could muster; the medal was a three-inch
hollow disk of silver, very light, likeness of President Jefferson on one
side, hands clasped on the other, Indian and white, with peace pipe and
war ax symbolizing whatever you liked. Watching the expression on
Black Buffalo's face Lewis remembered suddenly that awarding American military uniforms to favored chiefs had been Henry Dearborn's idea
and his opinion of the fat secretary of war sank further.

Lewis opened the rest of the bundle he had designated back in St.
Louis for this meeting and was dismayed by its scanty contents—three or

four knives, probably not as good as the English blade under the Partisan's belt, scissors, looking glasses, burning glasses, beads white and blue, red calico for the women, an awl, a packet of needles, a small iron mill for grinding corn . . .

When his audience realized that this was the end of the white man's largesse they responded with fury and contempt. This cheap display, coat that didn't fit, hat fit for a clown, handful of trinkets—the Partisan was up and shouting. He snatched the light medal from around his neck and pantomimed wiping his rear with it and then flinging the contents into Lewis's face. At this Lewis felt a burst of fury like nothing he'd known in years. His hand was on his pistol, his eyes felt bulged, his face was tight and stretched and burning, and Clark caught his arm and held him, whispering, "Easy, Merry, easy, for God's sake," and at once he regained control. The redness passed from his eyes, suffusion of blood subsiding, and he saw the Partisan gazing at him with something like fear in his expression.

Back in Virginia, Lewis would have killed the man who insulted him so, called him out, pistol to pistol, kill and maybe be killed at the same time, but the insult answered. Meanwhile, seeing the murderous passion pass from Lewis's face, the big Indian quickly recovered. He leveled a hand near Lewis's head as if measuring the white man's height, then lowered it swiftly to a foot off the ground, making a whistling noise as he went, clearly air escaping from a swollen bladder.

"We better do something, Merry," Clark whispered. "How about we take the chiefs aboard the big boat, as honored guests. We do come as friends, remember."

Cruzatte conveyed the invitation, at which the Partisan in particular brightened, a big smile creasing his face. All three climbed into one of the pirogues and the crew paddled them to the keelboat. The Partisan sat atop a couple of canvas-wrapped bundles. He raised a hand and his finger made little jumps in the air. Counting. The bastard was taking the opportunity to inventory what they were carrying but not offering to the Sioux.

Aboard the big boat Black Buffalo in his captain's tunic, cocked hat thrown aside, asked Lewis to open the hatch that covered the cargo hold that they might see its contents. Lewis saw the ploy immediately and shook his head. Passed some lame excuse to Cruzatte who stumbled through a refusal. Black Buffalo said something to the Partisan who nodded and paced off the probable dimensions of the boat's cargo hold, then snorted. Why, these stingy Americans who had given the Sioux owners of this land but a pittance had a fortune in goods wrapped and hidden. For what? Trade with the enemies of the Sioux? Who knew what might be so hidden, rifles, powder, fine steel knives, bundles of tobacco, kegs of whiskey, all material that in Sioux hands would make them the dominant trading power of the High Plains. Lewis knew he had to discourage this attitude. He showed the two swivel guns, each with its handful of musket balls. They moved on to the cannon. It was small, but pack it to its muzzle with balls and it would cut a swath that would leave dead and bleeding on every side.

But Lewis saw the Partisan glance at the other chiefs and shrug with a contemptuous grin. All show, he seemed to be saying, they won't have the nerve to use it. Lewis sighed. They had misread his fierce effort to control himself as cowardice and were acting accordingly.

As a last gesture, Clark agreeing reluctantly, Lewis poured a splash of whiskey into a cup for each chief. They brightened immediately, quaffed the drink in a gulp, and held out their cups for more. Lewis shook his head. They glowered. They stood and began to laugh and lurch about, feigning drunkenness. Indians did have notoriously poor heads for alcohol but not this poor. The Partisan lurched against Lewis, caught his arm, and told him right to his face—or so Drewyer confirmed after a sign language colloquy—that the cost of going farther on the river would be one of the pirogues with all its contents.

Outraged, Lewis ordered them ashore. They resisted. The two captains grabbed them and moved them toward the pirogue used as a ferry. They twisted from the white men's hands and trotted around the keelboat. Lewis called for help; it took seven crewmen to get the three chiefs in the boat and ashore. With a nod of agreement, Clark took the pirogue in while Lewis stood by on the keelboat anchored in midstream. When the pirogue ground ashore three warriors waiting there seized its mooring line while others jumped aboard and wrapped arms about the mast. The Partisan was yelling at Clark, Cruzatte on the keelboat translating for Lewis, Clark's face growing more and more explosively red, the Partisan saying the Americans would go farther only over his dead body, that they must pay tribute just to be allowed to live. This was his river, he shouted—no one traveled it without permission and without payment. Anyway, the pirogue was theirs, seized under Indian rules. The Partisan dusted his hands, dismissing any question of his orders.

From his post on the keelboat Lewis saw the Partisan belly up against Clark, pushing him and shouting into his face what clearly were personal insults. Even at this distance, Lewis could see the fury in Clark's eyes, and then Clark snatched his heavy sword from its scabbard and put the point under the Partisan's chin, ready to cut his damned head off. Warriors stood poised as if caught in surprised horror and then began stringing bows and drawing arrows from quivers.

"To arms!" Clark shouted. On the keelboat and the pirogue men reached for rifles and saw to the priming. Lewis was torn, seeing the ruin of their plans and yet glad to have it come to a head, ready to shake off the pressure of restraint. He realized he was smiling as he poured a dozen rifle balls down the cannon's elevated muzzle. Next he stuffed oversized buckshot into the blunderbusses on their swivels.

Clark, still holding the Partisan immobile with the sword point under his chin, shouted into his face, "You ugly son of a bitch, don't you ever fool with me!" and pushed him violently away. The Partisan stumbled backward out of Clark's range, then began to scream in fury.

Would it all explode? If an arrow flew, if a rifle fired, they would have a bloody war right here on the Missouri. In that shining moment when all stood poised, both sides with weapons cocked, ready to deliver death and destruction, Lewis with a firing taper glowing in his hand, there flashed through his mind an awful awareness of how far in the wrong direction he had brought things. He didn't doubt that modern rifles and heavy weapons would prevail, but what then? That the first act of the new government had been to start a war with a bloody killing field would echo across the years. Yet it would echo even louder if he was turned back here.

In the end the Indians broke. Black Buffalo, still in his uniform jacket, snapped orders to the men holding the pirogue. They let go, stepped back, and the vessel was released. The Partisan ran up a small slope to stand with his warriors with their strung bows, but Lewis noted that he scarcely spoke to them. Lewis had a taste in his mouth that he associated with the idea of ashes.

So it was over.

Three days later the Americans were on their way. In that time both sides had made belated efforts to soften rancor. But as the boats continued to fight the swift water, Lewis and Clark stood in the keelboat cockpit and agreed that they had handled it badly, letting it get all out of hand. Neither could see quite what else they could have done but knew they had not done well.

Just then Drewyer stepped down into the cockpit. "I been thinking," he said, "we done ourselves a good turn back with them Sioux."

Lewis looked at him. "How so?"

"Well, them bastards been threatening every trader who come through, just about robbing them, you know? But it didn't work this time and they was the ones backed off. Now word will go up and down the river far faster than we can go, word that says these folks are different, push 'em and they'll fight. I figure that's a good thing to have known out here where there ain't no law. Pave our way, so I see it."

Well, Lewis thought, watching the rough towers and cliffs of the Missouri Breaks, maybe old Drewyer's right. It don't hurt for people to know you'll fight if you're pushed. Don't hurt at all.

Twenty days had passed and winter was in the air when they sighted the Mandan villages.

25

The Mandan Villages, November, 1804

Winter was coming and in the final burst of fall's beauty, the high plains up in Dakota country showed it. The Mandan villages weren't far off now. The shadows were longer, the grass that the wind rippled in long furrows was recasting from green to gold, the hollows across the rolling prairie darkening more emphatically from light to dark. All this under a vivid blue sky with a hint of chill in the air, perfection only occasionally marred by a cloud.

The single V of southbound geese with soldiers honking for order in their lines had become dense clouds of migrating birds—geese, swans, varieties of ducks, cormorants, pigeons, white pelicans—whose very bulk and volume did darken the sky. Lewis had always supposed that darkening the sky was just a clumsy metaphor, but he was finding it literal fact in this bounteous range.

They were coming into grizzly country after weeks of hearing fearsome tales of the great white bear as some people called the grizzled animal for the white tips of its brown fur. Indians were afraid of it and didn't mind saying so. It was massive and unwaveringly ferocious. On its hind legs it stood taller than a man and weighed six to eight hundred pounds. Five or six solidly placed rifle balls wouldn't stop it unless they struck small vital spots.

The Corps of Discovery's first grizzly encounter fell to Cruzatte, the last man Lewis would have chosen. Cruzatte saw the great beast and with his teeth chattering threw up his rifle and fired. The ball struck the bear on the backside and he roared in outrage. He pawed at his rump, seemingly amazed, used to delivering hurt, not to receiving it. Cruzatte dropped his rifle, bolted into the nearby woods, ran madly to the river, and was ready to plunge in when he saw that the bear had not followed him. Thereafter he became more heroic with each telling of his adventure but never again went hunting alone.

Herd animals were gathering for the move to winter grounds before long. This was buffalo country and the shaggy beasts made dark seas against golden grass. Deer and elk formed in incredible numbers. Taking one was like taking a ripe apple from a tree. Lewis tramped for miles in a wondrous daze, Seaman at his heels seeming to share his master's awe.

Clark was more often in the boat, but Lewis made sure his partner got a full taste of this wild and wonderful prairie in the fall. Indeed, he shuffled the duty rosters so that every man, skilled hunter or not, had his chance to see this magnificence of season. It was a moment to make memories for a lifetime.

Lewis liked admitting mistakes no better than the next man but he knew that he and Clark had erred seriously with the Sioux and especially with that angry chief, the Partisan. They were the men of affairs, educated, experienced in the ways of the world, and he was none of these things. Yet in essence, he had dominated the situation, set its terms, and governed its outcome. Had he loosed his bow his warriors would have done the same and the little cannon and the blunderbusses and massed rifle fire would have roared and all of Jefferson's careful instructions would have gone up in gun smoke.

But as he approached the Mandan villages in late fall glory Lewis realized how dependent he was on the help of the people there. Trappers and traders had covered the river between St. Louis and the Mandans often enough that a general sense of that portion of the river was deep in frontier thinking. But no white man, nor any man with the wit and education to know what information was needed, had ventured beyond the Mandans. The latest maps were fables and fairy tales.

But the Mandans did know the ground to the west because they operated an intermediary trade bazaar between tribes far to the west and British and French traders in Canada. And their friends and allies, the Hidatsa tribe, regularly sent war parties west to and into the mountains on raids to steal horses, take women and children as slaves, and to gain standing by feats of valor. They knew the ground that the Corps of Discovery must cover. There must be no carelessness in dealing with them now.

The villages actually were two communities, one at each end of a long narrow island that had formed where the Knife River entered the main river, far up in the Dakota country. Three smaller villages of the Hidatsas lay a mile or two up the Knife.

People turned out by the hundreds from both villages to see the new-comers in their big boats as they went to the north end of the island and landed. There a mob of women and children jostled for better views. Drewyer, fingers flashing, learned by Plains sign language that all told the five villages had about four thousand people, which included some thir-teen hundred warriors. The explorers landed cautiously; Lewis would go into the village and connect to its leaders while Clark and the bulk of the men would stay aboard with weapons primed and ready.

But none of this proved necessary. The Mandans greeted him warmly, as if they had a natural sense for the importance of the Corps of Discov-ery. And perhaps they did. White men were not unknown in the village. The big trade fair came in August but several white traders had married into the tribe and lived among them. One of these men was René Jes-saume who was fluent in French, English, Mandan, and Hidatsa. After a few minutes' talk Lewis hired Jessaume to serve as interpreter for the winter. Thus was resolved one of the great faults of the Sioux encounter, the inability to understand each other. Next they dealt with the other problem of before, the Partisan's belligerent rage.

Each of the five villages had a chief and none was supreme, but it was quickly evident that Black Cat, who ran the upper Mandan village, had the ears of the other chiefs. And an hour's talk through the new inter-preter persuaded Lewis that Black Cat was a man of high intelligence with experience and diplomatic talents. He was about fifty, hair graying, a potbelly growing. He seemed genuinely amused when Lewis presented a captain's jacket, the more so when it wouldn't close over his belly. Indeed, he said, carefully pausing for Jessaume to catch up, his people would be pleased to have the whites winter among them. Tomorrow he and Lewis would go together up the river to find a suitable place for the small fort that Lewis said the whites would erect.

Lewis also felt that his growing liking for the Indian was reciprocated. But it became evident that some word of the Corps' progress up the river had already reached the Mandans. Quite bluntly, the Indian said that so many men with such a wealth of equipment should come armed with many presents to spread among the people. He had heard the American presents were noted for their cheapness and how little was given. He warned Lewis that such an error would alienate the Mandans and temper their warm welcome. This was especially important, he pointed out, because Lewis only minutes ago had been boasting of the quality of the trade goods the Indians could expect once relations with the new Great Father were well established.

Lewis hunted for language that Jessaume could translate adequately to explain their full mission—to go on clear to the Pacific, carrying with them presents for all the tribes they would encounter, having enough to buy what they would need, food and especially horses when they reached the mountains. All this must be carried with them, there being no resupply available, and then they must still have enough to make the return trip up to the mountains and across again and then down the Missouri back to the Mandans and then on to St. Louis—all on the stores they carried.

Black Cat listened intently, obviously struggling to grasp the magnitude all this involved. At last he made a curious seizing gesture with both hands and launched into rapid speech to which Jessaume listened carefully before nodding.

"I think it's working," he said slowly to Lewis. "That thing he does with his hands, it seems to mean he understands and accepts, offers no quarrel, you see. Then he talked awhile and I couldn't get it all straight but he seems to be saying that the meaning of your trip and your even being here tells him great change is coming. He said you'll have to bend yourself to Indian ways but Indians will have to bend to your ways too. Then he talked about the way people learn and grow and what all. I don't know what that has to do with anything but it's what he seemed to be trying to say."

Lewis nodded, more than satisfied. This was a very intelligent man, seeing far beyond Jessaume's grasp. The Indian was watching Lewis's expression intently as Jessaume talked. At last Lewis looked up with a smile and nodded; he understood and agreed. Black Cat looked thoroughly pleased. He called for pipes and they smoked together.

When Lewis returned to the boat he found Clark ashore with most of the men, so warm had been their welcome.

The captains agreed: it was a good beginning.

Big White was a handsome man, tall and heavy in the bone. He walked like a cat, lithe and swift, and was a famous hunter, said to be able to ease well within arrow range before game took alarm, and Lewis could believe it. He was popular and seemed to be a considerable wit since he often sent listening Indians into fits of laughter. His skin was so white that for a moment Lewis had taken him for an albino. He was just unusual enough in appearance to have had to develop wit and a natural authority of manner to escape the ostracism that often meets the simple sin of being different. But these same qualities had made him a chief, ranking under Black Cat but with considerable authority nevertheless. Black Cat seemed to admire him.

So Big White was there on a particularly cold day when Black Cat invited the elders to smoke and talk with the white visitor. Since the group seemed unusually receptive, Lewis decided to broach a new proposition that he had been waiting to advance. The new Great Father known also as the president was anxious for Indian leaders to make the long journey back to Washington that he might meet them in his dwelling and honor them and make them welcome. He wanted them to see the nation newly ascendant over their lands and their fortunes. A subtext that Lewis didn't mention was the expectation that the numbers of the whites and their wealth and power would awe the savages.

That was exactly how the president had put it, which had sounded all right at the time. Now, having grown to like and admire Black Cat and some of the others and seeing their ease of manner with each other and their near-perfect meshing with the land, Lewis found the term rude and ignorant. In fact, this particular assignment had especially irritated him. It had come very late in their planning, had come in an offhand fashion, and had seemed an unnecessary addition to burdens already considerable and somewhat unrelated to the march to the Pacific.

With Jessaume translating plus some help from Drewyer who already had the hang of the Mandan language, Lewis laid out the scheme—one of them to journey to Washington in the spring when part of the expedition would be going downriver. The Indians looked at him as if he'd suddenly lost his mind. Lewis talked rather desperately of the wonders they would see, all different from here, all the people, buildings of stone stacked to the sky, horses and carriages everywhere, lamps lighting streets at night, miles of fenced fields and pastures, harbors full of ships, establishments you entered unannounced and ordered any food you wanted—on and on he went, watching refusal unchanged in their eyes.

Black Cat was shaking his head but before pronouncing the utter failure of Lewis's argument he gave each man a chance to respond, which Drewyer said was Indian custom. Each grunted and shook his head. There was long hesitation when he came to Big White. Jessaume waited. At last, voice grave and portentous, he said by Jessaume's translation, "I will go to see these wonders and return to report to my brothers."

Lewis was delighted. He smiled and started to stand. But Big White was speaking again. Jessaume listened carefully, then said that he wanted the white man's promise that he would be returned to these villages fully protected. Now Lewis leaped up, nodding. "Of course," he said.

"Gonna take more than that, Cap'n," Drewyer said. "Give 'em a speech. Tell 'em your feelings are hurt they'd even wonder about safety. Try beating your chest—you're pledging your sacred honor, this man will be returned in perfect health to describe the wonders he certainly will see."

He gave them a bell-ringer, voice thunderous, gestures striking, as the two guides tumbled over each other translating. Black Cat smiled. Indians liked oratory and were good at it; he wondered if that related to their being of an oral culture, literature being foreign to their experience. But

more to the point, Big White stood with arms folded, waiting to be satisfied. At last he turned to Black Cat, who nodded. He extended his hand to
Lewis with a smile.

Later Lewis wondered just what had moved Big White. He had seen a
look of amused complicity in the big Indian's eyes and he had an idea that
more than anything, he wanted to do what his fellows feared or couldn't
summon the interest to do, which suggested in any case that they were
less men of power than was he. Questioning his safety and asking for
pledges, while reasonable on its face, might also have served to emphasize
his own courage in braving this unique journey.

But he also saw that Big White had put a hell of a serious obligation
square on his back.

Sixteen hundred miles up the Missouri, locked away from winter's worst,
ready to rest and restore and refuel, Lewis had a strong feeling of so far, so
good. Of course, he was only coming to the hard and dangerous part now.

26

Mandan Villages, December, 1804

Well, these Indians, they was of a different cut than them Sioux back
down the river. These Mandans were easygoing and laughed a lot and
seemed happy to deal with Americans. Shannon liked them instinctively.
And their attitude about women—oh, my!

The Sioux were as different as night from day, mean devils, arrows
drawn from their quivers and held across the bow, not notched, understand, but close enough to it—made you think of a rattler rattling away,
hasn't struck yet but you know he's got it in his mind. And then that big
Indian wiping his ass with the president's medal, plain as day what he was
acting out, and flinging a load even if imaginary right in the captain's face.
Well, God almighty, he realized in that instant that he hadn't seen the
cap'n really mad before and it was something he wasn't anxious to see
again, least of all if it was aimed at him. Face damn near black and eyes
bulging, them Indians staring like he was crazy.

So there they stood, motionless as one of them paintings you see behind the bar in a tavern, cannon and blunderbusses primed and cocked and matches lit on one side, arrows ready on the other, the ground about to be littered with the dead and dying, and just then Cap'n Clark, who'd been spoiling for a fight too, he got a look at Cap'n Lewis's face. And he said nothing more but walked over to the cap'n and put a hand on his arm.

Like that was a signal one of the older Indians yelled something and the warriors put arrows back in quivers and unstrung their bows, and Cap'n Lewis signaled to put out matches and it was over. But you knew if you hadn't before that Cap'n Lewis was not a man to fool with, not at all.

After they'd been at the Mandans for two or three days a big powwow was planned. The captains would get together with some of the chiefs and the leading men; Cap'n Lewis would give them his speech about the new Great Father and how they needn't look to the British no more, and then they'd feast and dance.

"And then," John Colter said, "the women."

They were sitting down by the river smoking a pipe. Cap'n Clark had given them a rare day off. Winter's chill had been in the air but it had passed for the moment and the sun was warm and soothing to sore muscles. Shannon had heard these stories along the river, of course, but had never quite believed them.

Well, it was true, John Colter said. First off, Indians had a lot different idea about the hungers of men and women from what most Americans Shannon knew believed. A successful warrior might have several wives, some stolen from enemy tribes, some local girls that had caught his eye. Apparently wives liked sharing a husband—and the work that went with marriage—with other women.

Then there was the conviction widely held among some Missouri tribes, including the Mandans and the Hidatsas, that when a man emptied his seed into a woman's womb some of his power, knowledge, intelligence, and skill went with it. And it lay in that warm repository until her husband took her, whereupon it flowed from her womb to his loins.

"Can that be true?" Shannon asked.

Colter shrugged. "Hell, I don't know. I've had plenty of women and never felt no power coming or going. But if they think so, maybe it works for them. Anyway, it sure can be nice for you."

"Aw . . ."

"Sure enough, George. You look out, big handsome feller like you, before long someone'll come up with a pretty little piece and tell you she'll be waiting in her buffalo robe. Think you know what to do then?"

"Well, I guess I'd say—"

"Naw, I don't mean talking about it. Nothing much there, you give him something, twist of tobacco, maybe, and some foofaraw for her—and it's not like a whore in a St. Louis crib, don't get that wrong. You give him something to acknowledge the value you place in the gift of his wife, and something for her, strip of red yarn to weave in her hair, maybe, letting her know you understand the honor they offer you."

He grinned, but Shannon saw it was warmhearted, not at all salacious. "No," John Colter said, "I mean when you get her in that buffalo robe, you know what to do then?"

Shannon glared. "Of course," he snapped. Hell's fire, everyone knew what to do then. Didn't have to actually have done it to know that. What did John Colter take him for?

"You ever done it, though? Really? With a live woman?"

"God damn it, John—what a thing to ask!"

John Colter laughed out loud. "Oh, George," he said, "you're all right. Tell you what—you just let her take the lead, she'll show you where to put it. Once you get it set, it'll all come natural."

And he jumped up and went off to wash his clothes and Shannon lay there in the sun dreaming of what might happen. Let her show you the ropes—come to think of it, that was a good idea and might solve his problem. After all, she would be an old married lady, she ought to know.

And sure enough, late on the next afternoon when the powwow was ready to commence, here come Drewyer with a young man in tow, him standing on one foot and then the other. "George," Drewyer said, "this here fellow, Fighting Cock, so's his name, wants you to have his woman tonight." He gestured and a slender woman in a buckskin sheath decorated with porcupine quills stepped forward. She looked at George and smiled. Her tongue slipped between her lips and she made a curious lifting motion with her belly that was so erotic that George felt momentarily dizzy.

"Tonight," Drewyer said. "After the powwow and the feasting and the dancing." He looked at George. "You understand—you'll want to have something for them, for each of them. When all the festivity's done, look for him. He'll come for you and take you to her."

At which George knew he was grinning like an idiot, and the slender Indian laughed out loud and clapped his shoulder, and the young woman giggled.

Then things were starting. The several chiefs, Black Cat in the lead followed by leading warriors of the five villages, filed into the shade of the sailcloth awning. An old man set out the ceremonial clay pipes and women brought in covered dishes from which savory smells flowed. Several of the men of the Corps who had been succeeding as cooks for the various messes had been up before dawn frying and draining the salt pork to make the crisp bites that everyone liked. The Indians uncovered slabs of roasted buffalo and large gourd dishes of beans and corn and squash stewed and seasoned, and everyone fell to.

When the food was gone—Shannon quite greedy, having found in himself a real taste for dog meat stew when the idea once had revolted him, sort of like eating your best friend for dinner—it was time to smoke. The pipe master, the old gent who tended them, had them properly packed now, and firing one after another with a coal from the fire, he got them drawing well and passed them to the chief who drew and then passed it over to Cap'n Lewis who passed to Cap'n Clark who passed it back to the chief ranked after Black Cat. By this time the bowl was hot; by the time it got down to Shannon it looked ready to melt and men took it gingerly, stem held between the fingers. By this time another and another had been lit and passed, and this went on for some time, solemn smoking, incantations marking the meaning, puffs of smoke and sometimes rings blown to the four corners and to the spirits that dealt with success on the buffalo hunt and rain to match the needs of corn and squash, not too much nor too little, and to the confounding of their enemies, to the virtues of the horse, the wisdom of the wolf, the cleverness of the fox, and certainly to the men whose spirit had entered these animal worlds. By this time Shannon felt he'd gotten the idea and could dispense with a few of the details, but he could see it was important to the Indians and dutifully contributed his *"Huh!"* to each prayer, all the while remembering how she had lifted her belly, like she was drawing him into her body.

When the pipes were put away Cap'n Lewis made his speech. Shannon thought the Indians seemed bored but maybe that was his own impatience. When the cap'n was done he thanked them for their welcome and signaled for the presents to be brought forth from the boats and unwrapped. A big stir of excitement went through the crowd, by now everyone outside where they all could crowd around. The cap'n held up things as he presented them, trying to make like it was something grand, but Shannon could see it wasn't at all grand. The disappointed sighs of the people, the way they looked at each other, some with dismay, some with disgust, told him the people were equally unimpressed. Then Black Cat stood up and began an oration. Sure enough, the people listened, at first politely, then with interest. Shannon could hear Jessaume translating for the captains; it seemed Black Cat was telling them these were token gifts compared to the spoils that would be theirs from the trade that the new Great Father even now was sending upriver to his new people, the Mandans and the Hidatsas, who could look for all manner of good things in due time.

The warm spell had held and they were outside, the people crowding around and watching to the pulsating beat of several drums of different size and tone. Now there were pipes that had a strange, shrill note that got your feet to tapping right quick, rattles and tambourinelike affairs that stepped up the tempo and the volume, everyone rocking back and forth. All this with a welcome hand from a curious drink of fermented berries that got them all into a first-class mood.

John Colter winked at Shannon, then dropped to the ground beside him to whisper, "Drewyer tells me a little lady . . ."

Shannon nodded.

"Sure you don't need no instruction?"

Shannon hissed, "Get out of here!" but he was smiling, and Colter danced away, leaving Shannon feeling warm all over.

He saw George Gibson unwrapping his old fiddle that he could make sing like a bird. There'd be dancing tonight. Shannon surmised the reason the captains had accepted Gibson for the corps was his fiddle playing, he not being worth much for anything else. But when they were leaving St. Louis and took on Pierre Cruzatte for his knowledge of the river they discovered he was even better than Gibson on the fiddle. Cruzatte was a funny little fellow, winked at you every time he spoke to you and since he had only one eye it gave a pretty odd effect. He said some sorry bastard had carved out his gone eye with a skinning knife. He played his fiddle sweet as maple syrup, picking up French voyageur tunes that had them tapping their toes and crying at the same time. But his real skill when the music got him excited and Gibson was playing away—why, he'd put down his fiddle and flip over and go to dancing on his hands! Not just walking, either, dancing, timing to the music perfect. Indians would shriek with laughter at the sight.

But it was York who really had them goggle-eyed. They'd never seen a black man and didn't believe there was such a critter. They would gather around him and try to wash off his blackness and get down to red or white or whatever he was underneath. One big fellow with a knife started to cut down and see where the black stopped and York hit him so hard he landed eight or ten feet away cold as a stone. Shannon liked the big black man and found a wisdom in him, too; it was good to talk to him, pretty soon he'd get you to thinking in a way you hadn't thought before. And then he was always cutting up and laughing and carrying on. It brightened the campfire to have York around.

He didn't take any lip, though. Dick Windsor got smart one night and York flattened him and Dick drew a big knife and said no nigger was going to hit him. Cap'n Clark told Dick that York would kill him about as quick as look at him and, my, that did take the wind out of Dick's sails. York was older than Cap'n Clark; he'd been tending to the cap'n since they was boys. But it all got Shannon to thinking, too, because it was hard to remember that York was a slave. Shannon had

known a few free blacks in Pennsylvania and while folks didn't always
want to socialize with them, they got along all right. You'd think that
would apply to York, too, but no, he was Cap'n Clark's slave. But York
didn't seem a slave; he was one of them, he lived and traveled, worked
and suffered as they did. He took the same joy in the way the sun came
cracking down the canyon in the morning and the smell of buffalo meat
on the spit and the taste of his pipe with a tin cup of coffee before bed-
ding down; he wasn't no different than any of them. Yet the cap'n owned
him and could sell him like he'd sell a horse he didn't need no more. It
just wasn't right. Shannon didn't know where he would end his days but
one thing he knew right now: it wouldn't be in the South where men
owned other men who were just as smart and brave and strong . . . men
like York.

About then the Indian men jumped onto the smooth, pounded council
ground and began dances of triumph, one by one reciting what heroes
they were, what devils in war, the men they had killed, the horses they'd
stolen, and the slaves they'd seized, Jessaume translating.

Then George Gibson broke out his fiddle and started playing Pennsylvania mountain music that had tracked over the water from Ireland and Scotland. Shannon recognized the tunes because his father's little brother had
come from Ireland with his fiddle and the consumption, hoping Pennsylvania air would cure him. It killed him instead but before he went he played
many a jig on that fiddle and you couldn't hardly keep from dancing.

So next thing you knew, fiddle music flying, the boys were up and
dancing, the Indians looking first startled, then delighted. And there was
big York in the middle, arms akimbo, rocking side to side with his feet
going just about faster than the eye could follow and Pierre Cruzatte
dancing on his hands with his one eye bulging. The Indians were laughing and yelling and tapping their feet, so York grabbed a fearsome-
looking fellow by the hand and dragged him up and got him started and
the sight of one of their own dancing to the strange music set them shriek-
ing with laughter. Well, next thing they all were up whooping and hollering and raising dust, and Cruzatte quit dancing on his hands and grabbed
his fiddle and went to dueling with Gibson till they were like a couple of
roosters seeing which could crow the best—oh, it was wild!

Finally it ran down, as Indians and whites alike began falling out from
exhaustion, and the music sort of trailed off. York staggered around like
he was drunk or exhausted and finally, maybe by accident or, Shannon
thought later, maybe not, he flopped on the ground right beside Shannon.
It would be a while before they went to the women and now they were
feeling easy.

Then to Shannon's great surprise York said in a voice quite unlike his usual bray, soft, kind of gentle, hardly a whisper, "George, you my friend, ain't you?"

Shannon reared up in surprise. "Well, of course. What kind of damn fool question is that?"

"Put your head down," York said, command in his voice. "Don't make it look like we're having a big talk, now. I want to ask you something."

Shannon put his head on his arms, lying so he could see York. "What?"

"Well," York said, his coal black face still shiny with sweat, "you see all these Indians, they free. They don't ask nobody nothing, they want to go hunting, go with a woman, go for a walk, go to hell, don't nobody say a word. Long as they don't step on nobody's toes, they free."

"That's right," Shannon said, seeing where this was going.

"Now, at home, they say black folks—niggers, you see—ain't as good as white folks. Ain't as smart or as brave. Say that's why we're slaves. Don't deserve no better. But these Indians ain't white and they ain't slaves neither. You see what I mean?"

"Surely do."

"Well, what I been thinking—see, I do as much work as any man on this here journey, don't you think? I'm as much a part of it as anyone. That's right, ain't it?"

Shannon nodded.

"Now, in St. Louis, I heard some talk, said if we really make this trip and get to the Pacific and get back, it'll be something special. Folks'll hear about it everywhere, they'll talk about Lewis and Clark and all of us, all over the West and maybe the East too. You think that could be?"

"I've heard the same thing from smart men and it makes sense to me, York."

"Well, since I'm part of this great thing we're doing and if we really do make it to salt water and all the way back—" He stopped, his eyes huge, staring at Shannon.

"Well, what? Come on, you can say it."

"You won't say nothing, will you? I got your promise on that, don't I?"

"Not a word. Not to a soul."

"Well, we get back and all, it's a big success and everyone's talking, what do you think if I ask Cap'n Clark to set me free? Manumit me, that's what they call it. You think I could ask?"

"Hell, yes—I think you should. You're as valuable as anyone on this expedition and smarter than most. Hell, yes, wait till we're back and just tell him."

"He probably beat the hell out of me."

"Why would he? God Almighty, you've earned it. Cap'n Clark, he ain't bad. Maybe he's never thought on it."

"That's the truth, I can promise you that. He's never thought on it and he ain't going to like it much."

"Maybe he will. We're going through a lot on this trip, him and us alike, and we're just getting started. It kind of glues us together, makes us look out for each other. We'll be different, we get back. You'll see. You ask him."

"Then you don't think I'm crazy?"

"God Almighty, York, you're about the sanest man I know. Smartest, too. What you're talking about, that's only right. You ask him, you hear?"

"When we get back."

"Well then, all right. But you ask him. Make sure you do."

There was a long silence. Then York's hand came out and Shannon grasped it and heard him whisper, "Much obliged, George. Maybe I will."

Then it was time to turn in and Shannon walked around looking for the slender Indian, wondering if the whole thing was a joke or a dream. Then as he was feeling sick with disappointment the young man appeared and beckoned and together they walked among the lodges. The Indian, Fighting Cock, Drewyer had said his name was, stopped at a lodge and stooped to crawl into the entrance tunnel. He beckoned, then ducked out of sight, and for a moment Shannon couldn't help a frisson of fear, wondering if the young man would turn on him with a knife. But it was too late now, he was in the lodge, he could hear stirring, and Fighting Cock led him to a bundle of robes. He spoke and the robe was thrown aside. She was there, naked, and she held out both arms to him and he sank into her embrace with a muffled cry of desire. She flipped the robe over his shoulders and kissed him.

But later, sated in a way he hadn't even imagined before, the young woman whose name he still didn't know already asleep, his head whirling with new knowledge, he thought of York. Back in Pennsylvania Pa had known some folks who were involved in taking care of runaway slaves, hide them when they came from Virginia or sometimes the Carolinas, get them on their way. He tried to remember what they'd called themselves — something about getting rid of slavery altogether — abolitionists! That was it! Paw had said that maybe their preacher was involved but nobody said much, one of those things it was best not to talk about. When the Corps of Discovery got home, maybe they'd be heroes and all, he might just go back and visit Ma and maybe look up that preacher. Maybe join up and try to do a little good in the world. Imagine York having to beg any man for the right to stand straight and do what he wanted. This slavery, it was just evil!

He sank back, warm, comfortable, calm, and then she stirred, awake now. She sighed again and touched his chest and instantly he was ready.

In the smattering of Mandan he'd picked up he managed to ask, "What's your name?"

She said something but he found it quite unintelligible and then she sighed again and drew him into her . . .

27

Fort Mandan, Late December, 1804

These were friendly people but Lewis didn't need Drewyer to tell him how rapidly things could change. He ordered construction of a small fort with seven-foot walls on an island downstream from the first village and posted guards around the clock. The day the fort was completed Drewyer brought in a stranger, forty-five or so, heavy beard, an uneasiness in his eyes. Two slender Indian girls crowded close behind him, glancing apprehensively at the whites. Drewyer said something to him in French and he barked at the girls, at which they stared at the ground.

"Cap'n," Drewyer said, "this here is Toussaint Charbonneau. French Canadian, he don't speak no English. Woodsman for the North West Company up in Canada, he knows Indian languages, he wants to get himself hired. Says he's an interpreter."

Lewis shook his head. "So are you."

Charbonneau launched a torrent of French, Drewyer nodding. "What he says, Cap'n, you're going in the mountains, you'll need horses. Well, the mountains, that's where the Shoshoni live, and they'll swap you horses. But his wives, see, they're both Shoshoni, they was captured in the mountains—he won 'em off the brave what took them. They know that country and they can talk—they can git you the horses."

The effrontery of this amused Lewis for a moment that slid into a spasm of worry. He sure as the devil would need horses. There was so much they would need to find their way, so much that could go wrong—he frowned and shook his head, at which the two girls cringed. He tried a smile to reassure them.

"I can't take two women into the wilderness," he said.

"Might not be such a bad idea. Woman with your party, it sure ain't a war party. Indians'll take note of that."

Yes, but it was the horses that were important. "I can take one," Lewis said, holding up a finger. "Not two."

Charbonneau thrust one of the girls forward, rattling something in French.

"Says take this one. She's the smart one."

She was slender, graceful as a doe, wearing a buckskin shift. Fourteen or fifteen. She gazed at Lewis and then gave him a slow, shy smile. She was as sweet as his own sister. She also was well along in pregnancy. He said as much.

"Drop her baby in two months, long before winter's done."

So he would go into the wilderness with a young woman carrying a new baby in a cradleboard on her back, suckling him every few hours. He glanced at Will.

"I like the idea," Clark said.

"What's your name?" Lewis asked. Drewyer spoke to Charbonneau who barked at the girl.

"Sacagawea," she whispered.

Well, it turned out that giving birth was no easier for Indian women than for white women. Especially when it was her first birth. And when she was slender with narrow hips, scarcely more than a child herself.

Lewis had given Charbonneau a hut in the fort for himself and his two wives, and it was here that she went into labor. Lewis had satisfied himself that so far as character went, Charbonneau was a sorry bastard while René Jessaume was only marginally better; Clark told him not to judge too harshly—out on the far frontier one tended to meet folks who were not knights in bright armor.

As it turned out, Charbonneau was gone on a hunt when Sacagawea's labor began. Jessaume's wife was serving as midwife with René translating as the ashen girl twisted and turned under her knowing hands. White women often died in childbirth and so did Indian women. Listening outside the hut to the high-pitched keening of the frightened girl, Lewis was seized by dread. He and Clark had talked it over and decided the only thing valuable about Charbonneau was his wife, but that she was very valuable with her capacity to talk directly to the Shoshones high in the mountains when winter would be near upon them. She could help persuade them to sell the horses without which the expedition must die on the spot. The more Lewis acquainted himself with this demanding and unforgiving land, the more he understood how naive had been his casual assumption that Indians had plenty of horses and would be happy to sell them.

He had started to pace up and down before the hut, drawing his coat tight against the cold, when the door popped open. Jessaume, looking drained, said, "Cap'n, you have any idea where we'd find us a rattlesnake rattle?"

"What the hell —"

"Well, Ma says the little gal's gone and gotten her baby sideways somehow and now the pain's so bad she's clamping down on it and won't let it go. Or somesuch — this ain't an area I know a whole lot about, you see . . ."

But Lewis was already running to his specimen bundles to find a rattle from a snake of monstrous size that he had intended to send to the president. He cut off two rings and broke them up with the butt of the knife. Jessaume brought him a cup made from a gourd and he stirred the rattle bits into water.

In the hut he found the girl whimpering and only half conscious. But she stirred when he lifted her head and put the gourd to her lips. She drank the whole potion, then lay back with a sigh.

Ten minutes later the baby was born, a handsome little boy red as a beet, whom Jessaume displayed as proudly as if he were the father. Lewis saw Sacagawea beckon to him. He sat on the edge of the bed and she burst into rapid talk. He made out only a word of it, Shoshone. He glanced at Jessaume.

"I think she's asking are you going to take her back to her people in the mountains?"

"Yes," he said with as reassuring a smile as he could muster. She drew his hand to her lips. He didn't know if that was an Indian gesture or one she'd picked up in the white world, but he knew exactly what she meant.

They had hired Charbonneau as a salaried interpreter with no special rights and he'd seemed happy to be chosen. But as the captains used him to translate their long searching questions to the Mandans on terrain, directions, distances, and landmarks, his wife's value to the expedition became more and more evident to him. So when Clark drew up a roster sheet that detailed his duties and salary and read it to him, Charbonneau being illiterate, he took it with an insolent smile, tore it neatly in half, and handed it back to Clark. It wouldn't do, not at all.

This was not the way to deal with either of the captains. Before Clark could slap him into courtesy, Lewis said, "Mr. Charbonneau, nothing has changed. You will go as equivalent in rank and salary to a private, you'll take your turn on the oars, you'll stand guard watch at night. That was what we hired you for and that's how you'll go."

In bastard French Charbonneau launched a tirade that Lewis understood only dimly. He would not row or stand watches, he would get his pick of their rations, he could leave the expedition whenever he chose and would expect a vessel, weapons, and food supplies to see his party back to the Mandans. All of which he wanted writ out on a piece of paper.

Lewis glanced at Clark, half smiling, and shook his head. Clark grinned and made a thumbs-down gesture.

"Pack your gear and get out, you and your women," Lewis said. "Clear the fort by sundown or I'll have you put out."

With what dignity he could muster, Charbonneau stormed out. The captains looked at each other. It was costly and painful to lose Sacagawea as interpreter to the Shoshones. There also was the loss of the goodwill that returning a daughter stolen from the tribe should earn the expedition. That was a costly loss, too, but Charbonneau had put them in an impossible position. He was an ignorant man, totally inexperienced in anything beyond trapping and woods lore, and of course couldn't see the damage that acquiescing to his demands would have done the expedition. At this point Lewis and Clark simply shrugged; they had done what they had to do.

At sundown Lewis walked down to the hut to find Charbonneau throwing his gear into a cart he'd found somewhere. Sacagawea was crying. She didn't look at Lewis.

Four days later a fellow trapper came over from the Mandan village as emissary for Charbonneau. The Frenchman, it seemed, was full of remorse, realized he had made a terrible mistake, and begged the captains to forgive him and take him back into the service on whatever terms they chose.

"Let him come and say so himself," Clark snapped.

Charbonneau appeared that afternoon. He was in tears. He had made a terrible mistake. Lewis told him to shut his mouth, listen again to the terms of his employment, and affix his X as directed. Sniffling, he listened, then made his mark.

The next day the captains sent Drewyer over to nose out what had changed the Frenchman's mind. He came back chuckling.

"It was that little gal. From the moment they left here she was on his ass. Telling him he'd thrown away his last chance to be a big man on the frontier—and for what? For his pride, that's what. Pride, nothing more. But whoever makes the journey, she's telling him, let alone someone who knows the way, he can count on wealth and position at the end. Now, I don't know if that's true, but it's what she kept hammering at him. Telling him he wasn't smart enough to see it so he threw away the greatest opportunity of his life. On and on she goes, giving him no rest. He slaps her, knocks her down, and she gets up with blood leaking out her mouth, and cool as a cucumber tells him he tries that again, she'll cut off his whang-doodle while he sleeps."

"Oh, no," Lewis cried, thinking of the tremulous smile she'd given him the day she'd joined the expedition. "That sweet little girl? She wouldn't say such a thing, I don't believe it."

Drewyer shrugged. "That's what Jessaume's wife says, anyway. Seems they've been close since the baby."

"Shoot," Clark said, and laughed. "I believe it. She's a strong woman and Charbonneau, he looks to me like he would grind easy." He glanced at Lewis. "Women are strong, you know," he said. "Strong as men, only in different ways. Stronger, sometimes."

"Well," Drewyer said, "the thing is, she wants to go home."

28

Mandan Villages, January, 1805

First sight of the Mandan houses had startled Lewis, for they were huge, nothing like the tepees he had seen so far. They were circular, made of sticks woven together and daubed with mud, maybe twenty feet tall or more and capped by a dome with a vent from which smoke poured.

Drewyer had chuckled at his surprise. "Winter comes, they quarter their horses inside with the family."

Horses in the house? "Cap'n," Drewyer said, "winter up here on the high plains'll give you a whole new idea about cold."

Now, well into a brutal winter, Lewis understood about the cold. The Indians said this winter was harder than most, but the mercury regularly dipped into the minus thirties and once was forty-seven degrees below zero. After that Lewis didn't question the Mandan view of architecture. At their own haven up the river—Fort Mandan—their horses and those loaned by the Mandans lived in shelters warmed by fireplaces.

Yet they had to eat and to eat they must hunt. Sometimes they joined Mandan hunts but more often went by themselves. At first this seemed to personify hardship but Lewis quickly discovered that if you kept moving a good coat was enough and there was a certain joy in facing the elements and plunging ahead and after days cooped in their fort the boys were anxious to go.

It seemed that Sacagawea had told everyone that the cap'n had saved her life and while that wasn't true, Lewis was the closest thing to a doctor in a thousand miles and the Mandans were quick to turn to him. Thus he wasn't surprised when a Mandan man came in tears carrying a little boy whose feet had frozen. The skin was already black and on the way to gangrene; the flesh came off when Lewis touched it. As gently as he could he cleaned off dead flesh. Tears streamed from the boy's eyes but not a whimper escaped him. By the next day it was clear that wasn't enough and the doctor was forced to remove the toes in hopes of saving the foot. This seemed to hold and though the boy would never be a great runner he would survive.

A few days later York asked to see the cap'n on a medical matter. York had been sought after more than any of the men for the transfer of power through love and had been working such transfers two and three times a day. The idea that York was the only black man on the expedition and so far as Indians knew the only black man in the world vastly increased the perception of transferable power. Finding York with hat in hand requesting medical aid, Lewis assumed it was a venereal problem, venereal diseases rampant among Indians, spread far and wide by visiting French Canadian trappers.

"Your apparatus leaking?" he asked York.

"No, sir, it ain't leaking. That ain't the problem. But, see, that Indian boy you worked on, well, I wouldn't want to start on that road—"

"What the hell, York. You let your toes get frozen?"

"No, sir, not my toes."

"What then—nose?"

"No, sir . . . well, you see—" He stopped.

"What?"

"Well, that cold snap yesterday, down in the forties below, well, I was outside just a minute, and I—well, I took a leak. Piss froze before it hit the snow. And since then . . ."

"Good God, York—you telling me you froze your pecker?"

"Yes, sir, I guess that's about the size of it. And after the way you took off that boy's toes, well, I'd hate to . . ."

Lewis nodded. "I see what you mean," he said. "Well, let's look at it."

Sure enough, the big man's penis had been nipped by the cold. It amazed Lewis that the cold could do that in the moment a man had his penis out of his trousers to urinate. But this was cold beyond any of their experiences even though the Indians seemed to thrive on it.

"It may be a little sore for a day or two," he told York. "Keep it warm.

Think you can find some nice warm place to put it? Might do it a world of good."

There was a gleam of humor in York's eyes. "Yes, sir, might be able to find such a place."

This was an ideal time to talk and Lewis and Clark went from village to village. It was slow with translations of language and sign talk filtering through but the Indians loved to talk. They knew the ground and the explorers didn't and that made the Indians feel pleased and superior. They were led from one elder to another. With each it was important to smoke, compliment the man on the arms and shields hanging from the frame that gave the odd house its strength, admire the finest of his horses. For each and for their women he had a bauble or a little sample of the artifacts of industry, a blade, a glass to make fire. Then after eating and sampling a wine that apparently was made from dandelions, they could at last talk.

Sometimes, sitting in a smoky lodge, women cooking, babies squalling, horses stamping, puppies tussling before the fire, smoke and odor pouring from the hole in the roof, he thought of Mr. Jefferson's study at Monticello where they had talked out their shadowy notions of the American West. He had spent hours there reading and poring over maps, a pot of tea handy, his pipe in his hand, and when he was done he knew as much as anyone in the world about the shape of the West. But that, as he also knew, wasn't much.

The Missouri's water source probably was snowmelt from mountains but you couldn't be sure. Could be rolling off a high plain of some sort. Still, there were lots of rumors about mountains, and it made sense there'd be something like the Blue Ridge matching, so to speak, in the West. Didn't have to be, of course, but you just figured. The mouth of the Columbia and the known area of the Missouri were about the same latitude. So looking at that, it made sense that the Columbia likely rose about where the Missouri did and there should be a neat portage across some height of land or other, a mile or two one hoped, that would readily connect. Northwest Passage.

The idea that the problem would solve itself so neatly remained a risky wager, but it had been said so often and for so long by such authorities that it had taken on a certitude that he could hardly deny. He had Aaron Arrowsmith's authoritative map of North America, published in London in 1802. He had the map Nicholas King had made for Mr. Gallatin and Mr. Jefferson in 1803 incorporating all the latest knowledge. Arrowsmith showed the mountains as a single ridge slashing down the continent. King showed mountains as hesitantly shaded entities with many breaks.

Facts and rumor intertwined, the result of years of thinking, imagining, correlating reports and estimates and rumors and dreams, all interworked with geographic logic—water flows downhill, snow melts in summer, springs emerge from underground streams, creeks become rivers, rivers must come from somewhere and must go to the sea, themselves or in bigger rivers.

But how different now from those pleasant speculative hours in Mr. Jefferson's study. In a smoky Mandan hut, watching a man he can't understand, it all becomes real, immediate, dangerous. The man sketches on a skin with a burnt stick, then pushes it aside in impatience to scratch in the ground, piling handfuls of dirt to indicate mountains, wild hand gestures to indicate cliffs and canyons, all with the force of authority— but did he really know? Did Jessaume even translate accurately? How different . . . and the thought formed again, locked in his mind in the same words—now it was real, immediate, dangerous. Now his and his men's lives depended on it. Now he had to know the way that lay ahead.

Gradually it came together. He and Clark listened and sketched. Indians had no compasses. They explained directions as angles drawn off the sun's course, distances by the days it took to travel them. The two captains decided a sleep was worth twenty-five miles, on average. It seemed the Missouri did indeed run from mountains that were high and dangerous. But no more so, the captains agreed, than the Blue Ridge at home, which rarely topped four thousand feet.

All the Indians agreed on the great trail of eastbound water. The river left the mountains, ran northeast, then veered east across vast distances to the Mandans. The Americans would be going *up*river—going west, then turning southwest. They would pass tributaries entering from north and south. Find the all-important Yellowstone entering from the south or the left. It was fed by the Powder and the Tongue and the Bighorn and the Indians said was named for yellow cliffs supposed to stand near its source though they knew no one who had actually seen this marvel. Sulfur had to be involved, Lewis figured.

Fight on up against the roaring current, come to more and more tributaries and then, at last, to the Great Falls of the Missouri. Now, that was a landmark that white men had picked up from Indian talk, though none had ever seen it. Rumors of it had reached clear to the East. Immense thunderous falls that hurtled into a hundred-foot drop with such speed and force that one could walk dry shod behind the crashing torrent. And an easy portage around the falls, half mile or so, Clark estimated. Beyond the falls come to the Three Forks of the Missouri; the right-hand fork carries you to the mountains. There it all became shadowy. They knew, they insisted, but when you pressed them they admitted that no, they themselves had not actually gone so far, but others had, it all was correct and certain. Headwaters of that right-hand fork will carry you to an easy pass and the far side you will see a beautiful open valley with water running to the west . . .

Lewis breathed a sigh of relief. It was there to be done, awaiting them, the way sketched out, landmarks in place. He felt as safe as he had in Jefferson's study. Almost as safe.

29

On the Missouri, April, 1805

When the air softened and the ice broke up and the first shoots of new green appeared, Meriwether Lewis led the Corps of Discovery out of the Mandan villages. At last he and his force—thirty-one men, one woman with her two-month-old son in a cradleboard on her back, and the big black dog trotting at Lewis's heels as he walked the high bank above the boats on the glittering water below—were leaving the known world to penetrate the unknown.

This was adventure, striding onto a whole that no man had assayed before. How many men get the chance to realize dreams? How many would even understand what that meant? But then, Lewis always had felt somehow alone. Even in boyhood life was at its best when he was on his own in the woods; there he felt he realized most fully an inner power, that quality that seemed to draw women and yet to frighten them. Perhaps that had to do with the bouts of melancholy that it seemed his own pa had bequeathed him, that even the president had noticed. But now all was changed as the greatest adventure prepared to unfold.

Ahead, much farther up the Missouri, lay the mountains; beyond them should lie the Columbia and passage to the Pacific. They need only find the mountains and that easy portage, then find the rising of the river known at its mouth as the Columbia and float on to the sea. Set aside two hundred years of wondering and conjecturing, theorizing and dreaming, and go and see. In doing so the Corps of Discovery would make itself central to ultimate national expansion, one of the great steps in opening the West.

But he was wise enough to fear such thoughts; his own reality lay ahead mile by mile, ascending the river, climbing the mountains, and plunging on. The Purchase meant he would be on American territory until the mountains, but at their crest he would pass onto land that world powers hungered for, Spain from the south, Britain from the north, Russia from the Arctic. It was time to reanchor the American claim.

Into the unknown, then, with a conjectural map based on scanty information conveyed in a language he didn't understand. There was immediate urgency. Snow would fly all too soon in the mountains. Then game would flee to the lowlands and men caught on the heights would be in starving time. He must get through before then; he didn't think he could survive defeat.

But forget risk. It was basic to life, present at some level in all one did. Focus instead on that alluring, mysterious, challenging sense of something out ahead that drew him ever forward. For much of his life he'd dreamed of walking into the unknown and now he was doing it.

He tramped along bluffs above the river where his two pirogues and six dugout canoes labored against the current. His rifle was slung across his back, his oak-shafted spontoon with its sharpened steel point was balanced in his hand. Seaman trotted close behind. Alternately he scanned the horizon for alarms and spied plants new and old, stopping to sketch and make notes, eyes keen for new birds and animals. His pace was long and steady and he felt tireless.

He was happy, happier, he felt, than he'd ever been. He felt whole in some new way, complete, fully in accord with what he was meant to be, old dislocations falling away. Even now, in the very act, he thought this tramping into the unknown, no matter the hardships, perils, weight of responsibility, would be the high point of his life. All that followed would be on a down slope.

From a bluff he looked down at his little flotilla, the slender dugouts black knife shapes in the shining water. He picked out Will Clark in the stern of a pirogue and felt a wave of affection. As co-captain, Clark was equal in command, equal in operation, and would be forever no matter what the War Department said. But it also was true that he was making a superb executive officer. Perhaps it was their differences that had drawn them together over the years. Clark was bluff, genial, hearty, good-humored but capable of startling anger, authoritative, intelligent, a natural waterman as Lewis was a natural walker. He was easy with the men who knew immediately that they could trust him. He was a happy man and always would be. But he didn't think and dream as Lewis did, or so Lewis surmised. He was steady, strong, sensible, stalwart in any crisis, and was Lewis's best friend; but he was not a dreamer and Lewis thought that was much to the better.

Looking down at his men, tiny figures in slender craft in glittering water, it struck him that Columbus could have been no more proud of his fleet and his men when he set out from Cadiz on a westerly course to find the Passage to India. Now, in parallel, 314 years later, Lewis's little party intended to complete what Columbus had started, make the new world whole, focus the continental nation, open that passage to the Orient.

When Cap'n Lewis had said it was about time to get on up the river toward the mountains George Shannon had clicked his heels with joy. He'd been ready! Felt like he just couldn't wait to see the sights out ahead, for them Indians had made the mountains sound like nothing you'd see back in Pennsylvania. And he'd been so sick of winter in the fort they'd built on that miserable island that he'd been about to pop a gut.

Wind screaming and moaning day and night, sleet cutting your face when you went out and found snow to your belt line, temperatures to freeze your eyeballs in their sockets or your pecker like poor old York — oh, but the boys did rag him after that, telling him his loving days were over, he'd done wore the thing out. Not to mince words, the plain fact was that if George Shannon never saw the High Plains in winter again that would be too soon. But now, on up the river a ways, winter memories were fading and he was full of joy.

He had the lead paddle in the second pirogue under Sergeant Ordway and that was an honor he would fight to protect. The long pirogue steered from the stern but the man in the bow had to be strong for he must react in an instant to claw the vessel off a rock that showed up from nowhere. Or a sawyer springing from the water like a ghost of the tree it once had been ready to punch out a boat's bottom. John Colter warned him, but Shannon didn't need no reminders; once you see a sawyer rearing out of the water like a sea serpent, you ain't likely to forget.

Paddle on one side ten minutes, then on the other. Current was running swifter as the terrain rose and the river narrowed. It felt like six or seven miles an hour, which meant they had to paddle that plus some more to make any progress at all. He could feel his shoulders and biceps growing; his shirts were tight to bust where they'd been a good fit when they wintered on the Mississippi. Indian girl had made him a buckskin shirt back at the Mandans else he'd soon be near as naked as the day he was born.

He heard a shout up ahead and saw Cap'n Clark gesturing to cross to catch the slack water on the inside of the turn. It was Shannon's job in the bow to keep her cocked on a forty-five-degree angle so no precious gain would be lost, digging as hard upstream as across, muscles aflame. Around the bend he saw with pleasure while others cursed that the river narrowed to a chute that the water rushed through. They tried it, paddling hard but making no headway as Shannon had figured, ahead a few feet, then back—watch the same rock for half an hour. Cap'n Clark signaled them ashore and they broke out the cordelles with their overhand loops to fit a man's shoulder so he could dig in his feet and drag the boat against the current. Shannon liked the cordelles because it put him ashore and let him use different muscles, but it sure enough was the hardest work of all. Naturally you didn't always get a nice sandy beach to stroll along. More likely you found rocks to climb over or thick brush to claw through or the cliff would come sheer to the river and you'd have to wade out in ice water up to your chest, slipping and sliding on mossy stones.

A couple of men stayed aboard to hold the boat off the shore with poles. On this particular day it was Shannon's turn to stay aboard so he was riding while the others worked. He was studying a magpie standing on a rock when the boat stopped moving. The towline was sawing between two sharp rocks. His warning was too late—the rope parted and the boat spun in the current.

He dropped the pole and scrambled to his paddle as the pirogue turned broadside. Then the boat hung on a rock, water pressure lifted one side, and water flooded in the other side. Shannon froze a moment. Then he saw the little Indian gal, her babe on that funny board she wore on her back, and she was catching boxes and holding them fast while the pirogue tipped farther and farther. She looked as cool as if she'd been back in some tepee cooking dog meat stew. Shannon reached his paddle and yelled at Dick Windsor in the stern and together they bent the boat off the rock and grounded it a hundred yards downstream. In camp that night Shannon told everyone about the Indian gal and the way she saved the supplies. Turned out all the expedition records was in one of them boxes. Only later did he learn that Sacagawea didn't know how to swim, she'd have drowned for sure if she'd gone in the water. Her and her baby. She had plenty of nerve, she did.

Every night when they went into camp she got the baby boy out of that contraption and warmed up some water and washed him good and then nursed him. She was a sight more tender than Shannon could remember his own ma ever being. Course, his ma had had a passel of youngsters. Cap'n Clark had taken a keen liking to the little boy. Sat him up on a blanket and played with him every night. The cap'n called him Pomp and said he was a fine little man with a great future and before you knew it the cap'n had laid out a whole life course for him, said bring him back to St. Louis and the cap'n would put him in the best school—well, by golly, he *was* a cute little tyke at that. It was surprising that an ugly bastard like Charbonneau could produce such a baby; Shannon decided Pomp took after his ma.

Of course risk was everywhere, clearly it was basic to life, and certainly Lewis had welcomed it across his own span of years as the spice that kept everything bright and alive. But a high-stakes whist game when the other side has marked the cards makes losing not a risk but a certainty. His mind flashed over those sessions with the Mandan wise men, the old Hidatsas who remembered the route from war raids that had carried them to the mountains, or almost to them.

Remember how they had sketched a rough map in the dirt, using twigs that soon wore down. Remember their quarrels over the positioning of this tributary or that, the hills and cliffs and gullies, put it a little more this way or that, smooth out the drawing here, extend the river there, while outside the wind howled and shook the lodge and snow on the ground grew steadily deeper. He remembered Black Cat's irritation when his prize pinto wandered into the circle, hoofs obliterating hills and valleys and turns of the river, how the Indian had snapped at his son, the boy looking hurt at this rare chastisement, telling him to get the beast back where he belonged, give him a piece of cottonwood bark, keep him happy.

He had read sincerity in these men's eyes and in their manner, but could he read accurately when he really didn't know their culture? Was translation even accurate? Or did it matter? His mission was to follow the Missouri to the mountains, which he could do without help. But the Indians had taken him right into the mountains, to the towering waterfall marked by the huge eagle's nest high in a dead cottonwood, used every year by the big birds, each occupant dutifully expanding it. An easy portage would surmount this obstacle and then they would follow the dwindling Missouri on to the three forks, where three smaller rivers joined to make the river he followed. Two would be dead ends if a man mistakenly followed those, but the third would take him to the crest, the stream steadily shrinking until it was a trickle that one could step over readily.

It was all there to be done. Right to the crest where the Shoshones, Sacagawea's people, lived with their many horses. Peer over the crest and you would see that which you sought. The men huddled around the map on the dirt floor of the smoky lodge admitted readily that they had never seen it but they were nevertheless entirely certain that you would find a broad, gentle plain, grassy and easy, sloping downward, a spring feeding a trickle that before your eyes grew into a small stream and then into a river that wound into the hazy distance and certainly was the great river to the west that they sought.

Now he must test what he'd been told.

His party had broken up at the Mandans. Corporal Warfington and his detachment were taking the keelboat downriver to St. Louis while the

Corps of Discovery moved upstream with the two pirogues and a fleet of six dugout canoes laboriously prepared over the winter. The keelboat was loaded with specimens and information for the president. It included live birds and several healthy prairie dogs, the latter sure to delight the chief scientist in Washington. Lewis and Clark each had written reports covering all that they had learned so far—details on terrain, nature of the soil, rainfall, suitability for agriculture, animal life, volume and flow of the river, nature of the Indian tribes they had encountered, fur trade patterns, and even offered opinions on why trees didn't grow on the prairie when the rich soil produced an abundance of grass that fed vast herds of grazing animals without ever growing thin.

They reported what they had been able to learn or surmise about each river that emptied into the Missouri below the Mandans. And Clark included his map of the river to the Mandans, which Lewis considered a cartographic masterpiece. This was a judgment he felt entitled to make given how closely he had studied so many maps, both those made in the field and those from, for instance, Arrowsmith's chart room in London. So the keelboat had cast off with shouted farewells and Godspeeds from both parties and the pirogues had started west.

The pirogue painted white was the smaller, a little under fifty feet, the red pirogue a little more. They were flat bottomed, rudder at the stern, mast a bit forward of amidships, rigged for a square sail when the wind was right, equipped for oars but usually paddled. The white was the more stable of the two and here the captains stored their writing materials, notebooks and records, and the precious navigation instruments.

It took a while for the men to fall back into the paddling rhythm that had brought them here, for now the river was shallower, the current swifter, the fight against onrushing water more difficult. Spring winds blew with what felt like tornadic force. Occasionally current and winds were too much and they took cover in a cove; sometimes a canoe would founder and douse its cargo. Then they must stop, empty it, unwrap everything, spread it on hot sand to dry in sunshine. No shortage of sand, of course. The howling wind picked it up in clouds and slashed it against faces and eyes. Venereal problems had left some of the boys with miserably sore eyes that the sand aggravated without mercy.

In deepening dusk one night Lewis came on Colter and Shannon talking in low voices. They were leaning against a downed tree trunk and Shannon appeared to be complaining about his eyes. With a chuckle, Colter said, "That's that little gal's present to you, George."

"Naw," George said. "You think so?"

"Course. Half the camp's got the sore eyes."

"But that don't mean—"

"French traders from Canada give it to 'em, that's what I hear, and they pass it right along."

"Go on. How could they do that?"

"Hell, I don't know. Reckon nobody does. Only it seems like it don't get passed 'til you take off your pants. On the other hand, who wants to keep his pants on at such a time?"

Both men laughed and then there was a long pause and Colter spoke more seriously. Lewis had to grin at his patronizing tone. "You see, George, ain't nothing in the world free. Little gal gives you joy, sooner or later she'll give you misery. Way life is, boy, and you better get used to it."

That night Seaman failed to return from some exploration of his own. Lewis walked out a ways and cut a wide circle, whistling and calling. Seaman could take care of himself, but if he met a bear he'd probably attack and would be sorely overmatched. He waited but no Seaman came crashing through the grass with his tail wagging. Lewis turned in that night feeling low and sorrowful, abruptly aware of how attached to the dog he had become. So in the morning when Seaman came bounding in he felt such a joyous surge of relief that he had to turn away lest damp eyes betray an emotion to the men that was not his idea of proper style for a man leading others across a continent. Under the guise of examining the dog's coat for wounds he managed quietly to express his affection, seizing Seaman by the muzzle and wagging him gently.

The Indian guides and mapmakers had been explicit—going upstream the Yellowstone River would be the first tributary of any size. It would enter from the left, coming from the west and emerging from a lush garden spot. No one Lewis met had actually seen the yellow cliffs that gave it its name, nor had anyone seen the geysers or boiling springs or mineral drips, all quite magical, from which it was said to rise, but they assured him that both existed. But such fanciful mysteries didn't matter much; what mattered was that the river fed the Missouri somewhat as they said.

Day by day he waited for the big river to appear on the left, sweating each turn as likely to unfold the treasure. He grew steadily more impatient, his faith in his informants shrinking, his fear of having been gulled growing. At last he decided to hurry ahead, making time by cutting across the river's looping turns. He took Drewyer and Joe Field and set out with Seaman close on his heels.

He always felt better when he was shaking out his legs and on the move. He followed broad trails of freshly turned dirt cut by moving buffalo herds, admiring the efficient way they went from here to there without a wasted step. They might as well have used transit and slide rule. The day faded away and Lewis pushed on, his mouth a grim cut in a hard face.

The sun winked over a crest ahead and left them in shadow. It was time to stop, form a camp, get a fire going, start turning chunks of the fat buffalo calf Drewyer had shot. From the corner of his eye he caught Drewyer and Field glancing at him, ready to suggest a stop.

But he didn't pause or speak and they marched on toward the crest. When they reached it he raised a hand to stop them. They were looking down at a broad valley through which a big river curled in graceful curves, sweeping back and forth into the distance. Remnants of sunlight were still in the valley, lighting extensive stands of timber so that new leaves glistened. Hurrying down the slope to the water they passed what seemed endless groves of fruit trees and berry vines, the fruit still tiny green kernels. They came on large herds—buffalo, elk, antelope—so unused to men that they walked among them without stirring alarm. Twice, indeed, a big critter approached as if to examine these strangers more closely.

Lewis slept that night with rare satisfaction. The Yellowstone was all that the Mandans had promised, as big, as beautiful, and when he paused to think it through, about where they had said as well.

In the morning he sent Joe Field up the stream as far as he could reach and still get back by nightfall. Lewis roamed through the river bottom searching out new plants and making careful entries in his notebook. In late afternoon Field returned to report that the current seemed gentle as the river swept to and fro in complex zigzag, often pausing to throw up sandbars. The valley continued broad and fertile. Presently Lewis heard the crack of rifles; Clark with the boats had reached the mouth of the river. With Drewyer and Field he walked down to greet them; he and Clark decided on the spot to hold an extra day in this magnificent garden; that night they had an extra dram of spirits, a dinner of buffalo veal, and a rousing party, singing and laughing and dancing, Gibson on his fiddle, Cruzatte on his hands, York's feet going about faster than you could see. The boys downright matched Lewis's mood, here at the mouth of the Yellowstone that was close enough to what the Mandans had said and making just the sort of garden they had described.

As they crawled on up the river that seemed to run a little faster each day the men began having too frequent encounters with the giant grizzled bears of the West. Lewis knew the Indians feared the beast but he figured that was because arrows were their primary weapons. Men standing fast with first-class 1803 rifles in their hands weren't likely to have much trouble no matter the creature's size. Put a couple of balls where it counted and he'd go down, all right.

They came to the Little Missouri River about where the Indians had said, and moving on, to the White Earth River coming from the right, sweeping down from Canada or at least near Canada, which wasn't all that far at this point. Lewis walked upstream two or three miles and sure enough saw the white patches of alkali in the banks that gave it its name. It was an important river in Lewis's view and he made careful notes. Now, in the spring, it had substantial water that was important because it ran near the south fork of Canada's Saskatchewan River and might make an avenue for American traders to tap the Canadian fur market. That would please the president, no doubt at all.

That night Lewis awakened to the guard's yells to find pandemonium. A huge buffalo bull swam across the river in the dark and collided with a pirogue. Apparently he took it for the bank for he scrambled onto one end. The boat bobbed violently, threw two men into the river, and nearly turned over as the bull slid off the other side. Now thoroughly rattled, the big beast climbed out of the river and charged headlong into the camp, heading straight for the neat tepee of tanned buffalo hide that Sacagawea put up with York's help each night. She and her husband slept there with Pomp, and the two captains who, without ever quite saying so, were making sure that the presence of a woman didn't lead to adventures that could destroy morale. At this Seaman leaped before it and barked and snarled so violently that the vast beast veered off and thundered out of the camp, men sleeping on the ground awakening just in time to scramble out of the way.

When dawn's light let them examine the damage to the pirogue, Shannon broke out the carpentry tools and set about repairs. Before noon they were on their way, and sure enough, came roughly on schedule to the next entering river, this one from the north. For reasons neither Lewis nor Clark could discover, the Indians called it "The River that Scolds All Others." Perhaps they had seen it when it was in hellish mood but it looked placid enough to Lewis; its color made him think of tea with milk and Clark penciled it onto the map as the Milk River. Next the Mussel-shell, translated from Mandan words describing the shell fossils found there. It appeared on schedule, almost on the day that Lewis expected it; the Indian geographers were proving out and Lewis was more and more content.

It was the damnedest howling yelling Shannon had ever heard, sounded like stark terror, couldn't tell if it were man or beast. Cap'n Clark signaled them in toward shore, and about then here come Will Bratton busting out of the woods, caterwauling like a damn banshee wailing someone's death notice. Shannon had never held Bratton in high regard, him having acted the fool a little too often, but something sure had him roiled up now.

When they touched the bank Shannon leaped out to lash the painter to a convenient tree. He yelled to York to break out a pole and hold the vessel's main body off the rocky shore. And Bratton come running up like he intended to jump into Shannon's arms as a child might, Shannon cocking a fist to let him have it if he tried such a damn fool stunt.

Instead Bratton fell to his knees, choking for breath, and finally gasped out his story. He had seen a grizzly, taken aim, and fired. He was positive he'd hit the critter dead center. But instead of dropping dead as Bratton had expected, the bear stood up and roared in surprise and rage and then tilted into a dead run, charging his attacker, his little eyes red, obviously planning murderous vengeance. Bratton threw away his rifle and fled through the woods. He insisted he could smell the bear's breath, the big beast was that close. Then, abruptly, coughing blood, the bear broke off, turned about, and trotted into the woods.

Shannon couldn't stand it. "The bear's breath, what did it smell like?"

Bratton glared, leaning toward Shannon, looking a bit like an angry bear himself. "I ain't in no mood to be played with, Shannon. What it smelled like, it smelled like fish. What he'd been eating, I reckon."

Shannon couldn't stop himself. "And you sure you hit him?"

"Hell, yes. Why else would he be coughing blood?"

Cap'n Lewis said they would go find this bear and see if he was kilt or what, and Shannon got himself into the front rank. Bratton showed them where the bear had turned and sure enough there were blood splashes on the grass and on tree leaves. They heard the bear before they saw him, a furious roaring that gave Shannon a shiver, though he'd never admit that.

The bear had crawled into a grove where the foliage was dense and had dug a pit a couple of feet deep, just big enough to lie in. Cap'n Lewis put two balls through his head and that finished him. They dragged him out of his pit and saw he was medium size, maybe three hundred pounds, and sure enough, the ball had gone right through his lungs and he'd still chased Bratton a mile or two and then retreated at least half that distance before he lay himself down to die.

"My God," Cap'n Lewis said, voice soft, sort of talking to himself like, "that is the damnedest animal I ever saw." But the cap'n still thought two hunters with 1803 pieces should be able to handle such a critter.

No one asked Shannon what he thought and he'd finally decided there might be merit in keeping his mouth shut, but if you asked him, he didn't much want to be one of them two hunters.

Well, Lewis told himself and told Clark, too, talking it over, Bratton hadn't shone very brightly. He should have shot the damned bear through the brain. But that wasn't fair, either, as Clark reminded him. If you're firing from a distance, and with a grizzly, that's where you want to be firing from, the brain is a pretty small target. No, what made the grizzly special was that when you wounded one of them, it didn't run off like a normal animal. It whirled about and charged, intent on tearing your head off when it caught you.

Part of the trouble lay in your weapon. The 1803 model infantry rifle, designed and manufactured at the armory at Harper's Ferry, was probably the finest and most modern rifle in the world. But it still took some time to load. Fire, then pull the rammer, splash a measure of powder from your horn down the barrel, lay a greased patch atop the barrel, put a ball thereon, ram it all down to the powder, then pop open the frizzen pan, put a dollop of powder there, close the pan, aim, fire, and start all over again. A trained rifleman could get off two rounds a minute, compared to the five or six arrows an Indian could fire in the same time, or the ground that a charging grizzly could cover.

A day or two later a couple of the boys, figuring two shots would be a sure kill, fired and found the bear hardly fazed. He locked on to them immediately and charged as they discarded weapons and ran along the riverbank. He ran along behind them, gaining. They jumped into the river from a twenty-foot bank. He jumped right in behind them and was swimming rapidly toward them when Drewyer killed him with a brain shot.

Only a day or two later Will was ashore with Drewyer and the Field brothers, Lewis left in charge of the boats struggling upstream. Early that afternoon he saw Will waving them in to a convenient landing place where a small stream entered the river.

"Let's strike camp here," Will said. "I got the damnedest bear you ever saw. He's in the river, on a sandbar, and I'll need a couple of the canoes to drag him in."

"He's alive?" Lewis asked.

"Oh, my God, no. We killed him but you wouldn't believe the fight he put up."

They took one of the canoes to a sandbar about half across the river, the three crewmen landing it well away from the body of the bear. Looking at the biggest bear he'd ever seen, Lewis whistled; thank goodness it was dead.

Still excited, his voice high and finding it hard to stay still, Clark said he and Drewyer had spotted the monster standing waist deep in the river and snatching out fish with lightning strokes of his big paw and tossing them onto the bank. He said he and Drewyer, moving very slowly, had concealed themselves in brush before opening fire from separate positions. The bear began to roar in obvious fury but it seemed he couldn't figure out the source of the attack and so had nothing to charge. Clark said he and Drewyer each got off five shots before the bear plunged into the water and swam to the sandbar that looked at least halfway across the river. Collapsed on the sandbar, it slowly died as it continued to roar in diminishing volume, and with a note of lament and dismay like the bear had never expected to come to such an end so suddenly. Lewis was surprised by this remark, coming from a poetic depth he hadn't expected in good old Will.

With a canoe and half a dozen crewmen they managed to get the beast into the water and then tow it ashore. When Lewis estimated the difference between how far Will and Drewyer were from the bear when they fired, and the distance the bear had traveled after they mortally wounded it, it seemed evident that had the bear figured out his attackers' location, as every other bear had done, Drewyer and Clark might be dead men now. But Clark could make the same measurement and reach the same understanding. No need to put it in words.

Struck with awe, Lewis measured the creature—from tip of nose to hind feet it was just under eight feet eight inches. They had no means of weighing it; Clark thought five hundred pounds, Lewis guessed six hundred, but as he studied the huge barrel chest he felt his estimate had been conservative. Might have been seven hundred, even eight hundred. When he dissected it he found five balls had passed through the lungs, while five lodged in other parts of the body, and still it managed to swim half across the river before it died. Lewis opened the huge jaw and saw that it was big enough to seize a man's head and probably strong enough to tear it off. He sighed and decided not to think further along those lines. Opening the carcass he found a heart the size of that of a large ox and a maw ten times the size of that of a black bear. The maw was stuffed with fish and with animal flesh that Lewis couldn't identify. When they rendered its fat for cooking it filled a small cask.

So here was a huge animal, fast, four-inch claws on the end of paws that he swung like a machete blade, able to outrun any man and most horses, capable of taking rifle balls everywhere but his brain while attacking at a dead run and showing a ferocious reluctance to die—he was indeed the king of the forest and he acted the part, walking with shambling assurance and hardly knowing the meaning of fear.

And this was the creature that Lewis had been entirely confident a couple of shots with a Model 1803 would drop readily. In his journal that night, describing the adventure, he observed privately that his ignorance was past and grizzlies intimidated him just as they did the Indian nations

as a whole. Clark never mentioned the event and Lewis surmised he had
learned the same lessons.

The boats clawed another fifty miles upstream, the river more shallow,
more turbulent. The country grew rough and broken with cliffs that
glowed in gorgeous colors when the sun was low. The Great Falls of the
Missouri couldn't be far now. The captains gave their exhausted men a
day's rest. And Lewis would go examine those distant cliffs and see what
lay on the other side. The explorer's hunger, to see what lies beyond the
far horizon.

The walk across four or five miles of floodplain covered mostly with
scrub willow, favored food for elk and other such critters, was harder
than he had expected. So was the climb up the cliff face. He wished now
he'd brought the Field brothers along with climbing ropes—some of the
passes were pretty thin to try alone. But it was too late to turn back,
which wasn't in his nature anyway. At the top he sat on a convenient
rock, drank from his flask shaped from a gourd, and looked around.

And there in the distance he saw a flash of white that looked too hard
and steep and sharp to be clouds. For a moment it seemed to disappear in
the glare. He shut his eyes, then shaded them with both hands and con-
centrated. And yes, there they were, mountains, huge mountains. And so
for the first time he saw the great mountains of the West.

He sat gazing with open mouth as hawks soared on sun thermals far
overhead. He was thrilled, excited, delighted—and, perhaps, a little dismayed as well. For these mountains were huge, vastly larger than the
Blue Ridge; forget all ideas of an easy transit. He was at least fifty,
maybe a hundred miles away, which meant he was looking at their tops,
the bulk of their bodies hidden by the curvature of the earth. Today was
May 26 and the peaks he must lead his men across were still packed
with snow. Would it be gone by the time he arrived? Would lower pas-
sages opening through the mountains be clear by then? If he could see
them at fifty to a hundred miles distance, how big must they be? How
much climbing would the expedition face? Talk of a gentle slope up to
meet a gentle slope down, manageable portage between, was suddenly
ridiculous.

Yet what a sight to see—the very mountains they had postulated and
dreamed about and wondered if they would ever reach. Did these mountains even exist? The Rocky Mountains, folks were calling them now, the
old names, Stony Mountains, Shining Mountains, fading before the new.
What this meant, the great landmark of the whole venture lying revealed

before them, it meant truly they were on their way. All they need do now was fight their way to those mountains and then across them and then . . . well, they had far to go and perhaps much to suffer, but the way was ever more clear. Think of it—the Rocky Mountains in sight . . .

30

On the Missouri, Summer, 1805

The water grew colder and swifter as they climbed; rapids appeared. They were using cordelles more often, frequently wading in paralyzing cold. It was brutal work and he and Clark made sure they took their share. He could see the pain on the men's faces but there was no slacking. As the days passed glimpses of the snowcapped mountains appeared more and more often, the men pausing to stare in awe. Lewis watched to see if he spotted fear on anyone's face and saw none; the closest anyone came was from the Field brothers. Joe asked somewhat plaintively, "Snow'll be gone, time we get there, don't you reckon, Cap'n?"

"Better hope it ain't," Reuben said. "Then we kin make us snowshoes or skis or somesuch and go sliding right over and never feel a bump. Ain't that right, Cap'n?"

"Leave me out of it," Lewis said, but he was reassured. They would be all right.

"Kiss my ass, Reub," Joe said, but he was smiling and Reuben laughed.

They passed from the mountains of color—towering cliffs with horizontal bands of white stone pierced with upthrusts of dark red stone that had eroded to leave towers and minarets, columns and pediments, pyramids and organ pipes and spires and niches in colors that glowed in the sun and merged to sheer white—and still it was all as expected, all that Black Cat had laid out while the snow flew outside the Mandan lodge.

It really was gorgeous country. Lewis swung along thinking of the bighorn sheep that he had just recorded for science. Big devils with curled horns poised five hundred feet over the river on a speck of rock, then leaping to another point, defying death as part of life. The country was mostly treeless, drier than one expected, but rich grass and willow brush in the breaks supported vast herds of buffalo, antelope, deer, elk.

They were eating high these days. Foxes, coyotes, and the gray wolf he had just identified for science hung on the herds, the wolves in alternating groups that relieved each other in chases that wore down the fleet grass-eaters . . .

The Great Falls, that magnificent landmark, should be but a few weeks on. He strode along full of confidence, Seaman investigating new odors, Drewyer and John Colter back a hundred paces, Lewis with rifle slung, notebook in one hand, spontoon in the other. Botanist, biologist, it didn't really matter—his journal was filling with exciting new discoveries. He could visualize appearing before the American Philosophical Society as a new elected fellow and laying out discoveries and findings that were spectacular—perhaps Mr. Jefferson would introduce him. Presently he veered back to the river to check his progress. He came to the lip and looked down—good God!

Ahead in the distance *the river forked*! The bottom fell out of his stomach. There wasn't supposed to be any landmark of any consequence, certainly not a major new river, between here and the Great Falls. The Indians had been positive about that, he remembered Black Cat jabbing the earth for emphasis, sweeping his hands apart in universal gesture, shaking his head, nothing! But what could it mean? That they were wrong? That they had lied, playing with him, damn fool white men thinking they can challenge the great country? Told him the truth on the near stuff that he could have found on his own and lied on what mattered? But he could not believe that. There had been conviction in their voices, and he was not sufficiently the fool nor they the skilled performers to make such grand deception likely.

He hurried back to find the boats. This was serious. They had far to go before new snow plugged those passes that the Field boys joked about. Walking and trotting, he reviewed the map in his mind.

They had started up from the Mandans, the turbid water growing steadily colder and swifter, but muddy as ever, the ground clearly rising. So far everything had been on the mark. Passed the Little Missouri and came to the White Earth River with its alkali banks. Just as was said. Then the mighty Yellowstone swept in from the south, its bottomlands full of rich growths of gooseberry, choke cherry, service berry, redberry, purple currant, honeysuckle, willow brush. The Missouri had even made the abrupt swing north and then the turn to the southwest.

But now they had come to a new fork, one that no one had mentioned, not a word in all those long smoky nights around lodge fires, Indians agreeing step by step on routes they all had covered in going after buffalo. Neither branch was a mere entering creek; both were substantial rivers flowing together where there was supposed to be no more than one. One was the Missouri, the other an unnamed tributary. But which was which?

Lewis hailed the boats ashore and told Clark the ominous news. Clark's mouth drew down in a hard line. It was at times like this that Lewis most appreciated his partner's cool head and sunny optimism. They camped that night on the point of land between the two rivers.

Could the Indians be so wrong? Clark thought it over and then nodded. Yes, they could be wrong. The problem might be that sharp turn to the north that the Missouri took, then the swift turn to the southwest. Remember, the Mandans held near their villages; it was the Hidatsas who had actually traveled to the mountains. And they were horse Indians who probably cut across the loop and missed this new river. Indians only went where there was reason to go. Lewis stood there slowly nodding; yes, that could be and the idea was certainly comforting. But it still left the difficult question; which fork was the Missouri?

In the morning they studied things. The right-hand or north fork was just what the Missouri had been for two thousand miles, the same muddy water that settled out a half inch in a cup, same turbid look and rolling motion. It ran from the west where the mountains were. It was two hundred yards wide, and deep.

The left or south fork was wider but not so deep. Its water was so clear you could see the round stones on its bottom. It was swifter and colder and ran with unriffled surface.

Stop and think, now. They were said to be approaching the Great Falls. But to carry such mud the north fork must cross hundreds of miles of prairie. The swift, clear south fork with its stony bottom was characteristic of mountain streams; it wasn't hard to believe its water had just come over the falls, that this, in fact, was the Missouri.

So they decided, but they returned to camp to find the men had decided otherwise. Pierre Cruzatte, his one eye full of fire, shouted that he had spent his life on the Missouri and he reckoned he knew his river when he saw it. The men agreed; the north fork was the Missouri. Hadn't they just traversed two thousand miles of this self-same river? They were amazed to learn their captains liked the south fork that didn't look a bit like the river they knew. Day-long patrols up each fork brought no answers.

This was a crisis. Time was short. They still must find the Shoshones, barter for horses, get across mountains that all aside from their formidable appearance, the Indians had made sound dangerous and near certain to be snowed over by early fall. If snow trapped them at altitude they would starve as game fled to the lowlands. They could eat their horses if they had horses but then how would they get out? So here, on this unexplained fork, if they chose the wrong way and had to turn and retrace their steps they could destroy the whole expedition. A serious delay would make them too late to get through. Supplies would run low with no source to replenish them in two thousand miles. No choice then but to retreat with tail tucked to the Mandan villages and then on to St. Louis. It would be total failure for everyone—and for American dreams.

This was a military expedition. Lewis knew he and Clark could simply order their soldiers forward. Discipline would carry them, but not willingly. He talked it over with Clark; forcing men is not leadership. Morale had been high, the men cheerful in the face of brutal hardship that certainly would get worse. But order them blindly on what they were sure was the wrong course and morale could collapse overnight. They'd better spend a few days examining each fork at length.

Lewis took the north fork and set out at dawn, Seaman at his heels, Drewyer and Sergeant Pryor with Shields, Windsor, Lepage, and the doubting Cruzatte. Low-growing prickly pear ripped their moccasins; they retreated to the bottoms and fought through brush and shallows. It was hard and his legs ached and mosquitoes were maddening, but he drove them thirty-two miles that first day, going due north. He catalogued five new birds; wild roses were in bloom. The next day and the next and the river didn't change.

He mounted a height from which he could see a good twenty miles and there was the winding ribbon undeviatingly coming from due north. It came on him now with the force of real conviction: this wasn't the Missouri. It was a big, powerful river coming from a great distance to account for all the mud it carried, probably rising up in Canada somewhere, maybe someday to provide a trade outlet that would let Americans tap Canadian fur, but in the present situation naught but a siren luring them toward the rocks.

He turned them and started back. Perhaps he would name this Maria's River, for a pretty cousin in whom he had absolutely no interest. But Clark had stung him a bit when he penciled in the most recent tributary they had encountered as Judy's River, for the cousin he figured would be old enough to wed when he returned. Probably it would work out exactly thus, Clark with his sunny temperament. Of course he'd have a girl he intended to marry, they'd have a passel of children and live happily ever after. Not that he begrudged ol' Will, who was a good fellow and deserved all the good fortune he could muster, but it set Lewis thinking about himself and all the times things went wrong. Miss Dolley's sister, Anna, she'd just been playing with him, he could see that now, careless young girl not knowing what impact she had and not much caring, either, but he had forgotten her. Doubtless she was long married now. It was a puzzlement the way pretty girls were drawn at first and then repelled. He thought about June Landros again, as he so often did, she'd really tickled his fancy there in

Philadelphia, and he thought again that there had been something real there, but it all blew up, and without any explanation, either. Well, forget it, never mind this eternal puzzling. Unbidden, her fatal words jumped again into his mind. *You scare me*, and this right in her father's drawing room. What? Why? But she'd shaken her head and run to the stairs and there was the butler waiting to show him out and the next day when he came by she was gone, to New York her mother said, very cool . . .

All the pretty girls . . . maybe Mary Beth Slaney was the only one who really had loved him, she'd begged him to marry up with her and have beautiful children. He still could remember the breathless hope in her voice but he'd been full of dreams and hadn't listened. Well, that wasn't fair, either. It wasn't a real regret, for he couldn't have given up his dreams and that was what she had wanted.

Probably he should find him a widow, a grown woman, but he was uncomfortable around grown women somehow. Tended to call them ma'am. I love you, ma'am. How the hell would that sound? Naturally he needed a woman's body as much as the next man, but that wasn't it. No man ever died for lack of a woman's body but he had an idea that they could and lots of 'em did die for lack of a woman.

Maria's River. That would do. They started back and a light drizzle began. They slept in puddles that night. Clay-based ground went slick as grease and walk slowed. The bank rose well above the river and they stayed up on it, sliding down only when necessary, then spending an hour or two clawing back up the slick clay track. Early on the afternoon of the next day they came to a high ridge, stony and abrupt. Going upstream they had been wading the shallows below and he'd scarcely noticed how rough the terrain was above.

He called a halt and pondered. Climbing the ridge would be slow and, for some of the men at least, dangerous. But they were ninety feet over the river and slipping and sliding down to the water, then wading the shallows, then clawing up the rain-slick bank might well take the rest of the day, and he was so anxious to get on their way, find the Shoshones, arrange for horses, and get over what the Indians called the Bitterroot Mountains before the snows came that he could hardly bear delay. Just then he spied a ledge down ten feet or so that looked to be a stone projection. More than ample for a man to cross.

He tied the rope Cruzatte was carrying and had himself lowered to test the projection. Sure enough, it was solid. The gods were smiling on them, for today, at least. He signaled the men down and set out in the lead, rifle strapped tight across his back, gripping his spontoon with both hands. It was a fine walk, a little narrow in places but not dangerously so. He passed the word back, don't look down when it narrows.

He was near the end of what he now thought of as a walkway when the wall turned slightly and revealed what had been hidden, a near equal distance. The ledge continued but now appeared to be more clay than bare rock and farther on it narrowed a bit. He hesitated but he judged they could make it and the penalty for going back now would be a whole day lost.

Slowly he moved along the ledge, and found the going not bad at all. Near the end he looked up and saw that the ridge they had avoided was falling off, leaving them a comfortable climb over tumbled stone to reach a fairly smooth top of the bank. Just get across this ledge and they would be fine. But then the walkway narrowed sharply, to a couple of feet, less in places. And here the stone projection seemed to have taken a coating of the slick clay gumbo that lay behind all their troubles on this difficult day.

He judged he could make it and if he could the men could. In his moment of hesitation it flicked through his mind that this was another decision of the sort that a man in the wilderness may make a hundred times in a day. Decision and action become one and if things go bad then it's time for new decisions and new actions and one just does his best. With a shouted warning to pass the word back for special caution here, he started across. Ninety feet below he saw rocks that they had climbed over coming upstream.

Half over his feet flew out from under him. His heart lurched. He went off the ledge but slammed his spontoon point into the clay. It held and he hung there, yelling to his men to go back. Then, elbows braced, hands locked on the imbedded spontoon, he swung his legs up, regained the ledge, and lay there panting. Yelled to his men again to go back. It was too dangerous and if they lost a day, so be it.

He began to inch his way on his belly, sliding to safety, the solid rock on the slope ahead that was steep but manageable, and was nearly there when he heard a voice stark with terror.

"God, God, Cap'n, what shall I do?"

He turned in horror. Dick Windsor, first behind him, had ventured out and fallen. He was flat, right arm and right leg hanging over the precipice, left foot and left hand scrabbling at the slick clay on the ledge. Never had Lewis felt so alone and so responsible. Windsor was one of his men. It was like seeing a child step before a runaway horse. His mind flashed over alternatives, but there weren't any.

"Easy, Dick." He smoothed a tremor from own voice. "Easy, now. You'll be fine. Dig your fingers into that clay, then what you do, you reach around behind you and get that knife on your belt. All right, there! You've got it. Now reach down and cut you a foothold in the bluff below you, like a step, don't you see—yes, that's it, now get your right foot into that step—got it? Right, now reach up and jam the knife into the ledge, dig it right into that clay, brace against it, between that and your foot in the step you can lift up—there! Now crawl, stab the knife in the ground each step, you'll be all right . . ."

Watching Windsor inch toward him, face white and drawn, Lewis wedged himself against rock, thrust the spontoon out toward him, anchored the crosspiece in the clay, and told him to come another couple of feet until he could seize the end of the spontoon and draw himself in.

"Thankee, Cap'n," Windsor whispered when he was beside Lewis. The captain wanted to hug him.

So they reached the fork in the Missouri a day late. Clark had returned and looked relieved when Lewis and his men appeared. The captains conferred. Lewis explained his conviction that the river he had followed that looked, acted, felt like the Missouri was in fact the tributary. Clark had passed well up the river that ran straight from the mountains just as the Indians had said, cold and clear with hardly a trace of mud as you would expect from water flowing over bare stone in the Rocky Mountains. Slowly the conviction had dawned for him that this was the Missouri. Hence a joint decision arising from evidence. They called the men together to announce their decision.

The men listened gravely. There was silence. Lewis knew this was the most critical decision since they left St. Louis. If the men still disagreed, it meant trouble.

Sergeant Ordway stepped forward and stood braced and blocky in his stained buckskins, black hair and black beard framing his eyes, and said, "Cap'n, I speak for the boys and they say they'll follow wherever you think proper to direct without no complaint, but they still think the north fork is the Missouri."

They were with him even if they were worried! He felt he'd run a dangerous rapid and splashed through. Still, it would be bad if he was proved wrong. He needed to give them something. He and Clark talked it over; Clark would start up the south fork with the boats while Lewis hurried ahead with a small party to find the Great Falls and make sure they were right. The men liked that; they danced to the fiddle that night.

They cached some of their supplies in the ground against their return next year, hid the larger pirogue in deep brush, and set out. He went ahead with Drewyer and three of the men, Gibson, Goodrich, and Joe Field. In midafternoon Drewyer killed four elk and they paused to skin them and make a hearty supper. But Lewis couldn't eat. He'd been ill the night before, guts throbbing, bowels gone to water. He'd taken one of Dr. Rush's fine thunderclapper pills that flushed a man out like busting a bottle, but now the pain was back. He was covered with sweat. He writhed, unable to hold still. Drewyer said he was pale like he'd seen a ghost. He realized his remedy kit was back with the boats. The men squatted around him; Seaman licked his face.

Jesus, this hurt! Dysentery, hazard of the traveler, all right, man expected some of that, but God, this was awful! He thought of Sergeant Floyd writhing in gut agony before he died. If Ma were just here, she'd know what to do, she was about the best herbal medicine woman in their part of Virginia, hell, half of what he knew had come straight from her, and he heard her voice clear as a bell in his ear and it said "choke cherry."

The men found a choke cherry and he directed them to cut tender twigs in two-inch lengths and boil them for an hour. The liquor turned black and bitter. He let it cool and drank a pint at sunset. An hour later he forced another pint down. The pain ebbed, then vanished. He slept peacefully. In the morning he drank another pint. He walked twenty-seven miles that day.

Twenty-seven miles but no sign of the falls. Thirty the next day. No falls. His guts throbbed and burned the way they used to do when he drank too much whiskey or let himself get enraged. Calling out that loud-mouth, stinker what the hell was his name? Now, gut hurting, he could not remember. He remembered the damned coward had run to General Wayne and found that Wayne figured pistols weren't a bad way to settle things. Lewis had had the dysentery for a week after that.

He came to a high place and climbed it to look west. There were the mountains, all right, calculated to inspire deep respect if not terror in any-one who planned to cross them. These looked . . . tough. They were jum-bled and piled above, masses stacked by careless sweeps of God's hand. Nothing like the single ridge Arrowsmith postulated, Arrowsmith sitting in London with a pencil in his hand. Lewis hadn't given up hope that the Missouri held navigable form and wound among all those piles so that the easy portage and the passage to India of which Mr. Jefferson dreamed might still be found, but that hope seemed more and more slender.

The river was running faster and colder now as they climbed. He went up a ridge and found it opened onto a plain that was studded with buffalo in incredible numbers. Thousands, tens of thousands, dotting the grass as far as the eye could see, fading off into a brown blur. What fantastic coun-try! But no falls.

He was getting uneasy. This had to be the way. If not it meant they were lost and what then? They had gone so far that if he were wrong the expedition might well be finished, a prospect he couldn't tolerate even in imagination. The next day the men fanned out to hunt for meat for the crews toiling upstream and Lewis plunged ahead with Drewyer in anx-ious search.

Presently he heard a muted roar that grew louder and louder as he trotted up one rise after another, spontoon in hand. It could be wind in a chasm, but he didn't think so. A tower of smoke appeared, whitish gray, boiling but not rising. Spray? He ran, stones bruising his moccasined feet, breath short, came to the lip of a bluff overlooking the river, the roar buffeting his chest with near physical force, knocked brush aside with the spontoon and stared at the Great Falls of the Missouri.

The whole river hurtling off the ledge above and plunging in a shivering curtain at least eighty feet into a boiling pool, roaring like a tornado, spray sweetening the air. He gazed entranced, his heart beating wildly— he'd known it was here and yet he'd been so afraid. With wild yells he scrambled down to stand at worshipful attention on a point directly before the falls, spray wetting his face, the water boiling at his feet.

He felt a deep humility. He and Clark had made the decision and the men had stood with them against their own instincts and it had proved out. Thank God, thank God, they were all right! The mountains ahead, a swift portage around the falls, and on to the Shoshones and their horses and the Continental Divide. They were on their way!

31

Great Falls of the Missouri, Late Summer, 1805

When Meriwether Lewis stood on the gravel shore of the pool into which the Great Falls of the Missouri thundered, spray splashing his face and cooling the air, he whooped with triumph. The sound, war cry and joy cry rolled into one, scattered birds in nearby trees and set that old woodsman Drewyer to laughing. Normally Lewis didn't take well to folks laughing at what he said or did but so joyous was his mood now that he laughed too.

Still, there were problems. It would be a tougher portage than he'd expected. The Mandans had said the move around the falls would be but half a day and from below he could see that that was wrong. This wasn't alarming, since you had to expect some confusion in roughly translated accounts, but hauling boats and supplies up an abrupt rise of a hundred feet certainly would mean a hard few days. And already days were shortening and time was running.

They dined on buffalo hump that night with a curious new trout that entered in his notebook as the cutthroat for the red slash under its jaw. In the morning he sent a man downstream to report their find to Clark and he put Drewyer and the others to work drying the meat they had killed the day before while he went alone to scout the terrain ahead. It looked like a rough climb so he left Seaman tied in camp and set out with rifle and spontoon. Rough climb indeed—it was brutal. He already could see that having cached one of the heavy pirogues in dense brush at Maria's River, they now must cache the other here and go forward with canoes.

And that meant—he couldn't deny a burst of elation—that his iron boat would save them just as he had imagined across the years. Thank God for such inspirational forethought! He had to laugh, thinking how the president's eyes would open when he came to this passage of Lewis's report and realized that the subaltern had been right all along! Of course, Lewis now understood that those days at Harper's Ferry when he had labored over the boat had been most of all valuable in and of themselves as he had been forced to take the command from the leader. But there still would be profound satisfaction in proving himself right in field judgment.

When he reached the top of the falls he saw that impassible rapids preceded the plunge. That would lengthen the portage. The Indians had said he would know he was at the top of the rough passage when he saw a huge eagle's nest high in a dead cottonwood. But he saw no eagle's nest. Of course, it could have collapsed and fallen over the years but he doubted that. So he marched on and to his dismay found that those impassible rapids extended over five miles of rapidly rising ground. He sat on a rock to contemplate this problem and in the silence became aware of a familiar roar. Hopped up and made the next turn and—oh, my God!—there was *another* falls! The Indians had said nothing of two falls. And there was no sign of an eagle's nest. But how many falls were there?

Now worried, he trotted along the sharp and difficult bank and soon came to a third falls, this a vast spread of nearly half a mile spilling over a lip some twenty-five feet high and beating into a huge pool. Hurrying now, half running, stones bruising his feet, prickly pear needles stabbing through his moccasins, he climbed to find a fourth falls, and then, rushing on, a fifth!

Above the fifth, oh, blessed relief, it was a different world. The river was nearly a mile wide, flowing at a sedate and placid pace. Wild geese by the thousands floated on the surface that was more like a lake than a river. The terrain was more a lakeshore than a riverbank; ending the portage and reentering the water would be easy here. But he estimated he had come twelve miles—add that distance to the awful climbing and they had a portage to curl a man's hair.

On a small island in the river he saw a dead cottonwood and high in its branches a bundle of sticks—the eagle's nest.

He walked on and came to a vast buffalo herd, the biggest he'd ever seen. They could use fresh meat for the night; he aimed and fired and then stood watching a fat cow fold to her knees, blood gushing from mouth and nostrils. Slowly she buckled and fell sideways.

As he watched this awesome sight, leaning on his rifle, he heard a shuffling sound behind him. He turned to see an even more awesome sight—a grizzly was coming straight toward him on all fours. Seeing the bear moving steadily closer he noted again how massive these animals were. If this one stood in attack mode it might be near eight feet and weigh six hundred pounds.

But then, grasping the way the bear came on in a steady, meaningful shuffle, eyes intent, Lewis realized it was attacking. He snapped up his rifle—and remembered he had not reloaded after killing the buffalo. No time now. He needed his dog but Seaman was back in camp tied to a tree. Well, try just walking away, treating it all casually. He started for a tree two or three hundred yards away, walking swiftly but calmly. But when he glanced over his shoulder he saw the bear pitch into a dead run, mouth gaping wide. A murderous roar tore from its throat. The river was his only hope now. Lewis bolted for the water, plunged in, and waded rapidly outward until he was near chest deep. He gasped, feeling a choking in his throat, not sure if it was the icy water or fear. For the bear came right in after him. Now, though, he did feel he had some advantage, for the bear would pretty well have to swim to continue the attack, denying him solid footing. He shuffled his feet and decided the river bottom here felt like sand, or at least was solid.

Rifle strapped across his back, Lewis grasped the spontoon in both hands and turned. The bear swam straight at him. Lewis raised the spontoon, taking aim. Maybe he could punch out its eyes. Even better, if it roared as they usually did with mouth wide open, maybe he could jam the spontoon down its throat. Force it to change its mind. The spontoon wouldn't kill, or at least not immediately, but it might inflict so much pain the creature would give it up.

The bear came on, roaring murderously. It flashed through Lewis's mind that the roar alone might subdue much of its lesser prey, cause little hearts to stop beating in pure terror, little animals to crouch, awaiting the end with eyes shut. He could smell its breath, fetid and foul and fishy, just as Bratton had said, Shannon ragging him unmercifully. Strange thought to flash in a man's mind—maybe the very oddity of it told him how close he was to meeting his maker.

He was holding the spontoon overhead, point bearing directly at that open maw, right hand grasping the rear of the shaft to provide the force of the blow it would deliver, left to guide the iron point down the throat all the way to the damned thing's gizzard if he could. Suddenly Lewis was boiling angry—who did this dirty damned bear think he was attacking as if he had his sights on some pitiful sitting duck floating blindly in the water waiting to make a meal for the king of the forest? Well, Meriwether Lewis was no goddamned sitting duck. He was incandescent with rage, let the bastard come on or Lewis would stalk him right here in the water and put out his eyes, jam the spontoon up his ass as he fled, give him something to remember this day by. Remember that the captain of the Corps of Discovery wasn't that easy to take.

And then, as he took a near-insane step toward the bear the huge creature stopped. He reared back, staring, and then all at once spun about in the water and hurried rapidly toward shore. Lewis stood, watching him go, spontoon still raised to smite him. The bear came to the shallows, bolted out and up the bank, shot across the sandy beach, and ran into the woods without looking back.

Lewis was amazed. Had the bear caught a whiff of the demonic rage that had been Lewis's reaction to acute danger? As a rational man and a scientist Lewis found that hard to countenance. But as a man who only now lowered his spontoon, only now began getting his breathing in control, it wasn't so far-fetched.

Could he be the first human being the bear had seen? They were notoriously nearsighted, but just the same it would be a strangely ignorant bear that had never seen a human when Indians hunted buffalo without worrying about the presence of bears. Bears and Indians seemed to have a live and let live attitude, though those bearskins in all the Indian lodges had to come from somewhere. And the bear-claw necklace and bracelets worn by that angry Sioux, the Partisan, suggested that bear fights happened.

Or maybe it was just that the bear knew murderous rage when he saw it and thought it too much risk for a dubious meal.

Suddenly, wading slowly toward shore in the cold water, he began to shiver. In a moment he was colder than he felt he could stand. Shock, he supposed, the shock of danger or perhaps of extreme fear, for sure enough, he'd been scared and still was somewhat. A man so chilled, his heart could stop, Lewis had seen it happen or maybe had just heard of it from old soldiers. Out of the water, wet shirt peeled off and luxuriating in a warm air current, he set about drying his rifle and, finally, loading it. Learned something there, didn't you, he was muttering to himself. Careless bastard.

He found Clark and the boats camped five miles below the first falls; the rapids had been too rough to come farther. That increased the portage distance to seventeen or eighteen miles.

But there were more immediate problems. Face white and drawn, Clark told him Sacagawea had taken ill and it looked to him that they might lose her. He had bled her several times, leaving her limp and drawn and she still burned with fever. Bleeding, the natural general purpose remedy that everyone used, hadn't done a bit of good. Made her worse, it seemed like. Dry, you see, like taking blood had dried up her liquid.

Lewis was their physician, though he knew so little. He thought of his celebrated mentor, Dr. Rush. But Philadelphia was far away now. And who could have imagined that on the far frontier he would be treating a woman? Still, he knew his patient; Pomp's birth back at the Mandans had been dangerous and though Lewis's main contribution had been to give the patient crumpled bits of a rattlesnake rattle, at least he had stood by like a consulting physician. Now he found Sacagawea under a rude wick-iup Clark had rigged. She was only half conscious. She gave Lewis a tremulous smile but screamed when he touched her lower belly. Her fever was soaring. He could find her pulse only in her throat, faint and irregular. Her breath came in gasps. Her arms and hands twitched in spasms. She was slipping away. The baby began to cry and she reached out but Lewis had to hold him to her breast.

As he sat watching the child's greedy suckle, the mother scarcely conscious, he was very frightened. If the mother died, the baby would almost certainly die too. But rivaling that dismal conclusion was his realization of the extent to which they had come to rely on Sacagawea to serve as entrée to the Shoshone tribe from which she had been abducted and then to serve as translator as they tried to express the need to purchase horses. That need would be desperate by the time they reached the high mountains.

With the baby sated, Lewis was free to begin his examination. Her lower belly remained excruciatingly sensitive to the touch. Charbonneau said she had had her regular bleeding but it had stopped a couple of days early. The trouble had started some ten days later. He couldn't stop weeping. Lewis told him to shut his mouth but the truth was he felt about the same himself. How terribly little he really knew! But he couldn't afford fear. He was all she had and he would do his best. Charbonneau said she had had a cold she couldn't shake and Lewis knew that venereal inflammations, spread by visiting traders, were rampant among Indians; logic suggested she suffered from an obstruction of the menses.

He mixed a dose of water with two parts ground Peruvian bark as they called the remedy brought along for malaria and one part opium and made a liquor he spooned into her mouth. Lewis thought her pulse seemed stronger. He gave her another dose. He mixed a poultice of warm water, flour, bark, and opium, wrapped it in a moist cloth, and spread it gently across her belly and between her legs.

She whispered inaudibly. Her lips were dry, her tongue swollen. He had seen a sulfur spring much like a therapeutic spring he knew in Virginia; it tasted awful and smelled worse but doubtless it had iron as well as sulfur and both were curatives. He sent a man hustling out with a bucket; she drank eagerly, Lewis raising her head with one hand, holding the tin cup to her lips with the other. He let her have nothing else. Pulse became evident in her wrist.

She lay back on the pallet with a sigh. Her pulse seemed stronger again and she breathed more regularly. Little Pomp awakened and wanted to play. Clark spread a blanket by the fire and the men took turns playing with him. Clark couldn't get enough of the child. The mother slipped into sleep. Late that night by the light of a candle made of bear's fat Lewis saw a gentle perspiration on her face. Her sleep seemed easier, the pain apparently abated. Finally he rolled in his blanket, his mind eased.

Sometime before dawn, the baby back in her arms, she awakened and Lewis gave her more sulfur water and a little more opium. He touched her lower belly; she breathed in sharply but smiled. The pain was receding. He made a new poultice with the same ingredients and applied it carefully. She touched his hand in gratitude.

By morning she was further improved and hungry as she nursed her squalling baby. Lewis fed her broiled buffalo with a cup of buffalo soup. Sacagawea gave him a happy smile. In two days she was up, cheerful, her old self, nursing little Pomp and, as always, making herself useful. Three days later a relapse. Alarmed, Lewis gave her niter to induce sweats and at ten that night thirty drops of laudanum in sulfur water. She slept. The next day she whispered that the captain had saved her life.

Lewis had no idea if he had diagnosed properly or if it was his treatment or the natural strength of the young that had pulled her through. But she felt he had worked a miracle in bringing her back from shadowy death. Lewis wondered if saving her had saved his expedition; looking back, he marveled at how utterly blithely he and Mr. Jefferson equally had assumed that when the time came they would find plenty of horses, Indians eager to help, ready to swap valuable animals for the trinkets in Lewis's peddler's pack. They were running late, everything taking too long. Now it would be late fall before they could reach Shoshone country, about the time the tribe would be pushing off for the annual buffalo hunt. Pressed themselves, anxious, excited, the Indians might not be in much mood for horse trading. Or they might already be gone when the white men arrived.

Time was ever more precious.

They were preparing for the portage that now stood at eighteen miles. They cached the pirogue in deep brushy cover as with the first one. Now they must depend on the iron boat to continue by water; it was rescue just as he'd always expected as he had faced down all the doubters. And now its use in the cold reality of wilderness a thousand plus miles from home would save them.

They found a cottonwood with a twenty-two-inch diameter, took it down, and cut rounds to make wheels. The rest of the felled tree was held in reserve; other smaller trees were cut into rude lengths to make a cart or wagon that really was a chassis, the body to be a canoe. The pirogue mast, cut in two, made axles, and willow branches made a long tongue or shaft that several men could pull at once while others pushed from behind. Onto this chassis or wagon they fixed one of the canoes and heaped it with some of the cargo from the pirogue, the powder and ball and flour and medicine, and the presents or trade goods to pave their way. There were six canoes. Each must ride up the brutal portage separately, dragged those eighteen miles of rough and very steep ground.

This would take days, during which Lewis and a picked crew of the most mechanically adept men would assemble the iron boat and cover it with elk hide that picked hunters would provide. Lewis calculated that elk hide would be less likely to stretch than buffalo hide when they covered the new boat. Of course the iron frame must go up on the first transit.

The men had an odd attitude toward the boat. They called it "the 'speerment" as if they would wait to see if it worked. But they were ignorant men. He remembered how the iron workers at Harper's Ferry had told him such an idea couldn't be done. Even Clark had seemed dubious. When he showed Clark the boat Lewis hadn't expected compliments, exactly, but he'd have liked at least an acknowledgment that it was a priceless idea that could save them when the day came. Still, fine as Clark was, imagination didn't seem his central trait. And then, perhaps no man is truly pleased by evidence of his friend's brilliance.

Across half a continent, Indiana Territory to the Great Falls of the Missouri, the subject had not arisen again. Everything had gone splendidly, not a whit of trouble over the shared command and divided duties. Not a word of dissent, not one clash. They had held together in the crucial decision at the unexpected fork in the river. And they weren't split now.

But like it or not, the boat must go over on the first portage. He said so with at least as much force as was needed. He saw anger and perhaps disgust blended in Will's expression and had to control his own rising temper. They were out of earshot of the camp, gazing over the tangle of steel rods, now rusting a little, and the tow sack of nuts and bolts. Clark's mouth was set, and for a dangerous moment Lewis wondered if it all would shatter here, so far in the wilderness. He remembered Clark's analysis of why Dearborn had resisted a joint command. What happens when disagreements arise in moments of crisis? Why does a ship have one captain, army unit one commander, be he corporal or general? He braced himself, determined to keep his own temper under control even as he realized he wasn't sure he could.

And then Will nodded. "All right," he said and turned back to the camp. His face might have been made of stone. He sat with his back to a log studying the fire and the men left him carefully alone. He posted the guards that night, he and Lewis on the first shift, positioned on opposite sides of the camp. But in the morning it seemed he had slept on it; he was his old self again. And the iron boat would be on the first load taken up the awful portage.

The portage was agony, the men under Clark dragging the heavy canoe-cart up slopes so steep their feet went out from under them. Sometimes they unloaded the canoe, dragged it up empty, then lashed sacks and boxes to their backs and climbed, clinging to rocks and clumps of grass for purchase as they went. When they stopped to rest they fell instantly asleep. Storms swept down the valley. Hailstones as big as lemons pummeled them and freak winds blew them off their feet. They double-soled their moccasins with buffalo hide but prickly pear needles still pierced feet and stabbed ankles. The long shaft on the cart broke; they replaced it with a willow branch. The soft cottonwood rounds began to crumble and they cut new rounds. One axle broke; they fashioned a new one of springy willow.

The frame for the new boat arrived on the first trip. While most of the men attended to the frightful labor of the portage, a few went meat hunting. Hunters went after elk for skins to cover the boat; they reported that elk seemed to have moved on. Quite inexplicably, herd animals will do that. Lewis chose the men who seemed most interested in the new boat and the most mechanically adept and started them assembling the frame.

Spring passed into summer and the days, until now growing reassuringly longer, grew shorter. Small difference, but he noticed it. They weren't progressing, the days were burning, the mountains were far away, the Shoshones would be off for the fall hunts before long, as Sacagawea warned again with a worried look. She was dreaming of seeing her people once more but she also cared for these men who had saved her life and treated her and her baby as good luck talismans. Lewis's stomach boiled, he hiccuped acid and his bowels ran like water. His appetite foundered. Day by day he forced an outward calm as the portage dragged on and the boat slowly took shape.

At last the elk hunters found some prey. To free men to prepare the skins Lewis took over the cooking, boiling buffalo stew and making suet dumplings as a treat. The men came by his fires and joshed him on his new importance; he realized with surprise that working without rank brought him closer; it made him one of them, which set up a round of self-questions that he finally dismissed angrily.

More days passed. It seemed there were no pines for miles—only cottonwoods—and that meant no pitch for caulking. They scoured driftwood piles along the river for the occasional pine log. He burned these, hoping to extract pitch, but they were too old and dry. Caulking loomed as a major problem. He settled on pounding charcoal to powder to mix with beeswax and bear tallow; it would have to do.

The frame was complete, looking very boatlike. Lewis enjoyed examining it from different angles, imagining it covered. It would be a beauty! The skins were ready, twenty-six of elk and two of buffalo as substitutes. The sewing began. The needles he had bought were triangular for strength instead of round. The holes they made in the hides seemed disturbingly large. The thongs laced through the holes didn't look as snug as he'd expected. He was worried.

Twelve days passed. The portage was completed. The exhausted men rested gratefully for a day but by the next day were restored. They poked around, watching the boat assembly, saying little. Clark came and stood with arms akimbo for nearly an hour, watching. He said nothing. Lewis, feeling more and more distressed and troubled, fought off the urge to challenge his co-captain to state his thoughts, out with it, damn it! The next day Clark assembled a party and led it off in search of cottonwoods big enough to make dugout canoes. "Just in case," he said with a faint smile. Lewis was pleased. They wouldn't need canoes, the iron boat would answer, but Clark with arms akimbo would be out of Lewis's sight.

More days passed. He was getting frantic. He and Drewyer rendered more tallow and produced a hundred pounds of the caulking mixture. July was slipping away with the speed of light. The whole year was turning, the snows coming on and they were stuck here!

The skins were laid on and snugged into place. Four men turned the boat over and suspended it above slow fires to dry the hides. Sure enough, as the skins tightened the thread holes gaped larger. A third of the way into July he was ready to coat it. He spread the warm mixture, smoothing it into the skins, larding it at the seams. When he was done it was thrilling—it looked just as a boat should, solid, strong, capable. He spread a second coat. It dried smoothly. Everything else had been ready for five days.

When the caulking mix covering it was perfectly dry, they launched the boat. It floated like a beautiful cork. He was suffused with a wild joy, he laughed and joked, he could hardly contain himself. They placed the crosspieces and prepared the oars. They loaded her and she took the weight as if she were prepared to cross the ocean. A ton or two in a hundred-pound boat.

Clark and the boys had returned—they had found the damned trees—and with profound satisfaction, Lewis gave the order to start in the early afternoon. But as they were ready to cast off, clouds came booming over the mountains, wind howling down the valley, whitecaps kicking up on the lakelike river. They hunkered down and waited and after a few hours of thunder and lightning the sun reappeared.

"Jesus!" someone said. "Lookee!"

The iron boat was settling. Water was pouring through parted seams. They splashed into the water and began unloading. When the boat was empty they pulled it ashore. The caulking compound had peeled off, the seams were bare, the needle holes had stretched and torn. It was a sieve.

It was finished. He knew in his heart and his gut that the great idea had failed. Solutions leaped to mind, give him weeks and months to obtain materials and try this and try that, it might still work, but now he knew further effort would be madness.

No one spoke. With a flick of his hand he directed them to drag it into the brush and forget it.

"Well, Cap'n," John Colter said at last. "It were worth trying. It really were."

Clark made no direct comment. He merely said they'd better turn to dugouts. The trees he had found were of a size to make one vessel thirty-three feet long, the other twenty-five. They dropped the trees and went to work with adzes and axes carving out the interiors. They would serve but at a bare three feet in width they would be desperately unstable. July was half gone when they moved out and they had miles to go before the mountains.

He said nothing to anyone about the iron boat and none asked him. Clark never raised the subject. But by God, Colter was right, it were worth trying, it were. That was command, which he had seized around this vessel, which seizure had been so necessary, and part of command is to try and live with failure and go on, wiser, perhaps, but undaunted.

They paddled hard upriver, bound for the next important geographic landmark, the Three Forks of the Missouri, only one of which led to the Shoshones.

32

Meriwether Lewis set the ash pole in the shallow, rocky bottom and held the canoe while Bratton and Shannon set their poles and lunged forward. As the vessel started to move he added his own twist of aching shoulders and they went ahead a few feet. He set his pole again. They were far beyond Great Falls. Somewhere up ahead, surely not far now, was that next landmark, the Three Forks of the Missouri, that would tell them they were headed right. As Lewis understood it, the Three Forks were three separate rivers that joined in one place to form the Missouri.

Day by day the water grew colder and swifter. Clark had gone ahead on foot. August already; they must find the Shoshones and get on. At a bend he saw a shallow ahead. When the boat grounded on rocks he held position with his pole while the others went into the water with a tow rope. When he stepped in the water the cold shocked him anew. The ache in his knee glowed.

They must drag the heavy dugout over the rocks. He lay the elk hide line over his shoulder, braced on mossy rocks, pulled—and his feet flew out from under him. He fell prone, a hip striking a stone. Icy water surged over his chest. His hip hurt. He stood, shivering, buckskins clinging coldly, and stepped blindly onto a rock so painfully sharp it must have cut moccasin and flesh. But he couldn't be sure, his feet so sore and tender from constant immersion, his moccasins beginning to rot, and he bent to the rope and pulled.

He was exhausted. His knees ached and every step hurt. His men were no better and many were worse. Half were running fevers with the ague if not the grippe. He pulled the dugout over the rocks and it caught on two submerged stones. He eased the rope and Shannon pushed it free. Lewis tried to swing it past the rocks and fell on the same hip. He struggled up, groaning despite himself. Shannon looked at him with concern. The boy was taking on a gaunt look, the more evident because he was clean-shaven, pulling out his razor most every day. The men ragged him; wanted to be ready to meet some Indian maiden out here in the wild and have a romance. Lewis thought it more likely that he doubted his ability to raise a beard.

"How do, Cap'n?" Shannon said softly.

"A little battered right now. How're you doing?"

"Well, Cap'n, what you told me back in Pittsburgh, you told me I'd have a lot of fun and there would be some rough spots, and what I want to say, you were right as rain on both counts."

Lewis grinned and took up the rawhide rope and threw his weight against it, fighting the swift current swirling at his aching legs. It was bad; they simply had to find the Shoshones and get on. These Indians should know the way ahead. The information from the Hidatsas at the Mandan villages was running out as the expedition passed far beyond the country those Plains Indians knew. They hunted as far as the Yellowstone; they only came here on raids for horses and women, not the stuff of careful geography. They had missed Maria's River, they reported one falls instead of five, imagined a half-day portage when it took twelve, thought the river beyond the falls was easy going . . .

Every time he mounted a height to stare ahead, the mountains looked higher and more ominous. There seemed to be endless ridges. Harder and harder to believe the Hidatsa report that up the final creek it was an easy walk to the divide and a quick portage across to the headwaters of the Columbia and a swift ride down. Well, well, Clark said, mountains are funny, water's got to come from somewhere, maybe it winds around — he wants to believe, Lewis thought, and God knows, so do I . . .

Time to get on . . . now the crucial member of the party was the quiet woman with her baby on her back. Lewis liked Sacagawea, though it was not in his nature to draw close to her and her husband, as Clark had done; Clark had a talent for friendship. But she was courageous and smart and held up for the hardest travel without complaint. She took good care of her baby but was always ready when the march started. She could dig in ground that showed him nothing and produce nutritious roots that held off the scurvy symptoms that follow an all-meat diet. Only Charbonneau could really talk to her, but maybe they were all a little in love with her and that sunny smile she gave so freely. They played with little Pomp as if he were a touch of home. Lewis noticed that after she came close to dying the men felt a new tenderness for her.

They were in the country of the Shoshones but they saw no Indians. Then a tower of smoke rose from a distant creek bed. A warning: armed strangers coming. It was a bad beginning. Sacagawea told him her people were terrified of the Plains Indians, the Hidatsa who had taken her but especially the ferocious Blackfeet who laid everything before them to waste. Not that her people lacked courage; they had only bows and arrows while the Blackfeet were well supplied with rifles from British traders. Once her people had been dominant, she said, and Lewis saw a

shine of pride in her eyes; tribal lore said the Shoshones were the first to
get horses from Spanish forces to the south and with the horse's mobility
and capacity for the lightning strike they terrorized the Blackfeet. But
then their enemies got guns.

The eternal cycles of war worked out on the western American plains,
the English long bow yielding at last to gunpowder, but Lewis seized the
opening it allowed him. American traders sure to follow him would bring
trade rifles that would allow these mountain people to hold their own if
not even the score. Now all he had to do was find the Shoshones to
advance this argument.

They had been climbing steadily for more than a month, the river sometimes rushing, sometimes limpid. The two captains long since had stopped
talking of western mountains to match the Appalachians in the East.
These were huge mountains that went on and on, patches of snow clinging to high slopes even under a blazing August sun that here on the river
was roasting them. They looked like paintings of the Alps in Europe that
Lewis had seen in Washington. The Blue Ridge? By comparison, it was a
mere foothill.

Things were getting serious. They had traveled twenty-five hundred
miles up the Missouri and had gained at least a mile in altitude. This
would be snow country in the winter. The game would start moving to the
lower elevations then and subsistence would become a real problem. That
was why the Indians must soon be off on their fall hunt, certainly any day
now, but it applied equally to Lewis and his men.

As they climbed the terrain grew steeper and the current swifter, the
water colder. Paddling became steadily harder. They broke out the
cordelles, men climbing the rocky shores and trying to avoid prickly pear
needles as they dragged the canoes forward step by step. When passage
ashore was too difficult they must wade out into the river with their ropes
but then they had to stop every little bit and let the sun drain the cold
from their muscles.

They came to spectacles and mysteries and wonders, omens and tests.
His notebook filled and he started a new one, storing the old in a water-
tight case with its predecessors. There was the awful morning still fresh in
memory when the canyon narrowed until soaring walls dropped sheer
into the water. As the walls closed the water deepened and seemed almost
compressed, the current taking new power. Now the water was too deep
to wade. They must paddle with desperate strength against current that
tested their best. Paddle wildly until muscles were ready to cramp and
quit, then drop a noose over a rock projection and hang on until quivering

arms quieted. Walls on each side rose sheer and threatening. They stretched toward the sky a good twelve hundred feet, framing a blue sliver far above, the canyon dark as dusk.

It felt like approaching the portals of hell, so ominous was this fading light. Lewis had been in plenty of tight spots and this was hardly the tightest, but the effect on spirits was extraordinary. In the canoe following his he saw Shannon, mouth a tight slash, muscles bulging as he dug frantically into the water. York glanced up and then toward Lewis with huge eyes. For once Reuben Field kept his mouth shut. Joe Field was behind Reuben and for a moment he thought Joe had winked at him, but it was too far to be sure. Still, it instantly lifted his own spirits. He felt as he did at such moments when men showed him gallantry of spirits despite their obvious suffering, a sort of love though he would cut his tongue before he would utter the word.

He entered a name for this portal in his notebook, underlining twice. *The Gates of the Rocky Mountains.* Then, abruptly, they were out of the chasm and the river widened and the current slowed and meadows came down to the banks and buffalo and elk came to drink. Lewis's mood soared and suddenly the men were all smiles, sporting and laughing as they drew up on the shore and kindled a fire and cooked enough buffalo hump to satisfy every hunger. Now Reuben chattered like a magpie, some of the men laughing with him, Joe giving him a tolerant smile. Now and again someone decided Reub talked too much and moved to take him down a peg, but the combination of both brothers and Reub's willingness to apologize when he had antagonized usually eased the situation.

Lewis felt and could see the boys felt a near physical pleasure, as if they'd come through a trial of passage. They laughed and frolicked and Cruzatte played the fiddle and some of the men found the strength to dance.

But as days became weeks the joy of that memory faded and there was harsh new reality to face.

Now they were far up the Missouri, surely near the three forks where the river originated. That meant they were deep in the country of the Shoshones but there had been no sign of the Indians except that column of smoke, rude alarm lifting into the sky.

Suddenly Sacagawea found her voice. She chattered loudly to Charbonneau, pointing. Yonder creek with white clay banks? Says that's where her people come for white body paint. Says the three forks must be just ahead, Charbonneau translating her words to Drewyer, he passing it on in English. Clark returned from foraging ahead. He was ill and his feet so torn with prickly pear that they ran pus. He had a roaring fever and his teeth chattered. He'd gone for miles and found nothing.

Then, a few days later, a strange river entered from the right, the mountain side.

"What the hell," Drewyer squalled in his shaky English. "Supposed to be three rivers. We better pull up here and take a look-see —"

"No," Lewis said, his voice snapping over the water to the other canoes, "keep on, keep on, this has to be it."

And sure enough, after paddling around two more bends, just around the third two rivers entered at once. The two just folded into one like the arms of a Y. They were maybe a quarter mile on from the first river. Found Three Forks. They made camp to spend a day recuperating exhausted men but so elated was Lewis at finding their goal that he whistled up Seaman and they went hiking up the riverbank, exhaustion forgotten. Yes, this was the start of the Missouri, three rivers pouring from the mountains to form the stream that would sweep across the Great Plains to the Mississippi. He entered names in his notebook — Jefferson for that first right fork that he intended to take, Madison and Gallatin, the treasury secretary, for the two entering together. It crossed his mind that naming one for Secretary of War Dearborn might be wise, but then he thought to hell with it. What had Dearborn done for the expedition? Gallatin had been an important source of information with his collection of western maps.

So they had reached the head of the Missouri River. But they had far, far to go.

That evening Sacagawea told them her story for the first time. They had camped, cooked and eaten, and now the sun was low in the western sky. The captains broke out a ration of tobacco. Supplies were getting low, it being crucial to save some for ceremonial smoking when they met Indians. But reaching the head of the Missouri was special. Clark had spread a blanket and was trying to teach Pomp to walk, the baby's legs folding beneath him. But Lewis knew he listened as carefully as did anyone.

Sacagawea said her people had been camped here on this very spot when the raiders came. She talked placidly and easily, her voice gentle, pausing for cumbersome translation. Five years had passed: she was ten then. The women were washing clothes in the river when lookouts galloped in shouting to take cover, Hidatsa were coming. But hiding was fruitless, the tools of washing scattered everywhere as sign of women's presence. Within instants, men mounted on their swift ponies were upon them with terrifying yells. She had a blurred impression of ferocious fighting, Shoshone men standing to the last, those fearsome yells, the screams of terrified women. She remembered the hollow, brittle sound of overshot arrows clattering against stone. She saw a man she knew, a friend of her father's, lunge at a raider with a knife and then collapse with an arrow through his belly. She remembered you could see the arrowhead bright with blood where it had passed through him. Then he fell prone, the arrow straight up, glistening in the sun. In her placid voice she made them feel the fight, see the fight.

She had been crouching in brush but she knew it was a hopeless hiding place and she erupted from cover and tried to dash over a river shallow. Then one of the raiders, a young man mounted on a huge warhorse, thundered up behind her, caught her arm, hoisted her, and flung her across the withers of his horse. It was a fine bay, she remembered, and sweating hard, her face jammed against its flesh. She arched her back, yelling and screaming, kicking the horse, fighting. He gave her a ferocious open-handed cuff on the back of her head and in that instant of pain she saw that he would kill her if he couldn't keep her, gut her and drop her by the trail to die, and she accepted the reality of capture. She cried herself to sleep that night and for many nights thereafter but beyond being brutally worked she didn't feel she was badly treated. Then Charbonneau came along and she caught his eye and he bought her. He didn't have to do it, but he said his church believed in marriage and since there wasn't a priest in a thousand miles he reckoned an Indian marriage would do just as well.

Now — she smiled at Clark and at Lewis — she was nearly home.

They started up the right fork, the Jefferson, toward the distant saddle that she said led over what Lewis knew as the Continental Divide and she knew as the place where water ran toward the setting sun to the west. The going was worse, ground rising rapidly, shallow water swifter and colder, rocks punishing, prickly pear everywhere. Awesome mountains rose around them, proliferation of distant and not so distant peaks showing snow even under the blazing August sun. The sight of these mountains, now viewed ever closer, reminded him every time he looked up that they were different from any he'd ever seen. Everything about this country was awesome and they were running out of time.

He decided he couldn't wait. The calendar was rolling toward September and already there was a cool bite in the air just before dawn. He must plunge ahead on foot and settle matters. Clark agreed — he would see the boats up the river until they could go no farther, nursing his wounded feet as he traveled. Lewis and a few men would rush ahead. This would put him at more risk when he met Indians but on the other hand, a small party would be less alarming and give him more chance to talk, through

Drewyer, in sign language. He deemed taking Sacagawea and the baby on foot put her at too much risk. He thought Drewyer could break the ice; he would need Sacagawea to persuade the Shoshones to part with their horses.

He took Drewyer, John Shields, and Hugh McNeal who carried an American flag on a long staff. They started, picking their way through cactus, the sun blazing, ground hot enough to burn. He couldn't always avoid the needles. Every hour he called a halt and they dug needles from their feet. The needles left little punctures that would fester and run pus. Lewis refused to let himself limp.

They made twenty miles on an Indian road and continued in the morning toward the divide that now was near. The sun beat down and wind swept over the crest. He could see forever. The creek they were following, headwaters of the Jefferson, dwindled to a trickle. It ended at a spring that dribbled eastward, the start of the magnificent Missouri.

They climbed onto the crest and stood on top of the world and looked down on the other side.

No broad valley awaited them, no major winding river twisting and turning in lazy S's on its way to the sea. Lewis didn't know just what he had expected, but he had hoped he wouldn't see what he did — range upon range of snow-covered ridges. Ridges through which he must find his way.

A little below he found a spring. Its waters ran westward. He took an icy draught from the start of the Columbia River.

Lewis's feet were torn, his whole body ached, he was hungry and half blinded by the brilliance of the sun on top of the world, but he still recognized a significance here that he knew would be lost on most of his men. For looking at that wilderness of ridges stretching into the distance he understood instantly that here lay the death of the dream that had held men for three centuries, that he knew glowed like hot embers in Mr. Jefferson's mind.

There was no Northwest Passage. No easy route by water to the Orient that would split the continent and finally complete the journey that Columbus had begun.

No Northwest Passage . . . he sighed and started down the long slope.

"Sign to him," Lewis said to Drewyer, "that we have a woman of his tribe. We're bringing her home. Hidatsas seized her these five years ago . . ."

The big Indian stared at him, his expression stern and dangerous. Plainly he was calculating. His name was Cameahwait, a man of Lewis's age with powerful intelligence showing in his eyes and the manners of a prince. He was the leader of the Shoshones and everything depended on his reaction. Lewis was alone in his village with Drewyer, Shields, and McNeal with the flag on a staff.

They had met the Shoshones when sixty warriors with bows strung galloped out to confront them. Lewis had laid his rifle carefully on the ground and walked toward them with empty hands spread. An old woman darted forward. Lewis had met her an hour before as she dug for roots. He had stilled her terror with gentle gestures and presents. Now, her voice shrill but proud, she introduced them as her find, pointing to their white skin and showing the gifts, little mirrors flashing in the sun.

So the deadly moment passed and the Indians made them welcome. They smoked and ate elk boiled with berries and roots and things were cordial. But when he asked for men and horses to recross the divide and meet Clark's party, everyone froze. More men with rifles coming? And Lewis hadn't even broached buying horses and getting directions. A young man whom Lewis saw would like to depose Cameahwait but lacked the weight and courage began to harangue the people. White men? What were they? No one had ever heard of such a thing. Suppose they were Blackfeet whitened in magical disguise, come to lure Shoshones to their deaths and take their horses? That made more sense than strangers dropping from the sky! O my brothers, this is a fool's errand!

A man close to Cameahwait signed all this to Drewyer who gave it to Lewis from the corner of his mouth.

Lewis leaped up. "Enemies?" he cried. "How insulting, how outrageous! We come as friends. We are Americans, come distance beyond imagining to meet our Shoshone brothers, and if we are well treated, American traders will follow with guns that will end Blackfeet threats forever!"

"Slow down. Cap'n." Drewyer muttered, fingers cramping. Lewis waited, then said they had proved their friendship by bringing a tribeswoman whom the enemy had captured. Family ties in American were central; were they less so among Indians?

As Lewis had planned, this gave Cameahwait his opening. Politics was the same everywhere. The tall chief made an oration around his responsibility to all his people, including a lost sister taken by the hated Hidatsa and restored by the grace of God. They would help the white men: it was their duty.

Still, when Cameahwait led a small band of men and a few women over the divide, the worried tribe singing the lamentations sung for men going to war, Lewis could see that his suspicions were aflame, his heavy, hard-slabbed face strong, eyes ranging for ambush. Near the fork in the stream where Lewis had suggested that Clark stop the boats the chief draped his ermine tippet around Lewis's neck. His men adorned the other whites. If

Blackfeet fire awaited them the whites would go down too. Fair enough.
Lewis put his cocked hat on Cameahwait's head.

But near the fork where Lewis had said they would find Clark he saw
with horror that the boats had not arrived. Cameahwait whirled on him,
his expression telling Lewis that this man would kill him in a moment if
he felt betrayed.

Instantly he handed Cameahwait his rifle. "Kill me first if the Blackfeet
come," he said. He felt as naked without his piece as if he'd stripped his
clothes; he was a soldier. Yet this Indian's manner even across the barrier
of language told Lewis that he could be trusted.

The next morning the boats appeared and Clark stepped ashore. Jubi-
lation and thanksgiving! Cameahwait embraced Clark as he had Lewis,
rubbing cheek to cheek. Before Lewis could present Sacagawea one of
the Indian women recognized her and rushed to embrace her with loud
cries. This, Cameahwait signed, was Leaping Fish, so named for the
agility of her escape through a river from Hidatsa.

At last they could talk, if circuitously—Sacagawea to Charbonneau, he
in French to Drewyer, Drewyer in English with who knew how much
error but better than signs. Before they could start she began to talk
loudly with extravagant gestures. Lewis assumed she was telling her
adventures and tried to interrupt but she waved him down. Charbonneau
and Drewyer conferred; it seemed she was describing the great white
world as she had gleaned it from French traders—rivers running beyond
imagination, vast lakes on both sides of endless land, people numerous as
ants living in houses of stone stacked one above the other . . .

Cameahwait rocked back and forth as he absorbed this torrent of concepts that Lewis supposed had never crossed his mind. When the parley
began Lewis laid out the great enterprise on which they were engaged,
their need to go on to the sea, their inability to move without horses, their
desire to trade from their storehouse of goods, their crying need for
directions—

Sacagawea screamed. She stared at Cameahwait, then leaped at him,
putting herself in his lap, arms around his neck, tears streaking her face as
she laved him with kisses. She cried something to Charbonneau. Cameahwait held her off to stare and then with a loud cry embraced her and continued to shout celebratory cries that the other Indians took up in
howling that amazed Lewis. Drewyer turned to him with a laugh.

"You ain't going to believe this, Cap'n. Shit! *I* don't believe it. This
here chief is her brother. She just recognized him. She's asking him
about Mama and Papa and he's telling her they're all gone, there's only
him and her left in the whole bleeding family. God Almighty! Would you
believe it!"

Lewis gazed in stupefaction. Heaven must be smiling on them with extravagant benediction. Surely no playwright would dare offer so outrageous a coincidence—he'd be shouted off the stage in a shower of vegetables!

The parley resumed on a new footing. They had delivered the sole remaining member of the man's family from distant captivity—and they brought the promise to trade guns that would let them meet their enemies on equal footing. If not placed in their debt, Cameahwait was at least convinced they were friends.

Willingly he laid out disheartening news. A river did run to meet the Great River of the West, but it was impassable, afloat or ashore. There was a trail to the west but it too was scarcely usable. We'll see about that, Lewis thought, and asked to trade for horses. Now Cameahwait's face darkened and a sharp murmur arose among his men. The annual buffalo hunt on the distant plains was starting now; the Shoshones should be there. Food supplies had shrunk, game was scarce, the people were hungry. It was time to go, now, not tomorrow or the next day, not waiting to help these strangers haul baggage over the divide. And they would need all their horses to haul home the spoils of the hunt, food and robes to last them for the whole year. Not a moment to spare—nor a horse to spare.

Here was crisis. They must have horses and there was no source other than the Shoshones. Failure here would finish them. Lewis launched an impassioned speech. They had come far, they were friends, they represented great power far to the east that could benefit the Shoshone people immensely—or leave them alone. If they were aided here they would send traders; if they weren't, the Shoshones would never see another white man, never gain the weapons that would allow them to turn on their enemies.

He could see Cameahwait torn by indecision, pressed by his worried tribesmen who saw the immediate as all that mattered. Lewis settled back, waiting; he had made his best arguments.

Then Sacagawea began to talk to her brother in a low, direct voice, Lewis listening desperately to the muttered translation, his heart in his mouth. There was something strong, even hard in Sacagawea's face. This man—pointing at Lewis—had saved her life. That he saved her saved her baby, who could not have survived on the trail without her. They had brought her distances beyond imagining over months and months and protected her constantly. Cameahwait was her brother; he and she stood alone with her baby at the end of their family; would he betray her now?

The tall chief stood and made a speech that took on a rhythm and rising power that made Lewis shiver even though mere bits came through translation. His judgment, he said, was that the white men's trade would free

them from the Blackfeet; the whites were demonstrated friends and he
would help them. If his people wished to go on the hunt without his leadership, that was their right. It was the ultimatum of a powerful man. Lewis
saw immediately that while there was muttering, Cameahwait had won.

The white men would get their help and their horses and then the trip
to the hunting grounds would start.

"She saved our bacon," Lewis said wonderingly to Clark.

"Sure enough. And did you see the iron in her? She's as tough as her
brother is, and I'd just as soon not tangle with him."

"Aye," Lewis said with a smile. "On both counts."

They had their horses. The Shoshones were sharp traders and the horses
were the scrub stock, but they would pack the expedition's supplies well
enough. What's more, three were mares with colts not yet weaned, consti-
tuting a walking commissary. The canoes were dragged into deep brush;
perhaps they would still be here for the return. The Indians gave them a
few of the rawhide pack saddles they used to haul home meat rations for
the next year from the buffalo hunt. They were ready.

They went to see Sacagawea. She and Charbonneau were in a lodge
with Leaping Fish and Leaping Fish's husband, mother, two sisters, and
assorted children. They had brought Sacagawea home and she had paid
her way. Would she stay here now with her brother and her people or
would she go on with them?

She glanced at Charbonneau and in that flashing look Lewis saw that
her marriage was one of convenience. Her husband had bought her when
she had been stolen by force. On the other hand, a marriage of convenience can prove convenient. She walked away, tapping her thigh reflec-
tively with a little stick she carried. She came back, looked at the captains,
and walked away again. She had benefited them greatly, her presence
telling all they encountered that they were not a war party. But they had
agreed they would not press her. Lewis felt he knew what was in her
mind. She had seen the world or at least more of it than anyone here on
the Shoshone ridge had seen. She had seen opportunity, she had listened
carefully to the stories of St. Louis and points east that traders described.
Now she looked around the conical lodges and wondered what home
really had to offer her.

She had gained a smattering of English. Turning to Clark she managed
to make herself understood. He had offered her baby an education, a
place in the vast culture to the east; had he meant that? Indeed, Clark told
her, raising his hand, honesty in his face palpable, he'd bring them all to

St. Louis, put Charbonneau to work and put Pomp in a fine school just opened by nuns.

Sacagawea smiled. Yes, nodding, she would stay with them, on to the Pacific, back as far as the Mandans, pause there until Pomp was a little older, then come to St. Louis. So, Lewis thought, in the end it wasn't the lure of civilization or the loneliness of this ridge; it was ambition for her child.

33

The Bitterroot Mountains, Late October, 1805

These mountains were . . . not frightening, not exactly frightening, but awesome. Yes, that was it, awesome.

The expedition had encountered massive mountains in reaching the Continental Divide, but somehow these were different. As he tramped northward along the gaily singing Bitterroot River they ranged ridge upon ridge to his left like great animals waiting with a malevolence that was stunning, direct, personal.

But that was instinct talking and he didn't like it. It flowed from the same deep well that supplied the melancholy that lived in the wings of his mind and he couldn't afford it. Not now.

Yet even gazing on these ridges—or perhaps because of them—there flowed from another well altogether a joy that he doubted life would afford him again. He had led his men across a continent to penetrate the heart of the Rocky Mountains. This was the ultimate challenge. And beyond it lay the ultimate reward—navigable water running swiftly down to the sea.

There was a trail of sorts, made by the Nez Perce who lived on the other side and crossed occasionally. The Shoshones had a man who had crossed it, a smallish, lean, grizzled fellow of forty or so with bad teeth and a nervous cackling laugh. His name sounded like Toby and so they called him. Yes, he could guide them but he demanded a small fortune in beads, for it was dangerous. Huge hogback ridges stood narrow and high and were blocked by jumbles of fallen timber. Summer snowstorms often obliterated the trail and if winter snow came early it could be fatal. Water and fodder for horses was scarce and there was no game but grouse. It was easy to starve on these heights.

What's more, Lewis knew they were starting weakened. His men had been hungry for weeks, game in ever shorter supply. The Shoshones, themselves starving, had shared berries and dried salmon but that didn't go far. The boys looked gaunt, cheeks hollowed and lips thinned, eyes shadowed. He knew he himself looked years older and reflections in still pools showed him the hunger in his own eyes. Hunger is cruel. The flesh weakens and then the spirit and then the mind. It erodes judgment and will. His men had used up much of their strength getting this far; there was nothing he could do about the fact that now, on the worst passage of all, they must run on muscle and grit.

It started well enough, which tells you something about fear. Toby seemed sensible, though communicating through Sacagawea was none too easy. At the Nez Perce Trail—marked by a creek gushing from the mountains—they spent a day hunting and bagged four deer and a beaver. Then up a steep trail through forest of spruce, fir, and pine so dense that branches must be cut to open the way for the pack train. They had thirty-nine horses, three of them mares with those precious unweaned colts, and a mule, these brutes hauling everything they possessed. The forest seemed dark and ominous. The trees looked black at any distance and the light below was shadowy and dim and the animals and the men leading them passed from sight almost instantly.

On the third morning they finished the last of the meat from below. Now they must rely on hunters. They set out in a chill drizzle and followed Toby up a long, narrow ridge in a taxing climb, horses breathing in heavy bursts. Lewis saw that this was a classic hogback, had you walking on a knife edge, steep drops on either side. You could get dizzy looking down on the tops of trees that seemed like arrows aimed at your heart, ready to be released with a twang of bowstring. The rock underfoot was either sharp enough to cut or coarse gravel that rolled under the horses' feet as they nickered uneasily. In every direction he saw more ridges with vast canyons between. The ridges were interconnected, the trail leading one to the next over a low saddle. Indians traveled on the ridges.

Lewis was content; he was getting the feel of new and remarkable country. But then Toby turned down, *into* the canyon. It didn't make sense, but the guide was adamant. Lewis talked it over with Clark: what choice did they have? But after a hard climb down, his knees aching, they advanced a few miles along a stream to find themselves in an Indian fishing camp! Quailing before their glares, Toby admitted he'd taken a wrong turn. He loosed a long, nervous cackle that made Lewis realize this was as hard on him as on them—and what if he decided to slip off in the night and go home? He clapped Toby on the back, smiling—it was all right, brother, what the hell, we all make mistakes. Toby grinned, relieved, and Lewis's impulse to knock him down faded.

"I could kill me a goddam Indian," Colter said, grousing to Shannon. "I knew this was a wrong turn."

Lewis was ready to take a hand—no talk of killing—but to his surprise the usually worshipful Shannon snapped back. "We all thought it a mistake, captains sure as hell did—"

"They say so?"

"Didn't need to say so. Anyone could see it on their faces. Anyway, you didn't say nothing, John."

Lewis saw Colter smile. "Hell, George, next thing you know you'll be growing up, sassing me like that." He clapped Shannon's shoulder. "Come on—let's get started up that damned mountain."

They'd gone too far down to turn back now. Lewis led them out in the morning, scaling a slope that from below looked nearly perpendicular. The climb proved as bad as it looked. "Let's go, boys," he said and took the lead, following the Indian, his loaded horse on a lead, doubling and redoubling on switchbacks that marched up the terrible slope in long sweeping zigzags on a slight trail cut into the rocky wall. Sharp rocks tore at his buckskins and cut the horses' legs. At a dribbling spring he showed the boys how to dress bleeding legs with mud poultices.

Seaman faithfully tracked Lewis back and forth along the ridge as the captain ranged up and down the line. But soon the dog was limping and Lewis saw the pads were ripped on all four paws. Lewis tried to wrap them with makeshift bandages but the dog worried them off immediately and lay there licking his paws one after the other. The captain tried getting him onto a horse whose pack had a level surface, but the horse didn't like it and Seaman liked it even less; immediately he jumped off, landing on sharp rock and crying out in pain.

So they marched, man and dog, the man's moccasins and the dog's paws wearing equally. Seaman regularly licked his paws, every animal's recipe for healing, and Lewis stopped trying to improve on nature. Maybe the torn pads would heal and harden; maybe someday this endless trek of pain for dog and men alike would reach its end. Seeing his dog in pain didn't hurt as much as it hurt the dog, but it hurt plenty. Still, wherever Lewis went, there went Seaman, back and forth along the trail, down the steep slopes when a horse fell and rolled, sharing his master's dinner, curled against him when he slept.

The hunters came in along time of dusk with two grouse scarcely bigger than pullets to feed a ravenous party. All right: kill one of the colts. They led the colt in one direction along the trail, the mare in the other till she was out of earshot. A blow to the forehead with the blunt side of an ax dropped the colt and Lewis cut its throat, catching the blood that gushed out for blood pudding.

There was nothing left in the morning but bones. When they set out along the ridge Pete Wiser was leading the mare whose colt they had taken. The horse was fractious, jerking her lead line, balking. Bratton was right behind and the mare's nerves infected the horse he was leading. It danced about, dangerously close to losing footing and rolling down the slope.

"God damn you, Pete," Bratton yelled, "I'll knock you on your ass, you don't get control of that horse."

"Come on and do it, you son of a bitch," Wiser shouted. Fists doubled, he let go of the horse and started for Bratton. The horse turned and bumped into Bratton, knocking him down on stony ground. Bratton howled, his hand came off the rock torn and bloody. He was scrambling up to attack Wiser when Lewis intervened.

"What the hell—"

"Mare keeps turning back, Cap'n," Wiser said. "Looking for her colt."

"That ain't no excuse," Bratton bawled. Lewis remembered Bratton and Wiser had clashed before. "Shut up, Bratton," he said. To Wiser he said, "You'll just have to keep her on a shorter lead line. Keep your hand right up at the bridle. Ain't a comfortable way to lead a horse, but she'll go over if you don't keep her tight."

He left both men glowering but too exhausted and ill to carry the quarrel further.

Wind or maybe fire in years past had taken down masses of trees that lay in jumbled piles like the jackstraws children played with at home. They must chop through some of the mess, the Field brothers filing their axes sharp every few minutes, but most had to be circled, men leading frightened horses off the trail where they plunged and nickered on the dangerous slopes of talus rock that shifted underfoot. Lewis fixed his horse to the several Shields was leading and posted himself at the bad spots to help his men across. Twice horses went down, hoofs flying out, falling heavily, rolling. One was stopped by branches and the other turned so it was on its belly with its head uphill, eyes wild and rolling. Each time he must slide down with a couple of men, get the pack off and the horse on its feet and back to the trail, then carry the load up and repack the brute and try to catch up with the train winding far above. It was dark when they reached the ridge, a four- or five-thousand-foot climb, and he was ready to drop, though he didn't let it show. Or thought he didn't. It grew steadily colder as they climbed, the air thinner and harder to breathe. They melted snow for water.

Sacagawea was on a handsome bay that her brother had given her. She rode it bareback, buckskin skirt tucked under her, reining with a simple bridle. The baby was in his cradleboard, usually on her back, though sometimes she hooked the cradleboard to the rude girth that she could cling to if the horse became unruly. Usually the sound of her voice was enough to quiet the horse.

Whenever they stopped she was off the horse and had Pomp out of his board to be changed and to nurse. But she was always ready when it was time to start again and Lewis saw that she was reading the nuances of voice and expression to know ahead of the others how soon the start would come. As the days wore on she grew thinner, her eyes seemed sunken, and you could see she was feeding the baby first, chewing meat until it was pulp, then giving it to him in little balls. You could tell that Pomp was cold and miserable but he rarely cried and immediately hushed when she picked him up.

Once her horse stumbled and fell. The cradleboard was on her back, as it always was for the more perilous points, and she stepped off the horse as it went down but clung to the reins to give it momentary purchase and a sense of direction and pressure. Horse Indians had care and handling of horses in their blood. Several of the men leaped to help her but she already had the bay on its feet and starting back to the trail atop the ridge.

With the previous night's colt but a memory, Lewis judged it time to try the great invention: portable soup. A Philadelphia cook had learned how to condense a rich, meaty soup and seal it in lead canisters. Thus the Corps of Discovery had hauled it across the continent. Open it, add water, taste it—well, it wasn't spoiled. It was an affront to taste, vile, in short, but it would keep you alive. The boys still had some spirit. Say, Cap'n, you flavor this here slop with panther piss? Toby made an awful face and spat out the soup and then joined the laughter that Lewis heard as music. You couldn't gripe about hardship because that made it worse and a dozen voices would tell you to stow it. Panther piss soup, you could laugh over that. But he saw they were taking on a newly ragged look. Clark agreed.

Lewis stood the first watch. The men slept rolled in blankets and he listened to them moan and mutter in their sleep. The night wind howled and groaned about the ridge, icy stars close enough to touch. When he passed the watch he rolled in both blankets fully dressed and was gone in an instant. Sometime later he awakened with his face wet and cold. Snow. Maybe an inch or two. He was asleep before it fully registered.

But at rollout it registered. Five inches and coming down hard. Clouds lay against the treetops like a big-bellied woman. It was cold but not the level of cold that comes with winter and the snow pack that would last till spring and be the death of men it caught. Not that. They broke camp and set out with empty guts through eight inches of snow, fat flakes falling steadily. Clark led, feeling his way, slow but moving. Lewis watched the boys stumble and stagger. He himself felt so weak and punished with hunger at a whole new level that he wondered if this was how real starvation began. The snow stopped and the accumulation grew thinner underfoot. Presently they passed onto bare rock. It had been a local storm. Saved again. Downhill now, the pace picking up; that was the way of these ridges, struggle up to a high place, a peaklike knob, and then down into a saddle where you might find a spring if you were lucky, and then the long, slow grind up the next height. They made eighteen miles before they camped. The hunters brought in another two grouse. They killed the second colt. Lewis saw new lines in Clark's face.

The horses were starving. The poor critters pawed through pine straw under the trees but found no grass. He left them unhobbled—they must be free to search out grass among the rocks—but that meant they were scattered in the morning and precious daylight hours and energy must be spent rounding them up. Late starts meant ten or fifteen miles instead of twenty or thirty before darkness swept in, coming a little earlier each day. Toby stood with hands on hips, looking impatient, but what the hell did Indians do in like circumstances? They had to care for their horses too. But then he realized Indians didn't try the crossing on the edge of winter. Indians minded their own business.

Sharp talus rock tore his moccasins and bruised his feet. He could ignore the pain, but he was stumbling more and twice he fell, banging knees and cutting his hands. Favoring his feet for the pain and hence clumsy or was he getting weaker? Or both? They cut through another deadfall. He made himself range up and down the column, talking to the boys, spelling those who looked ready to drop, sliding down the steep slopes to get behind horses that slipped from the trail.

Sunshine scarcely dented the cold north wind at seven thousand feet. They passed from one narrow ridge to the next to the next. Trees down the steep slopes were more than ever like deadly arrows. Rocks dislodged on the trail bounded until they vanished, into the canyon bottom hidden far below. They walked a tightrope on top of the world.

Colter passed him leading eight horses strung in single file. You could count on him; no man was more solid. Now, from the corner of his mouth, Colter murmured. "Better see about Willie, Cap'n." Lewis found William Warner on his knees, bent forward till his face in his hands was against rock, thin shoulders shaking. He knelt, rock gouging his knees, caught Willie's shoulders, and raised him. Tears streaked the young, gaunt face, eyes deep in their sockets.

"I'm gonna die up here, Cap'n," Willie said, more tears starting. "I'm so hungry and I'm weak and stumbling and cold and falling every minute and my knees is tore up and my hands and I can just feel my time running out—"

"Time running out?" Lewis forced a laugh. "Come see me sixty years from now, then we'll talk about time running out. Hell, man, you got strength you haven't even touched. You're not going to die 'cause I'll boot you right in the ass if you do." A grin flickered on Willie's face and his tears stopped.

The pack train was a quarter mile ahead, rounding a turn. Time to move. He stood and lifted Willie. "Come on, we gotta catch up." His hand clamped on Willie's arm, half holding, half propelling. After a while Willie walked without help. "Thankee, Cap'n. I guess you're right, I got a little more left in there somewhere." Lewis clapped him on the shoulder in approval.

But he knew how drained his men were from what this moment had taken of his own strength. Hunger was a deep, constant ache, muscle and sinew and organs crying for sustenance. The endless walking, the pain, the icy wind in the ears, the cold wearing you down and down the way pain will wear you, energy draining like a gut-shot critter pouring blood. More and more often he had to call a stop so they could rest. They dropped like sacks and dozed. Horses stood with heads down and legs quivering.

With Drewyer and a couple of others Clark hurried ahead. Late that afternoon, sun settling to the horizon and cold seeping into their bones, the main body followed blazes to the camping place Clark had found, ample water and fires already flickering a welcome. That night they killed the last colt. Lewis finished his portion feeling he hadn't eaten. He took the first watch. The fires burned down to coals. Far away wolves howled. He and Clark talked, everyone else asleep. Some of the men were near giving out. They could eat their own horses, but then they would have to abandon the supplies that were their lifeline for the return across the continent. But starvation, exhaustion, cold, and the diarrhea that now afflicted at least half the men were deadly in combination. A man could stand up to one but together they would drain away strength until grit wasn't enough. Grit would make a man crawl when he couldn't walk but when he couldn't crawl . . .

Best, then, if Clark hurried ahead with the six hunters to find level ground where there might be game to hunt. He could send food back or at least have it waiting when the main body came up. He left at dawn.

York and Shannon stayed with the main party. They seemed to have struck a special friendship. Both were extraordinarily strong and both were very willing. When a horse went down they were the ones who leaped to ease off the packs, get the brute back on its feet, and then hoist the heavy packs back into place. They were the ones likely to volunteer to search for firewood when camp was struck. York had a wise quality, mixture of experience and intelligence, and though he never pushed an opinion, Lewis usually waited to hear what York had to say before he and Clark decided anything. He had no idea if Clark noticed this respect paid the only slave and the only black among them. Shannon was different— young, not widely experienced, but there was a thoughtful quality about him. Colter had noticed it too. "That boy has a head on his shoulders," he'd said once, and Lewis had nodded. Indeed he did.

The next morning the horses were especially widely scattered because the mare whose colt they'd killed last had gone far back along the path looking for her baby. It was near noon before Lewis could get them moving and things quickly got worse. The ridge climbed up to a massive knob covered with snow and ice. A narrow trail, scarcely more than a trace in rocky dirt, edged around the base of the knob, and Toby led them onto it. In places it reduced to mere footholds. The men crept along, bracing themselves with their hands against the wall, horses nickering in terror as ground gave way under them.

Lewis was forward when he heard a wild yell and turned to see a horse tumbling down a long slope. It gave a nickering scream, the pack on its back smashed apart, and it rolled a hundred yards before crashing into a tree. He and Colter slid down the slope to the motionless horse. He saw it had been carrying a case of powder and a case of rifle balls, both heavy. They would have to butcher the carcass—

The horse snorted. Lewis saw its eyes were open. It waggled its head. He took up the halter and the beast lurched to its feet. It glared at them, its ears laid back on its head, and snorted again in pure rage.

Colter bounded up from a crouch as if he'd been struck. "Why, you clumsy son of a bitch," he shouted, "wasn't our fault you fell. Don't you go snorting at me!" They were all close to the edge. Colter was about the strongest but he was close too. Lewis ran his hands down the horse's flanks and legs. The critter winced a little but otherwise was sound. They repacked the cases on its back. "I'll be horn-swaggled," Colter said. Lewis figured he'd never see a more wonderful escape.

Yet even such an adventure was absorbed and forgotten as they slogged along this endless ridge, a ridge to the right and another to the left, canyons between so deep their bottoms vanished in gloom, black timber marching up slopes, scattered snow and ice on the knobs, everything slowly fading to blue in the distance, ridges without end—

"Cap'n," Johnny Potts said, "let me ask you something." Lewis had struggled up to the train's lead and now was letting it pass him so he could look at each man and judge his strength. He fell in beside Potts.

"You think we might be dead?" Potts said.

"Hell, no," Lewis said, alarmed. "What do you mean?"

"Like we all died, see, and this is hell and them ridges out yonder, they go on forever and we'll walk along 'em forever. Hell don't have to be all fire and brimstone like the Book says—maybe it's ice too. Them ridges, Cap'n, they go on forever, you can see that, there's no end—"

"That's enough, Johnny!" God, the man was on the edge of hysteria, let him cut loose and he'd have them all going and Lewis would have to slap him out of his moccasins. "You know better than that. We'll be out of here in a day or two. I don't want to hear another word of that nature, understand?"

Potts nodded, lips tight with momentary anger, and then that vacant look came back and he stared again across those ridges. Hunger and cold and exhaustion and diarrhea draining strength work on men's minds. No one can predict how taken together they'll impact, but certainly they dig out flaws and dislocations that otherwise are buried. He knew how dangerous this could be when you marched on top of the world three thousand miles from home.

That night they made more soup. He poured in the last of their bear oil and twenty pounds of tallow candles. The men gulped it down, then rubbed fingers in bowls for the last drops. The Indian looked at Lewis and smiled. Food, any food, was glorious.

At dawn he watched men hoist bundles to lash onto the horses. Too many then leaned against the horse, waiting for strength to return. Then they stumbled on. He marched at the head of the column, staggering occasionally when he was careless, torn feet aching, cold in his bones, it felt like his very life was draining away . . . in his mind he was back at the plantation, the smell of Ma's hickory smokehouse where Mr. Jefferson came for hams . . . pumpkin season coming on and she'd be making pies and the way she smoothed out smashed yams with butter—his foot hooked on something and he fell with a crash. Vivid pain shot through his knees and the torn palms of his hands, then slowly faded. It felt good lying here. Seaman licked his face. He chuckled and thrust the dog away. He didn't want to get up, needed sleep, long, long sleep . . . suddenly he was rigid with terror. No one spoke but he knew the train had stopped, they were watching—he bounded up with a boy's energy, horrified by the implications of that moment on the ground. Had his men seen that pause, the too sudden recovery? Of course they had—it mirrored all they felt, all they must fight. No one spoke. The train started again.

He walked on, now in an iron grip of determination, for himself, for them. Late that afternoon a vision of salvation came as if to give them strength. Climbing toward a sharp peak he glanced to the southwest and saw the first change in days. Mile after mile of broken ridges black with trees gave way at last to a dun-colored spread that widened steadily into the distance. It was prairie, level, an end to these awful ridges and slopes.

Toby strutted like a peacock, if a tattered worn-out peacock — he'd brought them through. March another day and all problems would be solved. There would be game on that level ground, deer and elk and fat bear and grass for the horses and they all would eat again! They stood there laughing like fools, shouting and pounding each other's backs. It was sixty miles away, but if they could see it they could make it, hold everything together and make it.

He shot a coyote late in the day. Hunters brought in a few grouse. They camped on a stream that yielded crawfish. It all went into a stew but the sight of the prairie was better than food. The next day they pushed hard down to lower altitude, the air warming. The following day Colter came running back from prowling ahead to say that Cap'n Clark had left them the better part of a butchered horse hanging in a tree!

Thank God! Good old Will! Found a stray and took it down and brought the boys back to life. The next day, moving down from the ridges, hurrying a little as the terrain spread out, grass in abundance, Lewis saw Reuben Field approaching, bowed by the heavy load lashed to his back. Reub had been with Clark and he was packing eighty pounds of a mix of dried fish and roots. Said he'd bought it from the Nez Perce winter stores. Said he'd packed it out for their dinner. They all laughed like hell at that, and Lewis heard the tinge of hysteria in their laughter. He could see it in their eyes. They were here, they'd made it, they were alive and past the worst that the Rocky Mountains had to offer. And they were on water that would take them down to the sea. The western sea.

Hallelujah!

34

On the Columbia River, December, 1805

God Almighty—forgive the blasphemy, Ma—but George Shannon was
one sick puppy! He was puking in the bushes every time he got a whiff of
vomit and you couldn't escape that because all the boys were sick with
their bellies blown, farting like drums, poor York holding his guts like he
figured they'd explode, Cap'n Clark muttering and cursing, John Colter
off a ways heaving up from his moccasins, oh! the pain shot through your
belly like someone had put a blade through you. Cap'n Lewis, he said it
was the diet switch. They'd starved in the mountains, then gorged on
dried fish hunks that might have been pretty ripe, all mixed up with roots,
and then they'd gorged again on fresh salmon, ate till their bellies was
taut, what you do when you've been on starvation rations. 'Twas to be
expected, the cap'n said, but Shannon thought it was mighty poor pay for
having starved.

"Ready to march, George?" Cap'n Lewis, standing there white as a
sheet, expression like he'd sat on a cactus.

"Yes, sir!" Shannon said. What he meant was he figured he was as
ready as anyone else and maybe readier than the cap'n looked from the
way he winced every time he moved. But somehow the cap'n managed a
smile of sorts and said, "Good, start packing."

So far as Shannon could see, the only whole and healthy person was
Sacagawea, little Pomp on her back in that pack she'd built, he cooing
and gurgling just like the river they now followed. Every now and then
he'd give a cry and she'd pull him out of the cradle and clean his little ass
and give him some tit and off they'd go. She dug those roots she seemed to
find by instinct and cooked them in bear oil and there she was smiling
when everyone else was heaving. And what a difference she made. Shannon doubted they'd have come this far without a fight if she hadn't been
with them. You could just see the change in the Indians they met when
they spied a woman with a baby—she was proof this was a party come in
peace even if they were packing plenty of weapons.

Shannon thought he'd never seen a stream so beautiful as what both
captains called the Clearwater. It was clear, all right, and he supposed

the Indians called it thus. It came gushing out of the mountains, cold as ice, sparkling, pure, a little touch of green but the bottom was clearly visible, each round rock sharply defined. It ran swift and true to the west, so said the Indians and surely they knew, to intersect with a still larger river from the south that roared on to feed what the cap'n said just about had to be the Columbia, the Great River of the West. But whether Cap'n Lewis was right or not, one thing was for sure—it would all be *down*stream!

Sick or not, they went on down the river a couple of days to the grove of giants the Indians had described, what the cap'n said were ponderosa pines. They reached to the sky.

"Didn't have none of these back on the farm, eh, George?" John Colter was feeling better. "Just look at them damn things!" He looked as proud as if he'd raised the big trees himself. "Everything's big in this wonderful country—we just seen the damnedest mountains there ever was. Biggest mountains, biggest bears, biggest buffalo herds, biggest trees—hell, George, this is the place to be! I'll bet it's got more gold, too, and I sure know it's a beaver trapper's paradise. I don't reckon I'm ever going home."

"What? Stay out here?"

"Why not? I want you to stay too. And York. We'll get York, he'll be good."

Shannon thought of York wanting to be free, wondering how Cap'n Clark would answer. If he stayed in the wilderness he wouldn't have to ask. A man like York, he shouldn't have to ask.

Then the seriousness of what Colter was saying sank in.

"How could you stay out here? What would you do? How would you live, all alone?"

"Wouldn't be alone if you came along."

"Yes, but close to it. Two or three men?"

"George, every creek you look up you see beaver sign. Every creek would yield you a fortune in fur. You saw at St. Louis how the fur trade booms—everybody in Europe and the East, they're wearing a beaver hat. Supply won't never dry up and it looks like the demand won't neither."

"But alone—"

"These Indians seem like nice folks, generally. I could live among 'em. And take my beaver loads down to the Mandans and in a few years I'll be rich."

"Or dead."

"Yeah, maybe, but what the hell—better than looking up a mule's ass bucking a plow back in Pennsylvania. So what do you say, you like the idea?"

Well, he did, of course, but somehow he knew he would be going back to Pennsylvania, not to the farm but back where there were lots of folks. But what he said was, "Well, it don't matter, you're in the army, a sol- dier — they made that clear right at the start. You can't just walk off."

"Well, shit," Colter said, nettled. "I wouldn't run off. Not so much the army but I wouldn't do the boys that way. They may need every gun before they're out of this. But we get back across the mountains, I'll ask the cap'n, and likely he'll give me my discharge. Why not? We've done what we come to do, soon as we get down to salt water. How could any- one deny us?"

He laughed, a big happy laugh, maybe because he wasn't puking no more, and he said, "You know what, George? You done made history, you done walked across the whole blamed continent, ain't nobody done that before. You're somebody, George!"

Such talk made Shannon uneasy. "Well," he said, "everyone done it."

At which Colter laughed like hell and slapped Shannon on the shoul- der and said, "You're a pistol, George!" Shannon didn't know what to say and then he decided he was pleased and he smiled. John Colter was really the pistol, but he'd made Shannon feel good.

The Nez Perce leader who had welcomed them when they came down from that brutal mountain crossing was called Twisted Hair, so his name translated. You could see in his face and his warm eyes that he was a kindly soul. The members of his tribe frequently sought his opinion, though not his permission, Indians not operating in the hierarchical fash- ion of white men. Children vied to climb on his knee. His big hand would curl around the little rib cage and he would talk placidly as the child studied his face. He had a way of laughing that made you want to laugh with him, and of course Clark had quickly made him a friend. Old Will had a talent for easy friendship that Lewis lacked. At the thought he shrugged. He didn't, so that was that. But Twisted Hair was a good friend.

"Merry," Clark said, "this here Indian says white men have settlements on the sea and he says ships visit, big canoes, he calls 'em — " He turned to the Indian, gesturing, and sure enough, Twisted Hair sketched shapes with his hands that clearly delineated a square-rigged ship.

"You've been there?" Lewis asked.

Twisted Hair stared at him blankly. Charbonneau and Sacagawea joined them. Bouncing language about, it came clear: no, he hadn't jour- neyed so far but the facts were well known, yes indeed. Well, Lewis thought, he believed the Indian because he wanted to believe, not because he was very convinced.

If there were settlements and storehouses he could replenish his supplies; he'd have a cornucopia if ships came. And a ship could carry word back to Mr. Jefferson. Lewis's message from the Mandan villages had said he would strike for the Pacific and then back to the Mandans to winter again. If he were at the Mandans now he could send a message downriver, so any day now the president would be expecting a message, and if it didn't come . . .

Then a new, more troubling thought—what flag would fly over these settlements if settlements there were? American traders or British, and if the latter, would a detachment of Redcoats be on guard? There always had been more to the journey than just the Northwest Passage and a route. Mr. Jefferson intended an American position on the Pacific and had all along. With the Louisiana Purchase that intention turned urgent. Lewis looked around the camp. Most of the boys had recovered from their blown bellies but they still were looking hangdog. Suppose he had to take a hard hand when he came to the Columbia's mouth? Could he start a war on his own say-so? One thing was sure, though—he wouldn't back down. That wasn't his nature. If the British pressed the exploring party would fight.

In this militant mood they went to work in the vast grove of pine that would yield the vessels to float to the sea. The boys took down several huge trees, trimmed branches and bark and suspended them over trenches of fire as the Indians directed. Every few hours they chiseled out the char and returned the log to the fire. Oh, if only the iron boat had worked! But he dismissed the thought. In ten days they had four huge dugouts and one smaller one, all hollowed down to thin shells with gracefully pointed bow and stern that glided lightly on the water. They loaded and ran downstream toward the sea.

It had to be a wild ride on rivers that fell from the same height but reached salt water in a fifth the distance the Missouri required. Running now with the current instead of against, paddles going deep and hard, they swept like a runaway stagecoach down the gorgeous Clearwater and into the sudden rapids. It was so deceptive, the river smooth and sweet, the sun still hot though the winter air was chill, and suddenly the surface crumpling and here we go!

Clark had the first canoe, while Lewis positioned himself in the second. At each rapid he and Clark pulled up, back-paddling as they studied the water ahead. They might go ashore and estimate the difficulty of a portage against the terrors of the rapids. Sometimes the water was so violent that prudence demanded packing the bundles on their backs and letting the canoes down on long elk hide ropes.

But more often they went straight in, Clark in the first canoe, Lewis in the second, each positioned in the bow to stand the vessel away from rocks. They crouched, poised paddle in hand, the smooth, silent current sweeping them more and more rapidly forward until with a perceptible jolt they were in the wild water. Every man was on his knees, paddles ready, the vessel bucking and plunging, foam and spray obscuring sight, the water's roar drowning their yells, rock looming from the mist, dig deep to hit it a glancing blow with the hull, not a head-on shattering blow, and just as a man decided anything worse would be the end, pop out into sunshine, gliding on smooth, sleek water, the surface creamy by contrast. And pull over into shallows and cling to a rock and try to get your breath as you watched the others come through, ready to rescue if necessary. Fifteen such rapids in a day, *bam-bam-bam-bam*, and sleep like the dead at night.

In two days they were on a majestic river that swept up from the south. Twisted Hair thought it all over and announced it was what he called the Snake. And in a few days a massive flow poured in from the north—the mighty Columbia, itself one of the great rivers of the continent with the Missouri, the Mississippi, the Ohio, the Hudson, and, Lewis soon found, a devil of a lot faster than the others.

Gone were the days when he could tramp along the shore with Seaman at his heels keeping up with his flotilla as it crawled up the Missouri. Now the river banged them along and he sat in a tight canoe, Seaman with his tongue hanging out, smiling whenever Lewis spoke to him. Well, maybe it was just as well, for this was uninviting country at best. Or maybe it was the contrast, coming from timber country to desolation sere as any desert. Whenever they went ashore, stretching and grunting, he set out on a quick botanizing tour and continued to find new species, but now he was afflicted with the feeling that somehow he wasn't really doing his duty that included, after all, a close accounting of flora and fauna, not just looking at a landscape like a passing tourist.

He tried to express these thoughts to Clark. His old friend looked at him oddly. "You ain't spending too much time in the sun, are you, Merry?" Lewis grinned and let it go. Will was right, of course; Lewis wondered if he just needed something to fret over. Still, he could see enough to see that this was some different country.

It was a great basin but radically different from the grasslands of the high plains through which the Missouri River flowed, where buffalo and other game animals roamed in huge herds. No sign of the friendly cottonwoods of the plains in groves along the river; here there were no trees at all beyond stunted willow brush. The soil was poor, the land covered with sage brush and bunch grass and prickly pear with even meaner needles. No buffalo grazed here nor much else. The Indians along the river lived largely on salmon that swarmed upstream in unbelievable profusion.

This was harsh country. For the first time Lewis found he must dicker and trade for firewood brought from afar. The people reflected this bitter terrain. They were small and often ill; they seemed grasping and demanding, nothing like the noble Cameahwait and his people in the mountains. Lewis often thought of the tall Shoshone; of course, as brother to Sacagawea you had to figure he would be strong for she was a tower of strength, endurance, and, so it struck him with faint surprise, good-natured kindness. He thought of that younger Indian who'd been on the edge of challenging Cameahwait. But his years in Washington had given Lewis some understanding of how power works, and he saw that soon Cameahwait would take that young fellow under his wing and put him to use as a favored lieutenant and, perhaps, successor when the great chief was ready to stand aside. But these Indians on the lower Columbia were scrawny and mean, and what the hell, maybe stealing was second nature when you were always hungry. But Lewis was far from home and supplies were running low and he couldn't afford pilfering scoundrels eroding what was left. And it infuriated the boys.

"Why, you son of a bitch!" Colter squalled one night about dusk when they'd put away stewed salmon. He was up in a flash and seized a scrawny Indian who had a blanket in his hand. He knocked the man down and knelt on his back and his knife was in his hand. "Time we teach these bastards a lesson," he bawled. Good God—they had miles to go and they would be returning this way too and hardly needed more hostility than they already had.

"Mr. Colter," Lewis shouted, "get off that man. Get your blanket and then let him go."

"Cap'n, I know rogue Indians, you got to teach—"

"That will do, sir. Off of him this instant!"

Colter stood. "Probably getting fleas off him nohow." He picked up the blanket and kicked the man who scuttled away.

In the morning Twisted Hair bade them farewell. He said he was far from home and wasn't sure he himself could get through Indians of this cut. Off he went smiling and waving after warmly embracing Clark.

Down, down, down the river, portage the Great Falls of the Columbia, on to what translated as the Short Narrows where the whole vast river compressed to a mere forty-five yards and went boiling and swelling through a mad gut, hold up and gaze at it and then run it like riding a cork blown from a bottle set in the fire. The Indians posted themselves on the banks to see the crazy whites drown after which they would garner the booty that would wash up along ten miles of riverbank. Lewis's canoe shot through it like a bullet, old Seaman on his feet and barking in excitement. Every vessel reached the smooth water below sound and secure. Lewis figured this survival disappointed hell out of those scavenging bastards who had been their hungry audience. Then with a whoop they hurtled on toward the Long Narrows.

Days passed, rapids becoming routine, some to be run in a wild rush, some to be treated with real caution, packing supplies across rough climbing portages as they lowered the canoes on taut lines. Then, one day, a breathtaking sight. They drew up on a sandy beach and Lewis climbed a promontory for a better view. Rearing right up to the sky was a perfect cone, obviously a volcano, dormant now, for it was covered with snow. It stood alone, huge and magnificent. With a start Lewis realized he was looking at what thirteen years ago Lieutenant Broughton of the Royal Navy had named for Admiral Hood.

And then, dead ahead, a new range of mountains!

Lewis spied them near dark as he prowled the shore. Saw them as a blur, fitted glass to eye, saw them towering, saw the river dwindling to nothing straight on the distance . . . oh, my God. More mountains to climb? It was horrifying. Then he realized that the men would react precisely as did he and he couldn't afford that. More mountains? Think, damn it. This water was hell-bent for the sea and either there was a lake the size of the Pacific Ocean this side of those mountains or the water already had cut its way through and made a series of gorges that ought to be something to see.

He came back to the smell of salmon stewing with those roots Sacagawea seemed able to find wherever she went and after he'd put away a handsome bowlful of stew he stretched and said easily, "Some hills out ahead of us, boys. Means the river cuts through, probably some gorges to knock your eyes out and a swift ride to the sea. We're almost there and by God, it'll be good to get there!"

A cheer went up. He saw Will giving him a knowing smile.

It was just as he thought, the river cutting the new mountains in a series of wild cascades that plunged down and down. He didn't name the mountains; place of the cascades would do. Sheer walls hundreds of feet high rose on each side. From both sides creeks poured into the river, plunging off the tops of the walls in feathery trails and, at times, thunderous waterfalls. Some were magnificent—one he measured by triangulation to be at least six hundred feet high and there were half a dozen three to four hundred feet plunging off the wall above into the river, spray soaking the men. What extraordinary country!

They came boiling out of these incredible canyons into a wide valley that amazed him—it amounted to a whole new world. The air was damp and chilly. Clouds looming close overhead leaked rain. Grass on the riverbanks was a luxuriant green. Trees were so big and so tightly clustered that when he stepped ashore and walked into them he had to twist and turn to make his way, passing from spruce to hemlock to fir to cedar. In a moment he was alone though he could still hear the men's voices, exclaiming in wonder. Many of the trees stood to a startling size, towering two hundred feet over-head, seven and eight feet in diameter at the base. Deeper in the woods, the sounds of the camp now more distant, he realized how easily a man without a compass could become disoriented and lost. Seaman, suddenly uncertain, walked close to him, his tail steady at half-mast.

Tales of childhood filled Lewis's mind, children stepping into an enchanted forest, Ma reading from that tattered book she had, he sitting at her knee by the fire and then, older, standing beside her to gaze at the drawings, his own vivid mind rendering the rough black lines into glow-ing color—great trees and woodsmen's huts and trolls and goblins and lit-tle boys and girls plunging bravely on . . . like the Corps of Discovery.

He heard footsteps and turned, newly conscious of being alone. His hand strayed to his knife; he hadn't brought his rifle. Then Will Clark stepped from behind a tree. He spread his hands, wonder on his face, and murmured, "What God hath wrought . . ." It came to Lewis as a prayer.

Waterbirds swarmed on the river, great clustered flocks of ducks, geese, brant, cranes, gulls, swans, cormorants—after weeks on a steady fish diet it was a hunter's paradise. That night, lying by the fire with a belly full of goose and brant, Lewis realized that he had come to a verita-ble rain forest in the midst of the American continent—and lying squarely against country that seemed like desert through which they had just passed. He lay there puzzling and gradually the lessons of the scien-tists in Philadelphia whom the president had insisted he see came back with a rush. Of course, air soaked with the moisture of the sea rolled in, struck the mountains, bounced up to altitudes where cold air leached out the damp in ferocious rains and sent the air on bone dry to the land beyond the mountains, leaving a rain forest here, a desert there. How strange and wonderful!

But in the days following even he, a natural-born enthusiast for new terrain, had to admit that it fell a little short of wonderful. The rain seemed never to stop, they were drenched day after day, they slept in rain at night, their buckskins began to rot. Another fifty-odd miles in the rain and as the river bent north he saw the unmistakable signs of what he had traveled across the continent to find.

The rock walls were wet well above the river's surface. He felt a shock like when you walk on a carpet from Persia and sparks fly from your fingers. Tidewater! He gazed at it openmouthed and started to yell and point it out and saw that all the men had noticed it and were staring. They floated, paddles athwart the canoes, gazing at this towering evidence; there was something reverent in this silent moment and then Clark yelled and waved his arm and they swept on toward the Pacific Ocean. On and on, another hundred miles, the river a magnificent surging body, its depth beyond calculating, running down between towering rock walls that reached toward the sky, everything combining to dwarf little men from the East in their knifelike slender boats . . .

"D'ye hear?" Clark shouted back from the lead canoe. He gestured forward. Lewis cupped his ears. Yes, he could hear it, a dull, continuous roar—already the boys with Clark were digging in their paddles and Lewis's boat came just behind, surging downstream as fast as muscle could add to current, and then they rounded a great turn and there spread before them was the Pacific Ocean, surf rumbling and booming against the shore.

Tears filled Lewis's eyes. They had done it; they had crossed the continent; they had come down the great river of the West and tied the continent into one. They had done it! And it was left to the ebullient Clark to put it into words, words that Lewis knew he would note for posterity.

"Ocean in view! O! the joy!"

They had crossed the continent, come from the East, come by land. O! the joy . . .

So they were here, arrived, goal achieved, desperate effort finally ended. Lewis felt a curious darkness, as if the saga completed had ended the tension and excitement and joy of the challenge itself. They had done it, won, come through alive and still strong. Would he find other mountains to climb? Would any compare to this most magnificent of treks?

The breakers they first encountered proved to be not from the ocean proper but from the great bay into which Captain Gray had piloted the brig *Columbia*. Clouds lay against treetops, rain poured, sunshine became a distant memory, the wind howled off the ocean, their slender dugouts swamped in rough water, wind-driven swells on high tides flooded their camp and they raced for higher ground—it did seem a hell of a note to come clear across the continent in triumph and find yourself shivering wet with a hole in your gut.

There were no American settlers here, no British, no Spanish. No traders, no Redcoats, no ships in the bay, nor had any appeared for many a moon, so said the Clatsop Indians, proprietors of these parts. The Clatsops were friendly, even gracious. Why in the world were the white men camping in this desolate spot? In a combination of much sign language and various back and forth efforts during which Lewis constructed a rough vocabulary of their language as he did of all Indians he met, they led the visitors to higher and drier land to the south where elk congregated. It took but an instant to decide they would winter here. Elk meat was leaner—you could stuff yourself and still feel hungry from the absence of fat—but there was more of it and elk skin made superior clothing.

But that darkness of mood held steady. The Clatsops said there was another bay to the north. Perhaps there were traders there and ships, but Lewis doubted it. He set out to see with Drewyer and Colter. They circled the new bay; no ships and no settlement. Drewyer bagged an elk and he and Colter set to roasting while Lewis went on to the beach. At last, alone as he preferred, he looked down miles of white sand drawn fresh and clean by magnificent swells rolling unbroken from the Orient to wash this white shore. Towers of dark rock reared from the surf, seals sporting among them. Waves thundered and boiled and ran up the beach to his feet with a dying hiss. The roar of the surf beat into his brain, gulls whirled and cried, terns ran across the sand with loud *kraaas*. As in the deep woods, Seaman stayed close at heel as if he were as awed as was his master at the unparalleled magnificence of the Pacific Ocean.

And here, alone, waves that began half a world away crashing at his feet, his mood lifted like a shaft of sunshine bursting through the dark clouds. It was near dusk and the eastern sky was darkening but to the west the clouds still glowed with inner fire over the limitless ocean. Standing on this opposite shore across the continent, he felt a sudden completion and satisfaction that he couldn't explain but knew was real. He thought nobody would understand this feeling unless someday he found a woman who matched his heart and probably not even then . . . but he felt enraptured in a moment of triumphant success that left him shaken and humbled. The Corps of Discovery had crossed the continent, cutting a path that in total was unknown to man or beast. It had marked a way that in full no one else had ever walked. They had opened the way and Lewis well knew that that changed everything.

In a narrow sense, perhaps Mr. Jefferson would be disappointed by the death of the dream of the Northwest Passage. But in leaving the terrain of the Louisiana Purchase when they walked across the Continental Divide and into Cameahwait's village and continuing on to the sea, the

Corps of Discovery had made the stretch to the sea peculiarly American. Let other powers compete, Britain and Spain and Russia, but deep in his gut Lewis knew that this far western stretch would be American, and when it became so the Corps of Discovery would be the foundation on which all who came after must build.

The thought was as exhilarating as the sea mist whipping his face and the wild gyrations and screams and shrieks of the pirouetting seabirds: the United States would be a continental nation fronting on the Atlantic and the Pacific.

And there was one other thing. Far to the north—too far to have real value—Alexander Mackenzie had struck a route and in vermilion had painted on a rock his name and the date and the magic phrase that had energized Mr. Jefferson, "By land."

Just yesterday Lewis had peeled enough bark from a huge cedar to cut his name deep into the wood. But it was the ebullient Will Clark who added the proper finishing touches. He peeled away considerably more bark and then, with ax and knife, wrote: "Capt William Clark, December 3rd 1805. By land. U. States in 1804–05."

That was the point. *By Land*.

PART THREE
DÉNOUEMENT

35

He noticed it the moment they started back on the course they had covered outbound, up the Columbia, across the Rocky Mountains, down the Missouri to St. Louis. Looking back he thought it might have started at the moment of triumph when rollers that had come unbroken from China died at his feet with a final hiss. But certainly now, embarked on the return, he noticed the down quality, a sense that the brightness had fled life. Almost immediately he saw that this was dangerous and he must hold it in control, which meant resisting its alluring darkness.

Yet it came to him repeatedly like those waves breaking at his feet. The happiness he'd known on this expedition, the challenge, the discovery of new plants and new creatures, could not be repeated. Well, he'd known that, hadn't he, told himself that his wild elation outbound was a once in a lifetime experience? Maybe that was just the way of things, the joy of youth maturing into more realistic and hence darker realms. But this darkness wasn't really new. It felt like an old friend, fitting like a much worn boot. He shook his head again. This was not good thinking. And he plunged ahead.

Up the Columbia, which was surely just as tough as the Missouri when you were in canoes going against the current, paddling furiously, portaging around the frequent falls, rappelling past boiling rapids, some of which they had shot on the way down. These Indians were master thieves and seemed to feel that whatever they could lay hands on became theirs by divine right. They kept Lewis on the edge of anger, but Clark calmed him, pointing out the impoverished lives they led, worse than any Indians they had met so far. But then three of them slipped into camp, untied Seaman, and led him away; clearly he would make a stew to end all dog stews. Lewis erupted; he was so angry he could scarcely breathe. In strangled tones he sent three men after the thieves with orders to shoot to kill. Later he thought that might have been a bit excessive; in the event the Indians saw they were being pursued and turned Seaman loose. The big black dog came bounding back looking as happy as when given a whole buffalo thigh to gnaw.

Then, with cries of thanksgiving, the party passed from the land of the thieving Chinooks to that of their friends, the Nez Perce and good old

Twisted Hair. Now they were poised to start on the terrible trail across the Bitterroots that had brought such pain and peril outbound. The Nez Perce gave them warm welcome but Twisted Hair warned them that though it was June, the snow was still ten feet deep and packed hard enough to support horses. But if they must go across now, he would send guides to lead them. The guides didn't appear on the day expected or the next or the next. Lewis gave the order to move out without them. He saw that look flash over Clark's face. Try that trail without guides, it under ten feet of snow? They set out. Presently they paused to rest the horses. The men were unusually quiet. Well, all right, Lewis told himself; he was impatient but he wasn't insane.

He saw Clark watching him. He raised both hands, palms up, in the universal gesture for what-the-hell, then jerked his thumb in the direction from which they'd come. Clark nodded.

"All right, boys," Lewis said, "this ain't working for sour apples. We'll go back and find that guide."

There was a muted shout of approval. Lewis led the way. As he passed Clark he winked. Clark grinned.

Still, with guides, the passage went well enough. Near the end of the trail, the way ahead marked so that even the white men could get through, the Nez Perce guides pulled out. Attacking Blackfeet had plunged the Missouri River into war from the mountains to the Mandans. The Blackfeet had attacked the Shoshones and Cameahwait had moved his people; where, the Nez Perce hadn't asked. Lewis glanced at Sacagawea. She absorbed this news without change of expression, though later, reining close to her, he saw she was crying. The Nez Perce said the chances of the white men getting through alive ranged from slight to none. They hugged and shook hands all around and then the guides turned back; "We proceeded on," Clark entered in his notebook.

He and Lewis talked it over. They didn't know the Blackfeet but they came in peace, with a woman, and had rifles in case their pacific intent went unheeded. They had gotten on well enough with Indians so far, even scraped through with the Sioux, so what the hell: they probably would be all right now.

On that basis they decided to split their force. Lewis would head north on the shortcut old Toby, their original Shoshone guide, had told them they could cut two months' passage to a week. If it proved out in bringing them relatively quickly to the Great Falls of the Missouri he would split his party again, leaving half to get the boats and the supplies out of the cache. With the other half he would take a serious look at Maria's River, that false stream masquerading as the Missouri as it came straight out of the north with its load of mud. Out of the north . . . did that mean out of

Canada and could that blossom into an American finger in the Canadian fur trade? Clark's party, meanwhile, would head south, pick up the Jefferson River back to Three Forks, then cross to the Yellowstone and explore it to its joining with the Missouri.

Later it did strike Lewis that splitting their party, each element much too far to support the other if attacked, was not his smartest move in the face of Indian war. But they were going back now and the report to the president was much on his mind, especially since it must start with the sharply disappointing news that there was no Northwest Passage, the dream of centuries could be cast aside and forgotten. Now he wanted his findings to be as rich as he could make them and hence wanted to cover as much ground as he possibly could and still reach St. Louis before snow flew.

Sure enough, Toby's shortcut worked just as he had said it would. Lewis led the way, the horses trailing behind him, each rider with a pack-horse's halter line in his hand. On he went, often dismounting to swing into the long strides that ate distance and soothed his roiling mind. For the more he thought of the report he must write the more troubled he became. What should it be, how should it go, what approach should it take? This would be a book for public consumption. It was one thing to draft a straightforward military report on what was done, what was found, conclusions, recommendations. Of course he would do one of those, forty or fifty pages in his narrow handwriting, but this was different. He had read a good many traveler accounts, they were quite the rage for a while—well, take Bartram's trek through the Carolina mountains, which Lewis himself had explored as a boy. But no, that wasn't at all the tone or form he wanted. Well, what did he want? He didn't know. He rode along, confused and angry.

As planned, he left half his party at the falls and with Drewyer and the two Field brothers, overall his best men, he started up the Maria's River. Still no problems. He was beginning to think this Indian war was less than his informants thought.

When they were well short of Canada the Maria's River degenerated into what Lewis named Cut Bank Creek. Star sights told him where he was with some precision and it was clear his fond hopes for this river named for a cousin had failed. Then as they swung south again to link with the Missouri and run eastward to the entrance of the Yellowstone where Clark should be waiting, their good luck in encountering no Indians of any stripe ran out.

On the particular day when it came undone, he had delayed starting in hopes of a clear sky and a sun measurement for a final positioning. But clouds held on and he gave the order to start. At noon they paused to eat and graze the horses while Drewyer went ahead to hunt along the river.

The terrain was gradually rising and Lewis with Joe and Reuben Field climbed until it leveled into a plain.

There Lewis was startled to see a herd of horses, twenty or thirty, perhaps a mile away. He focused his glass and saw a number of Indians sitting their horses and staring intently at the valley below. They almost certainly were watching Drewyer. And there almost certainly was a bigger party nearby to account for so many horses.

What now? If he and the Field brothers took flight the Indians would follow and their horses looked better than Lewis's hard-worn mounts. And that would leave Drewyer to their mercy.

"Break out the flag, Joe," he said. Field screwed the two parts of the flag staff together and unfurled the flag. The Indians were milling about nervously. As Lewis ordered the advance he said quietly, "Boys, we'll try to gentle them, but if they want a fight I might as well tell you I'll go till I die before I'll give up my gun and the papers — I'd like for you to stand with me."

Their mouths drawn into hard straight lines, both brothers nodded. With a wave of his hand Lewis started them forward. "Slow, now," he murmured. "Give them time to look us over." Up close he saw there were eight of them, all young, some mere boys. Suddenly one of them broke from the pack and galloped hard straight at them. Lewis immediately dismounted and stood by his horse, waiting. As if disoriented by this move the Indian stopped his horse. He was a hundred yards away. Lewis extended his hand, empty of weapon, hoping that looked peaceful. The Indian whirled his horse and galloped off. He had rushed in to count coup and Lewis's reaction had startled him. Lewis advanced slowly.

As he neared another Indian rode out and stopped. Lewis stopped the Field brothers and advanced alone, his horse at a walk. When he was close he offered his hand. The Indian clasped it and shook vigorously. Released, Lewis went slowly to the others and shook each one's hand while the first Indian greeted the brothers. The Indian pantomimed smoking. But the pipes and tobacco were with Drewyer. They all trooped downhill, found Drewyer, and agreed to camp together. That night they talked long through Drewyer's sign language.

The boys were Blackfeet. They said the warriors of the tribe were well equipped with firearms that came from Canadian traders with whom the tribe was close. They smoked for hours, everyone exhausted, and at last they turned in.

At dawn Lewis awakened to Drewyer's shout, "Damn you, let go my gun!" Drewyer was scuffling with an Indian over his rifle and another Blackfoot was running away with Lewis's piece. Lewis gave chase and when the Indian looked over his shoulder, Lewis showed his pistol and warned the warrior he would fire. The man slowly placed the rifle on the ground. The Field brothers ran up with rifles raised to kill the Indian. Lewis stopped them.

They blurted out their story. An Indian had taken their rifles. They had chased him. They had to tear the rifles from his arms. Reuben drove his knife into the man's chest. It must have sliced his heart for he died within seconds.

But before Lewis could digest this he saw two Indians driving off their horses. Frantically he ran after the horses, shouting that he would fire. One of the Indians turned and raised an old British musket. Lewis snap-fired and shot him through the belly.

A belly wound was almost always fatal. That meant two members of the Blackfoot tribe had died in meetings with the white men. They tried to give chase but the Indians were away. Indian horses as well as their own were milling about; they selected mounts for the trip on to meet Clark but before they went Lewis hung a Jefferson medal around the neck of the dead Indian. He wrote in his journal that he did so that there might be no question with whom they had tangled. When he wrote this he was boiling angry at the treachery of men willing to smoke with him and camp with him and then try to steal weapons and horses. But later, cooler, riding toward the Missouri, Lewis wondered how wise leaving the medal had been, pinning what the Blackfeet clearly would see as murder so directly on himself, establishing white men as enemies — except, that would be, for Canadian traders. Exactly the message Lewis did not want to leave.

But after that, fortune smiled on them. Without further encounter they followed Maria's River down to the Missouri. The rest of their party awaited them, having prepared the canoes they had cached there the year before. They turned the horses loose — bonus for the Blackfeet — and swept down the river toward the mouth of the Yellowstone where Clark would be waiting.

The big river from the south flowed serenely into the Missouri but there was no sign of Clark's party. Then Lewis saw an obviously fresh campsite and soon found a note left in a forked stick. Clark had been there the week before, found game scarce, and had gone on. Lewis would find him waiting downstream.

Fair enough. But they were low on provender and when he saw a number of elk in patches of willow in the bottoms he gave the order to put in. But then, as he told himself later while nursing the pain, he made a mistake. Cruzatte volunteered for the hunt and Lewis accepted him. He didn't pause to think that Cruzatte had just one eye and that one was nearsighted, not until a bullet slammed into his own rump, spun him around, knocked him down, gasping with pain and shock.

"Damn you," he roared, "you have shot me."

No answer. He shouted again. Silence. The sound of the shot had come from very close, within forty yards. Had to be Cruzatte. He shouted again, waves of pain running up his back. No answer. No sound. If Cruzatte hadn't shot him it must have been an Indian. If so, a single warrior or a war party? He yelled for Cruzatte to retreat to the boats and started his own retreat.

He tried to run to the boats. The pain slowed him, then stopped him. He fell, got up, fell again. Crawled finally until he could yell at the men in the boats. They examined the wound. The ball had struck just below the spine, penetrated the left buttock, emerged, penetrated the right buttock, and emerged.

He stuffed lint from his medicine chest into the wound to keep it open and rallied the boys. Cruzatte was out there alone and apparently unaware with Indians on the prowl. Lewis gave brisk orders. He would lead them out to find and rescue their comrade if he still lived. Within a hundred feet he collapsed, panting with pain. They carried him back to the boats and rushed off to find Cruzatte.

Lying there, he became conscious of a new discomfort. He was lying on a lump. He dug around and came up with the ball that had penetrated and emerged twice, leaving twin holes in his rump, and then, spent, trapped itself in his leather breeches.

It was a ball from a Model 1803 army rifle. Cruzatte's rifle. Just as he'd thought, the one-eyed Frenchman had shot him.

In twenty minutes the party returned with Cruzatte. Why, no, he hadn't been aware the captain had been shot or was in trouble of any sort, he'd heard nothing at all, he knew nothing, my goodness, he was shocked. And so forth. Lewis waved him away. It was done now. They laid him on his belly in the pirogue and headed downstream to connect with Clark. In that position, hurrying along after he had quieted Clark's concerns, Lewis had lots of time to think. And he found that the dark sense that life would not be so bright ever again stayed with him. His current situation, grunting with pain every time he moved, doctoring himself as much as he could twist and turn, seemed an ignominious end that somehow fitted his mood.

In another few days the Mandan villages came into view.

George Shannon sat leaning against a log in a shady spot near the lower end of the island where the breeze coming up the Missouri was cool and steady. They would be here a few days and Shannon was glad for the respite. He had been up much of the night tending to his duties with the wife of the same young man who had asked him as a special favor to transfer more of his power via the wife. It seemed that this fellow had been profoundly successful in the fall hunts. What's more, he had faced down an older Sioux warrior in a confrontation over a buffalo kill that had brought honor to the tribe as a whole. George glanced at the wife and saw that she eagerly endorsed this idea; indeed, when he'd left her this morning she had whispered "Tonight," and while her English left a bit to be desired he had had no trouble in figuring out her meaning.

This particular aspect of Indian relations was pleasing enough and yet when Shannon reflected on it he felt somehow uneasy. He thought maybe it was that he didn't really believe in this magical transfer of power and they did, though he had an idea the wife was as interested for her own sake as for her man's triumph on the hunting ground. But he couldn't escape the feeling he was taking advantage of at least the husband's credulity and he didn't like that but found it quite impossible to refuse. He thought he'd been too long away from civilization.

This led him to reflect that in a few more weeks they would be in St. Louis and he would be damned glad. He yearned to see streets and stores and church houses and God-fearing households in shuttered houses and folks going about their daily business—to see life at home, in other words. He was imagining such scenes, hands clasped behind his head, half asleep, when John Colter sat down beside him.

John Colter had two good cigars, tightly wrapped by someone who knew what she was doing, and he gave one to George.

"George," he said, "coming back along the Yellowstone with Cap'n Clark like we done, you saw what wonderful country it was, didn't you?"

"Well," Shannon said cautiously, "it was sure enough pretty." He had an idea where this was going.

"Well, God knows it was pretty enough, but I was talking more about the game and all."

"Buffalo heaven," George said. He was wide awake now, drawing on the cigar.

"Yeah, sure, buffalo and elk and bear and them damn goats leaping from pinnacle to pinnacle and I never saw one fall. But I was talking about beaver and mink, ermine, sable—guts of the fur trade. That country's a paradise like nothing I knew existed."

When John Colter got talking about wealth and position and power, which really was his subject now, his voice got hoarse, somehow. Shannon waited for what he knew was coming.

"See, George, you come out of that Yellowstone Valley with a bargeload of the finest fur in the world and you take it down to St. Louis and old Chouteau, he'll give you a fortune for it. But then, see, here's what's different. You don't blow it all in St. Louis. You stock up your kit, sure, and maybe you give yourself a night on the town, drink some whiskey, visit a whorehouse, you know, but next day you're going out again and that money, you've got it in the bank old Chouteau has set up."

"Bank?"

"Sure enough—just like Philadelphia or New York. Soon as he found himself an American protected by American law he was ready. Told me so himself when I went to see him one day. So next year I come back with another barge-load of fur. But this time I use the money in the bank to take it all to New Orleans and get five or ten times the price. Chouteau don't like it but what's he going to do? He'll send some toughs to catch me in an alley and I'll bust their goddam heads right open. And my next load, down to New Orleans and now I get me an agent in New York and London and now we're talking real business. And next year I'm back in that country and I got a handful of good men working for me and this time I come back with such a load you won't believe and my New York agent has a ship ready and off my whole load goes to China where they pay for fur like they've lost their minds, and by that time I may be back out mining the whole Yellowstone with a corps of mountain men, but I'll tell you, George, I'll snap my fingers and half of St. Louis will go to dancing, and some in New York, too. Then you got the door open to power—that's really what money's about, did you know that?"

Shannon shook his head.

"Well, 'tis," John Colter said. "That's how Chouteau uses it, where do you think all that weight he swings in St. Louis comes from? From owning things and assembling capital and having lots of folks' livings depending on him. Same with John Jacob Astor back in New York except he's bigger, he could eat Chouteau alive if he wanted . . ."

"Is that really what you want?" Shannon asked.

"Exactly what I want."

"Dangerous as hell," Shannon said. "We slipped around them Blackfeet this time but they ain't going to like the kind of operation you're talking about."

"I don't look to get killed, by Blackfeet or anyone else. It'll work if I have good men with me. That's why I want you to join up. We get around the Sioux in a bit and then I'll ask Cap'n Lewis and he's already pretty much said I can go, I help get them around the rough spots going home. So what do you think? You going to join me?"

Shannon hesitated, drawing on the cigar, thinking, but in the end he said, "I reckon not, John. Ain't no one I'd rather ride with but that don't sound like the life I want."

"You homesick?"

"I suppose. Not for my home, but for civilization."

John Colter nodded. "Well, I'm not surprised," he said.

"You think the less of me for it?"

"Naw," John Colter said, "I figured you'd know your own mind. You know, George, you done growed up a lot in this time. Let me ask you something, and I promise I won't tell no one. But back in Pittsburgh when Cap'n Lewis asked your age, you wasn't really eighteen, was you?"

Shannon hesitated. But John Colter had been a very good friend and now he was leaving and chances were but fifty-fifty they would ever meet again. He owed his friend something.

"Sixteen," he said, "nineteen now. But he'd never have took me at sixteen."

John Colter laughed. "That's about what I figured. My guess is that Cap'n Lewis thought about the same. But you've proved out right smart, I must say. You know when I think you did your growing? In that time you was lost."

Shannon smiled. "Found out I wasn't near so smart as I thought."

"Well, hell, that's the key to growing up." He stood then, throwing the cigar butt in the water. Shannon got up, took a final drag on his cigar, and tossed it.

John Colter put out his hand and Shannon took it. "I'll tell you good-bye when I cut loose, but this is really good-bye." He drew Shannon into a hard embrace, patting his shoulder. Shannon heard John Colter's voice go husky. "You take care of yourself, young fellow. Don't go forgetting all I done taught you."

"You've been a good friend, John," Shannon said. "The best a man could have."

Down the Missouri they went, digging hard to add to the current, racing for home. The party already was breaking up. Sacagawea and her husband and little Pomp had cut loose at the Mandans, where they had joined. Cap'n Clark had asked them to come on to St. Louis but they refused.

"Then send little Pomp," he said. "I'll raise him in my own house and I'll see he gets the best education ever."

Sacagawea shook her head. "Maybe next year," she said, Charbonneau translating. "When he's weaned."

When they were ready to go she came to see them off. The boys lined up and one by one took her hand and one by one she kissed each on the cheek. The captains were last. She felt they had saved her life once or twice with medical ministrations and saved her baby as well, and they had taken her home to her family and reunited her with her brother. If life didn't bring her back into her brother's welcome again, still their family was whole, Pomp its logical extension.

She took a hand of each, held it to her cheeks, kissed it. "Sank you," she said.

Well, Lewis thought, we should be sanking you — guiding us through those last days reaching the Shoshones, the wonderful fortuity of finding your brother the chief, getting us the horses without which we'd have failed, her own stoic acceptance of all the hardships of the trail, never once failing, always ready. What would the expedition have been without Sacagawea? Would they have gotten through at all without her?

But he didn't have the words. She was a woman, and an Indian, and at the moment he needed them, he didn't have the words. Clumsily, he patted her shoulder. Maybe she understood.

The Sioux were warring on all the tribes east of the Mandans, Lewis seeing the peace movement he had hoped to foster in ruins, but the boats swept along and as it happened they had no encounters. The twin bullet holes in his rump had pretty well healed, though he was still limping and glad to have the support of a cane.

When the day came that they saw milk cows in a field by the river and the critters ambled over for a better look they broke into cheers and their eyes weren't all dry. Within the hour they pulled into St. Charles, that last little settlement out of St. Louis. The people were stunned to see them and explained they long since had been discounted as lost, sure never to return. Lewis went ashore and bought a jug of whiskey and gave each man a solid drink. They fired their rifles, three rounds in unison, and the townsfolk returned the salute with their own fire.

Then they were off again and within another hour had pulled into Chouteau's docks at the city of St. Louis from which they had departed and stepped ashore, home at last, the voyage of adventure finished.

The same delighted surprise greeted them here, too. Lewis asked to hold the mail for his report to Mr. Jefferson, the request immediately honored. He had been working on the report for days, scribbling notes by firelight, then translating the scribbles into orderly prose that ran some sixty pages. It began with the bitter pill, that the Northwest Passage did not exist.

Then, as if to make up for it, he launched into vivid description of the country's great advantages — its game in tremendous numbers, its fertile soil that supported a vast sea of grass, its beauty, its wealth of plants and animals unknown in the East, its possibilities for the fur trade, the opportunities to unseat the inroads British and French traders had met. He laid out the Indian tribes he'd met, the kindly Mandans, the willing Shoshones, the always helpful Nez Perce. He dwelt on the Sioux and the Blackfeet with their innate hostility. He outlined a plan for dealing with the various tribes, noted that many chiefs seemed willing to visit the Great Father in Washington, including the Mandan chief, Big White, whom he reckoned would be in Washington now.

So rich was the outpouring of welcome that Lewis stayed two weeks in St. Louis before going on, to visit his mother through Christmas and then, just short of New Year's, go on to Washington. He had several fine suits of clothes made, visited a barber, scrubbed his hands until they were raw but clean. He and Clark stayed in Mr. Chouteau's handsome home but they were out most every night. He luxuriated in public affection. The leading people gave a dinner and a ball that lasted till near dawn and left Lewis with a brutal headache the next day. All those toasts . . . for a man who hadn't tasted a drop but for the drop on arrival since the expedition's whiskey supply ran out more than a year before. And he found he liked liquor. It warmed him, raised his enthusiasms, gave him an affectionate glow for the people he met, made their remarks attractive and his responses more striking and much more clever, so that groups gathered around him now, erupting in spontaneous laughter at his witticisms. He loved the way they listened with attention, asked questions, sought his judgments and advice, attended with obvious fascination to his stories of what he had seen far beyond their horizons. And the young women twitted about him like brilliantly colored birds and he saw they vied for the chance to partner with him in the dance.

Women on the street recognized him; they pointed, gabbling, and when he bowed burst into excited giggles. Men cheered him as he passed, often clapping their hands and calling to their children to witness his passage. Young men begged him to advise on all sorts of matters and the papers referred to him and Clark as "the young heroes." That first big ball had included every man of the expedition but York, who as Captain Clark's slave hardly counted for anything at all. Lewis and Clark in answering the multiple toasts spoke for the men, then offered the floor to any who wanted it. Few did in this exalted company. Lewis singled out Shannon as the youngest man in the party.

"How old are you now, George?"

Shannon stood. "Twenty-one, sir. Eighteen when we started." The room erupted in shouts and cheers, at which Shannon waved a hand blithely.

Later, though, Shannon said to the two captains, "York, he should have been here."

Something dark flashed over Clark's countenance. "He's a slave, George."

"Don't matter," Shannon said. He felt stubborn, moving his feet as when settling for a fight. "He did good as any of us. Better than most really."

Clark glared. "Course he did. That's what he's supposed to do. But he don't belong here." There was a moment of silence, Shannon feeling at a turning point, and then the two captains wheeled and walked away.

Well, Shannon thought, cooked my goose with Cap'n Clark.

But a week later the two captains bumped into him on the street. "What do you figure on doing with yourself?" Cap'n Clark asked.

"Well, sir, I like it here. Maybe I'll go back to Pennsylvania, see Ma and all, but after five minutes she and I are at loggerheads, so I won't stay there. Figure I'll come back here, probably find something."

"Good," Cap'n Clark said. "You belong in the West. Up and coming here, sky's the limit. But come back to Clarksville and see me there. I'll have something for you."

They walked off, leaving Shannon scratching his head. Looked like Cap'n Clark wasn't hot at him after all.

Stunning news had unfolded in their absence. Lewis and Clark sucked it up avidly. Of course, Mr. Jefferson had been elected to a second term as had been widely expected. The Federalists appeared to be a spent and dying force. Aaron Burr, vice president, had been booted out, or at least that's the way it looked, not just because he wasn't nominated this time but because of the way it had been handled. It had humiliated the man, who was a power in New York and had been largely responsible for swinging that state behind Jefferson in the first election. They had their reasons, Lewis understood that, but it was rough; Burr was polished, smooth, a devil with the ladies, and had always been gracious to Lewis in the latter's days as the president's secretary. He was highly popular in the West, having stood with the West repeatedly in the Senate.

Then he was scarcely out of office when he killed the great Federalist Alexander Hamilton in a duel on the Jersey bluffs over the Hudson. And now, just the other day, he'd been arrested on charges of treason. Though the story hadn't been proved in court yet, it seemed that Burr had invented the damnedest plot—he intended to take over the new Louisiana Purchase, steal it, actually, form it into a new nation rivaling the United States. Then, story upon story, the idea was to invade Mexico, throw the Spanish out, and divert the gold that now poured into Spanish coffers to the use of the new North American nation. General Wilkinson, commander of the U.S. Army and long regarded as a traitor in the pay of the Spanish, had broken up the plot and would be appearing against Burr, but the wise heads in the West seemed to feel that the whole plot had been Wilkinson's invention or at least that he'd been in on it from the start. Lewis didn't have any trouble believing that. He'd had dealings with Wilkinson when he was still on active duty and considered him the slimiest bastard he'd ever encountered. Of course this was all the talk of St. Louis; Wilkinson had been named governor of Louisiana Territory in addition to his army command and was well known here.

But too soon for Lewis, it was time to go. Chouteau gave a big dinner for them and again Lewis drank a good deal of whiskey. Again he found himself, with Clark, the center of attention and he reveled in it, enjoying it as much as the initial adulation. He said as much to Clark in the morning and his partner gave him an odd look.

"Well," Will said slowly, "I wouldn't pay it too much mind. I reckon they're happy with us 'cause we're fresh and bright, come back from a hell of a trip, and you cast that against all that's been going on, Burr killing poor Hamilton and this plot business, him going to steal the West, and Wilkinson, and you know what anyone who knows him thinks of him—hell's fire, we look clean and bright as a new penny."

Lewis frowned. It was a fresh thought and he didn't much like it. Everyone said they were heroes and he thought that was about right. He didn't want the idea stepped on. He shook his head.

Clark smiled. "I don't mind being a hero. Kind of like it, in fact. But, Merry, you don't want to take all this too seriously. Folks will turn on you with a snap of the fingers. I seen it with my brother. You watch out, now."

He felt a surge of affection. Good old Will. "I can handle it," he said.

36

Albemarle County, Virginia, Fall, 1806

"Mary Beth is in St. Louis," Ma said. "Did you see her?"

Lewis stared at her. He'd been home a week, had clasped his little brother Reuben who wasn't so little now in hard embrace and hugged Ma who didn't seem to age at all, and was remembering how much he had always enjoyed the smoked ham dinners she put together. The community had welcomed him royally. Already there had been a handsome testimonial dinner at which he'd made a quick speech. He drank some whiskey that evening, which seemed to surprise Reuben.

"I didn't know you took whiskey."

"I do, but that don't mean you should."

Reuben had smiled and let it go by. Whatever big brother the hero said . . .

Now, staring at Ma, he was trying to digest this news, and he asked rather stupidly, "What's she doing there?"

"Got a boardinghouse, her and Mrs. Parsons. Has a herbal medicine practice too, what all she learned from me. She writes every couple of weeks. Course, it takes a couple of months on the way, but we keep up. Anyway, she's doing right well. Says she and Mrs. Parsons got a nice bank account now with some Frenchman—"

"Chouteau. Fur company baron, opened the bank soon as Americans came in."

"That's it, the very name she mentioned. She went to Louisville, but when she realized the great purchase included St. Louis, she figured Americans would be flocking in there and they'd like an American place to roost, hang their hats, you know. And it worked out—she says they're full all the time, turn away new guests every day. Hard work, though, but she never shied from work. You didn't see her, then?"

"I had no idea."

"Whole town celebrating you like you said, I imagine she didn't want to interfere."

"Interfere?"

"You know, intrude."

He sighed. "Well, Ma," he said, "I expect you're right."

But it unsettled him, as mention of Mary Beth usually did, and he passed a somber afternoon and evening.

When Lewis came into Washington by stage, the other passengers pleasantly agog to be riding with him, he ordered his luggage hauled to the executive mansion but set out on foot himself, in no hurry and taking pleasure in the familiar city. Many of the folks he passed didn't recognize him, but enough did to make the stroll pleasant. But just the same, he found himself slowing down as he neared the mansion, in less and less of a hurry to get there.

His feelings about the president were considerably mixed. He was coming home a success but he had failed to find the Northwest Passage,

failed at settling Indian wars, and he had to admit he'd killed a couple of
Indians in acts that would not be forgotten soon among Blackfeet and
other tribes as the word spread. But that wasn't it, really; the problem was
that he had a bone to pick with the president and so the closer he came
the less enthusiastic he was and the slower he walked.

The president was expecting him; he had written ahead and Mr. Jefferson knew the stage schedules. So he came sweeping down the marble
staircase in his velvet slippers and enveloped the subaltern in a bear hug.
He led the way upstairs and called for tea, though Lewis would have as
soon fortified himself for this talk with a drink.

Mr. Jefferson seemed to bubble with pleasure. He said Lewis's report
had arrived within the week and he had read it half a dozen times, seeking
out its nuances and implications. He told Lewis it was brilliant work and
that Lewis must turn it into a book for the public. When Lewis mentioned
the Northwest Passage failure the president threw up his hand.

"Doesn't matter. You've done a great thing on this expedition. Tied
down an American interest in the Pacific Northwest that will stand well
when Britain starts to assert its claims. I think that will be one of the primary values we'll assign to all you've done, and of course there are many
others." He shrugged. "As for the passage, well, I've thought a lot about
it since your report came in and I suppose it never was very realistic,
more of a dream that we afforded ourselves when we knew so little.
Looking back, I can see that the idea that it would be so easy to find the
saddle and the portage and the river waiting to carry you to the sea as if
that was its only place in the scheme of things — well, those are ideas that
don't stand up so well in light of real exploration. But what we do have is
a great venture that succeeded magnificently. I do congratulate you most
heartily."

Lewis smiled. "Sir, no one could ask for warmer praise. I'll see that it's
conveyed to every man on the expedition."

"Tell you what. I'll issue a proclamation citing each man by name and
see that it's delivered to each on parchment."

"That will be very welcome, Mr. President. But raises a question I have
to put to you whether you like it or not. And I suppose you won't. Like it,
that is."

Looking not at all discountenanced, the president merely waited.

"Why did you let Mr. Dearborn deny William Clark the rank that you
had promised him?"

"Ah, yes," Mr. Jefferson said softly. "I thought that would come back
to haunt me."

"I took it as a promise," Lewis said. "I offered it to Captain Clark as my promise on your authority. And I can tell you, you have no idea the pain it caused—and the gallantry of spirit required to set it aside."

"Mr. Clark ob—"

"*Captain* Clark."

"Captain Clark. Sorry. But he objected?"

"Well, of course. I had been his lieutenant. He never would have accepted the secondary position. That's why I asked your permission to make the offer based on equal rank."

"But you persuaded him, then?"

"Yes—by pledging my honor that he would never be treated as lesser, that we would be equal in all things, the men would never know. I told him I couldn't make it alone. And that was true, too—then I surmised, now I know. I needed him. And he served as fully equal in every way. I want him treated so now, in pay, in honors, on that parchment you mentioned. Oh, sir, why did you let that go through? You and I had an agreement."

"Why? I'm not sure. I didn't recognize how seriously you—"

"Both of us."

"Yes, how seriously both of you would take it. And then, the secretary raised a military question. What happens if the commanders disagree? Reason ships have—"

"Yes, I know, only one captain?"

"Well, did you have disagreements? You and Captain Clark?"

"Once."

"You see? What was the issue?"

"The iron boat."

"Yes," the president said eagerly, clearly happy to change the subject. "How did that work, by the way?"

"No, sir. We'll discuss everything, but right now we're talking about why you betrayed—"

"Sir! That's a very harsh term."

"It's how I feel. I think it needs to be said."

"Tell me what happened on the disagreement. How did you settle it?"

"Captain Clark was big enough to ignore it."

"Really. To his credit, then?"

"Exactly. He was bigger than I was. He thought it would fail but he knew I was determined so he stood back."

"And did it? Fail, I mean."

"It did." He was surprised by how much it hurt to say those two words. He sketched in the situation for the president, who simply nodded.

"Well, Merry," he said, "I'm sorry. Convey that to Captain Clark and I'll write him a note. You've been around this town long enough to know that I don't wield all the power that people unacquainted with power imagine. I'll speak to the secretary about pay and titles. I'm not fully sure what good it will do, but I'll try."

Lewis saw he had gotten all he was going to get. "Well, sir," he said at last, "all that aside, I will say it was an extraordinary trip, never to be duplicated in quite its new wonder."

They talked for a couple of hours, the president plying him with interesting, incisive questions that forced Lewis to consider and reconsider. They were two naturalists, two students of Indian life and vocabularies, two statesmen considering the international implications of the trip, two storytellers marveling over the coincidence of Sacagawea's brother as the man to whom they must appeal for horses. As politicians they chuckled over Cameahwait's masterful handling of the young blowhard whom the big Indian was bringing along as he thwarted his hunger for the post before his time. Stories of the desperate passage over the Bitterroots made utterly clear why there was no Northwest Passage. They shared the sheer triumph of seeing those heavy Pacific breakers finally beating and then dying against the sandy shores of the Origan country.

At last the president sighed. "This is wonderful stuff, Merry. Earlier you had a phrase that struck my imagination. You called it a trip never to be duplicated in its new wonder. Now, that's what you must catch in your book. You must make your readers see and feel and understand all that you felt, all the way your heart swelled at sight of the buffalo in vast herds, the incredible grizzlies and your own narrow escape, those goats leaping from pinnacle to pinnacle, the miles of grasslands that must be rich to feed those herds, that's a critical point for readers who associate forests with fertility. Give them facts but make them feel the poetry of it all."

Again, Lewis felt the chill that had been striking him for months now. He didn't know how to accomplish this.

"I'm a little uneasy about it," was all he could bring himself to say.

"Oh, don't worry about that," Mr. Jefferson said easily. "There's enough poetry in what you've told me this afternoon to make a couple of books. You'll be fine. Just turn yourself loose, make the reader see and feel the way you made me see and feel this afternoon. It will be splendid."

Lewis let it go. They dined with several good wines and by the time they were done they were exhausted. The president had invited him to live in the mansion while he was in Washington, and soon they agreed to turn in.

But lying in the big, comfortable feather bed, Lewis had a pair of thoughts. He didn't know how to write the damned book no matter what the president said, and when you stop to look at it, there hadn't been a very clear explanation for what Lewis took as a fundamental betrayal, the rank question for Clark.

The War Department was in a little brick building on the mansion grounds, in front of the mansion proper. Lewis waited a few days before he called on Secretary Dearborn.

"Ah," Henry Dearborn said, "the wandering explorer."

Given that the powers of Washington had only the night before given Lewis a handsome dinner with no end of toasts with damned fine liquor, of which he had availed himself copiously, saluting him as the young hero of the hour, he thought Dearborn's greeting a bit mean. But what could you expect from a man as small in spirit as he was large in girth.

"Mr. Secretary," he said carefully, "I think we return with an expedition that produced many advantages for the nation even if it failed to find a Northwest Passage. Indeed, proving there is no such thing has a value of its own, even in its disappointment."

"Oh, quite," Mr. Dearborn said. "I understand you cut quite a swath last night, drinking at least as much as was good for you. I've watched you coming and going, you know, wondering all the while if you intended to come in and report. So you see, I'm glad that you've chosen to honor me today with your company."

"Sir, that seems less than fair—"

"Oh, then, permit me to withdraw the remark. Now, sir, you've been back these three months and I've heard nothing from you, but don't worry, the president was kind enough to have a copy of your report to him made for me."

Oh, God. "Sir, I thought it proper to report to him. He organized and planned—"

"Certainly, certainly, I understand fully. No more needs to be said. What can I do for you today?"

"Why, sir, I thought I might answer any questions—"

"Consider them answered. What else?"

Lewis hesitated, then plunged into how the Clark rank imbroglio looked to him and how he had promised Clark he would be treated and paid equally—

"You may treat Mr. Clark exactly as you choose, Captain Lewis. But his rank in the United States Army is lieutenant and that is how he shall be known and how he shall be paid."

He argued, wrestled, pleaded, quite demeaned himself when what he wanted was to slap a challenge into this oaf's face, settle their differences with pistols. But captains don't challenge secretaries and he knew the president would never stand for it and that everywhere he would be judged in the wrong and the secretary would triumph with no risk to his ugly hide.

At last, demeaning himself further, he pleaded. "Sir, I implore you to understand the situation. We led our men over thousands of miles of wilderness and every step of the way Captain Clark was my equal in rank, in command, in service, in importance. I understand you are not pleased with me, but please, let's not take it out on him—"

Glaring, the secretary said sharply, "That will do, sir. I take serious offense at your suggestion that anything but duty and departmental rules guide my actions. Now, sir, you have been long away from active military duty and perhaps you've forgotten your manners. Hence I am not going to call you before a court-martial for lack of respect to a superior, but I will tell you both that my message asking for a bill to pay you as captain, Mr. Clark as lieutenant, sergeants and privates according to their proper ranks has already gone to the House."

He looked at Lewis with what the subaltern could only read as disdain, then said, "Now, pray, have you brought your accounting?"

"Sir?"

"You've spent more than—let's see." Ostentatiously he rummaged on his desk to produce a slip of paper. "Yes, here it is—now, I see you have spent some thirty-eight thousand dollars, nearly thirty-nine—an absolute fortune—and you have not accounted for a single penny of it. It's been near four months since you've been back—I'd have supposed you might have found time to draw up accounts but apparently you've been too busy being an important man."

He raised a hand to silence Lewis's protest and said, "See Mr. Simmons of this department. He has all the figures and will receive—and evaluate—your report. And now, permit me to point out that there are many matters in the military beside your concerns to demand my attention, and so you are dismissed. Close the door on the way out."

"Sir—"

Dearborn slapped his desk, a sound like a pistol shot. "Dismissed!"

The president merely shrugged when Lewis reported this conversation. "I'm afraid he has the law on his side, Merry."

So much for presidential support. Lewis went on the Hill to prowl from office to office pleading with men there to set aside the secretary's bill and craft a new one treating Clark fairly. He got nowhere. Desperate, he proposed an appointment for Clark as lieutenant colonel, simply going around the secretary. But no, couldn't be done, unfair to other officers awaiting promotion. That Clark had no intention of remaining in the army so that it was all honorary seemed to make no difference. Congressmen might be willing to offer fulsome toasts to the young hero in a night of drinking, but in the light of day weren't ready to buck the secretary. Nor, as it turned out, was the president of the United States. And, thought Lewis as he drafted another apologetic letter to Clark and prepared to go, he would not forget the secretary. Or the president, both of whom had gotten what they wanted.

"Oh, my God," Dolley Madison said slowly. "That's terrible."

She looked at her husband. Jimmy was unrolling the hose he insisted on wearing even though fashion was turning to the new trousers that more and more men wore.

"Jimmy," she said, "that will ruin Merry."

He was sitting on the bench before her vanity. He looked up in irritation, rubbing a blister on his left foot. "Why? Named him governor of Louisiana Territory. That's quite a plum. And Clark, named him superintendent for Indian Affairs in the entire West. I'd say he treated both men handsomely."

"But isn't Merry supposed to write a book?"

"Yes. Tom is very enthusiastic about it."

"Well, how can he be governor and write a book at the same time?"

"Really, Dolley, how should I know? I don't write books. Hard enough to run the State Department, I don't need to think about books."

"Oh, Jimmy, you ought to get him to change his mind. Don't the territories come under the State Department's purview?"

"Yes, but if you think I'm going to challenge the president on what he sees as a very generous act, perish the thought."

"Merry will be a terrible governor. Here he comes back from a glorious venture, a magnificent success, whole country talking about him, and Tom drapes this office around his neck. God, what a pity. It may kill him, you know."

"Oh, for God's sake, that's the worst melodrama. Let him resign if he doesn't like it."

"He'll never resign. And he'll be delighted with the appointment."

"Then what—"

"I know him better than you do, Jimmy. He won't know how to write a book and that will weigh on him like a stone tied 'round his neck in the middle of a lake. And there will be endless trouble for you."

"Trouble I can deal with. Plenty of that already. As for Captain Lewis, I know you're fond of him but he has gotten very big for his britches. All these toasts and dinners and such, all this young hero stuff, the sooner that wears off and is done the better. He's treated Henry Dearborn abominably."

"Oh, Henry! He's an old ass and you know it."

"That's true, but he is the secretary of war and Lewis has no business forgetting that. All this western business, first this, then that, Tom talking about how essential it is to our democracy, lauding this young man to the skies. Louisiana Purchase—Tom thinks it's the most important thing since we threw John Bull out in the Revolution but a decade from now we may think entirely differently. May find it's a stone around our democracy's neck before we're done. Be a century or two just to get some people in there."

Petulantly, she thought—he could be petulant sometimes when he was tired—he balled the hose and flung them in a corner. "The tedium of the whole subject just exhausts me. Of course it was important and Lewis did bring it off well, but that's not to say that he doesn't live by accounting for his actions just like the rest of us. Only way government can function, really. If I'm elected to succeed Tom things in the West will be different, you may be assured."

"But, Jimmy," she wailed, "that's so unfair. Captain Lewis has done a great thing, surely you grant that?" He nodded, looking sulky. She dashed on. "Appointment like that will just ruin him and he's really a very decent young man, you always said that, have you forgotten?"

"No, but I don't know that the appointment will ruin him and it's none of my business and I'll be damned if I'm going to go tell Tom his act of generosity is a big mistake."

By now he was in the long nightgown he wore and he hopped into bed and snatched the covers up around his ears. She sighed and seated herself at the vanity and began the nightly chore of brushing her hair a hundred strokes on each side and the back. He was a wonderful, kindly, sweet man, her husband, but she knew he was not to be pushed. She was always careful in her choice of opinions to press on him. She thought he would be elected president and she knew she would not raise these points again. But just the same, the appointment was a terrible move that could destroy a fine young man.

37

Philadelphia, Early 1807

Philadelphia was a gracious city, the most smoothly urban and highly cultured city in America, natural magnet to scientists and savants. Tall chestnuts lined its cobblestone streets with brick sidewalks laid in intricate patterns and handsome brick homes of two and three stories. It was much cleaner than brash and hungry commercial centers like New York; a corps of sweepers tidied up after horses and it was unusual for a dead animal to remain on the street more than two or three days, a hog, say, or a spavined horse that had died in the traces and been cut loose and left to lie there. It even had streetlights and lamplighters who appeared at dusk and dawn to tend the lights. Lewis felt he belonged here, and now, with his membership in the cultural pinnacle, the American Philosophical Society, of which Mr. Jefferson was president, he did.

Naturally the Society president asked him to speak; he begged off with a note explaining he lacked time to prepare a proper address but would attend the next meeting. With the governorship of Louisiana Territory demanding his immediate attention, he was only here to see to the publication of his book and then must rush on to St. Louis. Of course he called on Dr. Rush and the others who had tutored him to tell them how useful their instruction had been. Dr. Rush listened gravely to his account of Sergeant Floyd's death, concurring with his surmise that a burst appendix had been the cause, which would have been beyond anyone's capacity to treat in the field. He asked eager questions about Sacagawea's illness and congratulated Lewis on handling it with aplomb.

Himself a leading member, Dr. Rush escorted Lewis to the next Society meeting and introduced him, then led the members in a rousing cheer. As an alternative to an address, he agreed to take questions and from an elevated dais, cognac in hand, explicated at length on the wonders that lay beyond the Mississippi and that few white men had seen. As the new governor of the whole province he dwelt on the vast responsibility and the immense opportunity to make this a glowing part of the American scene. When he was done the august members gave him a huge round of applause with cheers and then clustered about him for the rest of the evening. God, it did feel good! These were the men who were the intellectual heart of the nation; when they cheered him, why, the Dearborns of the world could just go to hell.

The vast Louisiana Purchase that accounted for about a third of the continent below Canadian holdings and north of Mexico had been split, a line drawn along the thirty-third parallel separating Orleans Territory with headquarters at New Orleans from Louisiana Territory headquartered at St. Louis, Meriwether Lewis, governor.

When Mr. Jefferson told him of the appointment Lewis had burst into an excited grin. Later, remembering, it seemed he'd damned near wagged his tail in his pleasure, which wasn't exactly the image he sought to convey. But the idea of running the place, having old Chouteau and all the others respectfully pulling their topknots when he passed, that had a rich, satisfying feeling that he'd never quite experienced before. Governor! In command of everything. Oh, yes, that felt good. Later he wondered if he hadn't just been getting that first taste of power.

He was thrilled with Clark's appointment, too. It was exactly right for him, Lewis thought later. He knew Indians and their attitudes and customs, had a feel for languages even though he wasn't adept, and best of all, he liked Indians. He found all their best qualities, understood their concerns and was always willing to deal with them, often chiding Lewis for impatience. They were a patient people and did not respect impatient men.

It was while thinking how the appointment fit Clark that he realized suddenly that he himself knew no more how to govern a province than he did how to write a book. The thought gave him a cold chill that ran right down his back and tipped his mood into darkness for the rest of the day. Fortunately, he was dining that evening with his old friend Mahlon Dickerson who was welcomed at all the best tables in Philadelphia and had introduced Lewis into this august society. A good dinner and a couple of stiff glasses of whiskey and they were ready for a long stroll on which they paused at numerous watering holes and made impromptu calls on homes where there was music and dancing and eligible daughters eager to meet the young hero of the West. He fell mildly in love with almost every young woman he met and dallied through evening after evening, which meant his mornings were consumed with trying to ease his headache and calm his boiling gut.

A letter came from Frederick Bates, who had been appointed secretary of Louisiana Territory, an office like that of lieutenant governor: respectfully welcoming, filled with best wishes, it noted that Lewis's presence as governor was urgently needed with numerous situations awaiting decision. Secretary Bates was anxious to serve the governor in every way possible.

A note came from Clark. He was in Fincastle, Virginia, where Judy was looking with high favor on his courtship. As an afterthought, he suggested Lewis keep a sharp eye on Bates. It seemed the secretary had expected the gubernatorial appointment for himself and was likely to be gunning for the man who got it.

Lewis put both letters in the bottom of his grip and went off to see his publisher. Philadelphia was the publishing capital of the nation and this was the real reason the president had sent him here. John Conrad proved to be a tall, courteous man who had gray hair on his chin and tufts of gray hair above his ears and spoke in little more than a whisper. He told Lewis that he regularly supped at five, went to bed at seven, arose at two in the morning, and reviewed manuscripts in his chambers until his neighbor's rooster crowed. He reviewed Lewis's journals for an hour while the explorer looked at other books he had published.

At last Mr. Conrad sighed and removed his reading glasses. "Brilliant work," he said, "and beautifully put in some places. Your journals make it all so vital and alive. I will be privileged to publish it."

Mr. Conrad cleared his throat. Lewis saw a startling expression of cupidity flash across his face. By the time it could register avarice had disappeared.

"Tell me, Captain Lewis," the publisher said, "do you and Captain Clark look for a return from this book? Personally, I mean, money that will flow to you?"

"Why, yes," Lewis said, startled. "We do hope for a return."

"But some of it goes to the government?"

"No—that has been our agreement from the start. Proceeds of our personal story go to us."

"So its sale matters to you, personally?"

He nodded, stopping himself from saying just how much it mattered. He saw it as his fortune. The plantation was his, but Ma and his brother had it for now. The book was his estate.

"Then," Mr. Conrad said, "you want it to succeed. To sell. So you don't want it to read like a government report. You know, dry, dull. You want plenty of pepper, stories, descriptions, adventures." He slapped the notebooks he'd been reading. "It's all in here, beautiful stuff, really. I congratulate you. You have a superb project. But it's not ready as-is. It's all day-to-day, fragmentary, some of it going to challenging a bear face to face, some with proposing government Indian policy. It wouldn't do to print these volumes verbatim but they contain material that's beautiful, poetic, wildly adventurous—really astonishing material. It will make a splendid book when you distill it out of this raw material. Then you can have something that will thrill the whole reading world. Just take a bit of effort on your part. But I'm sure you understand all this."

Lewis swallowed. "No, sir, I'm not sure that I do."

Mr. Conrad looked at him for a long moment. He made a curious clicking noise with his tongue. Then, his manner more kindly, he said, "I expect you need an editor, a professional, you see, who can take these journals, ask you a lot of questions and then help you fit the narrative into a shape that pleases you and that can be counted on to grip your readers." He smiled. "I can see it now. Thrill the public. This is a book that can be very good to you in a financial sense."

Ah. An editor. Yes, that made sense.

Mr. Conrad gave him the names of several candidates. Yet even as he took the list Lewis felt resistance building. Submitting the breadth and sweep of where he'd been and what he'd done and what he'd seen, to convey its utter magnificence, all to be masticated by a man who couldn't have the faintest idea of what—no, he felt the inner resistance growing.

Yet he knew he didn't know how to do it himself. But then he shrugged—he'd walked across two thousand miles when no one knew the way so he ought to be able to figure out this new problem too.

He engaged a mathematician to work his rough star sights into finished positions. He found an artist to render on paper the specimens of new birds he had brought home and another to draw illustrations of waterfalls and particular plants and trees and, of course, the mountains that crowded the sky. A cartographer would turn sketches into maps quite independently from Clark's map, which already was being readied for publication.

All that remained was a manuscript.

Before Lewis left Philadelphia Mr. Jefferson came to town for a meeting of the philosophical society. He dined with Lewis and of course, asked about the book. "You know, Merry," Mr. Jefferson said, "what you want from this book is to anchor what you have done, what you have learned, the sheer magnificence of your march through incredible hardship to the very shores of the Pacific Ocean. It is to crystallize in people's minds your name as the dominant voice in American exploration. Never mind Cook, Vancouver and the others—from now on, Lewis and Clark will be the voice of the West, of exploration." He wiped his lips with a napkin, his gaze fixed on Lewis's eyes. "Keep that in mind as you write."

Before Lewis left Philadelphia he called on the publisher. When Mr. Conrad asked how he fared Lewis frowned and admitted that this editorial fixing was all so new to him; he'd never done anything like it. He didn't mention the editor. But Mr. Conrad was in a mellow mood. "Oh," said he, "you won't have any trouble. Just follow your journals. They tell wonderful stories. Try a little nip of whiskey. They say that works wonders for the authorial impulse, though of course I never indulge myself."

As he saw Lewis to the door, Mr. Conrad patted him on the shoulder.

"Now, don't delay, dear boy. Put yourself full-time on this—St. Louis can wait, I expect—you want to strike while the iron's hot, as they say. Yes. Adventures like yours are perishable goods, you know. The public is so fickle—you're fascinating today, forgotten tomorrow. So hurry it right along. Get your editor set, agree on an approach and start sending him your material. You know the saying, 'let no grass grow under your feet,' eh? Good advice, doubtless everywhere but certainly in publishing."

Lewis next decided to visit his mother—St. Louis could wait—and to stop at Fincastle en route and meet Will's cousin Judy, whose portrait he had admired. In the flesh, she had blossomed into a pretty young maiden who to the visitor's practiced eye seemed downright anxious to marry Clark before a more sophisticated woman snatched him away. But Clark had waited these many years and insisted on taking things slowly, letting her get to know him as a man instead of as her grown-up cousin.

They made him welcome and a round of gay parties began. On the second day they went to Colonel Breckenridge's pillared mansion. The colonel came down from the veranda to greet them. A young woman, pretty in a plain way, was on the veranda and she came down too. He introduced his daughter, Elizabeth. She curtsied to Lewis and he saw a flash of interest in her eyes. The colonel held a militia commission and wore a sharply trimmed spade beard now showing a little gray that made him all the more distinguished.

Glancing about, Lewis saw a gazebo under a huge chestnut, and in it a slender young woman in a pale blue gown sitting upright in a plain chair with a book in her hands. Her neck was slender and bent at a little angle, and she held her chin lightly between thumb and forefinger. She was a study in concentration and Lewis felt himself drawn to her as a bee to nectar.

"Beth," the colonel said to his daughter, "run tell 'Titia we have guests." Just in time Lewis stopped himself from countermanding the order, so perfect was the picture of the lithe young woman in blue, beautiful neck bent over a book. Beth hesitated, giving Lewis a look that said she didn't want to go, then scampered away when her father glanced at her sharply. Before she turned Lewis gave her a quick, warm smile at which joy flashed across her face.

They were inside when the tall young woman in blue came in a side entrance and the colonel presented his oldest daughter, Letitia Breckenridge. She was beautiful. Utterly, fantastically, beyond belief beautiful, light brown hair cascading in gentle waves, eyes a dark blue almost like slate, lips that surely were made for kissing, a smile that lit the room, the afternoon, the day itself. Once he saw Beth staring at him with an expression of hurt anger but then he forgot her as Letitia warmed to his interest. Clark had told them lots about the expedition and about his friend Lewis, and now they plied him with questions and listened with bright interest. Sitting on a sofa with Judy's hand in his, Clark generously tossed out suggestions, tell 'em about the bear chasing you and coming near getting you, tell 'em about the prairie dogs.

Lewis felt her laugh was like a silver bell that responded to his witticisms and she had a way of swaying toward him when he seemed to please her with some comment. Sometimes he thought she would fall into his arms, but of course she didn't. They dined and afterward they danced as Beth played the piano and later still Letitia led him to a swing on the veranda and they sat in the dark talking. When she said something he particularly liked he took her hand and brought it to his lips. They sat thus for what seemed, oh, a very long time, and then she gently disengaged her fingers, letting them linger on his as she leaned toward him. The moment was charged as with summer lightning and then with a quick glance through a window into the parlor she leaned close and kissed him squarely on the lips. Later he supposed it hadn't lasted long but now it seemed to go on forever and he felt that he was melting. She pulled back with a little smile and said they should go in, and he followed her back into the house, in love as he thought he had never been in his entire life. It was time to go, a groom brought the carriage, he shook the colonel's hand, he bowed to Mrs. Breckenridge and to Beth, took Letitia's hand, felt her strong, steady pressure on his hand, bowed low and brushed it with his lips, and then they were off.

All the way back to Judy's house Lewis burbled over Letitia, her beauty, her charm, her intellect, her innate goodness of spirit. Clark and Judy said little, he giving them slight opportunity to speak. He intended to marry her, he would be speaking to her father shortly, he would press his suit for as long as it took, he would overcome any and all objections. At eight in the morning he rode over to the Breckenridges. The house seemed quiet. He went to the barn; hands told him the colonel was out in the fields and they expected the house wasn't up. He waited an hour, until a house servant came out, said the family had seen a strange horse and wondered who called. Lewis dashed a hasty note and sent it in. He had come in hopes Miss B would consent to go riding with him this morning.

The servant returned. "She say it gonna be an hour."

Letitia appeared in riding habit, the groom put a side-saddle on a gentle black mare, a black woman in a bonnet driving a light carriage came along as chaperone. But the day was brisk, clouds came on with a hint of snow and Letitia suggested they go back. She made hot chocolate and took two cups into a study off the drawing room and they drank in cozy comfort. Out of the corner of his eye Lewis saw Beth start to join them only to be called back by her mother. Good: the family apparently approved. He left before noon with a promise he could return for tea.

Back at the Hancocks' he found that Judy's little sister, Amelia, had spread the word far and near that Captain Lewis was sweet on Letitia Breckenridge. He thought that for the better, a way of announcing his intentions. Certainly Letitia seemed pleased to see him though this time her parents stayed in the room and he wasn't invited to dinner. As he rose to go, bowing gracefully to everyone, Letitia said she would walk him to his horse. They stood by the gate a long while, nearly an hour, his turnip watch later told him, talking in what seemed the easiest of intimacy. He rode away exulting in love.

In the morning, a rider with a note. Miss Breckenridge felt that the captain had made his intentions so evident that her staying here would constitute a challenge to him. Therefore she was going to Richmond with her father this morning for an indefinite stay. She wanted Captain Lewis to know that she wished him well in his new post in St. Louis.

He read this, then groped somewhat blindly for a chair.

"What?" Clark said.

Lewis handed him the note. "Same old story," Lewis said, his voice thick. "I thought this one was real. Thought it would take. God knows, she sent all the signals, I mean, I didn't think I was forcing myself on her. I don't know, though, maybe I pushed too hard, too enthusiastic, assumed too much. Maybe I scared her." Clark didn't answer and at last, knowing his anguish came through his voice, Lewis cried, "God, Will, I do want to find me a wife. You've got your Judy, look how happy you are. I want that too. Been wanting it for years. But it doesn't take."

That's what it boiled down to: he wanted a wife.

38

Albemarle County, Virginia, Late 1807

"Merry," Ma said, "ain't you supposed to be in St. Louis?"

"St. Louis can wait." He managed a feeble grin. "It ain't going anywhere."

"But, son, you're the governor, isn't that so? I mean, you've got things to do there. Don't you?"

"Well, Ma, I reckon, but I just don't feel like it. Like going. Like I give a damn if I ever see St. Louis."

"Don't curse."

"Sorry, Ma. But it's a fact."

"You've been here off and on for months. That letter come from the publisher, you left it open and I went ahead and read it, thought maybe it was good news. He said you ain't sent him a word in the whole time."

"I've tried. I mean—everything I put down seems wrong, seems silly, awkward, all awry, makes no sense."

"Aren't you supposed to get an editor—isn't that what the publisher said? You told me that."

"I don't want an editor—I mean, hell's fire, Ma, I wouldn't know what to say to him, and I don't have anything to send him anyway."

"You go out at night, don't you? Are you drinking?"

"Some. But it ain't out of control."

"It's dangerous."

"No, I can handle it."

"Your pa got like this sometimes. And your uncles, too. Your pa, he'd go for days with hardly a word, deep in the melancholies, and I'd go down and try to drag him out but it didn't do no good. What got him going again was work. Work his heart out, poor man, and then eventually he'd come out of it."

"What are you trying to tell me, Ma?"

"Well, your work's in St. Louis—maybe if you were there it would be better."

God, he had to laugh except it came out as a short, bitter bark from which she recoiled. But that was it exactly. He wasn't in St. Louis because he didn't know what the hell he was supposed to be doing when he got there. He said as much.

She stood in the doorway, looking at him as he lay on the coverlet of his bed. Her lips tightened and suddenly she looked much older and much harder and he felt a quiver of apprehension.

"If that isn't the damnedest fool thing I've ever heard," she said, forgetting her dislike of cursing. "If that don't take the cake—don't know what to do. Here you led a party of men across the continent where no man, white or Indian or anything else, had ever gone, not all told, and I guess you figured out what to do then, didn't you?"

"Will was there, remember."

"Well, of course, but when he was here he told me it was you that held it all together. I discounted that some, nice fellow telling a mother what she'd like to hear, but he ain't a fool and I looked in his eyes and I don't think he was lying."

But she couldn't understand, no one could—you had to live the sodden despair that he knew so well. It just made it worse, her trying to jolly him along. Her telling him that because he and Clark had led the trek—and yes, granted, it was one hell of an epic trek, but what did it all add up to? Not so much, after all. He looked back at those days and the boys and it all had a dreamy feeling, he saw Big White and Black Cat and fat old Black Buffalo in a haze, and Sacagawea and her brother, and what did those names mean, Sacagawea and Cameahwait, how had they come about? He didn't know, hadn't asked, the simplest human question and he hadn't asked. Suddenly this seemed like a vast failure of human spirit, an absolute sin, and he cried aloud.

He leaped up, drew on his boots, saddled the first horse he found in the barn, and rode hard toward the distant Blue Ridge. He had done well in mountains, that had been his glory days. But then as he considered it, it struck him that he had seen mountains that your average Virginian could hardly imagine, and why was he riding toward the Blue Ridge? He remembered Mr. Jefferson assuring him that western mountains could be no higher, no steeper, than the Blue Ridge. How little he knew, how proudly he postured. No one knew anything really, and everyone talked. Of course, that was why the book was important and the book, the damned book, he knew it was important, he didn't need reminders. He had heard little from the president but he had to admit that what he had heard had been gracious and kindly, gentle in its modest hopes that the book was coming along, that savants in Philadelphia as well as in Paris awaited it eagerly. Which was fine for them, they wrote things all the while, but God damn it, Captain Lewis was an outdoor man who could take you there and bring you back and if that didn't include being a great author, who were these men to criticize, they who would wet their breeches if confronted with a night alone in the wilderness—not that they had criticized, but still . . .

Darkness had fallen and presently light glowed ahead. Yes, the White Horse open for business where the regular patrons always gave him a hearty welcome. They paid homage to a famous man in their midst, and he liked that.

And then one day somewhat later, weeks or months, he awakened at dawn with the sense that all had changed, all was new. He had given up going to the White Horse and that probably was part of the clarity he felt in mornings now, but this was different. Well, it wasn't just chance that he had abandoned the White Horse, things had gotten out of hand one night and they'd had to pull him off some poor bastard who had offended him in some way long since forgotten and the proprietor had suggested that he was drinking too much and it would be just as well if he didn't come back. Meriwether Lewis the explorer barred from a miserable little log hovel of a tavern in Virginia! That sobered him up for a while and you may be sure it was an experience he didn't report to Ma or his little brother.

But that was all in the past now. On this morning dawn was just cracking. He felt real and whole. He hadn't gone out the night before, which was becoming more and more his habit, and he was reading again. Working on Shakespeare. Ma liked that, you could tell from the way she bustled about humming and the pies she baked. He had always liked dawn, its mysterious pale light revealing one object after another until the world emerged, fresh and new. In other days in what sometimes seemed a different world it had been the time of wariness, of expected and sometimes real attack. Now he lay on his feather bed as the Virginia countryside revealed itself and he realized that he felt downright good. Sort of a new man, so to speak.

He hadn't been totally idle. He had finished reports to the president on Indian policy and other frontier matters in light of the new territory. What he had not done despite Secretary Bates's pleas for help was go to St. Louis. In early letters Bates had said he would be warmly welcomed; now the tone had changed, he could count on finding plenty of men who would pick bones with him amid the rough new crowd that had flocked into town.

He laced his hands behind his head. Enemies, eh? Well, Captain—no, by crackey—Governor Lewis had dealt with enemies in his day and they wouldn't find him easy to take now. As he lay there he was overcome by a powerful feeling that things were different, everything had changed, things were falling into place with the satisfying click of a pistol's action. He tossed aside his blanket and leaped up. He thought of his morning drink but didn't want it. He pulled on trousers and boots, quickly buttoning his shirt. How long had St. Louis been waiting for him? Eight months? That was long enough. Of course he didn't know how to be governor in a new province that was exploding into action after somnolent decades of decadent Spanish rule—neither did anyone else. But he had never let that slow him before. Now he must hurry if he was to catch the afternoon stage.

39

Maybe, Shannon thought, lying in the rude little hospital in St. Louis with his leg throbbing, he had pushed his luck too far. One thing about the whole episode that made him think so was that the part of the leg that hurt so much, through the shin and down into the foot and even the toes, he could feel his individual toes, was the part that had been taken off. Amputated, the doc called it.

It was a damned outrage that the part that was gone should hurt the most. Wasn't it enough that he'd hobble around for the rest of his life? He'd figured that once they'd whacked it, above the wound, mind you, the pain would all be gone. That had been a major consolation as he faced the inevitability of surgery. He complained to the doc but that worthy gent merely nodded. "That's the way of it," he said, puffing that smelly corncob, "that's the way of it."

Sometimes he thought he should have stayed in Pennsylvania, taken over Mr. Stanley's feed store, gotten fat and slow and dull. At least he'd be walking on two feet. When the Corps of Discovery disbanded in St. Louis he had known he must go home, for a visit, at least—he owed Ma that much. He hadn't seen her, after all, since he and Pa went off to break new land in Ohio, a much bigger operation planned than they'd been able to afford in Pennsylvania. And Pa died and Shannon sold the place and sent the money to Ma with a note that he was going to the Pacific and that was the last she'd heard of him, so of course he had to go back. At first he'd been treated as a hero that he liked well enough except that a little of it went a long way. Old friends finding it hard to talk to him, that sort of thing.

But he wasn't back a week when Ma was all over him again. Same old story.

"Here's what I think you better do. I saw Mr. Stanley, he has the feed store, and he told me he'd like you to come see him about working in the feed lot for a while, year or two, get to know the business, then maybe take it over and then someday buying him out and owning it yourself and your future would be assured."

"But, Ma, I don't want to run a damn feed store."

"Don't curse, young man, and don't get too big for your britches, either. Mr. Stanley—"

"Ma, Mr. Stanley can go to hell."

Whereupon she burst into tears. "You haven't growed up at all. Same willful boy. I figured you going on this expedition, all them adventures, you might have learned what's real, but I see—"

He walked out, saddled a horse, and rode off to see friends, feeling very low. The next day he left.

She hugged him and whispered sadly, "I'm driving you away again."

"Oh, Ma," he said.

She began to cry. "Same as before," she said. He looked at her lined face, she not all that old, her life none too easy. Her bossy nature had driven Pa off and now her oldest son was following. Life was hard, that's all. It wasn't anyone's fault, really, she was the way she was and George equally was of himself and there it was. He went on to St. Louis where Cap'n Clark had promised him a place in his enterprises. And he felt so good just being here on this familiar ground that he realized this—the West—was his real home. Found him a place to stay at Miz Slocum's new lodging house and settled in. He liked Miz Slocum, an old Virginia lady, and she clearly had taken a liking to him. She was a good deal more warmhearted than Ma had ever been.

He was working for Cap'n Clark in the little fur warehouse the cap'n opened and generally pitching in wherever he was needed. The cap'n seemed to rely on him more and more, which made Shannon proud. Had to watch it he didn't get too proud.

About a year after he returned from Pennsylvania an Indian war had started along the Missouri, pretty much from St. Louis to the Mandan villages. Between the Sioux and the Arikaras the river was closed in a way that St. Louis folk had hardly seen. The Indians were furious about American trappers bringing out loads of beaver pelts that they believed were Indian property. Shannon didn't know who was right but certainly the fur trade was the only resource Indians had to bring to the white man's market.

Into this mess came Big White, the pale Mandan chief whom Cap'n Lewis had talked into going back to Washington for the big confabulation with President Jefferson. He'd had a high old time in Washington, from what he told Shannon, his quick mastery of conversational English quite surprising. But now it was time to go home. Mr. Jefferson had sent him back to St. Louis with an escort and orders for authorities here to figure out how to get him on upriver, which Shannon figured meant delivering him without an arrow in his gizzard.

Cap'n Lewis was supposed to be coming here, him the new governor and all, but he hadn't arrived and it was Cap'n Clark as Indian agent for all the West who decided we didn't have any option but to go ahead. He put together a little expedition, Ensign Pryor with a dozen regular soldiers and a few frontiersmen who knew how to handle a rifle. Shannon was flattered when the cap'n suggested he join up.

And then—go on, admit it—he'd been looking forward to another session with that pretty Indian woman whose husband believed his successes were due to the transfer of Shannon's power through his wife's body. Since Shannon didn't believe anything of the sort it was like taking advantage of the Indian to have his wife, though he remembered his qualms had been much stronger after he and the young woman finished than when they were fixing to start. Then, lying in the makeshift hospital looking for anything to occupy his mind except his own bleak prospects now, he thought again of the young warrior and laughed out loud—that Indian should see him lying here in this makeshift hospital. He wouldn't be so keen to share Shannon's power now.

"What have you got to laugh about, blockhead?" asked Jonesy, the little hospital's only other patient, in the bed next to Shannon's.

"Now, Jonesy," Shannon said mildly, "don't make me come over there and bust your noggin."

Shannon had his crutch and Jonesy's bed wasn't all that far away. But Jonesy laughed. "How you gonna do that?"

Shannon waved a hand. Jonesy could go to hell.

He lay there, reflecting on the way the whole thing went awry. They'd set out in a keelboat, fighting that fierce current with Big White tucked safely away in the cabin. Shannon was one of the few men experienced enough to know you wouldn't see Indians until they were ready to show themselves. Ensign Pryor kept rattling about how these Indians were overrated and when they saw soldiers and army rifles they'd run like rabbits and so forth and so on. Shannon didn't know a lot about war but he did know it was dangerous to hold an enemy in contempt. He tried to tell the young ensign but Mr. Pryor was in command and knew everything and Shannon saw he was so uncertain he couldn't hear a contrary opinion for fear his own view would collapse and die.

So Shannon was waiting and sure enough they came around the inside of a bend in slack water and he smelled trouble. Up ahead was a sandbar with enough growth to hide men. It was situated so that it left a narrow slot of river between it and the riverbank through which the keelboat must pass. It was a classic ambush site. He called to the ensign but the young man blithely waved them on into the trap and when they were fair in the slot a whole passel of Indians appeared on the right bank and on the island with arrows tipped into bows and strings half taut.

It was time to pull in, show a friendly hand, offer a few presents, propose a smoke with the leaders—probably wouldn't have done much good in the midst of war but they might have gotten the lay of the land and maybe impressed the Indians with their power, this being a military force more heavily armed than a regular trade group. But Pryor stood right up and shouted this was the United States Army and it was coming through.

Then arrows were flying and in a moment he felt that sting in his leg. What made it so bad, frontier lore said the Arikaras smeared their arrowheads with shit. So they said in St. Louis. Led to blood poisoning and gangrene. Somehow he'd understood this the moment he felt the fiery bite in his leg and looked down to see the arrow passed through the calf and hanging there, halfway through—like feeling the sting and looking down to see a big rattler gliding into the bushes, him having fixed you for good. He had broken the arrow back near the feathers and drawn the shaft out of the wound and wrapped a cloth tight around his calf, knowing that that wouldn't be the end of it. At last, with Pryor himself wounded and three of his men dead, the stubborn ensign called retreat and they let the current sweep them off. Turned back they were, a real blow to Indian relations, Indian figuring these whites could be intimidated easily enough.

It took more than a week to get back to St. Louis, even riding the current. Cap'n Clark was mightily perturbed and so was Shannon. Clark sighed and said to no one in particular, "What in hell are we going to do with this Indian?" Big White, he meant. Well, George could have told him, not by sending a handful of men with an idiot ensign and hoping the Indians would open the way by magic.

But by then George was really getting testy, the leg hurting more every day. He grunted with pain when the doctor felt around the wound, pressing firmly here and there.

"No sign of pus, eh?"

"No, sir. That's good, ain't it?"

The doc shook his head. He was young but seemed to know what he was talking about. "We look for pus. 'Laudable pus,' we call it. Keeps the wound washed out."

The wound was issuing a foul odor now. The flesh around it looked puckered and dead. Red streaks ran up his leg.

A strange doctor appeared. He said his name was Dr. Simpson and he was a surgeon, and Shannon knew the time had come. The doctor sat on the edge of the bed.

"I've done a plenty of legs," he said. He was smoking a corncob pipe and the smell made Shannon a little sick. Or maybe it was the idea of surgery. "Arms and legs, that's mostly what a surgeon does. Now, I'm good at it. Damned good." He crossed his legs. He was middle-aged, hair graying but still full, and his eyes were a very clear blue. Shannon began to feel more confident.

"You know what makes a good surgeon? Speed, that's what. It hurts, ain't no denying that, big fellow like you it'll take a half-dozen men to hold you down and you go right ahead and scream, it don't bother me none. But the point is, it'll be over fast. Under ten minutes, I promise you. Mark of surgical excellence. Now, are you ready?"

"Let's get it the hell over with."

"That's the spirit."

Afterward things were hazy. They gave him a few jolts of whiskey before they loaded him on a gurney and took him to a room where he had a glimpse of tools laid out on a sideboard. He looked quickly away. Six big men appeared and held arms and legs and one lay down across his belly till he felt he could hardly breathe and he was still protesting that when he felt the knife slice into the leg, cutting deep, skin flaps sliced away and laid back, later to cover the stump.

"Hold him now," the surgeon's voice low and tense, and then the most excruciating pain deep in his guts and he heard the rasp of the saw and he screamed and bucked, tried to throw off the big bastard, and he was still fighting when he heard the surgeon say, "There. All done." The big men — he didn't know their names, didn't want to know — trooped from the room without a word. The surgeon wiped Shannon's face with a soft cloth.

"There," he said brightly, wanting his own reassurance, "that wasn't too bad, was it?"

Shannon heard his own voice, pale and weak. "You ever had a leg took off, Doc?"

The surgeon glared at him. At last he sighed. "All right. I take your point. It was god-awful bad. But it saved your life."

Shannon managed to nod, drifting away. "Thank you for that," he murmured.

When Miz Slocum at the lodging house heard what had happened she came immediately to the little six-bed hospital. She looked down at the stump of his leg and murmured tenderly, "Oh, George." At which, quite inexplicably, he burst into a flood of tears, wondering even as he did what Jonesy would make of this. And Miz Slocum, she put her arms around him and he cried against her capacious bosom, cried for the shock and pain and dismay and fear for the future that he must live with a peg for a leg. She held him, rocking gently, and after a while his tears stopped and he felt calm and renewed.

Softly she said, "You'll be all right, George. You're the kind of man who comes out whole no matter what. You'll be fine."

That made him feel so much better!

When she was gone Jonesy sat up in bed. "That was a nice lady," he said. "You pay attention, George. She was right. Kind of fellow you are, you won't let a peg leg slow you down except for your walking speed. You remember what she said." Shannon decided Jonesy was more of a friend than he'd figured.

The pain lasted a long time, he doped on laudanum until he got tired of the dullness and decided to live with the pain. The dreams were the worst, that he hadn't been wounded after all, that the wound, the surgeon, the pain, were just dreams, and he'd leap from bed exulting only to scream and fall. Later they would fit him with a peg of some sort and teach him to walk, but that had to be after the healing had gone a lot farther. Now he faced a good while on crutches, leg of his homespun trousers pinned up lest it flap about and trip him in his unsteady passage.

40

St. Louis, Early 1808

When Lewis walked into the office of the territorial governor he found sitting at the governor's desk a middle-aged fellow carrying something of a pillow around his middle, much of his dark hair gone and what remained combed over his shortages, gazing with evident displeasure at a document he held in his hand. He wore spectacles that seemed to give him a squinting appearance, though when he removed them to gaze at Lewis with fierce irritation, the squint remained as if it were ingrained in his nature. There was something fussy about him as he straightened the desk, carefully aligning the ink pot with the sealing wax and the territorial seal, even as he glared at the intrusion.

"Secretary Bates, I take it," Lewis said. "I'm Governor Lewis."

A play of emotions rushed across the secretary's face, surprise, chagrin, and even fear as if he felt he'd been caught at something, and then something like defiance before settling into mulish hostility. He leaped up.

"Sir! We had no idea—"

Lewis smiled. "No, I gave you no warning."

"No, you didn't. And I must say, it's been long enough. I'd about given you up."

Lewis knew his face had hardened, but he chose to let the criticism pass unchallenged. He drew up a visitor's chair in front of the desk, dropped into it, and casually draped a leg over the chair's arm.

"Why don't you give me a quick overview of the problems, issues, questions facing us."

"This is a bad day, everything very crowded. If you had let us know—"

"But I didn't. Now, let's talk. And I'll want my desk back by the end of the day. You have an office of your own, don't you?"

"A small office."

"It'll have to do, I'm afraid. Now, as to the way things are?"

It was like busting a beaver dam, watching the water pour out, the way a mélange of troubles gushed from the secretary, whom Lewis saw immediately was in far over his head. Lewis might not be much better but he sure as hell couldn't be any worse. The trouble was that a tide of American frontiersmen had come flooding in to inundate the old French population. The newcomers saw themselves as the new wave for a new country and the old French regulars as foreigners who ought to be kicked out on their asses if they didn't conform to new ways. The old line Frenchmen saw themselves as aristocracy cleaving to old ways and traditions and the newcomers as arrogant barbarians who had no grasp of the real meaning of what Louisiana was or at least had been.

The Frenchmen also suffered under a profound sense of betrayal. Napoleon had decided to take the province back from Spain that had acquired it as booty in the pre-revolutionary French and Indian War. At this news the old Frenchmen, who had never become Spanish in manners and outlook, erupted with joy. Home again, back in the bosom of *La Belle France* at last! Then, cool as a farmer selling a hog at the stockyards, Napoleon had sold them to the outrageous, disgusting, barbaric Americans. Betrayal was the only word for their shocked disappointment, the man whom they had considered scarcely less than a saint selling them as on a slave block, which was one thing for African blacks, but they were French, and white to boot. And on the heels of this news had come a tide of the barbarians, hungry, ambitious men none too scrupulous and for many, at least, none too honest, or at least they seemed to the French to have the outlook that euchring a Frenchman wasn't really dishonest at all, more like driving a hard bargain.

This despite the fact that the laws still governing the province were written in French and had not been translated. Lewis decided his first move would be to hire a translator to render the legal code in English.

"And the fights—oh, my word," wailed Mr. Bates. Fists and knives every few blocks, each drawing a big crowd with entrepreneurs making book and sizable sums changing hands. Why, they even fought over the music played at public dances; in addition to ogling the French women, the barbarians insisted on raucous tunes that were right out of Scotland and Ireland instead of the easy melodies on which a Frenchman's heart could soar.

But Lewis could see that what truly galled the French population was that the new Americans had the drive, the energy, the money to lay their hands on the future and hold it tight, and any Frenchman not willing to accept that reality might as well catch a keelboat for New Orleans and thence a vessel for Marseilles. The future belonged to the Americans.

Bates whined that he hadn't been able to do much for lack of authority and anyway the problems were Lewis's fault for his failure to come sooner.

So Lewis found himself in a snake pit. French jousting with Americans, Americans with French, settlers hungry to flood the new territory, fur traders wanting the great land left undisturbed that their prey might prosper, Bates taking the settlers' side, Lewis the fur trade as the likely industry of the future, governor and secretary settling into what soon became open and somewhat disgraceful war.

And his journals from which the world awaited the story of the great expedition lay untouched in the bottom of his trunk. Urgent letters came from the publisher. Lewis ignored them. The president wrote; Lewis didn't answer. It seemed to him he no longer felt the same about the great man who once had given the boy full run of his famous library. Mr. Jefferson seemed somewhat the fair-weather friend, assuring you of his undying friendship when the going was easy, forgetting you when it got hard. Just couldn't bring himself to speak to that fat turd at the War Department, to use a little of his weight with the Congress.

Now what seemed to obsess him was the desire to get that damned pale as a ghost Indian chief, Big White, back to the Mandan villages, which already had cost three lives and poor Shannon his leg. And asking plaintively when the book would be seen, when an editor chosen, when the transfer of material from journal to book form was coming along even if the product had not been forwarded to the printer or a printer even chosen. Kept talking about the queries from the European savants as if his whole problem was that his reputation with them might suffer.

You could even argue if you wanted to, though Lewis didn't, but an argument could be made that this appointment as governor had not been entirely friendly. For Lewis understood that his real future depended on the book and understood as well that he was moving no closer to the goal. But here he was galloping about dealing with a thousand picayunish details when he needed to be organizing his notes into a coherent story, which he still felt he didn't know how to do. Get an editor, the publisher had said, echoed by the president, and Lewis himself thought that might well be a good idea, but days became months and months pushed at the year mark and he made no move. This when he was beginning to feel that the appointment he had greeted with such joy could kill him. No wonder he was drinking a bit. Well, more than a bit.

He wasn't well, that was the real problem. He took his medicine every day but since he felt he knew more than the doctors he didn't consult them but prescribed for himself. His guts were always in turmoil, boiling and belching. His head hurt, his belly hurt, he had chest pains and wondered about his heart. He tried all the tonics and herbal remedies he could find, strengthening them with morphine and sometimes, when morphine didn't seem to serve, with opium. Gradually he increased the doses. He had found a pleasant house to live in and a servant to provide meals, though he often dined with the Clarks and their new baby, and he kept a bottle by his bed.

A runner brought a letter that had gone to the office after Lewis had left. He saw at a glance that it came from the president. He ripped it open: what arrangements had been made to return Big White to the Mandan villages? And when are we to see the book?

When Shannon saw York in the street he advanced on his crutch with his hand extended but York put his hands in his pockets. White men didn't shake a slave's hand. Not in St. Louis. But York shouldn't be a slave.

"Did you ask him?"

York smiled and shook his head. Then, sighing, he said, "Well, you see, what bothers me, it's my wife."

"I didn't know you had a wife."

"And a daughter coming along now. They belong to a family in Louisville. When we lived in Clarksville I could just cross the river to Louisville on a Sunday and it wasn't bad. But here in St. Louis it's too far. I can't go to Louisville. Course, if I was free I could work for wages and maybe buy them their freedom, if the folks that own them would sell."

"Oh, York, you gotta ask. He'll never grant it if you don't ask."

"He'll beat the hell out of me, that's what he'll do."

"Not if he's a fair man. And I think he is. But you gotta ask."

A month passed before Shannon saw the big black man. He was limping. "What happened?" Shannon asked.

"I asked him. Like I figured, he got crazy mad and beat the hell out of me."

"But what happened then? He got over being mad, he said he'd do it?"

"Hell, no. Said he'd take a pistol to me if I kept on that kind of talk."

Shannon was stunned. He gazed at York in dismay.

York touched Shannon's shoulder and gave him a comforting pat. "You see, George, I know him better than you do. Known him since he was a baby."

It took Shannon a month to work up his nerve. He'd been working for Cap'n Clark all along, doing whatever the cap'n told him to do. Seemed like the cap'n trusted him more than anyone to know what to do and to keep it honest. Now, since they took his leg, he was mostly managing the fur warehouse till he could walk all right on the peg and throw away the crutch. So he saw the cap'n most every day but he found talking up to him wasn't all that easy.

When he'd gone home to Pennsylvania to see Ma, he had looked up that old preacher. Sure enough, he'd been part of a slave trail that took runaways and moved them bit by bit in the night. Said he'd finally quit. Folks in the North were getting less and less hospitable and the preacher was getting older. Shannon saw the palsied quiver in his hands. Felt he had done all he could. Shannon could understand that, especially now when he felt he had to go talk to the cap'n. In fact he realized he was looking for excuses to put off the talk and that made him see that Preacher Lorimer was dead-on when he said slavery was a fundamental human evil, ultimate expression of the strong oppressing the weak.

So when the cap'n was looking pretty content smoking a big cigar at his desk in his warehouse that didn't seem to clash with his duties as Indian agent for all the West, Shannon said, "Speak to you a minute, Cap'n?"

Clark leaned back with a smile and cocked his boots on the desk. "Say on, young fellow, say on."

"Well, sir, what I wanted to ask, why don't you turn York loose after all he done to make our trek such a success?"

Clark's smile vanished. He put his feet on the floor and sat very straight and there was a hardness in his face that told you what his usual good nature led men to forget at times, that this was a dangerous man. Shannon saw that he had gotten himself into deep water but he thought well, to hell with it, you have to stand up sometimes and this was one of them.

"York's been talking to you, has he?"

"More I been talking to him, Cap'n. He asked me once what I thought and ever since I've been urging him to ask you."

Clark stood abruptly. "And what the hell made you think that was such a good idea?"

Shannon had forgotten how physically powerful the man was. He swallowed. "Just come naturally to me. You've always been a fair and square man and slavery is an evil institution and York pulled all his weight and then some, and I just figured—"

"Well you figured wrong. You don't know a goddam thing about it, you open your mouth when a wiser man would keep it shut, and let me tell you, I don't take kindly to anyone giving my people a lot of dangerous ideas that just make trouble. And don't tell me about slavery about which you don't know nothing. Evil institution—who the hell you been talking to? Some ignorant northern preacher knows nothing about it?"

Now Shannon felt his own anger rising. "Didn't have to talk to nobody. Common sense told me. I don't see how you can argue like that, smart fellow like you."

Clark sat down without answering. He puffed his cigar back to life and leaned back. "George, I count you a friend. And you work for me too. You want either one of these to continue, we won't have this conversation again. All right?"

"Yes, sir," Shannon said slowly, "I reckon." What else could he say? Poor York.

That evening he saw Miz Slocum in the kitchen. She was working on lists for tomorrow's marketing. On impulse, he put his head in the door. "Bother you a minute, ma'am?"

She smiled and put down the pencil. "Coffee on the range. Pour us each a cup." She took up her knitting; she was making mittens for that youngster of hers, he getting to be a sizable critter now.

Both hands clasping the earthenware cup, he poured out the story and his feeling that somehow he himself had made York's situation more difficult and dangerous. He said he was thinking of taking the story to Cap'n—Governor—Lewis.

"What for?"

"Well, maybe he'd take a hand in it. He knows how valuable York was, he'll see how unfair it is."

She didn't answer directly but asked him to compare Captain Lewis with Captain Clark.

"They're the finest, strongest, wisest men I've ever known, and that includes my dear old pa. And it's even with the way Clark is treating York. But they're some different from each other. You take Clark, he's a fine commander, you never doubt he'll know what to do day to day, he won't get you in any fixes he can avoid and he'll get you out of those he can't avoid. In everything but this slave business, he's calm, sensible, balanced, and above all fair.

"But Cap'n Lewis, he's a great man. Thinks big and wide and deep when you get the feeling Clark skates on the surface. Lewis is all the commander Clark is, whatever I'd trust Clark for I'd trust Lewis just as much. But then there's a whole different element that reaches beyond Clark." His cup was empty as was hers and he hobbled to the range on his crutch to fill them. He fetched the cream from the window well, then put it back. She knitted in silence.

When he sat down he said, "You know, since this leg business, I been reading a good bit, read President Jefferson's book and a lot of others on how the country came about. And, you know, reading about General Washington, his manner, his quiet, the way he kept a lot of thoughts to himself and yet when he finally decided was pretty often right, I thought Cap'n Lewis is like that. Cap'n Clark is a fine man, all but this York matter, but Cap'n Lewis is a great man. That's the difference between 'em."

"Interesting," Miz Slaney said, "and I wouldn't doubt you're right. But I'd go slow on trying to use Lewis to sway Clark. Lewis is a slave owner too, you know. He's wealthy by inheriting the family plantation. His mother lives there now. Place couldn't operate without labor and in Virginia that means slaves."

Shannon gazed at her in surprise. "You know him, then?"

"Long ago. Long, long ago. Our place was a half mile from the Lewis plantation. My brother has it now."

"Have you seen him? Here, I mean."

"Of course not. When I knew him, that's in the past."

"But what I said about him, you think—"

"I think you're right. Fits the man—boy—I used to know."

Suddenly he understood. "You were sweet on him."

A deep flush flashed over her face but with it a distinctly stern look that wiped away his smile. "Yes, I was sweet on him. I guess we were sweet on each other. But that was long ago and things change and life goes on. Now, see here, George, this is none of your business and not another soul knows of it and if I hear it talked around I'll know it come from you and then we won't be friends any longer. Do you understand?"

Second time today he'd been threatened with loss of friendship. How strange. Cautiously, he said, "So I suppose you agree with them on slavery."

Again that sharp look. "No, I don't. Sarah Belle, she cleans the rooms, you see her, she's a free black. We pay her wages like anyone else. But I know how Virginians feel about slavery. General Washington, you mentioned him, he was a big slave holder there at Mount Vernon. Mr. Jefferson, his place about abuts ours, he keeps slaves. Sells them sometimes, too."

"But at least the practice dismays him," Shannon said. "I was surprised reading his book—let me go up and get it, I'll read you a passage." She said she'd wait while he negotiated the stairs. When he returned he had the passage underlined.

"Here—he's talking about slavery, you see: 'And can the liberties of a nation be thought secure when we have removed their only firm basis, a conviction in the minds of the people that these liberties are the gift of God? That they are not to be violated but with his wrath? Indeed I tremble for my country when I reflect that God is just; that his justice cannot sleep forever—' Well, there's more but that says it pretty clear, don't you think?"

She smiled. "It does, indeed. Says a lot for your reading, too. You surprise me, George."

He was pleased. "Well," he said, "turns out losing your leg gets you to thinking. What kind of life you'll have and how you'll lead it. And it makes you think you'd better know a little about the world, read some books. I mean, I ain't going to be dancing a lot . . ."

41

St. Louis, Spring, 1809

Eighteen oh eight bent into 1809, and it was at this time, when Lewis had been in St. Louis about a year, that he felt a sudden new turn, an abrupt sense that something was wrong. It was still distant, an ominous rumble that he caught on the edges of his senses, like the earthquake tremors he had heard on the Origan Coast that rainy winter when they lived on salmon. Very distant, stone grinding on stone, ominous movement, ominous sound. Something wrong.

Gradually this seemed to take the form of an attack on good spirits. Until now it seemed to him he had clung to at least some of the energy and optimism, the sheer enthusiasm he'd brought to St. Louis. But more and more often he found himself bereft of these bright qualities. Whiskey helped then, as did medicine, opium spiking even more effective than morphine. He found that thought of the book made it all worse, the president after him, savants impatient and demanding, and in Philadelphia, the publisher working in the night awaiting the neighbor's cock's crow, wondering when he would see a manuscript.

Oh, the book, oh, God, the book! He didn't know how to write the damned book! Didn't know how to start, how to finish, tone to take, form and shape and plans to make, knew nothing. It was unfair, it put all the weight on him when he was an explorer, a tramper over miles and miles with old Seaman at his heels, that was his strength, damn it, not sitting alone and building castles in the air. Don't think of old Seaman, kicked to death by an insane horse on the St. Louis riverfront, comrade through so many wilderness miles. And day by day that damnable darkness grew stronger and appeared more often and the distant rumble seemed louder and nearer. Something bad.

Secretary Bates proved to be an implacable enemy, just as Clark had feared. There seemed a madness in the man's twisted hatred. He was riddled with jealousy and filled with shameless hunger to replace Lewis. Wherever he went, whomever he met, he heaped criticism on the governor. When these stories came back to Lewis and he taxed Bates, the secretary denied them, a contemptuous grin lighting his face. He was tempted to give the man a thrashing but knew it would cost him heavily if he did so.

Sometimes he ached with loneliness. He desperately wanted a wife, as he lamented in frequent letters to Dickerson in Philadelphia and every other real friend to whom he wrote. The beautiful Letitia Breckenridge married his friend Robert Gamble; he brought himself with some effort to write each of them a cordial letter wishing them every happiness. Clark was as good a friend as ever but he had a pretty young wife now and a new baby with whom he was fascinated.

Lewis was fundamentally lonely, alone at a time when he badly needed company. His illnesses worsened, though he could get no diagnosis from the doctors and soon gave up trying and treated himself. He continued to expand his medicine chest with growing emphasis on opium, which seemed the thing best calculated to soothe his rumbling gut and ease his diarrhea.

What plans for Big White? Well, certainly not another handful of men as escort asking to be turned back by triumphant Indians. The trouble was, the army was already stretched too thin with all this talk of war with Britain. The Royal Navy was stopping American ships on the high seas and even in domestic waters ostensibly searching for their deserters, actually taking any likely looking sailor they could press into service. Ten to twenty thousand American citizens had thus been kidnapped. Now, the greatest indignity, a British warship had fired on an American naval vessel that was totally unready for war, this in Chesapeake Bay where the Briton was accorded the courtesy of watering and provisioning. Americans clamored for a war that the administration knew it would lose for lack of preparation. Lewis believed Jefferson and Madison would find a way to weasel out of conflict, but it was no time to ask for a diversion of soldiers to take an Indian chief home.

Then the perfect solution appeared. A group of leaders that included Lewis and Clark had formed the St. Louis and Missouri River Fur Company to exploit the incredible peltry richness of the Yellowstone Valley. Why not pay them to put together a sizable force of frontier riflemen, have them shoot their way through the Arikaras and Sioux if necessary, and deliver Big White? Clark thought it a fine idea and so did Lewis. They were on the frontier where army officers and other government officials regularly invested in private enterprises. Lewis thought of Colter out there alone on the Yellowstone; he'd bet that Colter was not only alive, but thriving.

Lewis drew up a contract by which the fur company would assemble a force of 125 men of whom fifty would be skilled riflemen, then deliver Big White to the Mandans for a seven-thousand-dollar fee payable when the Indian was safely home. Then the fur company would be free to go on to the Yellowstone Valley for trapping. Secretary Bates complained to Washington about the mixture of private and governmental funds without adding that he was in the sway of men who tended to prosper with settlement activity while Lewis and Clark believed western commerce would hang on the fur trade for thirty years.

The governor found his health improving as he plunged into the familiar details of assembling an important expedition. Soon he saw that more trade goods or presents for Indians would be needed and more firepower. He dashed off a voucher for fifteen hundred dollars' worth of trade goods and vouchers for five hundred dollars and four hundred fifty dollars for powder and lead.

For a couple of years now the two captains had been busy answering petty little question from petty little men who seemed to have taken a blood oath to guard departmental pennies. As Jefferson had intended when he gave an open-ended letter of credit to the expedition to equip itself as necessary, they had spent freely but always as necessary. Yes, Lewis had been a bit careless as Clark had warned him several times, but the amounts were small. But the clerks said of course this was never really an open account and every penny must be justified.

It infuriated Clark. "Bastards!" he roared. "Just what ruined poor George Rogers." Will had taken over the struggle to settle George Rogers Clark's debts from the Revolution now nearly a quarter century past, his oldest brother sunk in a morass of alcohol and despair. "You're the hero, you see, you saved the country or you marched to the Pacific or what have you. And now they're saying, Oh, thank you kindly for saving the West in the nick of time, holding off the Hair Buyer and his phalanx of Redcoats, but meanwhile here's a packet of pins you bought and we need an explanation in triplicate, why you needed pins, were there any alternatives, did you go to bids, were there other pins you could have had cheaper and so forth and bloody so on, all the time threatening, ready to refuse payment on that voucher for the goddamned pins and leave you to pay it out of your pocket. George Rogers never fully regained his health—remember him telling about plunging into water so cold they had to break the ice around the bank to get in, then marching a hundred miles in wet clothes that froze to your body? Of course he needs his drink, gets pneumonia every fall, hurts all over his body. It just breaks your heart. He served his nation when it needed him most and the thanks he gets is from a pissant clerk wouldn't recognize the smell of gunpowder if his life depended on it, trying to strip the man to ruin all in the name of proper forms and rules and so forth. Bastards!"

Then came a letter that was like a fist driven into his belly, leaving him gasping. It was from the new secretary of war, William Eustis, named by the new President Madison. Mr. Jefferson had retired to Monticello and seemed to see himself out of all the wars. Eustis found fault with the Big White arrangements without acknowledging that getting Big White home was both difficult and until recently, at least, an important governmental goal. He didn't like the combination of private and public monies, felt that the original seven thousand was adequate and the latter expenditures unnecessary. Hence payment would be refused on all Lewis's recent vouchers. Lewis could see Bates's gossipy hand in every phase of the letter; more than ever he wanted to use his fists on the secretary and knew he couldn't.

Thunder shook the sky and the ground. This was disaster, ruinous and complete. If his vouchers were not honored he was responsible for paying them himself. And that would strip him naked. His stomach boiled and howled. His body ached and his bowels turned to water. He threw down the letter and with pencil and foolscap estimated his position. He had debts of some four thousand dollars. His assets added up to some fifty-seven hundred but most of it was in land that could only be moved rapidly at a dreadful loss. Then he listed recent drafts on the government that this letter said almost certainly would be refused. They added up to almost seven thousand dollars. Paying them would destroy him.

Then his eye lit on another deadly passage. "The president has been consulted and the observations contained herein have his approval."

His door banged open and Clark stormed in. "Merry—what the hell's going on? Rumor all over town that Eustis is refusing your drafts. Everyone's in an uproar."

Lewis was stunned. His only hope had been to keep this quiet until he could turn it around in Washington or, at worst, have time to line up alternate financing and new debt, however unfair that would be. But make it public and creditors who would assume his ruin, probably quite correctly, would come storming in trying to get at least something from a diminishing pot. And now it was out and he would have no time to do anything. But how could the news have traveled so? He had just read it himself. Ah, Bates again. Lewis had received it already opened as usual by the clerk; the clerk reported to Bates and must have taken it first to him and he had run about spreading the news.

Lewis and Clark studied the letter together and now another and still more dangerous point emerged. A vicious rumor was running around St. Louis and now it had reached Washington, once again surely through Bates's agency. Gossip had been flowing that there was more to the Big White expedition than showed on the surface, the ultimate destination far beyond the Yellowstone, leading to the suggestion conveyed in hints and winks that something akin to the Burr conspiracy was afoot. Carve off a hunk of Louisiana, from there take Mexico with its rich gold mines, use their output to finance a new nation taken from American territory. Free-booting treason, in other words.

Aaron Burr had been acquitted of treason and no one really knew what he'd done, though there had been lots of smoke for no fire. Some argued the real villain was General James Wilkinson, commander of the army, whom Lewis considered capable of anything. The talk was that Burr had been Wilkinson's cat's paw. Who knew? What Lewis was sure of was that he knew of nothing in the Big White expedition to support such a wild rumor; returning Big White was its sole purpose. It hurt even to have to say so.

But if Bates had planted the rumor in Washington and it was believed, Governor Lewis was in desperate trouble that quite dwarfed financial ruin. He must go to Washington immediately with all his papers to accompany him in trunks; they would prove his innocence. Nausea on the rise, desperately wanting whiskey and realizing he had better not, he sat down to write Eustis. Betraying little of the shocking outrage he felt, he explained that he had accompanied every voucher with a careful explanation of its purpose and necessity. "I have never received a penny of public money." He hesitated, then dipped the pen and wiped its edges carefully that it might not blot, and added, "To the correctness of this statement, I call my God to witness."

Apparently representations had been made against him, he wrote, and it was clear the government had a derogatory view of him that he could only correct in person and with his records. He would leave within the week to come to Washington. Bitterly he denied involvement in any plot against the United States, adding, "Be assured, sir, that my Country can never make 'A Burr' of me—She may reduce me to Poverty; but she can never sever my Attachment from her." He told Eustis he would pass title to his land holdings to his creditors and noted that proof of his integrity would be found in the long run by the poverty to which his government had reduced him.

Then, with Clark's help, he set about gathering his papers, filing and annotating them, packing them in trunks for shipment, preparing to go. He would take a keelboat downriver to New Orleans and there catch a merchant brig for Baltimore and finally a coach to Washington. Traveling overland via Clarksville, Clark would join him in Washington to take part in his fight and to try once again to deal with the protested drafts that had ruined his brother. They worked well into the dark and then Clark took him home for a supper Judy was keeping warm. They ate in silence, the Clarks recognizing his mood. Clark urged him to stay there for the night but he wanted to go home. Clark walked him through the dark streets.

In truth, he wanted to be alone. The house was empty, his servant away. He lit no lamps, though the carefully banked fire was alive and a supply of tapers was on hand. Safely inside, he vomited. He cleaned himself and then the pan and sat by a window looking out on the dark and silent street. After a while he opened a fresh bottle of whiskey. He sat there a long time, the level in the bottle sinking. It all seemed so utterly rotten. The moon was up and he watched it inch across the sky and disappear. At last he stood, lurching, caught the bedpost in one hand and swung around to bury himself in the feathers and vanish.

42

St. Louis, September, 1809

He had a sense that he was plunging, falling from a high and barren cliff into a black sea, striking water that was neither cold nor warm, diving deep and then struggling upward, not concerned with breathing but with escaping that eternal darkness. Then he was up and out again, still alive again, hands at his throat removed for now, at least.

That distant rumble was no longer distant. Day by day it grew on him, stone grinding on stone, something wrong, something coming. Well, there was plenty wrong right now, he in deep trouble and struggling in his office with the door locked to gather papers. He really locked the door to keep Bates out; he thought he might kill the man if he saw him. Deep trouble, yes, indeed, but this wasn't it. This grinding coming ever closer was something else. But it was coming. Throbbing, urgent as a drum.

The door opened; Will with a key.

"How are you?" Will looked at him with that concerned expression. Good old Will, the only friend he had. Worried about him.

"Couldn't be better." He grinned. "Considering everything." He hadn't mentioned the drumming and didn't now; Will would worry without understanding. Clark asked how the packing was going and Lewis rather proudly mentioned two trunks packed and sealed with papers, more to come. When Clark was ready to go, Lewis swallowed, trying to keep tension out of his voice, and said, "One thing you could do, you go past the chemist's, Doc Berger, look in and tell him to make me some new medicine. I'm about out."

"You're taking a hell of a lot of medicine, Merry. And Berger, he told me what you're taking, it's mostly opium. You better go slow—that stuff will kill you."

Suddenly Lewis was enraged. "God damn it, Will, don't you turn on me, too," he shouted.

He saw a matching flash of anger splash over Will's face and then his old friend sighed, getting control of himself. "You know better than that, Merry."

Instantly contrite, Lewis nodded. "Of course. Yes, I do. Sorry, Will. But you'll get me the medicine?"

"All right. But listen—what did you mean, don't turn on me too? Who else is turning on you—Eustis, and Bates, sure, but who else?"

Everyone, he wanted to say. Everyone who mattered. But he knew Will would think him a little off, and maybe he was. He shook his head and didn't answer. Presently Will returned with the medicine and then went off to his waiting Judy. Lewis took another dose from the brown bottle and felt the calm overtake him. He walked home slowly in the dark, hat pulled low, and managed to pass without being accosted. He found that John Pernier, his free black servant, had prepared him a dinner but he was much too ill to eat. He packed an old corncob he liked and lit it with a broom straw thrust into the banked fire and poured a glass of whiskey and sipped it slowly though he was surprised to see how rapidly the glass emptied itself.

He thought about Clark and his question. But of course, his old friend couldn't see the vast conspiratorial apparatus arrayed against him. Old Will, good soul that he was, he would see the other side. Jefferson had given Lewis the great command that should entitle him to everlasting gratitude. And remember, Lewis had been late in arriving at St. Louis. What about the eight months he'd spent lazing around Virginia? Clark would wonder about the book too, he was involved, it was his expedition too; only his kindly good nature kept him from raising failure on the book.

So he pondered. Maybe he was a little off, but something in him rebelled at that, he felt it tore him from comfort for which his need was getting desperate. He poured more whiskey and he thought, God damn it, maybe he wasn't off, either. Maybe he wasn't.

Why had Dearborn been so hostile? Not just over the rank for Will;

maybe his complaint that two equal chiefs was militarily unrealistic even had a little merit at the start in terms of setting precedent. But refusing to treat Clark properly when they returned, why? Miffed after all these years because Lewis had paid too little attention to him at the start? Hard to believe anyone could be so small, but with Dearborn, maybe. But it was Jefferson's plan from the start and he knew it. Afraid to speak up to the leader, he vents spleen on the underling? Maybe. But why had the president let it go through?

Eustis . . . why didn't the new secretary send him a note, even ask him to come back to Washington and explain. He had to know that openly refusing the drafts would destroy Lewis, smash his credit, leave him naked to enemies. Did it as casually as swatting a fly. Or maybe his view of Lewis was exactly that, a household pest. But why? Or maybe the new president, James Madison, had ordered it. But why?

Or if Eustis was showing some old venom carried over from Dearborn, why had the president so willingly endorsed the action with its obvious disastrous consequences for Lewis? His mind ran back to Madison during Lewis's own period in the mansion, a fussy little man, punctilious and not very warmhearted, but they had never had trouble. Very different kind of men, granted, Lewis could smite him to dust, maybe he was uncomfortable around a man like Lewis and was taking it out now, but that was far-fetched.

Anyway, Madison had been very close to Jefferson for years, sort of a loyal underling himself. So why would he approve an attack on the man who, with Will, had successfully led the expedition of which Jefferson had dreamed for thirty years, the greatest venture in the young nation's history? And why wouldn't Jefferson intervene?

Lewis had been fond of Miss Dolley, though the semi-affectionate appellation stuck in his throat a little now. She had helped him understand a lot of things about Washington, but he knew she would never contradict her husband. Plead with him in private, maybe, but limit her complaints and urgings, and who knew if she had spoken for Lewis or even if she knew the whole sordid story.

The drumming seemed loud and steady now and he stood, perhaps to meet his demons, perhaps to greet them. He was coming to some grasp of things. With both hands gripping the back of a chair, he stared sightlessly at a wall asking himself, where was Mr. Jefferson in all this? His patron, his hero, the man who could do what Lewis couldn't, make the expedition happen, the man he had counted as friend almost since he could remember, a boy reading his books and learning from his gentle quizzing, the man who had chosen him for the greatest command since that of General Washington.

Where was he now with the trouble exploding? Lewis had done just as ordered, gone to the Pacific and established whether there was such a thing as the Northwest Passage. He'd brought back all his men alive except for poor Floyd, and Floyd's death had been from illness, not from an Indian arrow. He himself had been the only man wounded. He had brought back a wealth of botanical discoveries as well as animals and birds that had delighted the Peale Museum in Philadelphia.

He had carried out his end of the bargain while his patron had failed to carry out his. Even now, with his protégé being torn apart and destroyed, the patron sat serenely on his mountaintop watching flowers grow from seeds that Meriwether Lewis had brought home from the West. Couldn't burden himself to stay involved enough to know how his appointment was working out. To take a hand in the War Department's fury. Of course he was out of power but he was lifelong friends with the new president — could he not take a hand? Of course he could — the conclusion had to be that he just didn't give a damn if Captain Lewis was ruined.

And he was so terribly damned miserably lonely he could hardly stand it! Letitia — but it didn't have to have been Letitia. Not just anyone would do, but he was very lonely and had been a long time and things weren't getting any better. Old Clark married, Dickerson would marry soon, hell's fire, the whole world was married except him. An image of Mary Beth flashed into his mind, as she was that summer night when her laugh was like a silver bell and as she was now, a St. Louis hotelier, stout, skin coarsening, a power in her that he knew matched that of his own potent mother. What might he have made with Mary Beth? He didn't know. Skin coarsening . . . well, she was his age, maybe a year younger. His own skin was coarsening, wasn't it? Sun lines at his eyes from squinting. Different with a woman — or was it?

Now, as it so often did, his mind jerked sideways to the book — wasn't that the real source of all the trouble? But what made Jefferson so sure Lewis could quickly dash it off when he himself after a lifetime of erudition had written only one book and that as a list of questions and answers? What made him name Lewis to the territorial command when his own experience as governor and president must have told him it would be no bowl of peaches? Not when he was supposed to write a book. Not when his nature was to attack big projects, the reason he had succeeded so brilliantly in the field, and not the infinite daily detail of running a government. Suppose the president had sat the explorer down in a room in the mansion, given him a clerk for this and that, a supply of foolscap, new steel pen nibs and a bottle of pure ink, sat down beside him at a table and said, Let's see, now . . .

Jefferson had said he deemed Lewis capable of overcoming melancholy. But he should see the subaltern now, drowning in melancholy after his country had gotten his best from him, taken everything he had to offer while giving him nothing in return, and now cast him aside as so much refuse, hunk of bone tossed to howling dogs. The demons were laughing, he could hear them plainly. He sat there in the dark, frozen motionless, not sure if what he heard was in his head or on the street.

That thought jolted him and a sudden eerie silence overtook him and then he heard the drum start again in the distance, funereal taps coming steadily closer. Suddenly he wasn't sure what was real and what wasn't. He poured more whiskey and with the first sip a whole new line of thought seized him. This search of his papers, his plans for travel, his careful preparation of what he would say to the little Madison, all this was futile. A fool's errand. Their minds were made up. He dropped in a chair with a loud groan, the noise startling him. What the hell was he doing, groaning in the dark? He drank more whiskey and he thought, Futile? That is the goddamnedest most stupid idea he'd ever had, of course he would go there and in his eloquence make them see that they were the fools. Rub their noses in their own dirt, by God. Yes. At once he felt fine and thought he should get some sleep. But he didn't rise from the chair and after a while he slept there. Slid from the chair at some point, awakened enough to find himself on the floor, shut his eyes, and slept on.

"Cap'n," Shannon said to Clark as they closed the warehouse for the night, "not till you get back, of course, I'll take care of everything here long as you're gone, but I oughta tell you now I've got some new plans."

"Oh?"

"Yes, sir, I been reading a lot. Shakespeare, about how those kings were always cutting each other up, good many others. These crutches and all, I don't get around a lot like before. Been reading Blackstone."

"Master of English law? See? Even I know a little something. You thinking about the law, George?"

"Yes, sir. That's what I was going to tell you. Looking at the way all the world collides with itself, I'd like to be involved. Frick and Graydon, they said I could read law in their office for two or three years and they don't doubt I could take the bar."

Clark laughed. "You'll wind up a judge, George. I know you will, smart fellow like you."

"You ain't mad?"

"Hell, no." He extended a hand and Shannon took it. "Sounds good. I wish you the best, George. Now, there's something I been thinking about, what you said about York. Maybe you're right. Anyway, I'm thinking on manumitting him—turn him loose, free man. Ain't fully decided so don't say nothing to him yet, but I'm thinking on it."

"Wonderful!" Shannon seized the older man's hand again. "Think hard on it, Cap'n. You do it and it'll soothe your soul."

He saw Clark's eyes widen at that, and then they were locking the doors and in a moment parted.

The next night when darkness became thick and still, Lewis stepped into the street with his hat pulled low. His pistol was tucked under his belt, his coat pulled over it. He found the right street, then what he thought was the right house. He stepped onto the veranda and looked through a window. A group of men, some around a pinochle table, two playing chess, the others reading newspapers by bright oil lamps. He didn't see Shannon.

He walked around the house and entered through the kitchen door. A white woman and a black woman looked up, startled. Yes, he was in the right place, the white woman was Mary Beth's friend, what was it, Parsons, Mrs. Parsons? He bowed, a little unsteadily.

"Sarah," Miz Parsons said, "go get Miz Beth right now. Hurry."

Mary Beth walked into the room. Her eyes widened at sight of him. Wordlessly she took his hand and led him into a small sitting room. It was adjacent to a bedroom and before she closed the door he caught a glimpse of a lonely looking narrow bed neatly made.

"What is it, Merry?" Her voice was soft and gentle.

He gazed at her. "I don't know." He hesitated, then said, "I'm in a lot of trouble."

"I heard."

"It's betrayal. Sheer rotten betrayal." He poured out his story. But then, abruptly shifting his ground with scarcely a moment's pause, he said, "Or maybe it's all my fault. Dreaming too big, wanting too much. Maybe a little humility would have gone a long way."

He talked an hour by the little brass clock on her mantel, then started up suddenly. "I must go. There's so much to do."

She didn't ask why he had come. He saw that she knew even though he didn't. She stood too.

"Oh, Merry," she whispered, "I wish—"

"That we had married? I've thought of that so often. That night . . . but you were asking me to give up the dream. It doesn't seem so grand now but then . . ."

"Was I?" She sighed. "Yes, I suppose I was. And we were so young, you and I."

"Would it all have been different?"

She spread her hands. "I don't know. I just don't know."

Then, urgently, the distant drum tapping and tapping, he turned to the door. "I must go."

"Wait—you're in no condition to walk the streets alone." She opened the door. He saw the black woman waiting there and wondered why she waited. "Ask Mr. Broussard to come in," Mary Beth said.

A big man, mottled face scarred by pox, came in. He pulled off his hat and held it in both hands. His glance rested on Lewis for only a moment.

"Francois, will you see the governor back to his lodging? See that no one interferes. Anyone tries to talk to him, divert them."

"Aye, Miz Beth," the big man said. He put on his hat. "You ready, Governor?"

Mary Beth came close and hugged him. "Good-bye, Merry," she murmured. His arms went around her. How solid and sturdy she was. He thought of those willowy girls, of Letitia kissing him with her mouth open that first night, wrong, all wrong. His arms around Mary Beth felt good, he could have stayed there, he felt he could have gone to sleep in the aura of her comfort. But she stirred and he heard Broussard move his feet and he stepped back. They walked through the dark night and Lewis wondered what it would have been like. She wasn't a Letitia but she was strong. He didn't know how it would have been, but it wouldn't have been like this. Too late, too late.

In front of his house he offered Broussard a coin. The fellow smiled and shook his head. "Pleasure to do Miss Beth a favor," he said.

43

On the Natchez Trace, October 9, 1809

It was time to go, pack his papers in trunks and go to Washington to battle calumny and prove himself. The prospect of action always pleased him, but he couldn't escape the feeling that evil demons plagued him. Everything felt off-kilter.

He caught a keelboat for New Orleans on the St. Louis riverfront, his trunks in its hold, his precious journals with his pistols in two saddlebags. He had foresworn liquor, relying instead on his medicine, but then he decided self-denial was meaningless and cracked a flask. He liked to sit forward where the bowman stood ready to thrust the boat aside when the sawyers sprang up from the bottom with malevolence he felt might well be directed at him. The water was brown as chocolate. He leaned over the side to see it close, drawn to the idea of losing himself in its hidden depths. Perhaps he leaned too far for suddenly the brawny bowman seized him, shouting suicide. Ridiculous, not his plan at all, though the attraction of the idea was undeniable. A couple of days later he'd been inspecting his journals in the main cabin and John Pernier, his faithful but none too bright servant, had found him with a pistol in his hand and shouted the same thing as he seized the weapon. The donkey.

So the keelboat captain put him ashore at Chickasaw Bluffs, the new town at the west end of Tennessee. But this was just as well, for Lewis had decided that the sea passage to Baltimore was too risky, with the Royal Navy stopping American vessels to search for their deserters and kidnapping any likely looking sailor. The British would love to lay hands on his journals with their proof of his westward journey by land with all that implied for future sovereignty. The journals would disappear like water drying in the sun.

No, far better to go overland, east to the Natchez Trace that connected Nashville and New Orleans, north to Nashville, east to the Cumberland Gap and north again along the Great Valley to the place where the Shenandoah joined the Potomac, and then on to Washington to confront his enemies. He'd had enough of the boat, cooped up, imprisoned. He needed to be in the open air, astride a good horse, the sun warm on his face.

Well, maybe he wanted to be in the open because sitting motionless on the boat he had felt powerless to fight the dark sense that something bad and dangerous lay ahead, heralded by that tapping or rapping or pounding that ebbed and flowed but rarely passed entirely from his head. Astride a good horse, his precious saddlebags close behind him while his trunks went on by sea, things would be better.

Yet no sooner had he and Pernier mounted newly purchased horses than the old melancholy seemed to be crushing him. He felt he was gasping for breath, this dark thing riding his back, flogging him as a demon flogs, as a jockey flogs in the home stretch. Yes, that was it, distant laughter in the wings, something waiting for him, something toward which he rode, waiting to close with him.

They struck the Trace and turned north, riding slowly through giant oaks of virgin forest. He told Pernier that Clark was coming cross-country to meet them up ahead, and Clark would know what to do about everything. Pernier was puzzled but Lewis didn't bother to explain, having heard Clark's voice as plainly as if they sat together at table.

On the afternoon of the third day on the Trace they came to a rude inn known as Grinder's Stand, two small log cabins connected by a dog run. Nashville lay about seventy-five miles ahead. Mrs. Grinder watched Lewis and Pernier approach. She stood in the doorway, one hand out of sight; he was sure it rested on a shotgun. She said Grinder was away, cutting hay at a farm they owned.

Lodging for the night? Aye, Lewis in the second cabin, his man in the hayloft at the barn a hundred yards away. He studied his hostess. She was worn, no longer young, no longer dreaming. He asked for whiskey and she nodded.

But even as he swung off his horse the pain in his head and heart was such that he forgot her and was surprised when she returned with whiskey. She prepared a serviceable dinner but he couldn't eat and asked for more whiskey. He lit a pipe and sat with her in the cool air current of the dog run, watching the dying light in the western sky. The air was sweet with the scent of hay.

"Madam," he said, "what a sweet and gentle evening." She agreed, tight-lipped. He saw that he frightened her. Presently she went inside the larger cabin. He heard her bar the door. He told Pernier to spread a bearskin from the West on which he liked to sleep. All at once he couldn't stand further sight of his servant and told him to be gone, make his bed in the barn, sleep.

He was wide awake. The night was cool and he drew his coat tightly about him and thought again of the strange attacks made upon him. Had he really erred so greatly that he must be destroyed? The nation held him a hero still, along with Will and the men—and woman—of the Corps of Discovery. Then a new and exciting question formed in his troubled mind. It thrummed and twanged like a rope drawn tight.

How much of all this was really his own fault?

Had he yielded to deadly hubris, elevating himself to challenge the gods, seeking cosmic punishment?

These questions coming from nowhere that he could imagine were like an explosion that blew off doors and windows and roof and left everything flooded with bright light in which one could see farther and deeper than ever before. He felt shaken and rattled and somehow humble. At once he understood the change—he could see what before had been hidden. He felt newly in control and saw with a start how long he had been out of control, felt newly lucid and understood that lucidity had been lost and was now regained. He was in command of himself. Restored—surely by God's grace. A gift he must use with reverence. How much of the fault was his?

He filled his pipe and lit it with a straw thrust into the lantern's flame and looked at things. Hadn't he known all along that he would need records? Just as Will had reminded him. Hadn't he told himself he was too busy to do what in fact he simply disliked doing? Maybe Jefferson's easy instructions had seduced the subaltern, budget it at twenty-five hundred dollars to lull Congress at the start and then have merchants bill the president. But Lewis had known all along that brilliant as Mr. Jefferson was, he said many things without much thought. Of course someone somewhere would be keeping track of it all. He had known that. But before God, he had not turned a penny to his own use, unless you counted buying old Seaman. The image of the big dog lying on that rocky ridge licking his torn paws, then springing up despite the pain with that curious winning smile, brought tears to his eyes.

He relit the pipe. Go on. Look at it. Bates was a miserable creature, but what you do with men like Bates, you handle them. He knew that. And Dearborn—he should have paid more attention to the secretary of war when they planned a military expedition. He should have known that in the end the president, no soldier himself, would leave the subaltern holding the bag.

And he had been a poor governor, let's admit that. He had no experience and equal interest. The plan to return Big White to the Mandan villages had been honest enough but a wiser man would have spelled it all out to Washington and demanded written approval.

All right, grant all of that, but wasn't it still small potatoes against what they had accomplished? Yes, he was a novice in most things, but he and Will had proved themselves great explorers. They had led their men across a continent on a trek that no living creature had ever made, finding the way that in full no living creature knew. Now they knew the way and that changed everything.

A small flask of whiskey stood on the table by his saddlebags. He looked at it but had no desire to open it. Things had changed; he didn't need it. And he went on, considering and reconsidering.

Yes, ancient dreams of the Northwest Passage had died on those bleak heights. But now he knew their hard-rock replacement—up the Missouri 2,575 miles until its source, a creek a man could step over; overland for 340 miles, of which 200 were passable but 140 were over vast mountains and 60 were covered by snow for all but a month or two; and then run 600 miles of wild water on the Clearwater and the Snake and the Columbia.

But see—when they crossed the Continental Divide and walked into Cameahwait's village they passed from the Louisiana Purchase. From there to the Pacific was open, unclaimed by any power. Captain Vancouver had explored for Britain, Captain Gray in his merchant brig for the United States, while the Spanish looked north from California, the Russians south from the Arctic.

He remembered standing on the beach that triumphant final day of discovery, watching swells that came unimpeded from Asia break at his feet, terns squalling and sea mist whipping his face. And he saw that Lewis and Clark and the Corps of Discovery by crossing by land had solidified Captain Gray's claim. They had tilted the international balance and American settlers, coming in far greater numbers than other countries could muster, would do the rest. The nation was destined to be a continental power fronting on both oceans. It could not be denied now.

Could that triumph be stolen? Suppose the leader were to be revealed as scoundrel, traitor, malfeasant, a bankrupt fraud? He remembered Potts wondering if they were all dead and these endless ridges were hell. They had come through all that and now little men in the East who cared nothing for the West would steal it to advance their own petty designs.

When he had filled his saddlebags he had found in a side pocket the little knife that the old scout in North Georgia, Jack McIntyre, had given him. And what had Mr. McIntyre taught him? To see when he looked. Consider the rock formation belowground that shifted the flow of water this way and that. Find his own way. Believe in himself. Stand his ground. Do right. He remembered offering to teach Mr. McIntyre to read and write but the old man had shaken his head. He knew exactly who he was.

In that phrase, their own petty designs, he suddenly perceived a new motive for the strange attack from the East. Consider that a political battle still raged over the Louisiana Purchase. Fifteen million dollars, the cries went, a fortune that the nation might need a century to repay. And for what? For still more wilderness when we already drowned in wilderness with great reaches of Tennessee and Kentucky still untouched. It took a month for a letter—or a congressional order—to travel each way. Against all that we should weight our future with vast new tracts?

At least let us minimize interest in it, attention paid to it, resources wasted on it—let us do only the necessary and that barely. He remembered now that the new President Madison had never shared Jefferson's enthusiasm for the West. Remembered the dour looks that Madison had given him for encouraging the president's feckless dreaming.

But there was another factor, still more immediate. The Federalists, conservatives to the core, were out of power, their numbers shrinking. The East and especially the Northeast were their stronghold. The South and the West held to the Democrats. The West had vast tracts to attract land-hungry men; it certainly would grow while Northeast growth was essentially over. Leading the fight against the Purchase were desperate Federalists who feared western growth as a direct threat to their own futures.

Yes, that might explain a lot of the abuse of the explorer whose mighty feat had opened half a continent. Now in his blessed clarity, he saw he should have been prepared for that.

And how much had he done to keep Mr. Jefferson on his side? Suddenly he remembered that he hadn't written two letters in two years. He had answered none of those urgent queries about the book, driven in turn by those of the savants of Philadelphia and Paris. Suppose he had confessed his inability to write the book? Never mind his lament that it was too much for the world to expect from a sitting governor who didn't know how to do his job. Suppose he had humbled himself and asked for help? Put it back in the president's lap.

He knocked out the pipe, refilled it, lit it, and stepped outside to pace in the cool dark. The moon had set, the night was lonely and still, stars glittering. He glanced up, finding the familiar constellations, orienting himself. Then, like a flash of light, a new idea. Wasn't the book at the root of his troubles, the book and his failure even to begin it? He stepped back inside and spread his journal notebooks on the table, seeking comfort from their covers. It was all in there, every bit of it.

Now he saw it with utter clarity. It was the book, or rather its absence, that was killing him. Americans were fair and decent people. They liked their heroes and would stand by them but they needed a real sense of their deeds. The nation already was huge—the Census of 1800 put population over five million, an incredible figure. How to reach them all and make them see the trek and its hardships and its discoveries, all the new animals and birds and plants rewarding science? You had to get it down on paper, find the words to make them see and hear the burrowing prairie dog with his wild squeaking, see the bighorn's death-defying leaps, listen to the grizzly's awful roar when attacking. And make them understand what it meant to the nation.

That was his real failure, the inability to get all this down on paper so millions could experience it from afar. That was the real betrayal of those who had followed him. And in failing to capitalize on public affection and interest, he had made himself vulnerable to attack from little men with political axes to grind.

Now things could only get worse. He was going to Washington to fight these men with their petty accusations and not a friend to defend him, fight little men while the world forgot magnificent deeds. He thought of Will's map, the lay of the rivers pouring into the Missouri, the sense and shape of the land that tilted across those vast prairies until they rose into mountains that rivaled the Alps. The names he and Will had affixed to the rivers would be gone. The discoveries of plants and animals, all given proper Linnaean names, would be rediscovered at some later time by new and perhaps wiser explorers, men who could write books.

A couple of his men had published brief accounts, dealing mainly with adventures. But they lacked the knowledge to grasp what they had done while he lacked the ability to convey it. His failure . . . only he could do it and he couldn't do it. Of course he had thought of enlisting a writer to translate his notes and memories and visions but for better or worse, he was convinced that that would never work. The issue was dead—for as long as he lived.

What did he owe the world? Not much, maybe, but it had been given to him to see great things. He had had experiences that the Eustises and the Madisons of the world could not even imagine, things that beggared even Jefferson's imagination. He had known a continent at its rebirth. More men would come, the herds would thin, the animals would become commonplace, plows would break the prairie—but he had seen it whole, grasped it full when it had been in the stewardship of men who lived on and with the land instead of reshaping it to their own image. The men who were coming, Americans of European stock, would work great change. Now these men who feared the West were trying to destroy the man who had seen it whole and grasped it full.

But he didn't have to let them do their dirty work. He remembered Will saying with a laugh that they might make some history. Well, they had made history, all right, they were known across the nation and they were honored. He would not let them be dishonored. One thing he had still in his control—his destiny.

It was very late. He had been thinking for hours, the night now silent the way it gets when dawn's brightening is not too far away. The lucidity he had celebrated earlier stayed with him and looking back over the months and now years since they had come down the Missouri to triumph, his main feeling was one of exhaustion. He had carried burdens that had pressed him into the ground. Each way he turned had been the wrong way. He was more than ever exhausted now. He wanted to sleep but he had a great journey to cover, rest coming at its end.

He had been reading the classics again for their universal insight into the human creature, his well-thumbed copy of Shakespeare always close. He had chosen *Hamlet* for renewed study, acting out in his mind the vari-ous roles that he had heard so often from the stage, pondering the poet's inner meanings. A few lines from the great soliloquy lodged permanently in his mind, reverberating with passion:

"For who would bear the whips and scorns of time,
The oppressor's wrong, the proud man's contumely,
The pangs of despised love, the law's delay,
The insolence of office, and the spurns
That patient merit of the unworthy takes,
When he himself might his quietus make
With a bare bodkin?"

It was that bare bodkin that held his imagination, double-edged, glittering, and deadly as it comes sharp as a razor from its scabbard, brightly analogous to a modern-day pistol with its flint in place and priming powder in its pan.

His quietus make . . .

He loaded both pistols, splashed powder in the priming pan, and laid them on the table. He looked at them a long time. He was very tired. He yearned for rest beyond the journey. He could end the attacks, make them moot and pointless. He could fix himself forever with the Corps of Discovery and pay his debts to the men and the woman who had marched with him. Who collectively had made possible all that he had done. Let them not suffer for his failures.

He let his memory range, mind's eye seeing the great river bending and curling out of the west like a sublime serpent. He could see the gorgeous prairie, no tree in sight, the violet sky when the sun was gone, the deep-rooted grass that brushed his thighs, the magnificent herds that that grass supported, the vast open sky a great blue dome like that of a cathedral. He thought of the people who lived on the land, Black Cat and Cameahwait and the others, without whom the Corps of Discovery would have been lost before it started. Yes, and he remembered the way the land tilted gradually to the west, higher and higher, vast mountains looming in the distance. And the way a man's breath went short when he came to those mountains, the way walking their heights brought you close to God and close to death.

Much as he owed the men and the woman of the Corps of Discovery, he owed more to that splendid country. It was all there in his journals, noted as he saw it, all the description and color and sounds, the glare of the sun, the howl of the blizzard, the grizzly's roar, the singing rivers, the cottonwoods growing along every stream as God's gift to mankind in a sere land. All there in his journals. His own third act was ending. Let someone who could bring it all alive on the page step forward. Let the explorer step out of the way once and for all, bare bodkin all aglitter.

He put the pistol to his forehead and pulled the trigger. At the last instant the pistol turned slightly. Had he flinched? Had the pistol failed as they often did? He didn't know. The ball caromed off his forehead like a billiard ball from a cushion. A mirror told him he had a furrow across his forehead to go with his vast headache. He could hardly see.

Now he burned with thirst. He lurched to the door and called to the dark and silent cabin next to his, "Oh, madam, spare me a cup of water. Come heal my wounds."

No answer. Of course she was afraid, a woman alone. Mary Beth would not have left him alone to die in agony. But it was too late to think of Mary Beth, much too late.

He took up the other pistol and fired at his heart. The bullet crashed through his body. He lay on the floor, shuddering with pain and shock. He knew he was dying, but death took its own time. Pernier appeared and Lewis whispered, "I am no coward but I am so strong . . . so hard to die."

The sun rose abruptly, beautiful and blinding, and then just as suddenly it was night and stars blazed overhead. He saw he was traveling on life's arc, guided by the stars. He tried to read them to fix his exact position but the boat was going too fast, hurtling down the black river. He called to unseen hands to slow her for ahead he saw a vortex opening into the water's darkness. Then the boat lurched and dipped and with a gasp of thanksgiving he plunged into liberating darkness and was gone.

A Note on Methods and Sources

Meriwether is a novel and hence a work of imagination. But it is historically accurate to the extent I can make it, both as to what happened and the character and personality of the leading figures. As The American Story takes shape in five novels (*Dream West, 1812, Eagle's Cry, Treason*, and now *Meriwether*, with more to come, God willing) I call what I do telling the imagined inside of a known outside story. History is made by people acting on a broad political screen, and my own experience as a journalist covering first affairs in a single community, then in Washington around the Congress and the White House, makes clear to me the extent to which the hopes and dreams and dreads and furies of men and women affect our affairs of state.

History rejects this inner sense of story, as well it should. History depends on a paper trail as the only reliable source, and that often is as much cover as fact. But, of course, history's rejection of story opens the way to the storyteller, which is how I see myself—storyteller, not historian. Yet for my story to function its underlying fabric, the historical reality, must be told clearly and accurately. Hence *Meriwether* follows the historical record so far as that record is known. I have told Meriwether Lewis's factual story as correctly as I can. But in the end, following the facts, I must launch into interpretation, speculation, and finally imagination in order to tell a version of what I see as his complete story. Imagining lives lived two hundred years ago requires auxiliary characters, the servants and retainers, the friends, the women, and in the main these are lost to the historical record and must be imagined.

Language in the early nineteenth century bore a certain formality but I'm sure thoughts were as fluent, angers as quick, analysis as informed, and all were conveyed one person to another with the ease of human beings today. I have tried to reflect that quality in my dialogue, choosing language that avoids modernisms, and often sounds a little formal but probably less than the actual discourse of the day.

Party names can be confusing to modern readers. In the beginning an elite governed without parties. As objection to elitism rose, what then was called the Republican Party appeared under the leadership of Jefferson and Madison. From the start, its members were called Democrats. Soon it became the Democratic Republican Party and by the second decade was becoming the Democratic Party that we know today. The Republican

Party that we know today dates to the 1850s. I chose to list my characters as Democrats from the start to avoid inevitable confusion with modern politics.

I believe the central points of Meriwether Lewis's story are first the magnificent trek he and William Clark led and at the spectrum's other end, his suicide.

On the trek, I have followed it as closely as I can. The men on the expedition are accurately cast, I believe, except that I have given George Shannon more weight and used him for viewing matters more fully than the record supports. He was the youngest, was with Colter the first to be selected, did go off and get lost for ten days, did lose a leg trying to take Big White home. He did go into law and in fact finally was a midlevel judge. Colter went on to a famed career as a mountain man. Personal qualities given the men of the Corps of Discovery are largely my invention.

My presentation of Sacagawea follows the record in presenting her as a powerful woman with some imaginary details. Little Pomp did eventually come to St. Louis and live in Clark's home as a member of his family. He went on to a considerable career in the West.

The presentation of York is accurate, including his desire for freedom as deserved by the trek, and Clark's initial reaction to that demand. Probably York did come to freedom but the record loses sight of him. In later years Clark told people he had set York free. Further, Stephen Ambrose reports that years later an old man in the Louisiana bayou country claimed to be York and said he had run off from Clark. It hurts to read of Clark's reaction to honest York's desire for freedom that seems so dark in today's perceptions but there it is. In its small way it suggests the horrors of that evil institution.

The trek was a lifelong objective for Lewis, and it is hard to doubt that his problems when the trek was done turned around the fact that it was done. He did hear of Jefferson's plan when he was nineteen and applied for the command. Jefferson never bothered to answer, though Lewis as a child and youth was close to him as described. I use telling that story to introduce a major fictional character, Mary Beth Slaney.

She in turn goes to what I consider a central theme of Lewis's life, his problem with women. My depiction of him drawing women and then driving them away is accurate in a good number of cases. Letitia Breckenridge was a real figure, as was her little sister, and her brief romance is historically accurate. It seemed to me that Lewis desperately needed a solid woman his own age and that he might well have lived to a ripe old age had he found one. Mary Beth represents what might have been and hence has a recurring but not major presence in the novel.

Note that I introduce Webster's dictionary a few years before it was written. The evil General Wilkinson is accurately drawn in all reports. York's penis did freeze. Lewis's strange encounter with the bear is just as he related it.

The strain of melancholy in Lewis cited by so many is accurately presented. Today we would call the quality neurosis, and looking back, probably it is safe to say that his melancholy amounted to a manic-depressive streak. It did run in the family and Lewis was sharply aware of it. The same is true of Lewis's temper. Some Washington figures opposed his appointment as commander of the Corps of Discovery on the grounds that his temper would run out of control and make serious trouble.

This quality had heavy bearing on his suicide, I think. Of course, given that Lewis was alone at the time and two shots were fired, to his head and his body, there always has been some question as to whether it was suicide or murder. Various speculations, some quite fantastic, have been spun in support of the latter but historians today generally agree that Lewis died by his own hand.

The troubles that precipitated his depression at the end are accurately struck. He was careless in his accounts and he did delay the book, almost certainly because he didn't know how to write it and was frightened by it, common enough reaction for a man of action. But it seems extraordinarily obtuse on Jefferson's part not to understand that. As I have Dolley Madison note, the gubernatorial appointment was near a death warrant. How could Jefferson not have seen that? Despite Jefferson's undeniable genius, there seems to me to be a light and thoughtless quality in him as well. When he left office he seems to have abandoned his protégé, who admittedly was not cultivating his mentor. Blame on both sides, yes, but Jefferson was a man of such stature we might expect a bit of magnanimity on his part and a good deal more understanding. The feeling that he betrayed Lewis on the Clark matter and in his abandonment over the funding I find inescapable.

Certainly by the time Madison was in the White House and Eustis, a hopelessly second-rate figure, in the War Department there was no sympathy for an obviously distressed man who had served his country heroically. It all seems quite tragic and goes to my point on the extent to which prejudices and old angers dictate policy and the inside story. The fatal letter telling Lewis his accounts would be refused, the letter probably made public by Secretary Bates (whom I portray accurately but without sympathy; in reality he was probably no more than a pedantic bureaucrat) can be seen as a killing stroke. Had there been the slightest sympathy for Lewis's plight, represented by Dolley's remonstrance to her husband, he might well have lived to old age. That seems to me to be inherent tragedy.

As to my final chapter, how do you portray a man's mind as he contem-

plates suicide? Is he weird and wandering, out of his head, in such psy-
chic pain he can think only of relief? Or is he clear of mind, following a
course that seems best to offer preservation of what he has given his life
to, who he is, what he stands for? Meriwether Lewis led a magnificent
trek that changed history and was fundamental to leading the United
States toward becoming a continental nation washed by two oceans, and
much of what we know of our country today grows from that continental
quality. Lewis was never a fool and never psychotic, troubled though he
was and too heavily influenced by whiskey and opium. It's hard to believe
that he simply was out of his head.

In deciding to end matters here as petty enemies tried to drag him
down into the muck with themselves, was he preserving all he had stood
for and done? So I believe.

Finally, for factual matter and much insight I have relied on the late
Stephen Ambrose's magnificent *Undaunted Courage*. I turned to Mr. Ambrose
constantly for facts but I have been at great pains to steal none of his
words. David Lavender's fine *The Way to the Western Sea* refreshes the
Lewis and Clark story with his unparalleled knowledge and insight into
the ways and mores of the Old West. I turned often to my old favorite,
Bernard DeVoto, and to Donald Jackson's fine *Thomas Jefferson & the
Stony Mountains*, the Library of America's treatment of Bartram's *Travels*,
James R. Fazio's *Across the Snowy Ranges*, Paul Russell Cutright's treatment of Lewis and Clark as naturalists, Richard Dillon's biography of
Lewis, Henry Adams's magisterial if sometimes prejudiced history of the
United States in the Jefferson and Madison administrations, and of
course reading into if not every word of the journals. That only touches
my reading but accounts for the main elements. Finally, my deepest
appreciation to my editor, Robert Gleason, for a brilliant conceptual contribution.

And, my eternal gratitude to the New York Public Library, the Century Association Library, the Greenwich Public Library, and that magnificent resource, the Library of Congress.

—DN